# THE DIVIDED CROWN

TOR BOOKS BY ISABEL GLASS

*Daughter of Exile*
*The Divided Crown*

# THE DIVIDED CROWN

## ISABEL GLASS

TOR®

A TOM DOHERTY ASSOCIATES BOOK

NEW YORK

THE DIVIDED CROWN

A Tor Book
Published by Tom Doherty Associates, LLC
175 Fifth Avenue
New York, NY 10010

www.tor.com

Tor® is a registered trademark of Tom Doherty Associates, LLC.

Library of Congress Cataloging-in-Publication Data

Glass, Isabel.
    The divided crown / Isabel Glass.—1st ed.
        p. cm.
    "A Tom Doherty Associates book."
    ISBN 0-765-30746-4
    EAN 978-0-765-30746-0
    1. Kings and rulers—Succession—Fiction. I. Title.

PS3607.L369D58 2005
813'.54—dc22

                                        2004063751

First Edition: July 2005

Printed in the United States of America

0  9  8  7  6  5  4  3  2  1

# THE DIVIDED CROWN

# ONE

Work stopped at the port as the ship sailed into the harbor. Sailors, traders, and dockworkers lingered nearby, pretending to be busy, and beyond them stood a looser circle of craftsmen and merchants and servants and nobility.

It was a deep-hulled trading ship returning home, flying King Jerret's command flag with his two-towered castle. The crew made the ship fast to the pier and began to unload the cargo, chests and boxes of nutmeg and oranges and jade from the south.

The crowd moved restlessly. Around them dockworkers cursed and called out orders; seagulls squawked over fish. The passengers and horses began to disembark, walking carefully through the seawater and silver fish guts and broken packing crates that littered the quay. Finally, nearly at the end of the line, the people saw what they had been waiting for: the First Master of the College of Magicians and his wife the witch.

A murmur of dissatisfaction swept through the crowd. They looked so *ordinary*. Master Mathewar was not much more than average height for a man, though solidly built; he had blue-gray eyes and long, straight wheat-colored hair tied at the back. Folks said that he was the youngest man ever to be appointed First Master, but he was not young now. His face was brown with sun and white lines of age rayed out from his eyes.

His wife, Lady Angarred Hashan, stood nearly as tall as her husband, with darker blue eyes and a mass of red-gold hair that hung down her back. Both wore roughspun shirts and trousers and worn boots. They carried stained leather packs. Mathewar turned to Angarred and said something, and she laughed.

Fourteen years ago he had worked some magic to bring about the end to the War of All the Realms, though no one knew the full story. Folks told tales of his wife too, though these were even vaguer; they said that she knew strange magics, forest magics, enchantments that had never been seen within the walls of civilized cities and towns.

A delegation from the king moved forward to greet them, and here at last the crowd saw some of the splendor they had expected. The king's men were dressed in long gold and red cloaks; their surcoats had the king's double-tower emblem on them, and a single green jewel glistened from the brooches at their throats.

They spoke to the couple awhile and indicated the horses they had brought for them. These were docile and dun-colored, another disappointment for the throng, which had expected snorting jet-black stallions, at least. The Master and his wife mounted and followed their guides.

The crowd watched them go. Later a few people swore they saw something as the couple left—a presence, some tangible power—but their friends and neighbors laughed and said the sun had gotten in their eyes.

Angarred, for her part, looked around curiously as they rode through Karededin's capital city. She had not been to Pergodi for two years, since Queen Rodarren died. Rodarren's reign of nearly thirteen years had left the country prosperous and peaceful, and in the two years since her death it did not seem that Pergodi had changed much. People still thronged the streets, going about their business; carts rumbled over the cobblestones; folks shouted their wares at passersby; bells clanged as they tolled the hours.

Recently, though, she and Mathewar had received disturbing news from magicians who had visited the court. A man named Noldeth Haru, a minor courtier in Rodarren's time, was gaining influence

over King Jerret, Rodarren's heir; the boy-king had granted Noldeth
titles and land and castles, and seemed set to marry Noldeth's daughter. Then the magicians working for Jerret had returned to the College; they had been dismissed by the king, they said, but they seemed
certain that Noldeth was behind the decision.

Angarred remembered Lord Noldeth from Rodarren's time. He
had been a commoner then, in some minor capacity, officious and
full of opinions, a man who never missed a chance to make himself
seem more important than he was. She and Mathewar had planned to
visit the capital some time after the College term ended, to see if the
rumors were true and if Jerret needed their help. He was only fourteen, after all; he had been thrust into the kingship when his mother
died.

In mid-Spring, when the students at the College left for home,
they got a strange letter from Jerret, asking them to come to Pergodi
and "witness an important ceremony." At the end of the letter, almost
as an afterthought, Jerret wrote, "Oh, and I banished the Harus." By
this time word had reached the College that the Harus had grown
bolder, that there had been skirmishes and rebellions, and Angarred
and Mathewar had become increasingly worried. It seemed too dangerous to bring their three children to the capital; they asked Atte,
Mathewar's daughter from his first marriage, to look after them on
her farm. With everyone taken care of, Angarred wrote to Jerret and
told him they would come.

She didn't tell Mathewar her other reason for leaving. The College stood perched on a cliff overlooking the ocean, with the wild,
tangled Forest of Tiranon at their backs; she needed to get away, to
see someone other than students and masters and forest folk. She suspected Mathewar knew, though; they had been married fourteen
years and could sometimes guess each other's thoughts.

Now they followed the king's men through several neighborhoods
and over two of Pergodi's bridges. The houses around them grew
larger and richer, made of copper and marble, tile and wrought iron.

Finally they rode up the hill to Pergodi Castle, a hulking place of
towers and turrets and battlements. The castle had been built in levels
against the hill, each ruler adding to what his predecessor had done,
the stairs and corridors connecting them tacked on haphazardly. In

some places domes or arches were cut in half by walls, as a king ignored an earlier building to push on with his own vision.

As the party came closer the sun began to set, darkening the road before them; the air grew colder. Men holding spears stood at the outer gates and nodded to them as they went through. Their eyes looked blank, like flat pools of water; something about them made Angarred shiver. She had seen the same dead stare on other folks in the city, but she had assumed they were drunkards or sattery addicts. She turned to Mathewar and he nodded slightly; he had seen the same thing and it had disturbed him as well.

They rode through the courtyard, past a woman carrying a basket of squabbling chickens, and another woman with a bundle of laundry. More men came to take their horses, and some of these, too, had the dead eyes of the guards at the gates.

As they entered the castle a man came toward them, tall and lean, with gray close-cropped hair. Despite his age he walked firmly, his back straight. He wore a chain of office over the double-tower emblem; his eyes were alert, thank the Godkings, and he was smiling. "Lady Angarred, Lord Mathewar," he said, bowing to each of them. "I'm Dobrennin Under-steward. The king has asked me to tell you that supper will be in an hour, in the Lesser Banquet Hall, and to show you to your apartment."

"That won't be necessary, thank you," Angarred said. "I remember where my rooms are." As a noblewoman, though a very unconventional one, she had an apartment in the castle.

"Of course, milady," the under-steward said. "I'll come get you for supper, then." He bowed again and left them.

Though she did not come often to Pergodi, the castle servants had kept her apartment clean. She walked through the rooms, seeing their few pieces of furniture in the light from the western windows: a table, some chairs, a chest, and a large bed. She decided not to unpack. Jerret's ceremony would probably not take long, and they would return to the College and their children in a few days.

An hour later, after they had washed off the journey's grime and changed into formal clothes, Mathewar and Angarred followed Dobrennin through double doors into the Lesser Banquet Hall. Despite its name the hall was a large room with a high hammer-beamed ceiling. A long table of deep red wood stood in the center, lit by candle-branches every few feet; it was so highly polished it seemed a mirror for the candles, that shone almost as brightly upside down. A hearth-fire blazed along one entire wall, holding logs the size of small trees. The room smelled of roast meat and the sweet herbs thrown on the fire.

In the dim light Angarred saw Jerret heading toward them. "Master Mathewar, Lady Angarred," Jerret said formally. "I'm pleased to see you."

He had the brown eyes and hair of both his parents. His hair was wild, shaggy, a few days past trimming. He looked far too young to be king, like a boy dressing up in his father's clothes.

"Hello, Jerret," Angarred said. "What is this ceremony you wrote us about?"

Something stirred deep within his eyes, like a terrified animal running for cover. He twisted the ring of his office around his finger. She saw to her dismay that he was afraid, though he tried to hide it. He looked around the room, as if making certain no one could overhear, and said, "I'll tell you later."

A woman came up and took Jerret's hand. She had long, lustrous black hair and blue eyes with thick black lashes. Her skin was very white; a blue vein stood at her temple, near the hairline.

Angarred felt a brief shock, as if she were seeing someone she'd thought was dead. This was Lady Iltarra Haru, Noldeth's daughter. Hadn't she been exiled with the rest of her family?

She forced herself to cover her confusion, to look straight at the woman and not glance at Mathewar. "Hello, Lady Iltarra," she said.

Iltarra wore a mesh of jewels in her hair and a rope of pearls at her neck; the pearls, like her skin, seemed translucent, like clouds touched by the sun. "Hello, Lady Angarred," she said. "We've missed you here at court. And you, Lord Mathewar."

Mathewar stirred. He wasn't a lord and Iltarra certainly knew that. He nodded at her, saying nothing.

Iltarra ruffled Jerret's hair, then rested her arm on his shoulder. She was younger than Angarred remembered, about twenty, and stood a few inches taller than the king. He smiled up at her, and for a moment his strained, formal expression softened.

Jerret clapped his hands, and folks took their places at the table. Men and women came through a door carrying trays of food. Some of them had eyes as blank as newly minted coins; without looking at anyone they went to the table, set down their burdens, and left. Jerret watched them, and Angarred saw the fear return to his eyes.

The servants had brought out dishes of roasted boar and smoked fish. Folks began to eat, and for a while no one said anything; then murmurs of praise for the food rose from the table.

Conversations started up about trifling matters: clothes, hunting, affairs between people Angarred had never heard of. She did not see any of the courtiers she had known from King Tezue's time, or Queen Rodarren's. These new folks were younger and seemed to have come to prominence in the two years since she and Mathewar had visited the court; she recognized only one of them, Lord Talethe, a childhood friend of Jerret's.

Across from her sat a man who introduced himself as Lord Ezlin Ertig from the Finbar Islands. He spoke in a drawling voice to friends of his on either side. Angarred gathered that they were from Finbar too, but she had no idea where that was; she wished she had paid more attention to maps.

She turned to Mathewar, who would probably know. His normally tanned face had gone nearly as white as Iltarra's pearls. "What's wrong?" she asked.

"Later," he said softly.

That was the second time someone had told her to wait. She sighed and ate impatiently, eager for the meal to end.

Finally the servants came to clear the table and bring out more flagons of wine. "I'm very tired," Jerret said. "I'm going to bed."

"Good night, my pet," Iltarra said, kissing him on the cheek.

No one else showed any sign of leaving. More wine was poured; the talk and laughter grew louder. "I hear you're coming to the ceremony tomorrow," Lord Ezlin said to her and Mathewar. He had plain brown hair and eyes and was in his mid-thirties, too young for the sagging jowls that had already appeared on his face. He slouched in his chair, his face red and his eyes too bright; he had already drunk a good deal of wine.

"Yes, although no one's told us yet what kind of ceremony it is," Angarred said. "Do you know?"

Ezlin laughed. "I should hope so," he said. "Jerret's proclaiming me his heir."

Angarred must have looked startled, because Ezlin went on. "He's young, you see, and he's worried that he might die without sons. Of course, if he married and had children I'd renounce any claim to the throne."

He had said "if," not "when," Angarred noticed. "Are you—are you related to the royal family?" she asked.

"The Finbarek royal family, yes. Not to Jerret, though."

Iltarra joined them, sitting close to Ezlin. He straightened up and ran his fingers through his hair. "You want to know what qualities he has, why Jerret chose him," Iltarra said. "Show her, Ezlin."

"Don't be ridiculous," Ezlin said. Despite his words he sounded exasperated rather than angry with Iltarra.

"Go on," Iltarra said. "If you don't, I will."

Ezlin said nothing. To Angarred's surprise Iltarra put her finger in her mouth, against her cheek, and then pulled it out with a popping noise. "That's it," she said. "His sole qualification for rule. He and his family visited Pergodi once when Jerret was five or six, and Jerret loved to watch him do that. He would follow Ezlin around for hours."

"Nonsense," Ezlin said. "I'm certain he had other reasons."

"Oh, yes?" Iltarra reached out and brushed a lock of hair from Ezlin's face. "What were they?"

Ezlin laughed. "My ability to make men follow me," he said. He ran a finger over Iltarra's face in turn, though none of her hair had escaped her mesh cap. "And women." He turned to Angarred and Mathewar. "She's upset because Jerret exiled most of her family. What do you suppose your brothers are doing now, Iltarra?"

Angarred expected anger at this, but Iltarra continued in the teasing tone they both used. "Increasing the population of Ou, surely. But Jerret will invite them back—you'll see."

"No, he won't. That was the wisest thing Jerret ever did, exiling them to Ou. They had far too much power here."

"Ezlin hopes they won't come back," Iltarra said complacently to Angarred and Mathewar. "It was only the fact that my family is away that made Jerret brave enough to choose an heir. An heir who isn't one of my brothers, that is."

"Why should he bring them back?" Ezlin said.

"He knows he can't govern without my father. And if he hasn't worked that out yet, I'll explain it to him."

"Your father. It's unnatural how much influence that man has over him."

"Why did Jerret exile them?" Angarred asked, curious to hear Iltarra's answer. "We heard that one of your brothers—"

Iltarra shook her head, as if to signify that she was tired of the subject. She turned to Mathewar. "I heard a ballad about you the other day. About what you did in the War of All the Realms."

"You shouldn't believe everything you hear in ballads," Mathewar said.

Iltarra leaned toward him across the table. In the candlelight she looked white, as if she had drowned. Her black hair shone nearly blue, and the pearls in their mesh cap looked like small moons swimming in the night sky. "Why not?" she said. "Some soldier wrote it, probably, someone who might have been there. I almost don't know what to say. I've never met a hero before."

"Queen Rodarren asked a maker to write it," Mathewar said. "She thought it might help unify people after the war. I told her I'd write a song about her, see how she liked it. I never got around to it, unfortunately."

Iltarra laughed. "Do you write songs too? Could you write one about me?"

"You? I'd need to know more about you first."

"You know a good deal already. I'm beautiful, I'm talented—and I'm going to be queen of Karededin. There, you see. You never wrote a ballad about the last queen, but you can write one about the next."

"What about me?" Ezlin said, leaning back in his chair. "I might be king. Would you write a ballad about me if I became king?"

"How can you say that, Ezlin?" Iltarra said. Her tone was still teasing, as if she were talking to a fractious child. "If you became king it would mean that Jerret died, which the Godkings forfend."

"I'm sorry," Ezlin said. A look of confusion had come into his eyes; he didn't seem to know what he was apologizing for. A log fell in the hearth, cracking open to reveal its treasure of gold sparks.

"It's all right, my sweet," Iltarra said. She ruffled his hair as she had ruffled Jerret's.

"I've drunk far too much," Ezlin said. "Drank too much? How do you say that? Anyway, I should be clearheaded for the ceremony." He kissed Iltarra on the cheek and stood clumsily. "I'll see you all tomorrow."

"We should go too," Mathewar said, to Angarred's relief. "Good night, Lady Iltarra, Lord Ezlin."

They climbed the stairs to Angarred's rooms. "Holy Godkings, that woman!" Angarred said after she had closed the door behind them. "Do you think she's sleeping with him?"

"Who?" Mathewar asked.

"Lord Ezlin, of course." Then she understood his meaning; her eyes widened and she said, "Could she be sleeping with Jerret too? Thank the Godkings he isn't my child—I'd put a stop to that soon enough."

"I don't know." Mathewar sat on the bed and pulled his boots off. "Come here."

"Did you hear her? 'I'm going to be queen of Karededin,' she says. And she has it all planned out too—if Jerret dies she'll just marry Ezlin. And if that wasn't enough she seemed interested in you as well. 'Oh, Mathewar, I've never met a hero before.'" Angarred pitched her voice higher; she sounded nothing like Iltarra.

"I don't want to talk about her, not now," Mathewar said. "Please come here."

Suddenly she remembered his expression of horror at the banquet. "What happened during supper?" she asked, sitting next to him. "You said you would tell me later."

"I looked into the mind of a servant, one of those men with the dead eyes," he said.

He seemed reluctant to continue. "What did you see?" she said.

"Nothing."

"Noth—"

"Nothing at all. Oh, he knows how to dress and feed himself and how to perform his duties, but that's about the extent of it. No memories, no desires, not even his name."

"That's horrible."

"Yes."

She understood that he wanted to forget what he had seen for the moment, that he craved oblivion. Well, she could give him that, at least. She kissed him, and he drew her down on the bed. He reached back and pulled off his leather tie, and his hair fell around her like soft rain.

The next day Dobrennin Under-steward knocked softly and opened the door; he seemed to have been appointed to them for the length of their stay. "Would you like breakfast, milord? Milady?" he asked.

Angarred nodded. "I'm not a lord," Mathewar said.

The guide didn't seem to hear or to care. He took them to another, smaller dining hall, where they found bread and ale laid out on a sideboard. A blank-eyed woman set down a bowl of strawberries and walked slowly back to the kitchen.

"Where did those people come from?" Angarred asked, watching her as she left. "I didn't see any of them when we were here two years ago, for Rodarren's funeral."

"No," Mathewar said. They got their food and went to the table. "Someone must have created them. But who would do such a thing? And why?"

"Who would do what?" Iltarra asked, sitting down next to Mathewar.

Mathewar said nothing. Angarred, less discreet than her husband, said, "Those odd servants. The ones who seem dead."

"The Bound Folk?" Iltarra said. "My father or my brothers made them."

"What?" Angarred said. "How?"

"I have no idea," Iltarra said. "That's their business—they never told me."

"Weren't you curious?"

"Not really," she said, touching the strand of pearls at her neck. One of the pearls was larger and brighter than the rest, weighing the necklace down; it disappeared within her bodice and reappeared again as she moved.

"Why did Jerret send your family into exile?" Angarred asked again. "Everyone we talked to at the College had a different story."

"Oh, because of Drustig. He's the oldest, but also the most witless. He mismanaged his lands—he kept raising taxes, and he stole land that wasn't his and then killed the rightful owners, and there was talk of rape—not rape of farm women, which wouldn't have bothered anyone, but of noblemen's daughters. Finally his people couldn't take it anymore and they rose against him. And our father, who should have known better, joined Drustig, and then Jerret had to stand up for his people—there was nearly a war, but Jerret had more support than my father thought. He's a very popular king, Jerret is. And with his soldiers' help he sent Drustig and Cullen and my father to Ou— and now little Jerret's gotten brave enough to choose an heir." She shook her head in amazement.

"You don't seem too concerned for your family," Mathewar said.

"It will all work out," Iltarra said. "Jerret will realize he made a mistake and pardon them. All of them but Drustig, anyway—he's gone too far this time. But Jerret needs my father—he's never had an advisor as good as he is. Or I'll marry Jerret and convince him he was wrong to send them all away."

I was right, she does have it all figured out, Angarred thought. Thank the Godkings most of them are in exile—all the power-mad Harus at once would be terrifying. There had been a third brother, though she couldn't remember his name, and she wondered briefly what had happened to him. He had always kept to the background— he'd had some sort of infirmity. . . .

Dobrennin was coming toward them. "The ceremony will start in an hour, in the Hall of the Standing Kings," he said, then bowed and left.

"It doesn't look as if we'll be talking to Jerret after all," Angarred said.

"Oh, no, poor Jerret's far too busy today," Iltarra said. "Well, I should get ready."

After she left Mathewar said softly, "Someone should talk to him, though. There's a great deal wrong here."

---

# T W O

An hour later, dressed once more in formal clothing, they came into the Hall of the Standing Kings. When they died, kings and queens became gods and ascended to the Celestial Court; their statues of red stone, three times the height of a man, stood along the walls, Godkings on one side and Godqueens on the other. At the head of the rows were the first gods, Marfan and Mathona, holding their creations the sun and the moon. The other Godkings and queens held their attributes as well, a spindle for the Spinner, a ship for the Navigator, a sword for the Warrior. Torches smoldered at their feet, casting their shadows back against the walls.

Angarred had expected to see the religious in their drab brown robes, but it seemed Jerret had decided to perform the ceremony without them. After a moment's thought she understood why: the religious believed that the kings of Karededin descended from the gods, and if Jerret appointed an heir who was not of the royal family the kings would no longer be divine; the line of Godkings would come to an end. A brief picture came to her: the Hall deserted, the torches out, Mathona's moon fallen to the floor, and dust and spiderwebs over all.

"No religious," she whispered to Mathewar.

He nodded. "They probably want Jerret to produce an heir as soon as possible," he said. "He's the last of the royal family, after all."

"There's a rumor that King Tezue had a mistress," Angarred said.

"Where do you hear these things?"

"Lady Dubbish told me, of course," Angarred said, smiling. "But you can tell me something—where in the name of the Navigator are the Finbar Islands?"

"They're in the north, off the coast. They're not known for anything much—not until now, anyway."

They quieted as more people came into the Hall. King Jerret had chosen an odd group for his witnesses. Angarred recognized Talethe, Jerret's old friend; Chargad, the castle steward, Dobrennin's superior; and of course Iltarra, who stood next to Angarred, with the king on her other side. Ezlin, his eyes still red, arrived with two of his friends and a third person who hadn't been at the supper, an older man, balding and dignified.

Angarred counted to herself: five witnesses for Jerret, including themselves; three for Ezlin; and the king and his heir. Ten people, an even number, propitious to the Godkings, who went two by two throughout eternity.

Servants came in and set up a table between the rows of kings and queens. Other servants covered it with an old moth-eaten carpet and carefully put down some ancient relics: a sword, a crown, a key, a cup, and a few other things that looked like old junk, but that undoubtedly had some significance. Five of the Bound Folk took up positions near the wall.

Jerret motioned to the servants and they left the room. The Bound Folk stayed, though; Jerret hesitated and then turned away, clearly deciding not to challenge them.

Angarred frowned. They were an odd number now. It was superstitious nonsense, of course, but she felt uneasy all the same.

The young king began to speak. His voice wavered at first but grew stronger as he went on. He talked about peace for Karededin, and how important it was that the kings continued to rule justly and without a break. He introduced Ezlin, and spoke about the other man's life and works. Angarred grew bored and began to look around her.

Mathewar touched her. She followed his gaze. One of the Bound Folk had lost his blank-eyed stare and was watching the ceremony closely.

"Who is he?" Angarred whispered.

"I don't know," Mathewar said.

"Can you look into his mind?"

Most people learned to hide their thoughts without even realizing they did so; Mathewar could only read those who left themselves open. He shook his head.

They turned back to the ceremony. Jerret was wearing the crown now, and holding the sword. "Do you swear by Marfan and Mathona, by the great line of Godkings, to keep the laws of Karededin, and see that its people prosper?" he asked.

"I swear," Ezlin said.

Jerret asked more questions. Angarred looked away and saw to her horror that the bound man she had noticed earlier was now staring directly at her. She looked back at him, keeping her gaze level, trying not to shudder.

Ezlin knelt before Jerret. Jerret gave him the sword and set the crown on his head, then said, "I, King Jerret, on this day the forty-fourth of Spring, in the second year of my reign, in the year 898 after the founding of the College of Magicians, do proclaim and affirm Lord Ezlin Ertig, of the Finbar Islands, as my sole heir."

Ezlin rose. Angarred, who had forced her attention back to the ritual, hoped that this would be the end, but Ezlin began to make a speech.

She found herself looking at the bound man again. He was moving around some people to get a better view of another witness, the steward.

Iltarra said something. The king was going around the small circle now, asking everyone to swear that they had witnessed the ceremony and would uphold Ezlin's claim. Angarred, the last in the circle, swore in her turn, and then they all moved forward to sign a parchment with Jerret's proclamation already written out. Ezlin returned the relics to the table. He and the king laughed and slapped each other on the back, and the ceremony ended.

People began to talk, to joke, to congratulate Ezlin and Jerret. Servants came in to clean up, and then left with the table and relics. The Bound Folk, to Angarred's relief, went with them.

"Jerret," Mathewar said, when the king finally turned away from the others, "I'd like to talk to you."

"Later," Jerret said, grinning like a child. "We're having a banquet now, to celebrate, and then we're going hunting. Would you like to come?"

"No," Mathewar said. "When can I see you alone?"

"I don't know. Talk to my steward Chargad here." Jerret waved his hand, but the steward had already gone. "I've got to get out of this room—the smoke is making my eyes water." He headed out with Iltarra and Talethe and Ezlin and his men, all of them laughing and talking at once.

Angarred and Mathewar began to leave as well. Angarred stopped at the statue of Rodarren, the last in the row of Godqueens. She was called Robarren now; the names of the kings and queens were changed slightly when they died, to reflect the greater change they had undergone. Angarred had never gotten used to the new name, though; she had known the queen too well.

"I'm going to try to find that wretched steward," Mathewar said. "Do you want to stay here?"

"For a while," Angarred said.

She looked up at the statue, which held a sheaf of wheat; the religious had chosen the Sower as the name by which she would be worshiped. They meant to honor her for the peace and prosperity of her reign, but Angarred had always wondered if they were thinking of the birth of her son as well, which had happened almost miraculously when the queen was over forty.

It was no wonder, she thought, that Jerret had turned out to be a mediocre king. His father, also named Jerret, had died in the War of All the Realms, and her son was the only thing Rodarren had left of him. The boy had grown up spoiled and cosseted and made much of—and of course Rodarren had thought she would have years yet to teach him what he needed to know. No one expected that she would die of a chill at fifty-three.

Angarred turned to look at the statue of Jerret, now called Gerret. Rodarren had sworn she would never marry after her husband's death, but the religious had not believed her and had left Jerret's spot empty until she died. The queen had raged at that, but the religious, who liked to pretend that everyone had one mate for all time, were not willing to pull one statue out and put another in if she changed her mind. The scandal and embarrassment would have been terrible for them; no statue had ever been taken out of the line of kings since the founding of Karededin. Now that she was safely dead, though, Jerret stood facing her across the Hall, gazing at her for eternity.

Mathewar remembered where the steward's office had been during the reigns of Rodarren and Tezue, and he headed toward it, up several flights of stairs and through a hallway to another wing of the castle. Once there, though, he discovered only an empty room, and he cursed and turned back.

Perhaps Jerret had moved Chargad closer to the king's own apartments. He went down a flight of stairs and found himself in a dimly lit hallway. Someone came toward him in the gloom.

It was a bound man, the one who had studied the witnesses at the ceremony. Mathewar hadn't realized then how big he was; his shoulders seemed to brush the walls, casting the hall behind him into darkness.

Mathewar moved to the right to let him pass, but the man went left to intercept him. Mathewar stopped. The man came on, walking steadily. He was fifteen feet away, then ten. Something glinted dully in his hand—a dagger.

Mathewar looked around him quickly, taking in the man, the hall, the ancient portraits on the wall. He spoke a few words and a heavy painting flew at the bound man and struck his head, then fell loudly to the wooden floor. The man continued walking as if nothing had happened.

Mathewar glanced behind him and backed away down the hallway. A few doors lined the walls—but if he ran inside a room he would be trapped there. He flung another painting. The man brushed it away with no expression on his face.

The man was nearly upon him, and there were no more portraits. He spoke another spell, breathing hard. Red and gold fire coruscated between them—an illusion, but the man wouldn't know that. But to his horror the man stepped through the blaze as if it weren't there.

He had no instincts, Mathewar realized, nothing but unswerving obedience to whoever had bound him. Fire didn't frighten him. Knowing it was hopeless he reached out for the man's mind.

This time, though, he could read his thoughts; perhaps the man's deadly pursuit kept him so occupied he forgot to shield them. Mathewar observed the ceremony out of his eyes, saw him look at each witness in turn. He saw himself as he appeared to the other man, and watched the man compare that memory to the figure of Mathewar standing before him. And that was nearly all; he seemed focused on nothing but finding Mathewar and killing him.

He stepped forward and Mathewar stepped back, as if they followed the rules of a formal dance. The end of the corridor loomed; Mathewar could almost feel it behind him. The glimpse of the man's mind had given him an idea—a desperate idea, but he had nothing else.

He cast a glamour over himself. His hair turned gray and fell loosely around him, his face became lined, his eyes rimed over with cataracts. He stooped, and when he stepped backward he moved with the doddering gait of an old man. Another illusion, but one that felt real, unfortunately; the cataracts made everything seem vague, borderless.

The man looked around him and saw that the person in the hall did not match the picture in his mind. He was not human enough to look puzzled; he simply stopped walking. Mathewar tensed, ready to run. The bound man turned mindlessly away.

Mathewar leaned against the wall, catching his breath. I'm getting too old for this, he thought. He had not fought anyone with magic in fourteen years.

He pushed himself off the wall and followed the bound man. The hallway blurred before him. The man turned to go down the stairway. Mathewar drove his shoulder hard into the man's back. The bound man fell down the stairs, hitting the wall and steps heavily as he went. He reached the bottom with his head wrenched at an odd angle.

Mathewar returned to his own shape and hurried down the stairs. He glanced at the man as he passed but did not stay to make certain he was dead. He headed to the apartment first; Angarred had returned from the Hall of the Standing Kings, and he told her briefly what had happened. She put her hand to her mouth in horror. "What are you going to do?" she asked.

"I'm talking to the king. And this time he won't put me off."

He hurried down the hallway. She followed. "Jerret will be out hunting," Angarred said.

"Yes, but he said he'd celebrate first," Mathewar said. "I don't think he's going anywhere for a while."

They found Jerret and his friends in the Lesser Banquet Hall. "Mathewar, Angarred—come join us!" Jerret said. He leaned his chair back, nearly tipping it to the ground.

"Come with me," Mathewar said.

"I can't—my friends . . ." Jerret gestured to the others at the table.

"Come with me," Mathewar said. "I have things I want to say to you."

He used his commanding tone, the one that made anyone but the most strong-willed obey him. Very nearly all of Jerret's friends started to stand, compelled by the power in his voice.

"Just Jerret," he said. He left without checking to see if the king followed him.

"What is it?" Jerret said when they stood out in the corridor. Angarred closed the double doors behind them. "I've told my men to get my horses ready—"

"One of those Bound Folk attacked me," Mathewar said.

"What?" Jerret said, looking confused. "Why?"

"I don't know why. I suspect it's because he had orders to kill me if I came to your court."

"Why?"

"You should be answering these questions, not me. It's your court, your castle, your country. Who would have given those orders?"

"I don't—I don't know."

"Don't you?"

Jerret glanced up at him from under his thatch of hair. Mathewar had seen the gesture before; Jerret wanted to hide, to remain in ignorance of how things stood at his court. "One of the—the brothers I exiled," he said. "Or their father. Noldeth."

Mathewar nodded. "Why do you keep the Bound Folk in the castle?"

"I can't get rid of them! They won't leave!"

Finally, Mathewar thought, Jerret looked like the boy he very nearly was. He had needed help with the Bound Folk for a long time, probably, but he had also tried to ignore them, hoping the problem would go away.

"But you knew they might still be following Noldeth's orders," Mathewar said. "The Orator only knows what else he's told them to do. Why didn't you send for me earlier?"

Jerret rubbed his eyes and looked up through his hair again. "I don't—I can't . . . I'll have to bring the Harus back, ask them to fix it."

"Do you trust them, then?"

"I don't know! They've helped me, Noldeth and Cullen and Drustig—they know a lot of things . . . What would you do?"

Mathewar ignored this. "I saw something in that bound man's mind, something about the north," he said. "I think that's where these folk are created, or turned, or whatever evil is done to them. What's going on there? Is Noldeth or one of his sons there, creating more Bound Folk?"

"I don't know. Probably. Probably Polgar."

"Polgar Haru? Didn't you exile him?"

"No."

"Not him and not Iltarra. And yet you told us you'd sent the Harus away."

"Iltarra's not like the rest of her family. And I need Polgar. I put him in charge of the mines. I—I need money."

"What do you need money for? Rodarren left you a full treasury."

"For—for a good many things. You don't know what it's like, being king—you can't know." He looked up at Mathewar again. There was something sly in his eyes now. "For one thing, I've invaded Goss."

Mathewar folded his arms and studied him. After fourteen years of teaching he knew what expressions would terrify children, and Jerret proved to be no different from his students.

"What!" Jerret said anxiously. "I can invade Goss if I want to. I'm the king, you said so yourself. Do you think I'm too young to know about warfare? We're doing very well. We burned the king's castle and killed the whole royal family—we just have to put down a few rebels and the country will be ours."

"Whose idea was the invasion?"

Jerret stared at him mutinously. Mathewar's expression did not waver, and finally Jerret broke down. "All right, it was Cullen and Polgar's. But it's a good idea. We have the mines on our side of the border, but this way we'll have theirs too. We'll double our gold, our precious stones."

"Ah," Mathewar said softly. "So you struck the first blow."

"Yes, I did. We did. Why not?"

"Because in civilized countries there are certain conventions, which are intended to keep the land from constant warfare. And one of them is that you may not kill another king unprovoked."

"What—what do you mean?"

"I mean that if you kill a king, you forfeit your own rights. People will wonder why they shouldn't kill you too."

"You mean someone from Goss? But they're scattered, disorganized—"

"Someone from Goss, yes. Or one of these Bound Folk."

Jerret looked around him fearfully, as if he expected an assassin to leap at him from the shadows. "Why should they?"

"Why should they try to kill me? I don't know what Noldeth or his sons ordered them to do."

"They would never . . . They're my friends."

"They've given you very bad advice, for friends."

"You don't understand! I had to invade Goss. I need the money. There's nothing left, and I owe—I owe some people . . ."

Mathewar raised an eyebrow. Once again he said nothing; Jerret wanted to talk now, and his part was to listen.

"I gave the Harus some money," Jerret said. "Well, I had to. I raised them to high positions, and I gave Castle Haru to Noldeth so they'd have a last name, and then I had to give the sons castles as well. Castles are expensive—you have no idea how much it costs to run them. And then they needed servants, and clothing, and horses . . . They started as commoners, they had nothing . . . What should I do?"

"If I told you that, then I'd be the one doing it, not you."

"Don't talk in riddles, please. I need your advice."

"All right," Mathewar said. He had frightened poor Jerret enough for one day. But how had things gotten so bad so quickly? Jerret looked up at him, and he had a quick memory of the boy who had been charmed by his magic, who had watched with shining eyes as an apple appeared out of nowhere. "Your parents were two of the finest people I knew, and I see them in you, both of them. Know what happens around you, in your court, in your land. Think. Learn. Remember. Work and sacrifice."

Jerret nodded. He seemed puzzled, but Mathewar had the sense he would at least mull over what he had been told. "Go to your friends," Mathewar said.

Jerret ran toward the dining hall. "Oh, and send someone to the north wing, one flight down from where the steward's office used to be," Mathewar called after him. "I think I killed that bound man."

Jerret turned briefly, a horrified expression on his face. Then he opened the double doors, and the loud greetings of his friends rolled over them like a wave.

"Was I too harsh?" Mathewar asked Angarred.

"Well, you terrified *me*," she said.

He laughed. Then he said, more thoughtfully, "I don't like what's happening here. He said he exiled the Harus, and yet he's kept Iltarra and Polgar. And these Bound Folk . . ."

"Why did that man want to kill you?"

"I don't know. Perhaps he had orders from the Harus, as I said. Noldeth has to know that I disapprove of what he's done here, that I'd advise Jerret to get rid of that family and never allow them back . . . Perhaps Noldeth ordered a few of the Bound Folk to kill me if I ever came to court." He thought a moment. "I'll have to go north," he said.

"North? But—but what about Jerret?"

"I was hoping you'd stay here and keep an eye on him. I don't like the way he's talking about the Harus—he seems ready to bring the rest of them back again. And I can't think he's getting good advice from Iltarra, or his friends there in the dining hall."

"I'd rather go with you. What if something happens to you?"

"Nothing will happen. I'll ride up, look around, and come back, that's all. I'd be in more danger if I stayed at court—someone wants to kill me here."

"But there's war in the north, and people's minds are being destroyed—"

"The war is over the border, in Goss. And I won't get close to whoever's creating the Bound Folk."

"But why do you want to go? Because of what you saw in this man's mind?"

"Yes. His mind wasn't completely gone, not like that other bound man I saw. He seems to have been created more recently—perhaps that's why he still remembers a few things. And if I get closer to whoever's doing this I might find someone who remembers more—someone with a memory of how he was changed, even."

Angarred sighed. "All right. But what do you want me to do with Jerret?"

He laughed again. "Oh, convince him to withdraw his troops from Goss, and see that he doesn't invite those dreadful Harus back, and keep him from spending money he doesn't have . . . Seriously, though, I don't know. Try to teach him some things about being a king. About responsibility." He frowned and was silent for a while. Then he said, "These Bound Folk—whoever is creating them is worse than a murderer. At least the dead can rest. And there's nothing I can do about them—I can't see any way to free them, or even if they can be freed. Do you know who I'd love to talk to?"

"Tobrin."

"Yes." Tobrin was a very old, very skilled magician. Mathewar had no idea where Tobrin lived; the old man visited him occasionally at the College, and more rarely in other places. "And I'll wager we won't see him for a while now. He always seems hardest to find just when he's needed the most."

"He'll only say what he always says—that the problems of the realm don't concern him."

"I'd like to see him say that about the Bound Folk. It's perfectly possible that Noldeth or one of his sons could create enough of them to take over Karededin."

"When are you leaving?"

"It's too late today. And I'll have to say farewell to Jerret. Tomorrow, I suppose."

They walked back to their apartments. Mathewar packed, and Angarred started a letter to Atte and the other children.

She missed them all keenly; she had thought she would be returning home by now. They would be disappointed with her news. She hesitated with her pen over the paper, thinking of them.

Atte had married a farmer and moved away from the College. Despite having grown up around magicians and forest folk she had become a remarkably practical and level-headed woman with no ability for magic of her own. Angarred's three children with Mathewar— Sorred, Berren, and Eliath—had been raised on magic, and they had looked forward to visiting their half-sister and seeing something as exotic as a farm.

Sorred had shown talent at an early age, and now, at thirteen, he studied magic constantly, even sitting at supper with a book propped up in front of him. Angarred knew that Sorred felt himself to be in the shadow of his famous father, that he hoped to reach or even surpass him; and she worried about how serious the boy always looked, and how unhappy.

The second son, Berren, was eleven, and looked to become a good magician as well. Unlike his brother, though, he was easy-going and good-natured and he rarely studied, hoping to get by with the least amount of effort. Angarred worried about him too, about his lack of ambition, but Mathewar said he couldn't really blame the boy; he had done the same himself for a while, and like Berren he had never fallen behind in his studies.

Eliath, their daughter, was six; if she had any talent in magic it would start showing up soon. Mathewar had told his sons what to watch for while they were away, but Angarred wondered if they would: Sorred ignored everything but his studies, and Berren, though he loved Eliath, seemed to treat her as a pet.

Angarred sighed. She started a description of Jerret's ceremony, leaving out all mention of the Bound Folk.

# T H R E E

**O**ver three hundred miles to the north, in Goss, a group of friends and family had gathered for a party. Candles shone luminous from the iron wheels overhead—good wax candles too; no expense had been spared for their guest. Garlands hung from the ceiling, and the tables, also strewn with colorful flowers, had been pushed back to the walls. Three musicians played in a corner while folks in their best clothes danced on the plain wood floors, and two or three on the tables.

The guest himself sat on a chair in the shadows and looked on uncomfortably. He had washed for the first time in weeks, tied back his long wild dark brown hair, and dressed in his cousin's clean clothes. When he'd looked in the mirror he'd seen a stranger, someone far older than his twenty years, unrecognizable except for the grief and horror that showed in his brown eyes. He felt at a great distance from these people, as if a wall had been erected in front of him, one hard as iron but clear as glass.

He glanced at the food on one of the tables, piles of cheeses, bread, apples, pears. He knew that Aspen Valley, hidden in the hills away from the Karedek forces, was as pinched by hunger as everyone else, that they had brought out what they had to welcome him. Still, he could not help but think how his men would fall on this food, how they could feast for days on it.

"Do you want to dance, Brangwin?" someone asked.

He looked up. A woman stood there, smiling down at him. Her expression seemed odd, and he realized that he had not seen anyone smile in a long time. Then he blinked and she became his cousin's wife, a woman no longer young with worried blue eyes and a circlet of yellow flowers in her yellow hair.

"No, thank you, Lirden," he said.

"You can't just sit here in the shadows and not talk to anyone. They went to a lot of trouble to arrange all this, you know."

"I know," he said. For a moment he had the wild idea that he could tell her about the last few months. He had written poetry, back in his other life, but in the hills it had seemed frivolous to play with words, and here all the words had deserted him, perhaps in consequence.

"Any woman here would be happy to dance with you," she said.

"I know," he said.

"It's not so hard, dancing. You'll probably remember it once you get started."

"I'll try."

She smiled once more and left him. He watched her as she went, saw the light from the candles fall on her as she came into the center of the hall.

Brangwin looked around him again. He had never been to Aspen Valley; refugees from the farms and villages around his castle had built it while he had been fighting the Bound Folk. Most places in Goss were made of stone, but there hadn't been time for that here; the meeting hall still smelled of cut pine, and the walls shone white with new wood.

His cousin Madaroc headed toward him; Lirden must have told him something about his bad behavior. "You could at least make an effort, Brangwin," Madaroc said.

I am, he wanted to say. Instead he said, "I haven't rested like this for nearly half a year. This is the best gift you could give me."

"I'm glad you like it," Madaroc said. Brangwin could not tell if he spoke mockingly or not. "Some of these boys want to join you, to go fight the Karedek. Do you want to talk to them?"

"Later."

"We've been training them to fight with swords and axes. And a few of them are strong enough now to pull a bow."

Brangwin nearly laughed. He would wound his cousin terribly if he did, though. "The fighting—it's not like what we learned as children. There's no graceful give and take. The Bound Folk—the Bound Folk keep fighting until their life's blood is all spilled. They don't feel pain or fear. They can go on even if they've lost an arm, or their stomach has been ripped open."

Madaroc flinched. He had gone too far, Brangwin saw. What was a commonplace in the hills was here something too dreadful to speak aloud.

"For Tashtery's sake, why don't you stop this?" Madaroc said angrily. He had wanted to say this all along, Brangwin realized. "What's keeping you out there? Is it honor? Some stupid idea of honor?"

Madaroc had said *awith*, "honor" in old Gossek. Words in Gossek were formed from roots; their meanings changed according to changes in prefixes or suffixes or vowels. "Honor" was related to "promise" and "law" and "word," and more distantly to "heritage" and "story." Brangwin hadn't thought of honor in a long time. He shook his head.

"Why don't you come live in Aspen Valley with us?" Madaroc said. "For every one of the Bound Folk you kill, that Karedek devil will make two more. And people who have been to his fortress say he has hundreds of them, maybe thousands. If you go on like this you'll only get yourself killed, which would be a stupid waste."

He might not get himself killed, though. Worse could happen, though Madaroc didn't know it and Brangwin was not about to tell him. He could be captured and turned into a bound man himself. A week ago he had fought and killed one of his men who had been changed this way, and since then he had been unable to command, or even to make the slightest decision. Finally he had decided to accept his cousin's invitation and come to Aspen Valley to rest.

Why didn't he quit? Why didn't he marry one of these women, settle down in the valley and raise crops and children like everyone else? He honestly didn't know anymore. One memory kept him fighting, something he had encountered in the hills. He had been bathing in a stream when he had seen what looked like logs heading toward him from the south. But as they came closer he realized that they weren't logs but men, dead men, at least a dozen of them.

The Bound Folk wore out quickly from their ill use. More and more had to be made, to work the mines in the south, to fight the Gossek, to guard the Binder's fortress. In time the Karedek devil would discover the valley, no matter how well hidden it was. Brangwin saw all of these people, dancing, laughing, eating, all of them happy and alive—he saw them walking in step, chanting to the monotonous rhythm of their march. Everyone would die or be enslaved—it was only a matter of time.

"I have to get some air," he said to his cousin.

When he came back the tables and benches had been set up in the middle of the room. Women came out from the kitchen bearing platters that smelled deliciously of mutton. Madaroc stood at a table at the front of the room and motioned to Brangwin to join him.

Brangwin went to his cousin and started to sit next to him. "Stand up," Madaroc whispered. They stood together, both tall and rangy like most of their family, with the same brown hair and eyes. Madaroc had grown softer in the valley, though; his face was rounder, his hair had been cut, his gaze was unconcerned as he looked out over the room. "A toast!" he cried, loudly enough to be heard to the end of the hall.

Men and women hurried to their places and poured red wine from the flagons on the tables. Madaroc held out his own goblet. "A toast!" he said again. "To my magnificent cousin, the scourge of the Karedek, the Binder's fiercest opponent, Prince Brangwin!"

Brangwin flinched when Madaroc shouted his title; the Karedek did not know that a son of the royal family had escaped the castle fire and still lived. But of course that was no secret in the valley; everyone here knew who he was, and saw him as the hope of Goss.

Madaroc indicated that he should say something. "I thank you," Brangwin said. "I'm unused to—well, unused to a great many things, and one of them is hospitality. I thank you greatly for yours, which I will treasure always."

The people cheered again and sat down to the meal. Brangwin ate sparingly, unable to forget his men in the hills, who lived on what they hunted and what the folks in the surrounding farms could spare. The Gossek farmers helped them as much as they dared, but for the most part they had been terrorized by the invaders. They might have died for their beliefs, but few of them would risk becoming slaves with no will and no memory of who they used to be—and Brangwin did not think he could blame them.

A small hum of conversation started up in the hall. Someone at Brangwin's table said, "I don't understand why we simply can't rout this man, this Binder."

The man was a minor court official who had been promoted above his stature. A distressing number of people had risen this way; most of the king's advisors and officials had died in the burning of the castle. Brangwin could not remember his name.

"Brangwin, what do you say?" the man said around a bite of rabbit. "Destroy the Binder. Once he's gone the Bound Folk will have no one to obey—they'll probably simply drop in their tracks."

"Well, for one thing we don't know what the Bound Folk will do," Brangwin said. "It's possible they'll continue to follow their orders, no matter what happens to the Binder. And for another—"

"Yes, but why don't you try it?" the man asked gruffly. "I don't understand what you've been doing all this time."

Brangwin breathed deeply, using discipline he had learned in battle to keep calm. "For another, we did try to slip inside the Binder's city. There are hundreds of Bound Folk there, more than we could count. My men tried to pass themselves off as Bound Folk, but they were discovered—I don't know how."

"Then watch the city, learn how to impersonate them."

"Impersonate" was the wrong word, Brangwin thought. It implied the existence of a person, and the Bound Folk were not people. "We've tried that too," he said. "It's too dangerous. It's possible that he—that the Binder—sees into the minds of the people he controls, and that he became aware of us because our minds were hidden from him. I'm not willing to lose more men that way." He stared into the shadows of the hall, remembering.

"You think," the man said. "You don't know, do you?"

"You're welcome to look for yourself if you like," Brangwin said, his politeness slipping. Madaroc kicked his ankle, and he bent to his supper and said nothing else for the rest of the meal.

Finally the feast ended. One of the musicians began to sing, a ballad in old Gossek about Prince Irru's miraculous victory over the

Karedek. Karededin had invaded and occupied Goss and Finbar and Ou many times over the years, but they had always fought free. They had ended up speaking the usurper's language, though, and it had become the fashion among the nobility to study Gossek, to go into the isolated eastern valleys and learn the language from folks who still kept the old traditions, or to hire these people as servants and caretakers for their children.

Now, listening to the song he had heard in the cradle from his old nurse, his defenses weakened by food and drink and fellowship, Brangwin felt himself horribly close to weeping. What next? he thought. Was he about to stand and sing along with the musicians, tears streaming down his face, as he had seen old soldiers do?

To his relief the ballad ended. Another started up, this one in Karedek but hauntingly familiar. Finally he recognized it, and he turned angrily to his cousin.

"Are you going to let them sing that song?" he asked.

"I wasn't listening," Madaroc said, startled. "What is it?"

"Lies about that Karedek sorcerer. Mathewar."

"Mathewar? I don't . . . Wasn't he the one who ended that war in Karededin a while back?"

"So they say. And if he could end a war, he's powerful enough to create the Bound Folk."

"You think Mathewar is—is the Binder?" Madaroc asked.

"You mean you don't know who the Binder is?" the dreadful official said. "By Tashtery, I would have thought surely that by this time—"

Brangwin stood and left the hall. Once outside he slowed, then stopped and gazed up at the stars for a long moment. "Brangwin," his cousin's voice said behind him.

"Is this why I fight?" Brangwin asked, still looking at the glittering sky. "So that these idiots can stay safe and warm and satisfied, and tell me why my tactics are wrong?" He turned to Madaroc.

"I don't know why you fight," Madaroc said. "I told you, I think you should stop. And I say this as someone who will inherit, or whose sons will inherit, if you die."

Inherit a country of dead men, Brangwin thought. He could not trust himself to say anything more, and he headed toward Madaroc and Lirden's house, where Lirden had prepared a room for him.

But after he had climbed into the huge featherbed he could not fall asleep. His stomach ached from the rich food he had eaten, and the bed was far too soft for a man who had been sleeping on a cave floor; he felt he might sink into it forever, until it swallowed him. He thought of his men shivering in the cave, and from there his mind turned to his usual litany of worries: their small store of food; the dwindling supply of blankets, of weapons, of the herbs they used to treat their wounds; the men who deserted, more and more of them now.

He remembered one man in particular, Gorren. Gorren fought day after day with few complaints; in fact, he seemed to grumble only because the other men expected it from him. Then one day they had an unusually easy skirmish with a company of Bound Folk, a battle in which they killed a good many and lost no men themselves.

For some reason, though, it was this fight that made Gorren run mad. Afterward he attacked invisible men, or trees, or his fellow soldiers; he wandered far through the forest, talking intently to himself. Several times he had ordinary conversations that ended with him shouting about mundane things—the laundry, for example, or the weather. Finally one day he had left the camp and never come back.

Brangwin grew sleepier. The nightmares that had plagued him since he had started to fight returned, and in his drowsy state he could not struggle against them. What if he had to fight people he knew? What if the Binder had enslaved his parents, his brother and sisters, his friends and servants? He felt certain they had all died in the firing of the castle—died while he had been out singing foolish songs to someone, he could barely remember who—but what if they hadn't?

And tomorrow, he thought, he would have to speak to some young men about fighting the Bound Folk. Their heads would be as stuffed with foolish thoughts as his bed was of feathers; they would talk of adventure and bravery and pushing the Karedek back over the border. And he, Brangwin, could not frighten them too badly; none of them would volunteer if they knew what lay in store for them.

The featherbed claimed him; he fell down into it and drifted off into his haunted sleep.

# FOUR

Farther north, in the icy country of Ou, Caireddin and her friends sat in a tavern at night and looked out at the fog. It ebbed and flowed, and sometimes when it swept back it uncovered not the sea and the rough sand they knew but a round bone-white tower.

Magic lay thick in places in Ou. Stories abounded of folks picking up strange knives or beads or books, and the horrible fates that awaited them. Everyone knew to avoid certain places, to stay behind locked doors at the dark of the moon, to turn away at the least sign of anything uncanny. Nine hundred years ago the Sorcerers' Wars had laid waste to the country, and it had taken centuries for the land to recover.

In the south, folks had heard, a magician named Tobrin had bound most wild magic into a stone. Tobrin had never reached the north, though, had never climbed the passes through the mountains on the border between Karededin and Goss, or walked the frozen wastes of Ou. And so people feared magic here, and no magician had ever gone from Ou to the College in Karededin, and if a child showed an ability to work magic he or she knew to say nothing about it.

The tower seemed to draw Caireddin's friends. "What would

happen if we climbed it?" Jofre asked. They had all had a good deal to drink, as usual.

"What would happen?" said Tarkennin. "It would dissolve, probably, and we'd find ourselves five stories in the air, with nothing beneath us."

"There might be something inside," Jofre said. "A charm or talisman that no one's seen for centuries. We could gain unlimited power."

Tarkennin's family had a tarnished old armband that they claimed held power from the Sorcerers' Wars. Tarkennin had once taken out a carved box and shown it to Caireddin, though he hadn't let her touch it, and took care not to touch it himself. All of his family seemed to be wary of it.

"All the more reason to stay away," Tarkennin said now. "You know how dangerous those things are."

"Are you afraid?" Jofre asked.

Of course he was afraid, Caireddin thought. He'd be a fool if he wasn't. She said nothing, though. She was the only woman among them, and the youngest at eighteen, and sometimes she thought that they only tolerated her.

"Not at all," Tarkennin said. "I'm merely being sensible. Someone has to."

"Sensible, though," Suby said, struggling to turn some thought into speech. "Sensible means what you can sense, right? What you touch or see or hear. And so if we can touch the tower—" He nearly lost his idea, groped for it a moment, found it again. "If we can touch it that means it's real. We can climb it."

"All right then," Jofre said. He grabbed his cloak and hurried to the door, and the others followed.

"It's only real at the moment we touch it, though," Tarkennin said, going slowly. "It might not—"

No one paid any attention to him. They paused only to take several torches from the walls. The taverner scowled at them but said nothing. These young men, and the young woman too, were minor children of nobility, folks who had nothing better to do than sit in taverns and run up reckonings that might never be paid—and he could do nothing about it.

They ran out into the icy cold night, toward the fog. They stood and watched it, gathering their courage. It rolled back and revealed the tower.

Jofre hesitated only a moment. Then he gave a loud cry, ran toward the tower, and hit the wall with his hand. They all heard the loud slap.

Caireddin ran after him, terrified. She struck the wall; it was as real as anything she had ever touched.

"Look!" Jofre said, pointing to a door in the wall. Caireddin didn't remember seeing it before; perhaps it had only come into existence in the last few moments. It stood open, revealing darkness beyond.

Jofre ran through it. "Hey!" Tarkennin said. "You shatterpated lunatic!"

"Victory favors the mad!" Jofre shouted from inside the tower.

Caireddin grabbed the hilt of her dagger with her free hand, then shouted and rushed through the door. "You said you didn't want to live!" she called back to Tarkennin.

Everyone laughed. Tarkennin had written a poem to a woman he claimed to love, telling her he couldn't live without her. No one had believed his protestations for a moment, though.

Inside, in the dim light, Caireddin saw green marble stairs spiraling up against the circular walls. A torch flared above her and she ran toward it. Footsteps clattered behind her: Tarkennin and Suby had braved the door. Voices shouted up and down the stairs, calling out encouragement.

Several turns of the stairs later she slowed to a walk. Her companions' footfalls sounded different, more muffled; the steps here had changed from marble to wood. She heard cries of fear, distorted by echoes, and she turned back to see only darkness; at least one of the torches had gone out.

A cold wind came from somewhere. She shivered within her cloak. Her torch blew out. "Hey!" she shouted. "Hey, Jofre, wait a minute! Wait—I need light!" The small red light above her receded. She began to run again, trying to keep it in sight.

The light disappeared. Was it out, or had Jofre simply gone one level up and out of her sight? Or—she shivered in the cold—had Jofre extinguished his own torch, was he waiting in the darkness for her? He had played a good many pranks like that before; he was not, as her mother never stopped reminding her, a kind person. She imagined him in front of her, his bitter cold hand reaching toward her from the shadows, and she shuddered again.

Well, there was no point thinking of her mother now. She rushed on ahead. Something cracked beneath her, and she fell. She held her breath, terrified that she would tumble to the bottom of the tower. But she stayed where she was, and she realized that her leg had gone through one of the wooden steps. "Help!" she called out. "Help!"

No one came. She wrenched her leg up out of the crack. Her heart was beating fast, too fast for her to feel any pain, though she knew that would come later.

She turned and went down as fast as she could in the dark, her hand brushing the wall for guidance. No one passed her; Tarkennin and Suby must have gone back as well.

She wondered if the door would be there, or if the tower would dissolve around her, as Tarkennin said. She forced herself to go slower; she could not risk another fall.

To her relief she finally saw light coming through the open doorway. Outside the sun lay on the flat plain to the east, glowering red below the fog.

She turned. The tower wavered like smoke and then disappeared. Beyond it she could just barely see the waves of the ocean washing to the shore and back.

What had happened to the others? She looked around frantically and saw Tarkennin staring gape-mouthed at the vanished tower. She ran to him and they held on to each other, something she could not remember ever doing with any of the companions. "What's this?" Jofre said from behind her. "Found another lover so soon, Tarkennin?"

She spun around, letting go of him. Jofre grinned at them. "Where—where did you come from?" she asked. "We saw the tower disappear. . . ."

"Nonsense," Jofre said. "I just walked through the doorway." He turned back to where the tower had been, and for a brief moment a look of terror appeared on his face. He composed himself quickly; they all prided themselves on their coolness in the face of danger.

Jofre had once said that if he had to ride to war his battle cry would be "Imperturbability!"

Caireddin moved away from Tarkennin, trying not to let her fear and worry show. "Where's Suby?" she asked.

"What?" Suby said. He stood some distance away on the plain, gazing around him with a look of befuddlement. "I'm here—where else would I be?"

The sun rose higher, burning off the fog. It was only then that she remembered her mother wanted her home by daybreak, though she had forgotten why. Well, she would be late again. It didn't matter; it did not do to give in to Efcharren too often.

"I've got to be going," she said to the others.

"Is your mother calling?" Jofre asked. He put his hand to his ear. "Oh, yes, there she is. Caiiii-reddin, Caiiii-reddin . . ."

"I think that's your mother," Tarkennin said to Jofre, "moaning because her son is such a blockhead."

"I'm just tired," Caireddin said. "Aren't you?"

"Not at all," Suby said. "The night is young."

Jofre snorted a laugh. Tarkennin laughed with him, and Suby joined in, and suddenly all three of them were howling with hilarity, clutching each other for support, as though Suby had told the funniest joke they had ever heard. Caireddin turned and went back to the tavern for her horse.

Her mother, as she had feared, had stayed up all night waiting for her. She looked as composed as always, though, her fine brown hair gathered neatly in a bun and her eyes sharp and alert. She had grown stouter as she had gotten older, but the years had done nothing to her beauty; it was easy to see what about her had attracted great lords and kings.

"Hurry up, go wash yourself and get dressed," Efcharren said. "You smell like a brewery."

"A winery, please, Mother," Caireddin said. "Give me credit for some standards."

Efcharren ignored her. "And you've ruined your clothes again. And is that blood on your leg?"

Caireddin looked down and saw the long tear in her trousers. "I think so."

"Holy Marfan and Mathona, have you been dueling again?"

"Well, I have to. You know I can't let challenges go unanswered."

"How many times have I warned you about dueling? You have to be careful, especially considering who you are. Well, don't just stand there. They'll be here any minute."

"Who?"

"And do what you can with your hair. And try to wear something nice for a change . . ."

Caireddin left her in the middle of a sentence. As she went she realized she could have told her mother the truth about her bleeding leg; a night in an enchanted tower would be every bit as frightening to her as a duel. As it was she had only dueled once—well, twice, really, but the second had been more of a brawl.

She waited for Shorry, their only servant, to heat the water for the bath. She settled in, washed off the blood and dirt and spilled beer, and scrubbed her hair. A thread of pink drifted up from her cut leg, which throbbed painfully in the hot water.

She sat for a long time while the water cooled around her. Her mother had been King Tezue's mistress; Caireddin was Tezue's illegitimate daughter. That meant, as Efcharren never tired of telling her, that she and King Jerret were the only members of the royal family left alive.

It didn't matter to Caireddin; she knew she would never be a queen, probably never even see Karededin. But Efcharren had intrigued a great deal for Caireddin over the years. She had wanted to return to Karededin during the War of All the Realms, when the succession had seemed uncertain; and she had almost claimed the crown for her daughter when Tezue died, and again after Rodarren's death. But travel had been too dangerous during the war, and afterward the crown had been handed down peacefully from Tezue to Rodarren and then from Rodarren to Jerret.

Caireddin's eyes closed and she leaned back in the bath. She was tired, and still a little drunk from the night in the tavern. She forced her eyes open and got out of the tub.

When she went to her bedroom she found that Shorry had set out one of her dresses, no doubt under orders from her mother. She ignored it and put on clean trousers and a shirt and belted on her dagger.

She stopped briefly to look in the mirror. Visitors from Karededin had commented on her resemblance to Queen Rodarren, and she could only think that Rodarren had been a remarkably plain woman. Caireddin had unexceptional brown hair that, to her mother's despair, she wore in the same style as her male friends, in waves that fell to her shoulders. Her face was too long and looked unhealthily sallow, and there were dark hollows under her eyes—though that, of course, could have been from staying up every night.

As she headed down the hallway she could hear her mother talking to two or three men. One of the men coughed loudly for a moment and then continued, saying something about the war in Goss.

She walked through the cluttered room where her mother received visitors. Three men turned to look at her. Two of them had striking good looks and seemed enough alike to be relatives; they had very pale skin, lustrous black hair, and blue eyes. The third looked as dull as she herself did: brown hair, hazel eyes, brown clothes.

"There you are," Efcharren said. She frowned at the clothes Caireddin was wearing. "At last. This is Lord Noldeth Haru"—she indicated the older of the two handsome men—"and his sons, Lord Drustig and Lord Cullen. And this, of course, is my daughter, Lady Caireddin."

They bowed to her, and the other handsome man—Drustig—grinned. He had a wolfish smile, with very white teeth; it seemed to promise all sorts of forbidden excitement. She found herself grinning back. Shorry brought in a tray of bread and cooked meat, and before she could set it on the table Drustig helped himself to both with one large hand. He already held an empty goblet in his other hand, and he waved it around until Shorry set the tray down and refilled it.

"Lord Haru and his sons have been Jerret's trusted advisors since the coronation," Efcharren went on, motioning to the men to sit down.

They picked up their conversation where they had left off, talking about Goss. Caireddin listened without interest as Lord Noldeth spoke of troop strength, weapons, towns and cities she had never heard of conquered. "Goss is practically a part of Karededin now," he said. "There are only a few rebels left in the entire country."

She should say something, if only to let them know she was still here. Her head was still muddy from drink and lack of sleep, though, and she had a hard time following the conversation.

"I've heard talk of a rebel leader who won't give up," she said, cutting off Noldeth in the middle of a sentence. "Some even say he's a member of the royal family."

Noldeth looked at her in surprise. "Where did you hear that?" he asked.

Her friends learned a great deal of gossip from brothers and sisters and cousins who paid attention to politics. "Oh, everyone seems to know it," Caireddin said airily.

"You have some knowledgeable friends, milady," Noldeth said.

Efcharren said something about the Gossek royal family. Noldeth began to cough, and everyone waited politely until he finished. Caireddin's attention strayed; she found herself looking at the room with the eyes of her visitors. King Tezue had settled a good deal of money on Efcharren, but for her part she had had to agree to leave Karededin. The room, like the rest of the house, was crowded with family relics and gifts from Tezue and objects Efcharren had bought in various places; Tezue's generosity had not run to a bigger place to live.

Massive pieces of furniture lined the walls, in places two and even three deep, jutting out awkwardly into the room. Suits of armor leaned against them, and lamps and candelabras and glassware covered every surface. There was a stained-glass window in a corner where the sun couldn't reach it; Caireddin didn't even remember what it showed. Rugs piled up on top of other rugs, in places so deep the unwary could sink into them. Paintings and banners, tapestries and coats of arms obscured the spaces on the walls that remained, some of them on top of others, waiting until Efcharren could decide which she liked best. The room had a persistent smell of mold; Shorry had never been able to discover where it came from. There was little space to walk, though she and Efcharren had marked out paths over the years.

Efcharren looked up sharply at something Noldeth said; Caireddin saw that the two of them were finally nearing the reason for Nold-eth's visit. "What about him?" her mother said.

"King Jerret is ill, they say. Very ill."

"Is he?" Efcharren said. She looked sorrowful at the news, but Caireddin knew her well enough to sense the stark interest beneath her sadness.

"Some are even whispering that he isn't expected to live," Nold-eth said.

"May I ask a question?" Caireddin said. Her mother scowled at her. She went on without waiting for an answer. "You say you're the king's counselors. What brings you to Ou?"

Efcharren scowled harder. Noldeth grinned, a less crazed version of his son's expression. "That's a very good question, Princess Caireddin." Now it was her turn to scowl; she had no right to that ti-tle, and he must know it. "We've been exiled, I'm afraid. There's a faction at court that's turned Jerret against us, seduced him with pretty promises . . . He's really very young, you know, only fourteen years old. Well, he'll call us back when he realizes what bad advice he's being given. Either that or . . ."

Caireddin heard the words as clearly as if he'd said them aloud—"or he'll die." No one would speak plainly here; everything would be couched in coded words and vague phrases. "How very interesting, Lord Noldeth," she said, her tone implying just the opposite.

Noldeth saw he was losing her. "Unfortunately, it looks very much as if poor Jerret will die without an heir." He waited for her to ask a question; when she didn't he went on, speaking faster. "There are only two men who can possibly succeed him, and they stand here before you, Lords Drustig and Cullen. They've been with Jerret since the beginning of the reign, you see—they know how to manage things, how to do the country the most good."

"What about you, Lord Noldeth?" Caireddin asked. "You would make a wonderful king."

Noldeth looked startled. She had interrupted his speech; worse, he seemed to sense the mockery in her tone. "I thank you, milady," he said. "Unfortunately, I am too ill to take the crown. My sole hope is to see one of my sons on the throne before I die." He cleared his throat; it turned into a cough that went on a while before he brought it under control. "If Drustig or Cullen becomes king, though, the line in the Hall of the Standing Kings will come to an end, since we are not descendants of the royal family. It's rank superstition, of course, but the people care about such things. And so . . ."

She had seen where this was heading from the moment Noldeth had mentioned Jerret's illness. "Oh, you flatter me, milord," she said.

Efcharren scowled again. "It's no mere flattery," Noldeth said. "Either of my sons would consider it an honor to marry you. And think what it would mean to you. Queen of Karededin. Your heir a king, your name remembered as a god when you die . . ."

"I hear Jerret's thinking about proclaiming an heir, though," Caireddin said. "Someone from Finbar, or Emindal, one of those islands."

"Now that is absolutely untrue," Noldeth said. His pleasant expression slipped; he looked furious. "And believe me, I would certainly have heard such a thing."

His eyes shied away from hers as he spoke. She realized that he was lying, though whether about Jerret's heir or the extent of his knowledge she didn't know. She felt suddenly tired of all the fencing; even the fact that she had angered him no longer seemed like a victory. He began to talk about the parts of the country he commanded, the popularity of his family in Karededin and how quickly either son would be acclaimed king, but she paid little attention.

Finally they rose to leave. "Well, we'll certainly think about what you've told us here," Efcharren said. She would not commit herself to anything without seeing what happened in Karededin, Caireddin knew; Jerret might truly have chosen an heir, or could even recover from his illness.

Drustig took Caireddin's hand and kissed it. "I'll be made king," he said softly as he raised his head to her. He grinned. "I'm the oldest."

"You?" Cullen said in a louder voice. "You'll never be allowed back in Karededin. Not after—"

"Not after what?" Caireddin said, as innocently as she could.

"Come, both of you," Lord Noldeth said. "Thank you very much for your hospitality, Lady Efcharren. Princess Caireddin."

He bowed. Efcharren led him and his sons out of the room; Caireddin could hear him coughing as he went down the hallway.

"I don't know about that Lord Drustig," Efcharren said when she came back. "He seemed . . ." She shook her head.

Caireddin understood him very well, though. She and her friends played at moral irresponsibility, but Drustig wasn't acting. He truly did not care about anyone or anything. Though perhaps he cared about her; the look he gave her at the end had been deep, searching, the expression of one rebel recognizing another. She shivered, not entirely pleasantly.

The most amusing part was that her mother could not disapprove of him; he might, after all, become king. She grinned to herself, and wondered what he had done in Karededin.

# F I V E

Only one man could have made Mathewar delay his trip north, and he came to Pergodi early on the day Mathewar was to set out. Mathewar had gone to a courtyard in the middle of the castle, a place he had found long ago but which no one else seemed to know about. There was a dry fountain, crumbling a bit at the edges, in the center; he sat on the fountain's lowest steps and leaned back, his eyes closed, facing the Spring sun.

He had come here to be alone, to think about the Bound Folk, and about magic. His thoughts turned to Jerret instead, and then to his own children. How well would they do if they had become king at such an early age? Suppose they had no one to advise them; or rather too many people, and no way of knowing which of them to trust? He thought they would do well, but then he knew himself to be biased.

He forced himself back to the Bound Folk. He had never encountered anything like them, but he knew there were a good many things he had never seen. Despite all he had learned at the College, despite the books and scrolls and maps and scraps of parchment in the College library, he was coming to understand that he and the other masters knew very little.

There were said to be strange relics in Ou, for example, cups and rings and mirrors that held dangerous magic from the time of the

Sorcerers' War. The library had some books from Ou and Goss, but they were in languages he didn't know, with words that shifted like the fog in those lands, seeming to change their meaning with every reading. In his spare time he was trying to teach himself Ounek and Gossek, but, well, he had no spare time.

Then there was the mystery of women's magic. His magic, the College's magic, dealt mostly with seeming, with illusions. Those taught by the College could do a few other things—see into minds, sometimes, or move objects—but he was coming to think that these abilities were limited, almost trivial.

Fourteen years ago he had seen the forest folk work magic, and it had been a revelation. The women, and some of the men, knew how to change shape, to assume the bodies of animals; they had flown as crows or brought down trees as bears. It was a magic of becoming, of actual transformation.

When he became First Master he had invited women into the College for the first time since its founding nine hundred years ago. Some of the older masters had objected, but he had ignored them. What would happen if the two magics were joined, if one could become a thing instead of seem it? If magic were truth instead of illusion?

But since then he had come no nearer to solving the problem. Some of the students had learned shape-shifting, and some had learned the more traditional magic—it seemed to depend on which they studied first, as if no one mind could hold both. What was more galling, though, was that *he* could not master the magic of transformation, despite all the attempts he had made, with and without Angarred's help. And Angarred, who had learned how to change shape from the forest folk, felt frustrated as well.

The masters who had objected to allowing women in the College now wanted to see them gone. Nothing had been gained by their presence, these men said. Women had their own magic—let them go to the forest if they wanted to study.

The sorcerers had known the answers to these questions. Nine hundred years ago—

"Good morning, Mathewar," someone said.

Mathewar opened his eyes and squinted into the sun. A short, thin man stood in front of him, his wild white hair shining in the light.

"Master Tobrin!" he said, getting to his feet quickly. It was no co-incidence that Tobrin had shown up just as his thoughts had turned to the old sorcerers; he must have had some sense of the man. He wondered briefly how Tobrin had found him, but he knew better than to ask. "You've come to help me with the Bound Folk, then?"

"No, not at all," Tobrin said. "I'm here for a game of kettim."

Now Mathewar noticed that Tobrin was carrying a wooden box under his arm; he had known that Mathewar wouldn't have bothered to bring his own set from home. He sighed. He and Tobrin had played numerous games of kettim; however, Mathewar played a deeper game of his own as he tried to ferret out the secrets of To-brin's vast abilities.

As a boy Mathewar had been taught that Master Tobrin had lived nine hundred years ago, that he had founded the College, that he had bound all destructive magic into a Stone and so stopped the ruinous Sorcerers' Wars that were tearing the realms apart. Fourteen years ago, though, he had discovered that the truth was much more com-plex: Tobrin had transformed *himself* into the Stone, and so had kept watch on the land through the ages. But Tobrin cared nothing for what he called politics, the problems of the realms; his only concern was to see that the Sorcerers' Wars did not flare up again.

Tobrin, like the forest folk, had the ability to shift his shape, and he knew the magic of illusion that the College taught as well. He was the only person Mathewar knew who had mastered both—but he refused to give up his secrets, saying that they were too dangerous.

Mathewar had spent fourteen years of frustrated talk with the man. Now whenever they met they seemed to engage in a duel, with every move a part of the contest.

"Well, what are you waiting for?" Tobrin said. "Let's go to your apartment and play."

They went inside and up the stairs to Mathewar and Angarred's rooms. Mathewar worried that the climb might be too difficult for the old man, but he looked as tireless as ever.

"Master Tobrin!" Angarred said as they came inside. "Hello!"

She saw the box under his arm. Mathewar knew that she felt im-patient with their long games, that she did not believe Tobrin would ever part with any of his hoarded knowledge, either purposely or by accident. But she gave no sign of her feelings; she said only, "Here—I'll get the table ready for you."

He and Angarred used the table for more than meals; she had to clear off books and scrolls and scraped parchment, quills and inkstands, cloth and needles and thread. Then she left them; she had told Mathewar once that if she had to watch another game of kettim she would not be responsible for her actions.

Mathewar and Tobrin sat and laid the board on the table. Tobrin had the most beautiful set Mathewar had ever seen. The board was marble, the squares outlined in gold, the stones fashioned of jade and onyx, ebony and amethyst, chalcedony and figured glass. The stones were round, curved at the top and bottom like shells, so that they wobbled for a while after they were set down.

The two men tossed for the first move. Tobrin won and pushed a stone across the board.

"Have you seen the Bound Folk in the castle?" Mathewar asked, making the first move in the other game they played. He placed a stone on a square in front of him.

"Always so impatient," Tobrin said. "You might ask me how I am first. Or how my journey went."

"I might, but I think this is far more important."

"I'm fine, thank you. And I had a wonderful journey."

"Where did you travel from?" Mathewar asked. He glanced up, one eyebrow raised, knowing that Tobrin would never answer that question.

Tobrin set down a stone near Mathewar's and studied the board.

"Did you see any Bound Folks on your journey?" Mathewar asked.

"Yes."

"An answer, praise the Orator. Do you know who created them?"

Tobrin said nothing.

"Do you know the Harus?" Mathewar said. "I think they're the ones making them, but I don't know how."

Silence from Tobrin.

"You can't say this isn't your responsibility," Mathewar said. "The Bound Folk could overrun the realm, destroy Karededin. Isn't that what you stayed around to prevent—the misuse of magic?" He moved a stone. "If you know how to stop this and you won't tell me you're as culpable as whoever's doing it. Every time he binds someone it's as if you did it, as if you took away their memories, their histories, their life. As if you enslaved them."

"I told you—these things are not my concern," Tobrin said, making another move.

"Well, they ought to be your cursed concern!" Mathewar took a breath to calm himself; he could not let his anger overwhelm him. "Have you seen their minds? It's an abomination—there's nothing there, nothing except whatever orders they've been given."

"Yes."

" 'Yes' what? Yes, you've seen their minds, or yes, you're listening to me?"

"If you concentrated more on the game you wouldn't lose so often."

"I win more times than you do and you know it," Mathewar said, then realized he had fallen into Tobrin's trap and changed the subject. "Maybe I *should* lose—maybe I should work harder on asking you questions."

"It's your turn again."

"I don't understand how you can sleep at night."

"I sleep very well, thank you."

They played for a while in silence. Mathewar tilted the back of his chair against the wall. The wall was too close and the chair fell forward again, and he spoke a few words of magic to keep it where he wanted it.

Tobrin frowned; clearly he did not approve of Mathewar's frivolous use of magic. He had become more irascible over the years; sometimes he even lost his infuriating calm. Probably it was infinitely easier being a stone than a man. All to the good—if Mathewar goaded him enough he might make a mistake.

"Here's what I know about the Bound Folk," Mathewar said. "They were created by someone in the north, probably one of Noldeth's sons, probably Polgar. They're being used to work the mines—Jerret's spent all the money in the treasury and needs the wealth the mines can bring him. It's possible the Harus will do more with the Bound Folk—that they'll create enough men for an army, and, as I said, all of Karededin will be overrun."

Silence from Tobrin.

"I was about to leave for the north today, but then you came by," Mathewar said. More silence. "I'll go tomorrow instead."

"I've never been to the north," Tobrin said.

Mathewar looked up. In all the years they had played together Tobrin had never said anything about his history. Was this a clue, did Tobrin's words mean more than they seemed to? No, they couldn't possibly.

"I'd write you about it," Mathewar said, "if I knew where you lived."

They reached the endgame. Mathewar studied the stones, gold and black and ivory. He made one last try. "I could use the Stone to free the Bound Folk, you know," he said.

"The Stone is dangerous," Tobrin said.

"It is," Mathewar said. "Dangerous to use, and dangerous not to." He dropped the front legs of his chair to the floor and pushed a piece across the board. "You're going to lose in three moves."

Tobrin studied the board for a long time. Finally he nodded, slid the stones off the board, and set up for another game.

"Why do you play with me if all we do is argue?" Mathewar asked.

"You're the only one I can talk to," Tobrin said.

Mathewar thought of their conversation and began to laugh. The laughter went on and on, with a touch of hysteria in it: he was playing for such high stakes it was a relief to relax.

"You call this . . ." He was unable to speak for a moment. He wiped his eyes on his sleeve. "You call this talking?"

"I don't see what's so amusing," Tobrin said. "Toss for the first move."

A few hours later, after Tobrin had gone, Mathewar went to bid farewell to the king. As he expected, Jerret did not like the idea of him leaving.

"I don't understand why you have to go away," Jerret said. "I already told you what's happening in the north. Polgar's there—he's working the mines for me."

"Don't you want to know who's creating the Bound Folk?" Mathewar asked.

"I suppose so. But why do *you* have to go? I could send someone else."

"Who? Anyone you send might be working for the Harus."

"I think you're obsessed with the Harus. They're not as bad as you think—they've helped me a lot."

"They revolted against you."

"Just Drustig." Jerret seemed about to say something else and then stopped, as if he realized that this was an argument he could not win. "It isn't fair for you to leave right now. You told me I'm not supposed to listen to the Harus, but if you go away there won't be anyone left to advise me. And Ezlin's leaving too—he's going home in two days."

"Angarred will be here."

"I don't want Angarred," Jerret said unreasonably. "I want you."

"What happened to Rodarren's councilors?" Mathewar asked.

"They—I don't know. They went home, most of them, after I dismissed them."

"Why did you dismiss them?"

"The Harus—the Harus thought I should."

Jerret was becoming more honest, Mathewar thought. He couldn't criticize him now; he had to be patient, let the boy come to his own conclusions. "Is that why you sent all the court magicians away?" he asked.

Jerret nodded. "Noldeth didn't think the magicians would be completely loyal to me."

Mathewar felt a rising anger. Noldeth had wiped all the other players off the board, even the magicians who had been sent to help the king. In the end, Jerret had seen no one but the Harus and his frivolous friends. Let him not pardon that family, Mathewar prayed, though he did not believe in the Godkings.

"Perhaps you could send to the College for more court magicians," he said, as calmly as he could.

"Perhaps," Jerret said. He did not sound certain.

"I'll be back as quickly as I can. We can talk about this then."

"All right," Jerret said. He seemed to remember his manners and said, "May the Navigator guide you on your journey."

A few nights after she had met the Harus, Caireddin sat in the tavern again, watching Jofre methodically strip a trader of his money. He had played a few games of cards with the man, losing them all, and then had won one at the very last minute, making it look almost an accident. The trader had stared in amazement at the pile of coins Jofre raked toward him; clearly he had not been keeping track.

"One more game," the man said. "Give me a chance to win my money back."

"What if you lose?" Jofre asked. He laughed stupidly, as if to say he couldn't imagine such a thing happening.

"I'll double the pile there."

"All right," Jofre said.

His languor fell away. He had grown bored with the game, and he set about winning it as quickly as possible.

Jofre had the most money of any of them; what he won at cards was a pittance compared to the earnings from his estates. Caireddin didn't understand why he enjoyed taking money from innocent travelers but he seemed to grow alive during the games—at least until the end, when his mask slipped and he lost the look of an amiable, slightly foolish lord.

Caireddin looked away; she had seen Jofre do this at least a dozen times. She glanced around her at the small warm room, the torches on the walls, the smoke-blackened beams, the same dark color as the beer. Beyond the window the waves came into shore, edged by foam that glimmered in the darkness. There was no sign of the tower; it had not returned in the four days since that one wild night.

Her eyes met the taverner's, who was watching them with disgust. He had asked Jofre many times not to cheat his customers; it was bad for business. More than that, though, Caireddin guessed that he probably made less in one week than Jofre won in a single night.

The trader stood; he seemed to have suddenly understood the trick that was being played on him. He took a handful of coins from his purse and flung them to the table. Their spinning and ringing was the only noise in the room until the trader slammed the door loudly behind him. A cold blast came into the room.

"Maybe now you'll pay your reckoning," the taverner said.

"A gentleman never pays his reckoning," Jofre said. "That's how they know he's a gentleman. We'll have another round here."

They sat back and drank. "Do you know—" Caireddin said. She hesitated; how could she ask what she wanted to know without giving away her interest? "Have any of you ever heard of a man named something like Drustan? Or Drustig?"

"Of course," Tarkennin said. "He and his family were advisors to King Jerret before they were exiled."

"But why were they exiled?" Caireddin asked. "Drustig seems to have done something horrible, but no one will tell me what it was."

Tarkennin laughed. "I'll say it was horrible. His vassals rose up against him—he did some very bad things, though I don't know exactly what. The king supported them, and Drustig, instead of backing down, made war against him."

"Against—against King Jerret?" Caireddin asked. She felt the same perilous excitement as when Drustig had grinned at her. She and her companions had stolen, and knocked down a fence or two, and chased animals out of barns, but she had never known anyone audacious enough to war with his king. The sheer size of the man's ambition took her breath away.

"That's what they say," Tarkennin said. "They also say he's completely mad. Well, he'd have to be, wouldn't he? To fight against the king?"

"Maybe King Jerret slighted him in some way," Caireddin said.

"Not that I heard," Tarkennin said.

"Why do you ask?" Jofre said. "Do you fancy him?"

"Of course not," Caireddin said. Jofre had always guessed her secrets quicker than anyone else; she hoped she sounded truthful. "My mother introduced me to him and his family—she has some idea that he'd make a good match. It doesn't look as if he'll become king anytime soon, though."

"Is that what you want?" Tarkennin asked. "To be queen? Queen Caireddin?"

"No," Caireddin said. "But if I'm to marry a madman I'd like some compensation."

They laughed, and Tarkennin ordered another round.

For the first few days Mathewar enjoyed his journey. Crops grew in the Spring sun; sheep, heavy with fleece, came up to their fences to watch him pass. The walls around the towns and villages were sturdy, the houses clean and the streets well swept, the people contented if not happy. Queen Rodarren had left the country prosperous, and so far it had withstood whatever Jerret and Lord Noldeth had done to it.

Mathewar could have stayed with any of the magicians the College had sent to the small towns over the years, but he preferred to stop at inns and talk to the folks there. Here too, he saw evidence of a thriving countryside: the inns served good food and ale, and the beds he slept in were comfortable and free of vermin. Best of all, every inn seemed to have a garrulous old taverner, a friendly man or woman eager to gossip.

But as he rode farther north he began to notice Bound Folk. At first there were only a few of them, carrying burdens or repairing houses or working in the fields. One day, though, he saw a cloud of dust on the road ahead, and after a moment he made out a great company of them heading toward him. He had joined a group of travelers on the road for safety, and they scurried aside, leaving the road free. The Bound Folk marched in step as they passed, singing a monotonous song of only two notes.

He asked questions about the Bound Folk, but no one would answer him directly. He did not use his commanding voice; people became different, more circumspect, around magicians.

The next day he spotted a large group of people clustered ahead of him. As he rode closer he saw that they were standing on a riverbank, looking at the current below. No one spoke.

He dismounted and made his way to the river. A body floated past him; he could smell the stench of death from where he stood. More came, and still more; a few piled up at a bend in the river like a grotesque logjam. "Who are they?" he asked the man next to him, though he knew quite well. "What happened to them?"

"They're Bound Folk," the man said, very quietly, as though to name them was to draw them down upon the crowd. "They work 'em too hard, and then they die."

"Who are Bound Folk?" he asked.

"That's nothing I want to know—and you shouldn't either," the man said.

Mathewar turned away from the river and continued down the road.

As night fell he found a tavern, the Cat and Stars. He heard only silence as he stepped inside, and at first he thought that the tavern must not attract very much trade. But as his eyes grew accustomed to the gloom he saw some people he recognized from the riverbank, and he realized that the folks here did not want to talk about what they'd seen; it was as if they'd been struck dumb by the sight.

Two musicians began to play a lute and smallpipes in the corner, and a woman sang; the taverner no doubt wanted a little noise and gaiety around the place. But no one joined in, though the songs were surely familiar to everyone there.

Mathewar got a beef pie and some ale and went to sit at a table. Another song started. He did not think of himself as easily embarrassed, but his face grew hot as soon as he recognized it; it was the ballad about him that Rodarren had commissioned.

Someone sat at the table across from him. "Don't worry," the man said. "I won't tell them who you are."

He looked up. "Dorrish!" he said, pleased to see a familiar face. "What brings you here? Wait—this is where you went after you finished your studies, isn't it?"

"That's right," Dorrish said.

Mathewar remembered more now. Dorrish had been an uninspired pupil at the College—not bad, and certainly hardworking, but without the flashes of brilliance Mathewar sometimes saw in his students. Two years ago, when the small town of Hoy had asked for a magician, the masters had offered the post to him. "Do you like Hoy, then?" Mathewar asked.

"Very much," Dorrish said. "It's a quiet town. Peaceful. And the people are friendly—well, usually friendly." He frowned and glanced around him at the tavern. The folks looked stunned, as if they'd survived a disaster—not just the ones who had been on the riverbank but all of them. In the silence the woman continued to sing about the brave magician who had saved Karededin.

Dorrish lowered his voice. "That's why you're here, isn't it? Because of the Bound Folk?"

Mathewar nodded. He was beginning to think that Dorrish wasn't as dull as they had all supposed, either that or he had flourished here, in this small corner of the realm. "What do you know about them?"

"Nothing I can tell you in a tavern," Dorrish said. "Would you like to come to my house?"

"Yes, very much." He finished his ale, then stood and pulled on his cloak. The woman had reached the end of the song, praise all the Godkings.

"Sometimes the students would sing that when you weren't around," Dorrish said. "But I always thought you hated it."

"You have no idea how much," Mathewar said.

They headed through the quiet twisting streets. There were no lights along the paths, and the moon was dark; they had only stars and a few bright windows to show them their way. A cat passed in front of them, walking purposefully, its eyes shining yellow.

Despite his new confidence Dorrish seemed almost unchanged. He was a plump man, with wide gray eyes that looked perpetually amazed. He had started to lose his light curly hair even as a student, and now only a wild fringe remained. "I got married here, to a woman from Hoy," he said.

"Did you? That's wonderful."

"Yes, it is. Sometimes I wonder if you and the other masters knew what would happen when you sent me here."

Mathewar said nothing. Every magician knew this trick, the art of staying silent to seem wiser than you were. Dorrish probably knew it as well. Still, perhaps one of the masters had seen something of Dorrish's future, or guessed.

Dorrish led him up a path to a thatched cottage and opened the door. Light and warmth spilled out over them, and as they went inside Mathewar saw a young woman sitting by lamplight, mending an old shirt.

"This is Master Mathewar, the First Master at the College," Dorrish said. "And my wife, Bergad."

Bergad stood quickly, the clothes on her lap falling to the floor. She had a round face, and wavy hair a bit like Dorrish's. "Hello," she said, flustered. "Please, sit down. We have some ale, but there isn't much else, I'm afraid." She looked reproachfully at her husband.

"We really don't need—" Mathewar said.

"Stay there, Master Tobrin," Bergad said. Magicians were called Tobrin after the founder of the College. "Please."

She rewound the fall of string and folded a shirt and hurried into a room beyond an open doorway. Dorrish shrugged apologetically.

"She's a very calm person, usually. I've told her about you, I'm afraid."

They sat at a table around the lamplight. "Can she hear this?" Mathewar asked.

"Oh, yes. I tell her everything."

Bergad came back and gave them mugs of ale, then built up the fire in the hearth. Mathewar had thought her plain before, but now he noticed a beauty in her, especially when she smiled.

"Master Mathewar wants to know about the Bound Folk," Dorrish said. His wide eyes no longer looked amazed; he was as serious as Mathewar had ever seen him.

"Oh!" Bergad said. She put her hand to her mouth.

"I'd like to know why no one wants to talk about them, to begin with," Mathewar said.

Bergad sat slowly at the table, her hand still at her mouth. "Well, because—" Dorrish said. He stopped a moment, as if gathering courage to speak. "Well, we keep seeing more of them. They're coming farther and farther south. And we know that when they wear out they make even more, and it's possible—well, it's possible we could be overrun and captured. And then . . ."

"People are starting to disappear," Bergad said. "No one who would be missed—single folk mostly. But we think . . ." She trailed off as well.

"Who makes more of them?" Mathewar asked.

"We don't know," Dorrish said. "They call him the Binder. We've sent petitions to the king but no one ever comes to protect us, so we think he may have a hand in it somehow. That he might have even sent the Binder here."

Mathewar frowned; Dorrish's guesses hit far too close. By the Balance, why hadn't Jerret thought of the welfare of his people first? "Where is he, this Binder? Do you know?"

"We think near the mines. We see caravans pass by on the road, loaded with gold and precious stones and guarded by Bound Folk. Someone's getting very rich in the south."

"Have you ever looked into their minds? Or tried to free them?"

"Free them? How can I—how could anyone free them? Can you?"

"No. But someone might be able to—what's made can sometimes be unmade. What about their minds? Have you seen anything?"

"I've tried, but . . . No, Master Mathewar. Nothing."

"You're fortunate, then."

"Have you?"

"Yes, I have. Their minds are almost completely empty. There's nothing there but the task they have to do." A shiver passed through him, though the room had grown pleasantly warm.

"How—how terrible," Bergad said.

"It is terrible, yes," Mathewar said. "Have either of you heard of Polgar? Or Noldeth or Cullen?"

"They're advisors to the king, aren't they?" Dorrish said. "Hoy belongs to Cullen, actually, or belonged to him. But we heard they've been banished—they couldn't have anything to do with this."

"How far are the mines from here?"

"You're not thinking about going to the mines, are you?"

"What else would you suggest?"

"And why shouldn't he go there?" Bergad said. "If anyone can help these poor Bound Folk it's Master Mathewar."

"I doubt I can help them," Mathewar said. "I'm only going to look around, see if anything can be done."

"It's impossible to get very close," Dorrish said. "The Binder's surrounded by hundreds of Bound Folk, maybe thousands by now. The traders are saying they've built him an entire city."

"Well, but how far is it?"

"About a hundred and fifty miles," Dorrish said. "You're closer to it now than you are to Pergodi."

"All right." He stretched. "I'm too tired to think of any more questions. Does the tavern have rooms for the night?"

"The tavern!" Bergad said, outraged. "You're staying here, in our house, and no arguments."

"I wouldn't dream of arguing," Mathewar said. "Thank you very much."

Bergad flushed, as if she'd remembered who it was she had just ordered about. Mathewar grinned, and she smiled back shyly. "Look at this," she said. "You haven't had any of your ale."

"I had some at the tavern," Mathewar said.

"Oh, ours is much better than that rat piss they serve—"

"Bergad," Dorrish said.

She smiled again at Mathewar, bolder now. "Come with me, Master Mathewar." She lit a candle from the fire and led him to a small room with a featherbed and a down quilt.

"Thank you again," Mathewar said.

"You're welcome, milord," she said.

"I'm not a lord. Just call me Mathewar."

She shook her head, clearly unable to imagine taking such a liberty, and backed out of the room.

The featherbed was as soft as he had imagined, but he could not get to sleep. His errand seemed to grow more urgent the farther north he went; every day he did not act meant more men and women enslaved to the Binder.

He lay on his back, staring at the ceiling. The song Rodarren had commissioned ran stupidly through his head. He hated it not for its simplicity, or for the way it got the events entirely wrong, but because he did not recognize the person in it. Certainly that person wasn't him.

He had been addicted to sattery then, one of the strongest drugs in all the realms. He had started drinking it when his first wife Embre died; ironically, it had first been prescribed by a doctor, and it had nearly killed him. He hadn't cared, though. If Embre was dead he hadn't wanted to live.

And he hadn't wanted to fight for Karededin; he had gone to Pergodi, half mad with hatred and grief, to revenge himself on the magician who had killed her. Angarred had saved him; she had helped him stop drinking sattery, and had shown him that he could love again. He had been terrified of the idea, certain that anyone he loved would die.

Fourteen years later he still craved sattery, still woke every so often shivering and sick to his stomach. Angarred woke along with him and piled blankets on top of him, but the cold was not the sort that could be banished by blankets. He would lie awake until dawn, thinking only that one sip of sattery would fix him, just one sip and he'd be fine . . .

That was why he hadn't drunk Bergad's ale. He knew how easily he became addicted, and he had already had one mug of ale at the tavern. He was careful around drinks, and herbs, and anything else he might start to crave. Angarred thought him overly cautious, and probably he was, but he felt safer with at least an illusion of control.

And so he cordially loathed Rodarren's ballad. He hated being confused with the brave man folks had heard about in every tavern, hated it when, like Bergad, they acclaimed him as a hero or looked to him for answers. When he'd first heard the song he'd told Rodarren that he would write a ballad as well, this one about what had really happened. The queen had answered, calmly, that people needed heroes to help unify the country. Perhaps they did, he'd said to her much later, but those the people chose as heroes could not help but be changed, and sometimes not for the better.

He woke early the next morning and dressed quickly, anxious to be away. Dorrish sat in the front room, waiting for him. "I'll go with you to the mines, if you need me," Dorrish said.

Mathewar shook his head. "I don't think I'll need anyone," he said. "But thank you."

"Is it because I'm frightened of the Binder? Is that why you don't want me to go?"

"You should be frightened of him. Anyone with any sense would be. I'm terrified myself."

"Then—"

"The best thing you could do is to stay here. Folks need a good magician in their midst. Help their crops grow, make their houses strong. And you might have to face the Binder yet—it's possible he'll come this far south. Build some walls around Hoy if you can, see that they're guarded, make sure the weapons are sharp."

Dorrish seemed to shine from within when Mathewar called him a good magician; even Mathewar's prediction about the Binder didn't daunt him. "All right," he said. "The Navigator guide you. And be careful."

"I will," Mathewar said. "Thank you both for everything."

# S I X

Lord Ezlin Ertig and his retinue sailed for the Finbar Islands the day after Mathewar left. Angarred kept watch on the court but nothing unusual happened for nearly two weeks.

Then one day, while she was walking near the king's apartments, she heard a scream. She broke into a run and saw a huge man knock Jerret's friend Talethe to the floor.

Without stopping to think she changed into a leopard. Her muscles coiled and she sprang toward the big man, feeling exaltation at her sudden strength. With her new keen sight she saw a dull glint in one of his hands, and she realized he was holding a dagger.

He lifted the dagger to Talethe's throat. She lunged at his back and tore a great gash with her paw, then set her teeth—her sensitive teeth, which could feel almost as well as fingers—at the delicious spot at the top of his spine.

Yes, a voice said within her. Yes, it is lawful to kill this one. She bit through his bones. They made a satisfying crunch, like an apple. He went limp beneath her.

She turned him over with a paw. Talethe scurried away, but she ignored him and continued to nuzzle at the dead man. His smell was strong and vivid, filled with exciting information. Someone screamed.

She lifted her muzzle and saw a man and a woman coming out into the hall.

They were brighter than the man on the floor, dressed in rich gold and green and red, but not nearly as interesting. She lowered her head and returned to sniffing at the dead man. The woman screamed again. Stop, Angarred's inner voice said. You may not eat him. You may not. Change back.

She shifted back into her human form and stood up. Smells and colors grew dull around her; it was like visiting a dimmer, slower, stupider world. The woman—Iltarra, she knew her now—scuttled away, terrified. The man followed her and put his arms around her, his eyes wide with fear. "You have—you have blood on your mouth," the man—Jerret, the king—said.

Angarred wiped her mouth with her sleeve. She remembered the sharp tang of the blood, and she felt a familiar mixture of longing and disgust.

"Is he—is he dead?" Iltarra asked, staring at the body with horror and fascination.

Angarred nearly laughed. He had better be, she thought. "Yes," she said. She glanced at the man and realized she had seen him before, at Jerret's ceremony. So he had been one of the Bound Folk. She hadn't been sure, and the leopard hadn't cared.

"Holy Godkings, look—he had a dagger," Iltarra said.

"Who was that man who ran away?" Jerret asked.

"Your friend," Angarred said. "Talethe." She had a horrible thought about the Bound Folk and the people they attacked, but she did not want to mention it in front of Iltarra.

"Holy Godkings," Iltarra said again. "He was trying to kill us, I know it. Why else would he be in this part of the castle?"

"Are you certain he was one of the Bound Folk?" Jerret asked, looking down at him. "He has those dead eyes, but that could be because he"—he laughed nervously—"because he's dead."

"Yes," Angarred said. "I'm certain."

"You have to ask my family back, Jerret," Iltarra said. "My father knows how to control these people."

Angarred, still feeling the thrill of the hunt, nearly growled at her. She forced herself back to human politeness. "I'm sorry, but that's the

worst thing you can do," she said to Jerret. "It's as Iltarra says—the
Bound Folk follow Lord Noldeth's orders. They're killing because he
told them to."

"That's nonsense," Iltarra said. "Why would my father want to kill
Talethe, of all people?"

"You tell me," Angarred said. "He's the only one who could have
ordered that bound man. He and your brothers."

"This wasn't my father!" Iltarra said. Her voice rose shrilly, and
Angarred had to remind herself that the woman was still frightened.
"That man was going to kill me next. Me and Jerret. My father
would never order that."

Angarred didn't think Iltarra would have been next, but Jerret
looked down at the dead man and nodded, agreeing with her, and she
said nothing.

"My lord, please," Iltarra said. "Revoke my father's banishment.
He'll know what to do."

"If you bring him back he could have his Bound Folk kill us all,"
Angarred said.

"I don't know, Angarred," Jerret said. "They're killing us now.
Maybe I should."

"That would be wonderful!" Iltarra said. She leaned down and
kissed him.

Jerret frowned. "On the other hand, if I ask your father back I'll
look weak. People will think I don't mean what I say. They did raise
an army against me, your father and brothers."

"Drustig raised the army, mostly," Iltarra said. "You can leave
Drustig in Ou, make an example of him. You'll look strong then, believe me."

Jerret shook his head. "No, they all fought against me."

"But they said they were sorry!" Tears formed on her beautiful
black eyelashes. "They said it was a mistake."

"Maybe," Jerret said. "I'll have to think about it."

Angarred saw with disgust that Iltarra's tears moved him more
than any of her arguments had. She had to speak, had to tell the king
what she suspected. "There might be more going on here than you
know, Jerret," she said carefully. "Do you remember that bound man
who tried to kill Mathewar?"

"Yes. But what—"

"And now another one attacked Talethe. They were both at the ceremony, remember?—the one where you proclaimed Ezlin your heir. What if the Bound Folk are trying to get rid of all your witnesses? With the witnesses dead there would be only Ezlin's word that you wanted him to follow you as king."

"Are you saying that my father—that he would kill—" Iltarra could barely get the words out.

"Lord Noldeth would never do that," Jerret said slowly.

"This woman slandered my father," Iltarra said. She looked at Angarred for the first time. "What are you thinking—that my father disagrees with Jerret's choice of heir? Maybe that he wants to be king himself, is that it? There's no one in this castle more loyal to Jerret than Lord Noldeth." She turned back to Jerret. "Send her away, Jerret. Exile her. She belongs in the forest with the other witches."

"Who else knows how to control the Bound Folk?" Angarred said.

"Wait," Jerret said, trying to calm them both. "Didn't—didn't Mathewar say that the bound man only wanted to kill him? And none of the other witnesses have been harmed."

"Mathewar might have been wrong."

Jerret frowned, struggling with the idea. It was as if she had told him the Godkings didn't exist, Angarred thought—he had worshiped Mathewar as a child, before his allegiance had shifted to Ezlin and Noldeth and others.

"Be careful, in any case," Angarred said. "Don't go anywhere without your bodyguards. And tell everyone who was at that ceremony to be careful as well. Write to Lord Ezlin—he needs to know about this."

"All right," Jerret said. The fear lurked in his eyes again, and he looked up at her through his unruly hair, trying to hide it.

"Come on, Jerret," Iltarra said, putting her hand on his arm. "I can't stand to be in her presence a second longer."

Jerret hesitated a moment between Iltarra and Angarred. Finally he nodded to Angarred and headed to his rooms with Iltarra. "Please talk to me before you decide, Jerret," Angarred said.

Iltarra looked at her with dislike, but Jerret, still troubled by the decisions he had to make, did not see it.

So Mathewar had been wrong, she thought after he'd gone. She felt nearly as surprised as Jerret. The bound man who had attacked Mathewar had probably not even been looking for him. Mathewar had been up where the old steward had had his office; probably the man had been searching for Chargad instead. Of course when he'd seen Mathewar he'd seized his opportunity.

She knew that Mathewar would never have left her at court if he thought she would be in danger. But she couldn't write and ask him to come back—for one thing, she didn't know exactly where he was. More importantly, though, he had to find the man who was creating the Bound Folk. Anyway, she had proved she could take care of herself.

Jerret and Iltarra headed back to Jerret's rooms, which formed an entire wing of the castle. As soon as Jerret closed the door behind them Iltarra put her arms around him and held him close.

"That was terrifying," Jerret said. "Thank the Godkings Angarred was there."

"Angarred terrifies me as much as anything," Iltarra said. "There was a moment when I thought she'd kill us all."

"She'd never do that," Jerret said. "She's protecting us from the Bound Folk."

"Maybe," Iltarra said. She sounded doubtful. "But she can't watch out for us all the time. It's as I said—you have to pardon my father, bring him back. He knows everything there is to know about the Bound Folk."

Jerret moved out of her arms and went to one of the room's many comfortable chairs. He said nothing.

"What is it, love?" Iltarra asked.

For a moment Jerret thought about not answering her. She came over and sat next to him in the huge chair. He ran his hand over the soft, cool flesh of her arm. He loved her with a single-minded desire; he had ever since she had shown herself to be interested in him. He knew, of course, that she was attracted to him partly because he was king, that she wanted to be queen and share in his power. But she had to love him, he thought, if only a little, or why would she spend so much time with him?

"Something Angarred mentioned," he said finally. "Mathewar told me that the Bound Folk wanted to kill only him, but Angarred said that Mathewar was wrong."

Iltarra laughed, a little cruelly. "And that bothers you? That he might have been wrong? He's certainly not infallible, you know. I could tell you stories . . ."

"What—what stories?"

"Oh . . . Well, for example, he's a sattery addict."

"What!" He knew what sattery was, of course—the most addictive drug in all the realms. "No, he isn't. I've never seen him drink sattery."

"Well, he says he stopped. Maybe he did. But he'll start up again, you'll see. They all do. Anyway, people's minds are destroyed if they try to quit—they become idiots, or madmen. Mathewar might have been a good magician once, when he was younger, but you can't really trust anything he says now."

Jerret fell silent again. Could Iltarra be right? Could he have relied on someone with such faulty judgment? "He never told me anything about—about any addiction."

"Didn't he?" Iltarra murmured.

It was all so difficult. He shouldn't be asked to make these decisions; he was only fourteen years old, after all. But a part of him knew that this was a poor argument. He enjoyed the privileges that came with being king, enjoyed sharing Iltarra's bed, among other things. Shouldn't he take on the responsibilities along with the benefits? Wasn't that what Mathewar had said, that he should work and sacrifice?

He didn't want to start working and sacrificing just yet, though. Anyway, Mathewar could be wrong—even Angarred had said so.

Lord Noldeth never said anything about sacrifice. And Noldeth never left him when he needed him, either. If Mathewar had wanted him to do something, he should have stayed around and made certain the thing was done. Instead Mathewar had gone north and left him all alone.

"Maybe I will invite your father back," Jerret said.

He reached for Iltarra but she stood up. "It's been a very trying day," she said. "I'm too worried to be good company. I'll see you at supper, love."

He watched her go. Sometimes he wondered if she used her favors as a sort of blackmail, a way to get him to do what she wanted. If she would have bedded him if he had pardoned Lord Noldeth on the spot. He shook his head. No, she had to care for him. He couldn't be wrong about that.

That evening at supper Jerret announced that he would pardon all the Harus except Drustig. Iltarra looked elated. "Jerret—" Angarred said.

Jerret shook his head. "I've made up my mind," he said.

For the first few days after leaving Dorrish's house Mathewar passed through villages that looked much like Hoy. People rarely spoke, not even when he stopped for a meal or a bed, and none of the magicians he visited could tell him as much as Dorrish had.

Then the land began to rise, the air became colder, the villages grew farther apart. The houses so far had been made of wood, but here they changed to heavy red stone, with bright painted trim and small leaded windows. They huddled closer together too; he supposed that Winter here was fierce.

Bound Folk worked out in the fields or walked along carrying heavy loads. Every so often a company of them would march through, and people would flee to the sides of the road. Once an old woman ran too slowly and the Bound Folk mowed her down, as unmoved as if she hadn't been there, as if they didn't hear her screams.

At a tavern he managed to coax a woman into a disjointed conversation, and she told him that troops swept the roads and villages every so often, looking for what she called the Free. So far no one had paid any attention to him, but he knew it would be only a matter of time. He had an idea he was more conspicuous on a horse, so he stopped at a stable and asked the man there to board his horse until he came back.

The stabler regarded him suspiciously. With the stubbornness of a madman he asked Mathewar over and over again why he was leaving his horse, what he wanted in the north, who he was, and whether he had been sent to create more Bound Folk. He disbelieved, with a fine scorn, Mathewar's reply, that he wanted to learn more about the

Bound Folk and the man who created them, and finally Mathewar had to settle the matter with a handful of coins.

The stabler turned out to be the last person he spoke to on the journey north, the last human contact he would have for a good long while. Almost immediately the land around him changed for the worse. Whole villages lay empty, streets gutted with fire, doors smashed in, houses pulled down stone by stone. In some towns a few people still remained, scuttling like frightened mice from one building to the next. These seemed almost more terrible than the deserted places; the folks here looked dazed, as if they had survived a deadly plague. And in a sense they had; the rest of the villagers must have been taken away to be enslaved.

Miners had laid waste much of the land; mountains in the distance had been leveled and heaps of slag lay around for miles. And yet men and women still went down into the mines, bringing up what little remained.

Bound Folk worked in the fields as well, though in many places the crops grew wild or choked with weeds, the farmers gone. The Folk planted their crops in severe regimented rows: they looked like hair drawn back too tightly and twisted viciously into plaits. They worked in a dull, simple rhythm, each of them carrying buckets or bending to pull weeds in time with the others, and as Mathewar drew closer he could hear the monotonous drone of their song.

A tall mountain rose in the distance, its peaks white with snow even this late into Spring. People he traveled with had spoken of Iliardim, the great fortress and castle and mine of the Binder, and he realized that the road he was on would end there, at the gates of the mountain.

The road became steeper yet, the going difficult without his horse. The wind cut through his cloak. None of the inns were open, of course; he spent the nights in abandoned fields and houses and ate food that people had left behind, though it made him uneasy to do it.

He began to notice the searchers that the woman in the inn had warned him of, their eyes slightly less dead than the other Bound Folk. They were looking for the slightest deviation from the Folk's dullness, he knew, and he took special care around them.

Soon there was no one but Bound Folk on the road. They had divided into rows, those headed south to the left and the ones going north to the right. Some of the men and women heading south led caravans of carts and horses; probably, as Dorrish had said, they were bringing spoils from the mines to a king who had plundered his mother's treasury. The Folk and horses traveling north carried tools or lumber or bricks for the Binder's city, or food for his slaves. People spoke rarely, and only to exchange information.

The Bound Folk marched in step in a way that was horribly difficult for one of the Free to mimic. Several times Mathewar caught himself walking out of rhythm, too fast or too slow, though fortunately no one else noticed.

Four days after he left the stabler he saw a wall looming in front of them, built of irregular red stone; probably it had been made from the destroyed houses. Two enormous standing dragons, carved from stone, reared up on either side of the gate. The line narrowed to pass through the gate, and as they came closer Mathewar noticed guards watching through the dragons' eyes.

Why did the Binder need guards? he wondered. Everyone did his bidding: what use did he have for armed men, for coercion? Mathewar's mind was guarded as closely as he could make it, but he still felt uneasy.

These thoughts were nearly forgotten at his first sight of the Binder's city. He stood on a slight rise and the city stretched out before him, the largest he had seen since Pergodi. It looked like something built by a madman, but a madman with unlimited time and workers and materials, one capable of satisfying every whim.

The city was so big it seemed to swallow the Bound Folk who entered it, though streets and squares in many quarters were empty, deserted. A few great statues and towers rose up over the rest of the buildings, which were a jumble of houses and factories and barracks. Some of the houses were opulent, shining with marble and tile and what looked like pure gold or silver, but others lay in ruins or had never been finished, as if the Binder had lost interest. Steam rose from beneath the city, bursting forth in places with a loud whoosh.

He realized he was standing and gawping, not at all the way one of the Bound Folk would act. He moved forward, trying to match the gait of the others, to look as if he had a purpose.

As he walked through the city he noticed more signs of the Binder's neglect. Fires burned out of control in places; he saw a huge statue of a woman with flames dancing in her eyes. A tower had fallen, lying diagonally across several buildings. Bound Folk working on a half-finished castle had thrown up quarters for themselves along the walls, tiny shacks of ill-fitting stones that would leak at the first rain. Someone had written "Destroy the Binder" in dripping black paint on an arch; the arch itself stood at the end of a street, leading nowhere.

An alarm bell rang, sounding hideously loud in the silence, and a company of soldiers marched through a street ahead of him, their footsteps echoing from the vacant buildings. He moved quickly in the opposite direction. A woman ran past him into an empty square.

Mathewar saw her for only a brief moment but she seemed panicked, terrified by something. He hurried after her, walking as fast as he dared. A blast of steam shot up in front of him, making him cough, and when he could see again the woman was gone.

He headed through the square with some idea of following her. Not everyone here was bound then, he thought. Someone had set at least some of the fires, perhaps only to warm themselves, and had written the phrases on the walls. The word "Kill" loomed ominously on the statue of a king in the middle of the square. He looked up; the king's crown shone in the weak light, as if plated with real gold.

At one corner of the square stood a great tower, taller than any building he had ever seen. How did anyone get to the top? But it didn't matter; the Bound Folk would do whatever the Binder ordered, no matter how difficult. As he watched a man threw something from the roof. It arced toward him and resolved itself into a bird and then flew away toward the mountain.

It was probably carrying a message from the city to the Binder. The thought made him uneasy, and he headed quickly away from the tower. But there were other great structures, and someone could be watching him from one of them even now. Tall statues of a man and a woman stared at each other through the gulfs of distance between them, and he ducked down a narrow alley, out of their sight.

For two days he simply walked through the city, trying to fathom the mind of the man who had built it. He found very little to eat; there were places that distributed food but the Bound Folk visited them only in groups, and he thought that he would be discovered if he tried to join them. He ate what he could scavenge in vacant houses, and then, if the place seemed warm and secure enough, he slept there as well.

Twice he saw one of the Free: a woman whose walk didn't match the Bound Folk's, and a man who ran through an alley filled with scraps of stone and wood, looking nervously over his shoulders. He tried to follow them but lost them both; clearly they knew the city better than he did.

On the third day he headed back toward the gate. A company of Bound Folk walked in front of him, slowing him down. The Bound Folk slowed even further when they reached the dragon towers; then, without speaking, they narrowed their line to fit between them. They were nearly through when the shrill alarm sounded and a voice shouted from within the dragon's head. Archers lined up at the dragon's eyes, their bows pointed downward.

A man at the end of the company turned and ran. At least a dozen Bound Folk ran after him; several reached him at once and knocked him to the street. Two of them pulled him up roughly and marched him between them to the gate.

The alarm bell had been ringing continuously. Now, when the Bound Folk brought the escaped man back to the guards, it finally stopped. The archers lowered their bows, and then soldiers came down from the dragon towers, took hold of the prisoner, and forced him back into the city.

Mathewar walked away as quickly as he could, profoundly disturbed by what he had seen. The guards were there to keep people in, not out. They would let any number of men and women into the city, but if these people were not bound they would be captured when they tried to leave.

And where were they taking the prisoner? Probably to the Binder, but if that was so then there was another gate somewhere else in the city. That gate would be as strongly guarded, if not more so; he would not be able to escape that way.

Could he mimic the Bound Folk well enough to fool the guards in the dragon towers? He wanted to leave soon; Angarred would worry if he stayed away too long. Besides, he was getting hungry.

He decided not to test the guards right away. He slept that night in a vacant house he had discovered, and in the morning he went out with some idea of finding the other gate.

The city's streets curved and twisted, many of them ending abruptly. At one point he came to a square marked off with a pattern of lines, and he realized it was a great kettim board, that the Binder probably played kettim using Bound Folk as pieces. He wondered who the man played with, and what happened to the folks on the losing side. He passed houses scaled like dragons, and domes and arches and bridges, and stairways leading up into houses or down to the sewers. He quickly became confused, though he thought he still knew where north lay.

A few hours after he had started out he found himself in an unfamiliar square. The sound of men marching in unison came toward him, and he hurried to a shadowed side street. As he watched, a column of troops came through the square, then continued up another street opposite.

One of the men dropped behind, then started walking away cautiously. Mathewar moved back toward the square to follow him. The man was very young, maybe eighteen or so. He turned a corner into a narrow street; Mathewar nearly lost him in the shadows. The boy peered into buildings as he passed, starting at every noise or a blown bit of paper. Finally he came to a half-completed manor house and went inside.

Light streamed in golden bars through an unfinished section, illuminating walls of painted tile and floors of green and gray marble patterned with gold. Trees carved in green stone bent toward one another, creating leafy arches; dim rooms stretched out beyond them, impossible to see how many.

The boy sat near a pile of wood scraps. Now Mathewar saw that despite his youth he had pure white hair, the color of ice. He took out a flint and laboriously made a fire, heedless of the destruction to the floor, then leaned against a wall and held his hands out to warm them. Mathewar reached cautiously into his mind.

He had not been completely bound, Mathewar saw. The Binder

had taken his thoughts, his memories, his desires, the total of what made him, and had walled them off from the rest of his mind. For some reason though, perhaps the young man's strength, perhaps a small magical ability, the Binder had not been able to finish building the wall; some part of his mind had broken through.

Mathewar moved toward the breach in the boy's mind. He struck at the wall to the side but it threw him back. Startled, he touched it gingerly; it was hard as iron, far stronger than it looked. He threw himself against it again and managed to dent it slightly.

The blow weakened him. His attention still on the boy's mind he reached blindly for the wall of the manor house and fell against it.

He took a breath and lashed out again. The wall in the boy's mind buckled some more. He threw everything he had learned against it, hitting it over and over. He could barely stand; in the world outside the boy's mind he felt himself drop to the floor, exhausted.

He cursed all the Godkings and went back to battering the wall. This time when he stopped he saw that he had knocked down a good deal of it. He waited for the boy to venture outside of his binding but he stayed where he was, perhaps too frightened to move.

Mathewar felt very tired now. He redoubled his efforts for one final attack, and to his great satisfaction he sensed most of the wall falling inward.

The boy slowly became aware of himself. He lifted his hand and studied it, turning it over, then looked around him at the fire, the tile and marble house, the man sitting next to him. His name came back to him, or part of a name—Nim.

Mathewar left his mind then; the College taught magicians never to violate a person's privacy except at greatest need. Like the boy he had to force himself back to his surroundings, to realize that the leg he saw against the floor was his own.

The boy stood and came toward him, loomed above him. His eyes were pale gray, nearly as white as his hair. "Why did you do that?" he asked. He sounded hoarse; he had not spoken in a long while. "Is this some new trick of the Binder's?"

"No," Mathewar said, or thought he said. The room slipped upward and turned black, and he fell to the ground.

# SEVEN

As the days passed Angarred became ever more watchful. She made it her business to know where Chargad the steward was, and Jerret's friend Talethe, and Iltarra, and she studied the Bound Folk carefully.

Ten days after the attack on Talethe, King Jerret knocked at Angarred's door and showed her a letter. "It's from Ezlin," Jerret said. "He has some news."

"Come in, please," Angarred said. She led the king inside and they sat at the crowded table. "Would you like something to drink?"

Jerret shook his head miserably. "Just read the letter," he said.

Angarred knew that Jerret had written Ezlin about the attacks by the Bound Folk. But this letter couldn't be a reply; there hadn't been time. "What is it?" she asked.

"Read it."

Angarred opened it at the broken blood-red seal and began to read. "Dearest Jerret, My Favorite King . . ." She skimmed over the usual good wishes. "A strange thing happened on our way back from Karededin," she read. "Two nights out, at about the middle of the night, I heard a loud splash. I got out of bed and ran up on deck, and as I went I heard another splash.

"Other people were on deck when I got there. We helped the crew shine lanterns out over the ocean, but the night and the water were so dark we couldn't see anything. Then we counted everyone on deck, and then went below to count the people who had stayed in bed.

"Only one man was missing, though—Lord Aglar. Do you remember him? My father sent him along with me to observe things. I'm sorry he's dead, of course, but the cursed man's caused me no end of trouble—because I couldn't (and still can't) explain his disappearance my father seems to think that I've done away with him for mysterious reasons of my own.

"The captain told me something disturbing the next day, and it's the only explanation for the whole mess I've heard so far. He said he'd seen a number of the Bound Folk come on board in Pergodi Port. He didn't mention it to me at the time—he'd assumed I'd asked them to help us with our baggage, though of course I would never do anything of the sort. The captain said he had watched them closely, but he had a lot of other things to do and it could be that one of them hid himself on the ship. Then, when we were well under way, the bound man could have forced Lord Aglar overboard and jumped himself.

"What I don't understand, though, is why he would do such a thing. Lord Aglar annoyed me tremendously, but that's no reason to kill the man, and I can't think of any other reason anyone would have wanted him dead. But on the other hand he was certainly not the sort of man who would kill himself. If you can come up with any explanation for this mystery I would be truly grateful. Your humble and obedient servant . . ."

Angarred looked up, troubled. "This Lord Aglar," she said. "Was he the bald man at your ceremony?"

Jerret nodded.

"Another witness," she said. "Another witness attacked by Bound Folk. Do you believe me now?"

"I believe you about the Bound Folk," he said. "But I can't believe that the Harus are behind this."

"Who else could it be? Don't you find their actions at all suspicious?"

"No."

"Then why—why did you wait until they were gone to proclaim Ezlin your heir?"

"Well, they would have been upset if they'd been here. They'd have tried to argue with me, tried to convince me that one of them would be a better choice. But that doesn't mean that they would—that they would kill—"

"Are you sure of that?"

He nodded again, though he did not look very certain. "It's too late to change my mind, anyway," he said. "My letter's probably reached Ou—they've probably started back already."

"Well, remember what I told you," she said. "Be careful. Don't go anywhere without your bodyguards."

"All right," he said again. He stared down at the letter, then went to the door and opened it without saying good-bye.

Mathewar woke to see light coming through a window. He sat up; his head pounded as he moved, reminding him of the worst of his sattery days.

He was in a room lined with beds. He had slept on one of the beds, apparently, and there was another one, empty now, above him.

Where in the name of the Navigator was he? A few people lay asleep on other beds, but he hesitated to disturb them.

He still had his cloak with him, thank the Godkings. He stood and went to the door. There were more people outside, standing or walking or sitting with blank expressions against a wall. "Excuse me," he said to the man next to him. "What is this place?"

The man laughed harshly. "Hey!" he called out. "This fellow wants to know where he is."

Several men and women turned around. One or two of them laughed as well, but for the most part they simply stared at him, emotionless.

"It's a simple question," Mathewar said. "Are you going to tell me, or shall I ask someone else?"

"Oh, I'll tell you," the other man said. "You won't like it much, though. We're in Tashtery's kingdom underground, waiting to be sentenced for our misdeeds."

Mathewar turned to a woman near him. "Where are we?" he asked.

"We're in the Binder's prison," the first man said wearily. "He holds us here until it's our turn to be brought before him."

He didn't go on. He didn't need to: everyone there knew what would happen after that. Someone must have carried Mathewar there after he lost consciousness; perhaps they had seen him talk to Nim. He looked around him, horrified. No wonder these people seemed lifeless; their life would truly end for them in the space of a few days.

Well, he had to get out. And when he got back to Pergodi he would describe to Jerret every atrocity he had seen, all of them done in Jerret's own name; he would singe the boy's ears off. "Thank you," he said.

The man turned away, saying nothing. And why should he, Mathewar thought. His life had been pared to the bone, nothing but terror and boredom; what good would politeness do him?

He spent the rest of the day going through the prison, looking around him. Most of the people moved without any purpose, simply walking from one spot to another. A few of them stared ahead, their eyes blank, gone from the world before they ever saw the Binder. For the second time that day he thought of sattery addicts; they had the same empty expressions.

He went past the precise rows of huts, all of them like the first one he had seen. Finally he came to a high stone wall; a gate stood some distance to the right. He headed toward it.

Soldiers peered down from the guardhouse to one side, armed with swords and bows. They seemed bored, and so, perhaps, easy to fool. Mathewar hid in the shadows of one of the huts and spoke a few words to make him appear to be one of the guards.

Nothing happened. He tried again, wondering which of the words he had gotten wrong, but his appearance stayed the same. Perhaps he had forgotten the spell, he thought, though he knew that was impossible: he could recite it in his sleep.

The next spell he tried did nothing either, and the one after that. He looked around him, panicked now, unable to hide from himself what had happened. Freeing Nim had taken all his magic; it was all gone.

He sat against a hut. His heart beat so hard and quick it was difficult to think. Concentrate, he thought. But another part of his mind gibbered like a mad thing: you're going to be a Bound Folk, a Bound Folk, a Bound Folk . . .

His mouth felt dry, his breath came fast. Thoughts swirled chaotically: what about Angarred, would anyone ever discover what had happened to him, what about the children, would Jerret learn where he was . . .

Finally he managed to isolate one thought and follow it to the end. He had seen Polgar a few times at court, back when Rodarren had been queen, though the man had been overshadowed by his father and brothers. Polgar might recognize him as well, might remember that he was a friend of the king, and First Master at the College.

But what if he didn't? Undoubtedly any number of people, when brought before the Binder, had claimed Jerret's friendship; and possibly one or two of them had been telling the truth. Mathewar could not prove any of it, not even that he was a magician. Perhaps Polgar could send a letter to Jerret—but Mathewar couldn't believe that he would even bother.

He had been without magic before, though in that case a magician had used the Stone of Tobrin to take it away. That time he had been certain—well, fairly certain—that it would return. Perhaps now he was just exhausted from freeing Nim, perhaps he had to wait and he would heal; it would all come back.

But do you have time? the other part of his mind asked. What if they take you to the Binder before then?

He ignored the thought as best he could and headed back to his hut.

Mathewar and the other prisoners were not made to work; no doubt the Binder wanted them rested and healthy when they began life as his slaves. They got two meals a day and could sleep whenever they liked. All in all they were treated well—except, of course, for the horror waiting for them at the end.

Mathewar still wandered between the huts, though now he did so aimlessly, not certain what he was looking for. For a while he talked to other people, and when a man in his hut woke screaming he went over to comfort him, though everyone else stayed in their beds. But as the days went by he saw the prisoners taken away one by one, and he realized what his fellows had known all along, that it did not do to get to know any of them. Once or twice he caught himself becoming as lethargic as the other prisoners, waiting fatalistically for the end.

On his fourth day in the prison he spotted someone with white hair standing a little ways from his hut. Could it be Nim? He had wondered what had happened to the boy. He hurried down the row.

It was. "Hey, Nim!" he called, pleased. "Nim! Over here!"

Nim turned and headed toward him. He walked belligerently, scowling, and Mathewar realized, almost too late, that the boy's fists were clenched, that he wanted to fight. He spoke the spell to call up the illusion of fire.

Nothing happened. He cursed; he had never fought without magic before. As he tried to remember how to counter Nim's attack a fist swung toward his eye, and once again he fell into blackness.

This time he woke only a few seconds later. Nim still stood over him, rubbing his fist with his other hand.

"Why did you do that?" Mathewar asked. He sat cautiously. The back of his head throbbed. He reached back to touch it and only succeeded in sharpening the pain.

"Why shouldn't I?" Nim said. "I'd do it to any of the Binder's men."

"You think—you think that I—"

Nim moved closer, furious. "No tricks!" he said. "I know you work for the Binder."

"Then why did I free you from his binding?"

"You wanted me bound more securely. You wanted me here, safely under his control."

"What am I doing here, then? I'm about to be bound myself."

"I doubt that," Nim said. "You're his spy—you're here because you work for him. You led his soldiers to me. They captured me just after you freed me, the same time they took you away."

Mathewar shook his head. Red and gold sparks flashed in his left eye, the one Nim had hit. He got to his feet and leaned against a wall. "They took me to bind me," he said. "I would never work for him. I freed you because I wanted to see if I could do it. To see if the Bound Folk could be freed."

For the first time Nim looked uncertain. "Why me?" he asked. "Why not someone else, someone important?"

"Because you weren't entirely bound. I couldn't free anyone who was. Why weren't you, do you know?"

Nim glanced around him, his expression filled with fear and mistrust. He shook his head.

"I don't work for the Binder," Mathewar said. "Truly."

A long moment passed. "I don't know," Nim said. "There are some of us who aren't. The Half-bound, we call ourselves. Sometimes our bindings become weaker, or disappear entirely. Usually it's only for a little while, but I've known people who were able to get away. The rest of the time we have to work like the others." He shivered.

"I have an idea why," Mathewar said. "I think it's because you have some magic, though you've never been properly trained. I think—"

Nim backed away. "No," he said. "No, you're wrong. I'm not a magician."

"What frightens you about that?"

"I'm not frightened! I hate magicians, that's all. He's a magician— the Binder. An evil sorcerer. I won't have anything to do with magic."

"There are other magicians besides the Binder," Mathewar said. "Most of them don't work evil. I'm a magician."

Nim moved sharply; he wondered if the boy would hit him again. But Nim just backed away, then turned and ran off.

Mathewar watched him go. A thought had come to him while they had been talking, a way they might both avoid being bound. A desperate chance, but better than nothing.

He found Nim again that evening, in one of the dining halls. Even here, with people sitting at long trestle tables and eating, there was very little conversation, only the sounds of spoons clattering against bowls, or chairs scraped against the floor. He took his food—stew made of nothing he could identify, ladled from a huge cauldron— and went to sit next to the boy.

"Listen," he said. "I have an idea—"

Nim shook his head. "I don't want to hear it."

"Just listen." He spooned out the one piece of meat in his bowl, but it turned out to be mostly gristle. "We'll appear before the Binder together. If they come to get you first, I'll go with you. And if I go first—"

"If they get you first I'll wave good-bye as they carry you off. I'm not seeing the Binder one moment before I have to."

"When we get to the Binder we'll tell him that I freed you, that I'm a magician. I'm certain he'll be interested—he probably doesn't even know that it can be done."

"And then what? He'll bind us anyway."

"Yes, but we'll gain some time. He might spend a while questioning us, or working with me to see how I did it. . . . And maybe we can escape, or learn how he binds people."

Nim shook his head again. "You've lost your wits. It happens to people here—they think about their binding and they run mad. What good does a few days or weeks do us? We'll still be bound at the end of it."

"Maybe not. And there's another reason you'll have more of a chance if I go with you. Polgar might remember me from court."

"Do you think he will?"

Mathewar found that he couldn't lie to the boy. "I don't know."

Nim shook his head. "You've lost your wits, as I said."

"Well, can I follow if they take you?" Mathewar asked.

"Do whatever you like—I certainly can't stop you."

By that time Mathewar had seen a number of people taken away. The Binder's men seemed to choose folks at random. Sometimes they grabbed the first people they saw, the ones who had so little hope they didn't even bother to run. Some of them liked to chase prisoners down, or go into huts and kitchens and other hiding places, searching for those who tried to escape. Almost everyone they seized tried to get away, kicking and screaming and biting, but the soldiers always overpowered them.

He had to wait a long time, two weeks by his count, before the Binder's men came after Nim. They caught him one morning after a brief struggle, then chained him by his ankles to a line of prisoners. Mathewar put himself in the way of the soldiers and they took him as well. Nim sneered at him, disgusted.

"Listen," Mathewar said to the soldier shackling him to the chain. "I have to talk to the Binder—I have something important to tell him. Could you bring this boy and me—"

"Don't worry—you'll see the Binder soon enough," the soldier said.

"Yes, but we have to see him together. Believe me, he'll want to hear me out. And he'll reward you for bringing—"

"Silence!" the soldier said. "No talking. You'll see him soon enough, as I said."

The soldiers ordered the line of prisoners to march. They set off, their chains clanking. Then the soldiers led them out the gate in the high stone wall, stopping briefly to greet the men in the guardhouse.

The road outside curved up the mountain. Iliardim, the Binder's fortress. A woman near the front of the line started to cry, the tears running quietly down her face. Incredibly, the guards began to talk and joke with each other.

Could he do this? Or was he as big a fool as Nim thought? He had no magic to show the Binder, only Nim's word and his own wits.

What if the Binder refused to listen to him? Angarred had said— a number of people had said—that he was overconfident, that he thought he could do anything. She would certainly accuse him of over-confidence now, if she could see him. But she couldn't, of course; she would probably never know what had happened to him if he failed.

The air grew colder the higher they climbed. A man dropped to the ground, screaming. The line clanged to a halt. Soldiers hit and kicked the man until he got up again. Folks on either side of him supported him as they walked.

Halfway up the mountain the road turned in at a doorway made of stone. Guards at the entrance handed out torches to the soldiers, and they continued on by the smoky light.

They were in a cave. Wonders opened to them in room after room, lit by the torches: billowing curtains made of stone, stone ici- cles, glittering pillars, floors and ceilings the color of pearls. Colors glinted as the torches passed, revealing veins of jewels: gold, green, a red like fire. A stream of metallic blue ran within a carved channel, and pale eyeless fish swam through it.

No one seemed to pay attention to the marvels, though. Mathewar tried to keep track of their twists and turns, but he doubted he could find his way back. They squeezed between wet glistening walls, clambered over rocks, followed their guides to the left or right when the paths forked. He became aware of how cold the cave was, or perhaps it grew colder as they went farther in. Sometimes they felt gusts of chill air around them, twisting through the hollow places like a river.

Once their way opened out and they entered a cavern larger than any hall he had seen in Pergodi Castle. It was unguessably vast, the far wall and ceiling lost in shadows. Fantastic towers of flowing stone shone out of the darkness as they walked through, and the clinking of their chain echoed and re-echoed from the walls.

A short time later they came to a small room, and the guards motioned them to stop. Two men fastened the length of chain to a metal ring driven into the floor. Then the guards left, taking their torches, leaving them in darkness.

The room was icy cold. Some of them rubbed themselves to keep warm, shaking their chains; others moaned or cried out. The air smelled of metal and water, and they could hear the trickle of a stream somewhere beyond the walls. "Get me out of here!" Nim said to Mathewar, naked panic in his voice. "Please, get me out!"

Mathewar sat on the floor, which felt as chilly as marble. Waves of exhaustion and terror passed over him, sometimes both at once. He kept his arms crossed to warm himself, but it didn't seem to do any good.

One by one the guards came for them, their torches briefly lighting the darkness. Folks wept and shouted and begged as they left; one man laughed like a mad person, as if he had been told the best joke of his life.

Finally two guards motioned to Mathewar to stand. "Can you bring this man along too, please?" Mathewar said. "I'd like to show the Binder—"

"I don't care what you'd like," one of them said. "Only one person goes in to see the Binder at a time. That's the rule."

"But he'd be interested—"

The guards said nothing, just unfastened Mathewar's shackle and gripped his wrists, then half pulled him into the next room.

# E I G H T

Candles cast their luster over the room; they looked like the stone formations growing up out of the floor. Stone like white swords pointed downward, seeming about to fall at any moment. Shadows flickered. A man wrapped in several blankets sat on a slab of stone carved into a chair. The guards brought Mathewar to him and then disappeared back into the darkness.

The man was not Polgar. He was thin, with a narrow, foxy face, dark red hair, and a pointed beard.

"Where is Lord Polgar?" Mathewar asked, amazed his voice didn't shake.

"Silence!" the man said, his voice echoing through the room.

"Polgar knows me from court," Mathewar said. "I'm Mathewar Tobrin, First Master at the College of Magic. I have some interesting information—"

"Yes, yes," the man said. "You're the tedious man who keeps talking about showing us something. We've seen pretty much everything, you know. And don't think you can trick us—no one leaves this room unbound."

"It's no trick, milord. I freed one of the men out there—Nim, his name is."

"Our business is binding, not freeing." The man glanced at a pillar of muted gold at the side of the room; in the dim light it appeared to be melting. His eyes glinted as he turned.

"I looked into his mind," Mathewar said. "There was a wall around his thoughts, and I knocked it down." He had already decided not to tell the Binder about the Half-bound.

"I'm not interested, I said."

The man looked to the side again. A shadow separated from the pillar and came toward them. No, it was another man, hobbling as he walked; now Mathewar could see that one leg was shorter than the other, the foot turned inward.

"Lord Polgar," Mathewar said as he came closer.

Polgar sat and pulled blankets around him. He had thick black hair, blue eyes, and long black eyelashes like his sister, though his face was rounder and his hair untidier, and he was a good deal fatter. His skin was paler even than Iltarra's; it looked like candle wax. He and the other man together seemed like some unholy parody of a king and queen on their thrones.

"Did you hear what I told your—your assistant?" Mathewar said. He used the word deliberately, the way someone might poke at an anthill to study it.

"I'm no one's assistant!" the man said. "My name is Lord Annin Damazue."

Mathewar nodded. The "ue" at the end of his name meant that the man was related to the royal family. He pronounced it the old way, as two syllables.

"You said you freed one of our Bound Folk," Polgar said. "And that you're First Master at the College—"

"Of course he is," Damazue said. "We've had people here claiming to be just about everyone, a Mathewar or two among them, I believe. Someone even said he was Lord Noldeth—do you remember him, Polgar? And the woman who claimed to be Queen Rodarren? I suppose she hadn't heard the queen was dead these two years."

"Hush," Polgar said. He studied Mathewar awhile, a bit uncertainly, but if he recognized him he gave no indication. "Go on," he said.

"It's true, my lord. You must remember me from court. And I assure you King Jerret will be very angry if you bind one of his magicians."

"Yes, they all claim to know Jerret too," Damazue said. "Well, if you're a magician, why haven't you used your talents to leave this place?"

"No, wait, Annin," Polgar said. He turned to Mathewar. "Tell me again what you did. I might want to free some Bound Folk myself."

"What?" Damazue asked. "Why?"

"I don't know," Polgar said. "Because—because some people might be more useful unbound. And if my father comes back from exile I can show him how to do it."

"Your father wants you to bind people, not unbind them," Damazue said. "Anyway, you worry too much about him."

With that sentence a good deal became clear. Polgar was not a strong warrior, like Noldeth's other sons, nor a beautiful woman, like his daughter; in Noldeth's eyes he had no worth at all. When the Harus had challenged the king and ridden off to war Polgar had been unable to fight along with them, and so he had not been exiled with the others. Because he was allowed to stay in the country Noldeth had charged him with creating more Bound Folk—the first time, probably, his father had given him something useful to do. And Jerret had gone along because he needed the treasure from the mines, and did not want to look too closely at how he got that treasure.

"I went into his mind and broke down the wall around his thoughts," Mathewar said.

"Let's bring him here," Polgar said. He clapped his hands and the guards moved forward out of the shadows. "Go get me—what was his name?"

"Nim."

"Nim, yes. Go on, bring him."

They said nothing until the guards came back with Nim. His white hair looked pale in the candlelight, the color of the fish in the stream. He looked around the room, his eyes wide, and then nodded shortly to Mathewar.

"Did this man free you from your binding?" Polgar asked.

Nim nodded.

"Oh, for the Godkings' sake!" Damazue said. "What did you think he'd say? They worked this up together."

"Look into his mind," Mathewar said. "Or into mine—"

"Don't be ridiculous," Polgar said. "I can't see into people's minds."

"How do you bind them, then?" Mathewar asked.

"You don't ask questions here," Damazue said.

"No, it's a good question," Polgar said. "My father could look into minds, a little. When he put on his head the——"

"Enough, Polgar!" Damazue said. "Do you want to give away all your secrets? He's heard too much already. Bind them now, and make them forget everything you've said."

Polgar looked startled at the other man's harsh tone. Polgar was still in charge, then, whatever Damazue might think or want. "But what if—what if he can do what he claims? I do think I recognize him. He was at court, I'm fairly certain of it."

"Well, then, don't just take him at his word. Have him unbind someone here in front of you."

A man came into the room, breathing hard. "A message, milord," he said, handing Polgar a piece of paper. "They say it's important."

Polgar held the paper to one of the candles. He looked at it and then looked away, staring for a long moment at the moving shadows on the wall. "He's coming back," he said finally, his voice expressionless. "Cullen wrote. He and my father are coming back. Jerret's pardoned them."

"What difference does that make to you?" Damazue asked.

"He wants me in Pergodi. My father. He wants me to give Cullen the—the thing that I use for binding." Suddenly, astonishingly, he grinned. "Well, that settles this problem, anyway. I don't have time for these two—I have to go pack."

"Are you just letting them go?" Damazue said, astonished.

"Why not? I know I've seen this one before. King Jerret might be angry if I bind him. Or—or my father. And if he's really nobody, I won't be making too much of a mistake by freeing him. Come on, Annin, let's go pack."

"You don't have to leave right this minute. Your precious father can wait an hour or two. Bind the rest of the men, at least."

"No." Polgar grinned again. "I'm never binding anyone else, ever again. It's Cullen's problem now." He clapped his hands and the guards came forward. "Take these two outside. And unlock the rest of the prisoners and take them as well."

"No, wait," Damazue said. "Leave this one, Nim. I want to ask him some questions."

Nim looked frantically at Mathewar. "I'm not binding him, Annin," Polgar said.

"I'm not asking you to. I have some questions for him, that's all. How it feels to be unbound, that sort of thing."

"I thought you didn't care about unbinding," Polgar said. "Anyway, I thought you didn't believe them."

"Yes, but now your father's here. And you're right, we should tell him about this. You!" Damazue said to one of the guards. "Take everyone else outside. And you"—to the other guard—"stay here until I'm done with him."

"Mathewar," Nim said. "Mathewar, don't let them—"

"Lord Polgar, do you promise you won't—" Mathewar said.

"That's none of your business," Damazue said.

"I won't bind him, I promise," Polgar said.

"Mathewar, please—"

"I can't do any more," Mathewar said. "I'm sorry."

The guard seized him and took him back into the other room.

The other prisoners were slow to understand that they had been freed. They rubbed their ankles where the shackles had bitten, then murmured among themselves, wondering if this was some new trick of the Binder's.

"We're free now," Mathewar said. "Truly. Come on, this man will take us outside."

One by one they formed a ragged line near the guard, then followed the flickering torch out of the mountain.

The sun was setting in the world outside, but all of them, even the guard, stood for a while blinking, the sullen red light the brightest thing they had seen for a long time. It struck the Binder's city, which burned white in the setting sun. The city looked like a toy; Mathewar had the odd feeling that he could step forward and crush it under his boot.

The guard left them, saying nothing. Men and women milled around a moment, then, in ones and twos, they set off down the mountain.

When they had all gone Mathewar went to stand behind a grove of trees. He wanted to see what had happened to Nim, if Polgar had kept his word and not bound him. More than that, though, he wondered what it was that Noldeth had ordered Polgar to bring to Cullen, the "thing" they had talked about. It would probably be packed away, carefully hidden, but it was just barely possible that Polgar would be carrying it. Or wearing it—Lord Noldeth had put it on his head, Polgar had said. A hat? A crown?

A while later a guard led Nim out of the cave and went back inside. "Nim!" Mathewar said, stepping out of the trees. "Nim! Over here!"

Nim looked around, showing no surprise at seeing Mathewar. "What is it?" he asked.

"How are you? They didn't bind you, did they?"

"No, thank all the Godkings. They just asked me questions, like they said."

"Thank the Godkings," Mathewar said reflexively.

"What are you still doing here?"

"I wanted to see if you were all right." The boy said nothing. "And I want to watch them leave."

"Why?" Nim asked.

"Hush," Mathewar said. "You can stay with me if you want, but we have to hide, and you have to remain silent."

They went behind the protection of the trees and stood awhile without talking. The sun dropped slowly to the horizon; the air grew colder. If Polgar and Damazue waited any longer, Mathewar thought, it would grow too dark to make them out.

Finally he saw movement at the doorway. Someone stepped outside, one of the guards, he thought. The guard dragged a cart behind him; it bumped over the steep road. A few more people came out of the door, carrying bundles, and then Polgar himself.

"There he is!" Nim shouted. "It's Lord Polgar!"

"Hush!" Mathewar said.

It was too late. Polgar turned toward them, squinting at the trees. "Who's there?" he asked.

"It's us," Nim said, coming forward. "Me and Mathewar."

"What in the names of the Godkings are you doing here?" Polgar said.

Nim said nothing. At least, Mathewar thought, he knows enough to keep quiet now. "We were too tired to walk down right away," he said, stepping out of the trees. It sounded feeble.

Polgar must have thought so too, because he said, "Why were you hiding, then?"

"We weren't hiding," Mathewar said. "Just resting."

"Well," Polgar said, shrugging, "farewell to both of you." He turned to Mathewar. "If you truly are who you say you are, I suppose I'll see you in Pergodi."

More carts and men came out of the cave, Lord Damazue last. Whatever the device is, Mathewar thought, it's well and truly hidden now, if it wasn't before.

Polgar and Damazue mounted their horses and the caravan headed down the mountain. When they were far enough away Mathewar said, "What did you think you were doing there, if you had any thoughts at all? I told you to keep quiet."

"I don't know," Nim said. "You said you wanted to see Lord Polgar, and, well, there he was . . ."

"Yes, and I said I wanted silence too. I was looking for something."

"What?"

A horrible thought occurred to him. "Are you telling the truth about not being bound?"

"Yes, of course."

It was a ridiculous question anyway, Mathewar thought. The Bound Folk said whatever Polgar told them to say. He didn't think Nim had been bound—but then why had the boy cried out? Had he wanted to give him away?

"You can look into my mind if you don't believe me," Nim said.

"I can't," Mathewar said. The two words rang in his head like a death bell; he wondered how many times he would have to say them.

Nim didn't respond. It was past irony, Mathewar thought. He had given the most important part of his life to this wild surly boy, and Nim didn't even realize it—and probably wouldn't care if he did.

They started down the road. "What are you going to do now?" Mathewar asked.

"I don't know," Nim said. "I'd go back to my village, but it was destroyed when they took me."

"How long have you been bound?"

"Two years, I think."

He had been one of the first, then; the Harus had probably started their villainy shortly after Jerret became king.

"Do you want to travel with me?" Mathewar said. "I'm going to Pergodi, but after that I'll head back to the College. You could see whether you have any talent in—"

"No!" Nim said. "I don't want to be a magician, I told you!" He ran down the mountain and disappeared into the darkness.

Mathewar watched him go and then continued walking. A while later he came to a fork in the road; there was just enough light to see that one path led away from the Binder's city. He followed it to where it ended, at the base of the mountain.

The light was completely gone now. For the first time he realized he hadn't taken his cloak with him from the prison; he had been too terrified to notice before. The wind gusted in the trees; he felt very cold. He made a bed of leaves and curled up to sleep.

Brangwin studied the ragged army in front of him. Some of them had followed him from Aspen Valley and now stood looking around them, eager for their first confrontation with the Bound Folk. They seemed like children to him, or puppies excited by some new toy. Well, he thought, their first battle will change that. He always felt sorry to see it.

He gave the signal, and his men faded back into the trees. The green and brown clothing over their armor made them hard to spot; the Bound Folk would not see them until they were upon them.

The trees shaded a wide road, whitened with dust: a trader's road, though no one traded much anymore. Brangwin listened for the Bound Folk's footsteps, a dull marching sound he sometimes heard in his sleep.

A noise came toward them. It sounded nothing like the Bound Folk, though, and he peered out from behind the trees to look. One of the boys from Aspen Valley stood so far from his hiding place he was practically in the middle of the road; Brangwin hissed at him and motioned him back with a rough gesture.

He saw nothing on the white road; it stretched to the horizon, the color of a dull sky. But the noise grew louder, still heading toward them, what sounded like men talking and laughing and singing, and the steady clop of horses. Not Bound Folk, then. Other men began to look out at the road and he waved them back.

A great company appeared far ahead of them. They were surrounded by dust and too small to make out, but as they came closer he saw that the men on horses wore armor and carried spears. "Is help coming, sir?" one of his men whispered.

He had never thought these men might be allies. But then who were they? "Hold on to your weapons, boys," he said.

And then the world exploded. He felt heat and cold at the same time, sharp knives and soft blankets, loud jangling noises and exquisite music. Someone babbled to him urgently: his mother, or his brother, or maybe the Binder himself. Sharp jagged colors rained down like falling stars. The trees careened around him like wind blown leaves, and then his men, and finally the road itself flew off the face of the earth and twisted up into the sky.

He tried to move away, to run. He saw one final illusion—a man on a rearing horse, his sword upraised, a half a crown on his head. Tashtery, he thought in terror, the god of dark fire and death. Then he stumbled away from the trees and knew nothing for a while.

People thronged Pergodi Port, some of them the same as those who had seen Mathewar and Angarred arrive. They stood silent, watchful, as the wide-bellied ship from Ou was made fast to the pier. They were not merely curious, as they had been earlier; some had come to welcome the exiles back, some to vilify them, and some had not yet made up their minds.

The Lords Noldeth and Cullen Haru came down the plank. Their clothes and jewels blazed in the late Spring sun: fiery rubies, leaf-green emeralds, glinting and clinking gold. Some in the crowd gasped at their splendor. Their servants followed, and their great horses, richly caparisoned and hung about with bells.

Noldeth and Cullen mounted and rode off. The crowd parted for them. The lords nodded to the left and right, and waved to a handful of officials in red and orange cloaks waiting to escort them to the castle. A group of people called out, "Long live the Harus!" Later, some folks said that perhaps they had been hired for this purpose. But more people cheered, and still more, until a wave of acclamation swept over the port. Noldeth stopped at the edge of the crowd and scattered a shower of coins behind him.

In the excited talk that followed, most folks agreed that Jerret had done the right thing by pardoning the exiles. They commented on how well the Harus looked, the father with his striking black hair, blue eyes, and white skin, and the son—well, people said, it was a pity he had not inherited the family's good looks, but still he seemed fit and healthy. A few men and women pointed out how easily the crowd had been won over, with just a pretty show and a few coins, but they were soon drowned out by the rest.

The two lords rode through the city. At the base of the hill where the castle stood Noldeth began to cough. He reined his horse in; the coughs grew louder. Cullen glanced at him, worried. Holy God-kings, he thought, what if he dies right now? Finally Noldeth was able to take a deep breath, and they continued up the hill.

They went into the castle. Nobles who had heard about their arrival rushed up to meet them, hangers-on from before they were exiled. Cullen turned, grinning, trying to greet them all at once.

"King Jerret," Noldeth said.

Cullen looked up, shocked. Jerret was ill, Noldeth had said so several times. And yet here he was, striding up to them, filled with excitement. Iltarra clung to his arm.

Jerret moved forward to hug Noldeth, then Cullen. "Welcome back," he said. "I've missed you both so much. I don't know where to start—"

Noldeth raised his hand. "We've had a long journey," he said. "We'd like to go to our rooms and see you at supper tonight. We can talk then, if you like."

"Of course," Jerret said.

Noldeth and Cullen gave Iltarra a quick embrace. Servants took their bags, and they made their way to their rooms. The Haru family had an entire wing in the castle to themselves, with an apartment for each of them. When he was certain they couldn't be overheard Cullen said, "You told me Jerret was ill."

"Let's go to my room," Noldeth said. "I need to talk to you."

Cullen sighed. He wanted an answer to his question, but not if it meant listening to another of his father's lectures. "I thought I'd rest a bit," he said.

"You'll rest when you're dead," Noldeth said. He opened the door to his rooms and they stepped inside.

Noldeth's apartment was the most luxurious in the wing; it had a hearth in every room and was crowded with gifts from Jerret: thick colorful carpets, soft beds and chairs, and bright newly woven tapestries. Light came in from the great windows.

Noldeth went immediately to his bed and fell on the fur covering. He was breathing hard, and a blue vein beat at his temple. He raised his hand, and Cullen waited. "Long trip," Noldeth said finally.

"What about Jerret?" Cullen asked. "You said he was ill."

"Well, he may become ill," Noldeth said. "Any number of things might happen."

Cullen felt foolish. Why had he believed his father when the man had proved over and over again what a good liar he was? "I don't understand," he said, trying to follow the twistings of his father's mind. When Drustig had lost the king's favor, Noldeth had finally given up on his firstborn, and Cullen had dared to begin to hope that his father would work to make him king. But now it seemed that Cullen wasn't about to become king after all, that his wretched sister Iltarra would be queen. "Why do you want me to court Caireddin then? What good is Caireddin to us if Jerret is still alive? Iltarra will just marry Jerret and become queen."

"Have you ever played kettim?"

"What? A few times." He had hated the game too—it was far too complicated. He liked simple things, a horse and a sword and an enemy before him.

"You have to arrange for every possibility," Noldeth said. "Suppose Jerret doesn't want to marry Iltarra?"

"Of course he does—"

"Or suppose Iltarra disobeys me and decides to marry someone else? It won't be the first time she does something foolish. The Godkings know what she's been up to while we've been gone."

Cullen heard the violence in his father's voice, and a shudder runneled through him. He was a child again, seeing Noldeth's hand swing toward him, feeling the crack to his head and the sickening fall to the floor. He was watching Noldeth advance on Drustig or Iltarra, his hand upraised, a look in his eyes they had all come to recognize. He was hearing Polgar scream from his room—poor Polgar, who had gotten the worst of it. His limp enraged Noldeth; their father seemed to think the boy had somehow caused it.

Noldeth no longer hit them, thank all the Godkings. He had beaten their mother once too often, and she had died shortly afterward—something had torn inside her, the doctor said. The next time Noldeth had raised his hand to them Drustig had challenged him. Drustig had not reached his full growth then—he was still several inches shorter than Noldeth—but a wild light shone in his eyes; he seemed prepared to battle to the death, his own or his father's. Noldeth had backed down, not wanting to lose a fight in front of the family.

Noldeth could still do a good deal of damage to Iltarra's standing at court, though. Perhaps all Cullen had to do was wait, and Iltarra, like Drustig, would make a fatal mistake.

"I would need another plan if that happened," Noldeth said. "So I would move up my next piece—you—and you would marry Caireddin and assume the throne."

"But how could that happen unless Jerret died?"

"There are always other possibilities. He might go quietly."

"But what if he didn't? What would you do then?"

"Stop asking all these questions. If only Drustig hadn't gotten himself exiled—he would never have questioned me like this. But I have to work with the materials I've got. Do you want to be king or not?"

"Yes. Yes, I do."

"Well, then. Have you written to Polgar?"

It was typical of his father to assume he needed several reminders to do something. "I told you—I wrote him before we left Ou."

"Good. He should be here soon, then, with your . . . inheritance. And then I'll do as I've promised—I'll give you control of the Bound Folk."

Cullen felt as if an oppressive weight had fallen over him. He hated the Bound Folk, the ghoulish way they looked, their dead eyes and unchanging movements. In Pergodi his father had ordered several of them to be his bodyguards, and every so often he would be startled to find one standing near him in the shadows or walking far behind him down a hallway.

The worst, though, was the idea of having to create more Bound Folk. He had seen it done, of course. They came before his father in chains; they screamed and fought and cried out to the Godkings; they promised Noldeth incredible wealth or favors, but all of them left the room docile, with no stamp of personality upon them at all.

His father had spoken of giving him the Bound Folk before, but he had never set a time. Cullen had begun to hope he had forgotten it, but of course his father never forgot anything.

"Father, I—I'd thought to use very few of the Bound Folk when I—"

"Nonsense," Noldeth said. "We need an army, and most of the rabble in Karededin supports little Jerret. Well, we saw that when Drustig moved against him. The Bound Folk are a tool, just like anything else. You don't have to like them—no one does. You just have to know how to use them."

"But if I can raise an army on my own—"

"On your own? Do you fancy yourself a leader of men, like Drustig? Do you think the Karedek will flock to your banner just because of your charm? I've known leaders, and believe me, you don't have the authority, the personal power, to make men follow you."

Cullen flinched at the comparison with Drustig, but Noldeth hadn't noticed. "All my life I've worked toward the throne," his father said. "I started from nothing, don't forget that. We were carpenters for generations—my father's last name was just Carpenter, and so was his father's, and his father before him. I gained Jerret's trust, I became a lord and got a true second name . . . I'm dying now, but I haven't come this far to see it all thrown away. Iltarra will be queen, or you'll be king, do you understand me?"

"Yes," Cullen said.

"And you'll create an army that will follow you."

"All right."

A knock came a short while later. Noldeth quieted immediately and sent Cullen to the door. Bound Folk stood there, with their bags; Cullen shuddered to see them.

———

For the most part Angarred had stopped dining with Jerret and his courtiers. She knew all sorts of people in Pergodi, everyone from bakers to lords and magicians, and she had started to visit them, catching up on the news of the last two years.

But she felt she had to be at supper for the Harus' first day back, had to watch Noldeth and protect Jerret. She had begun to understand the scope of the game the two of them played, and she realized to her dismay that Noldeth was a far more experienced player. Drustig had been a small piece; Noldeth had never expected Jerret to invite him back and could afford to lose him, to leave him in Ou. Jerret didn't realize that, though; he thought he had executed a brilliant move by keeping Drustig banished. He had tried to take more of the family's power by proclaiming Ezlin his heir, but Noldeth had countered that by killing the witnesses to his ceremony one by one.

Jerret had opened the Greater Banquet Hall to feast his friends. The room had the same double doors and beamed ceiling of the Lesser Hall but held half a dozen more tables; tapestries on the wall kept away drafts, and there was a small alcove set aside for musicians. Only one table had been prepared for the meal, with candle-branches casting light upon it every few feet; the other tables were dim shapes, or hidden away completely in the gloom. Great logs blazed in the hearth closest to them.

Two dozen or so people headed toward the table, and Angarred quickly found a place near the Harus. Jerret sat across from her, with Lord Noldeth to one side of him and Iltarra to the other; Lord Cullen took the seat next to her.

"Ah, Lady Angarred," Lord Noldeth said. "It's good to see you again. May we hope that your illustrious husband will join us for dinner?"

"He's away right now," Angarred said.

Noldeth smiled. She had the idea that he knew all about Mathewar's journey, that he had spies everywhere in the castle. The first course came from the kitchen, and Noldeth turned his attention to the food.

More courses arrived, boar from Jerret's hunts, pheasants brought to the city at great expense, eels caught near the College. There was a flagon for each of them, and the servants never stopped pouring wine into cups of alabaster and gold.

No one said anything of consequence for a while: the Harus spoke of the weather on their journey to Karededin, and Jerret told them proudly how he had speared the boar. When the servants came to clear away the table Jerret pushed his chair back and said, "Lord Noldeth . . ." He stopped, clearly uncertain how to go on.

"Yes, my son?" Noldeth said.

"I—well, I need your help," Jerret said. The fright Angarred had seen in his eyes was back. He glanced quickly at one of the bound servants coming toward them with another flagon of wine.

"Anything," Noldeth said, prompting him.

"Well, I've been having trouble with the Bound Folk."

"Nothing simpler. You tell me what you want them to do and I'll have them do it."

"For one thing—for one thing there are so many of them."

"I'll stop making them, then. I was going to anyway."

Jerret leaned back. He seemed relieved. Angarred looked from him to Noldeth and back again. Was that all he was going to say?

"What about your family?" she asked Noldeth.

Noldeth looked at her in surprise, as if a piece of furniture had spoken. "What do you mean?" he said.

"Will the rest of your family stop binding people as well?" she asked. Jerret scowled, but she thought it would take more than Jerret to deter her.

Noldeth looked at Jerret. "Is this woman doubting my word?"

"No, milord," Angarred said, forcing herself to be polite. "I just wonder about these people. Who were they before they became Bound Folk? Binding them like this—it seems worse than imprisonment. And how were they bound?"

Noldeth waved his hand airily. "No need to concern yourself with that, milady. Believe me, they all deserve their fate, harsh though it may seem to you."

"But so many of them—"

Noldeth turned away from her to Jerret; he had clearly finished with her. Angarred began again. "I'm afraid the problem is greater than Jerret made it sound, Lord Noldeth. The Bound Folk tried to kill several people while you were gone."

"That's impossible," Noldeth said, grudgingly turning back to her. "I would never order them to kill anyone."

If she hadn't heard Mathewar's story and seen one of the bound killers for herself, she might have believed him. She was watching him closely, though, and she thought she caught a telltale shift in his eyes.

"But you're the only one who can control them, aren't you?" she said. She was close behind him now, feeling the excitement of the hunt. "I saw one of them attack a man myself. My husband was attacked by another, and we think one of them killed Lord Aglar."

"So we have only your word and that of your husband for these accusations, then," Noldeth said. He turned back to Jerret. "I know you trust this woman, my son, but I've heard some rather dreadful things about her. They say she's a witch, that she can take the shape of animals . . ."

"She can—I saw her myself," Jerret said. "She saved my friend Talethe when one of the Bound Folk tried to kill him."

Anger flared in Noldeth's eyes as he realized his mistake. He spoke calmly enough, though. "You'll have to forgive me, Jerret," he said. "I didn't know you'd seen these attacks as well. Of course your word is beyond doubt. But I have to say I don't understand what's happening here. As I said, I would never order these men to kill."

Once again Jerret seemed inclined to accept whatever Noldeth said. "There's more to it than we've told you, milord," Angarred said. "The Bound Folk are attacking the witnesses to a ceremony, one in which Jerret proclaimed an heir to the throne. We think that if they kill off the witnesses, it will be Lord Ezlin's word against—"

"Against mine, is that what you're saying?" Noldeth said. "Jerret, do you see the lies this woman is spewing, the calumny against me? She hardly knows me, but for some reason she thinks I would fight you over your decisions, that I would actually kill—" He began to cough.

"Please, both of you," Jerret said. "Please don't fight. You're both my friends—I want you to like each other."

"If there's another explanation I'd like to hear it, milord," Angarred said, as politely as she could. "Your daughter Iltarra saw the attack on Talethe as well—she said she thought she might be next."

"Yes, and that proves my father could have nothing to do with any of this," Iltarra said. "He would never harm me."

Noldeth started to say something, but another coughing fit overtook him. The candles had sunk lower; the hulking shadows of the other tables seemed to gather behind them.

Finally Noldeth took a deep breath. "Thank you, Iltarra. Do you honestly believe I would hurt my only daughter? Of course there's another explanation. There has to be, because I would never order anyone at the castle killed. And when I discover it I will let you know, and you will apologize."

"If you convince me, I'll certainly apologize," Angarred said.

Noldeth slammed his open hand on the table. Conversation stopped; she saw Talethe, farther down the table, look at them and then quickly look away. "I don't have to convince you!" he said. "I'm accountable to my king, and to him alone. But here's an explanation, if you like. I heard you say 'we think' a few moments ago, as if you were part of some great influential circle. But 'we' consists only of you and your husband, doesn't it? My allies told me how you tried to keep me in exile, tried to turn Jerret against me—believe me, I was very well informed about what went on here these last few months. I heard how you and your husband started a conspiracy of whispers against me. But everyone knows Master Mathewar is incapable, besotted by sattery—and you, as I've said before, are a witch."

Angarred found she was shaking at Noldeth's accusations, not so much the ones directed at her but his inferences about Mathewar. "I'm afraid your news is a good many years out-of-date," she said, trying to keep her voice even. "Mathewar hasn't had sattery for a long time."

"But don't sattery addicts start drinking again?" Iltarra asked.

"That's true, Iltarra," Noldeth said. "Usually they do."

"Your lies are more poisonous than any potion, Lord Noldeth," Angarred said. "Wait until Mathewar comes back before you question his judgment."

"I object to being threatened this way!" Noldeth said.

"Oh, for the love of the Godkings, I wasn't—"

"Please," Jerret said again. "Please don't argue like this. I wanted this day to be special—"

"She provoked me—" Noldeth said.

"I'm sorry, Jerret," Angarred said. "I can't get along with this man, and I won't pretend that I can." She gathered her skirts and left the room, hoping no one saw her trembling as she went.

# NINE

He had stopped running sometime back. It seemed as if he were waking up now, becoming aware of his surroundings. He looked around and saw that he was walking on a dusty white road.

Someone was calling him, an unfamiliar voice. "You there! Boy! Yes, you. Where are you going?"

An old man, a farmer probably, walked a path through a field toward him, hobbling with the aid of a stick as fast as he could.

"Where are you going?" the man said. "It's not good to be out in the open like this—the Bound Folk might get you."

He had heard of the Bound Folk. He didn't want to think about them, though. He ignored the man and kept walking.

"Well, you can't say I didn't try to help," the man said. "Most people wouldn't have taken the time to help a vagrant. Suit yourself, then."

Vagrant? He stopped and lifted his hand to his face and was surprised to find that his beard and hair had grown filthy and tangled. "Where—where am I?" he said.

"On a trader's road, headed to Forrel," the man said. He took the last few steps to catch up to him, breathing hard.

The name meant nothing to him. The man must have seen his puzzlement because he said, "Goss. You're in the kingdom of Goss."

He nodded. That sparked some distant memory. "Marfan and

Mathona help us, though," the man said. "We're not a kingdom, really, not without a king. And now we're being pressed between the Bound Folk and this new enemy—"

"What new enemy?"

"Come on, we have to get out of the road," the farmer said. "Let's go to my house—I can give you a meal, at least. Nothing special—the Bound Folk got all the cattle."

The farmer went back down the path and he followed. "New enemy, yes," the man said. "Drustig the Half-crowned, they call him. One look at him and you're entirely confounded. You run as fast and as far away as you can, you're that terrified of him. You forget everything, even your name . . . Oh."

"I—I saw him," he said. "I thought he was Tashtery, but Tashtery doesn't wear half a crown on his head . . ."

"Tashtery, yes," the man said. "Don't talk yet—see if you can remember anything else."

He remembered Tashtery and his wife Lammergil, the Pale Lady. Folks in Goss and Ou and Finbar did not worship the Godkings, who had once, after all, been kings of Karededin. They believed in Marfan and Mathona, who had created the world and the sky, and in their doubles and opposites, Tashtery and Lammergil, the lord and lady who ruled under the earth. Tashtery brought death and catastrophe; his wife, the Pale Lady, blighted the crops in Winter and strangled babes in their cradles. He had grown up with terrifying tales of their misdeeds.

Now he remembered more. He had grown up in a castle; his parents had been king and queen, and he—he had been a prince. Prince Brangwin. And with that everything came back: the burning of the castle, his long and hopeless war against the Bound Folk, his last moments of sanity before the world around him burst apart.

He looked down. His clothes had turned to rags and he had lost his armor; he had a vague recollection of taking it off so he could run faster. Scars covered his arms, from battle wounds or from trees scratching him as he fled. He felt exhausted, as if he had raced for miles.

His strongest memory, though, was of hearing the madil-bird as he ran, Tashtery's harbinger, singing its shrill evil song: "Tash-teeer-reee! Tash-teeer-reee!" At home, when the madil-bird sang, they said it meant someone was about to die.

The old man reached the farmhouse. It was small, built of stones that fit snugly against one another. The farmer wiped his feet on the mat and stepped inside, and Brangwin came in after him.

They went through a sparse, clean common room and on into the kitchen. A pot hung over the hearth. The farmer peered into it doubtfully, then started a fire to warm it.

"Sit down, sit down," he said to Brangwin. He took one of the chairs around a scarred pine table, looking grateful to be able to rest his feet, and Brangwin sat opposite him. "My name's Hartil, by the way. Have you remembered anything else?"

"Yes. Almost everything, in fact. My name—my name is Brangwin."

"Like the young prince that was?" Hartil asked.

"Yes," Brangwin said, too tired for explanations. "But tell me about Drustig. Who is he? What devilish forces does he command that he can—"

"Brangwin," Hartil said thoughtfully. "There's a rumor that one of the princes survived the burning of the castle. That he's fought bravely against the Bound Folk ever since, protecting his people from the Binder. Now you're the right age, and you look a bit like a picture of the king I saw once . . ."

Hartil stood slowly. Brangwin saw, horrified, that he was about to bow, though Marfan only knew how he would get back up again.

"Sit down, please," Brangwin said. "Please, it's all right. Yes, I'm Prince Brangwin. I was. And I fought the Bound Folk. But now there's this new enemy . . ."

Hopelessness smothered him like gray fog. He couldn't stand against Drustig. No one could, not when the man destroyed your own sanity. And Goss, his beloved Goss, was caught between Drustig and the Bound Folk, squeezed in a trap. His people would either be bound or go mad. He had reached the end.

He didn't weep; all his tears had been burned out of him long ago. "Tell me who Drustig is," he said.

"You have to have heard of him," Hartil said. "He's all folks have been talking about these last few days." Brangwin shook his head. "He was some sort of advisor to the king of Karededin—"

"May Tashtery take him and torture him," Brangwin said.

"Yes, well," Hartil said. "King Jerret exiled him to Ou for some reason. Ou is filled with wild magic, dangerous magic, and folks think Drustig found something—probably the crown, that half crown he wears—to use as a weapon."

"But what does he want with Goss?"

Hartil stood with difficulty and went to the hearth, then brought two bowls to the table and gave one to Brangwin. It looked like vegetable stew—of course, Brangwin thought, the cattle had been stolen—though it was so thin perhaps it was meant to be soup. It didn't matter. He ate it gratefully, wondering when he had eaten last.

"No one knows," Hartil said. "Some folks say that he doesn't want Goss at all—that he's simply marching through us to get to Karededin. That he's revenging himself on King Jerret for exiling him."

"It's a pity they don't fight each other and leave us out of it," Brangwin said.

"Yes, indeed. But when two lions fight, the mouse looks to his own safety."

Brangwin's nurse used to say that; it was an old Gossek proverb. He nearly wept then, but he continued on, savagely ignoring the emotions Hartil had raised. "What is that crown, though? How does it . . . it makes men run mad . . ."

"You can answer that better than I could," Hartil said. "You've seen it, haven't you? Can you remember it?"

To his surprise he found that he could. "It was—it was white. Not silver, though—something brighter and harder, white gold maybe. It was fashioned into spikes, and there were pearls on the spikes, black pearls. He wore it on the left side of his head, I think. His horse was rearing over us, and he was—Drustig was laughing . . ."

"Yes. They say he's completely mad. Some think he doesn't want us or Karededin after all, that he fights for absolutely no reason."

"He enjoys it, though," Brangwin said bitterly. "I could tell that much."

They finished their meal in silence. The light beyond the windows failed; Hartil stood and lit some lanterns. "What are you going to do now?" Hartil said. "You would honor me if you stayed here for the night."

He did not know whether to laugh or cry. Hartil undoubtedly had only one bed; he would force Brangwin to take it and then lie in pain all night on the hard wooden floor. "Where am I?" he asked.

"Near Forrel, as I said."

Brangwin shook his head. Clearly the old man knew little beyond the nearest market town; he had probably never traveled anywhere else.

"I knew a man who journeyed to Ou once," Hartil said. "He said it was about a hundred miles from here."

That near? Brangwin and his company had been pushed farther and farther north by the Bound Folk, but he knew they hadn't come that close to the border of Ou. He must have run—he thought a moment—perhaps fifty miles. No wonder he felt so tired.

But where could he go? He couldn't fight, his castle had burned . . . For a moment he wanted to slip back into madness, to slough off all his worries and responsibilities and let everyone else fend for themselves until the end came.

No. He couldn't do that; he was still a prince of Goss, after all. And with that he knew what he would do. He would return to Aspen Valley, see his friends again, live as best he could until they were overrun by one side or the other. He would work the crops they had planted, though he would probably not live to harvest them. He remembered the laughter and music in the meeting hall, and for the first time he felt something in his heart besides despair.

"I'm going home," he said.


Mathewar woke to what looked like red and gold and black rain. A moment later he realized that he was still seeing sparks in his left eye; he closed it and the sparks went away. Then he looked around for Nim but found no trace of him; the boy was probably long gone. He set off down the southern road.

Around midday he came upon a group of people traveling together for comfort, and he joined them. No one in the company spoke; everyone looked anxious to put as many miles as they could between themselves and the Binder. Nothing around him looked very different from his journey north: Bound Folk still worked in the fields and carried heavy loads; whole cities gaped open, everyone bound or fled. Other towns had been spared, and the people bent laboriously over the crops, watering and weeding. He caught the lush, heavy scent of growing things as he passed, and he realized that Spring was about to turn into Summer, if it hadn't already.

He found he had a few coins left, enough to get him to Pergodi if he was careful. He gave thanks that no one in the Binder's city or the cave had had any use for money. At the next town he bought a knapsack and cloak, a blanket and some food and a bottle for water.

For a wonder, his horse was still where he had stabled him. The stabler grumbled as he led him out. "There won't be any bindings for a while," Mathewar told him. "The Binder's gone south." The stabler grumbled again, disbelieving.

He did not visit the magicians in the towns he passed, and when he came to Hoy, where Dorrish worked as the town magician, he found himself walking a long way around it. He did not think he could bear to talk to the man, or face his wife's hero worship. Still, he found that he could not stop thinking about magic.

He remembered entire lectures he had given to new students. They thought of magic as something exciting, even perilous, he told them, but they would learn that the study of magic was far duller than they had ever imagined. The most important skill a magician could have was a good memory—and they would soon set to work memorizing hundreds, even thousands, of spells, whole reams of them. And after they had learned a few hundred of the most important they would study ways of combining them, and the nearly infinite number of new spells this produced. And that, he said—always seeing their faces fall at this part—would occupy them for their next few years at the College.

After memory, a magician needed to be able to think quickly. It would do you no good to have these spells at your fingertips, he told them, if you could not think of the right one, or the right combination, when a man came at you with a sword. A few of them always laughed at that; they were very young.

It was only after you learned all this that you came to magical power itself. They all had that power, he told them, the ability to infuse words with strength, to call them to life, and eventually they would learn ways of using it. At this point, of course, their faces would open and they would watch him raptly, as if he knew all the secrets of the world.

Perhaps he had been wrong, he thought now. He still remembered nearly all the spells he had ever learned, and he could come up with the one he needed instantly—and none of that learning helped him at all.

For the first time he thought about his future. The new term started in Autumn, and he and Angarred had to be back at the College by then. The more traditional masters might cause some mischief otherwise, might undo the changes he had made over the years.

He longed to see his children as well. Was Sorred still as serious, and Berren as careless? Had Eliath shown signs of magical ability? They were growing so fast, facing so many problems; they needed him there, him and Angarred . . .

And he wanted to look through the library, to find in some book or scroll or manuscript a suggestion that might help him. And he could ask Tobrin, if Tobrin came to visit—and if the old man said it was none of his concern he would wring his ancient neck.

But how could he teach his classes once he returned? And if Jerret had invited the Harus back to Pergodi, how could he leave the boy alone with them? Angarred couldn't stay with him; she had classes to teach at the College as well. He would have to convince Jerret to accept court magicians from the College, but what if the Harus had gotten to him first?

What could he do at either place?

He tried not to fall into self-pity; it would do no one any good. But he felt as if he had been paralyzed, had lost the ability to move or function. He didn't know how to *be* in the world. What was a magician without magic?

Once again the countryside south of Hoy looked in better condition than the rest of the country. People appeared more talkative, villages and houses tidier, roads in better repair. He joined a company of travelers going to Pergodi; a few of these even seemed in good spirits, singing and telling stories. Perhaps the land was already feeling the effects of the Binder's absence, he thought. Or perhaps he only hoped that was so, that something good had come to Karededin at last.

On his third day from Hoy someone in the group noticed a lone rider following them. They all turned back to look, murmuring among themselves, worried he might be a bandit or, worse, a spy from the Binder. But when a shaft of light struck his hair Mathewar recognized the boy immediately. Nim had found him.

Nim kept the same distance from the company all day. When night came the group settled down to sleep, and Mathewar wrapped himself in his blanket.

He came awake to a soft noise. Someone was rifling through his knapsack. Nim. He reached out and grasped the boy's wrist.

Nim became utterly still, too startled to pull away. He was still holding the dried meat he had taken. "Why do you steal what I would freely give you?" Mathewar asked.

"I—I don't know," Nim said.

Mathewar let him go. Nim grabbed a dried apple and a half loaf of bread and ran off.

He wondered where Nim had gotten the horse. Then he remembered that he had seen one or two riderless horses on the road; probably they had belonged to folks who had been captured and bound.

Nim continued to come to him at night, so regularly that Mathewar set out bits of food for him. He wondered where the boy would go when they reached Pergodi, whether he would become lost among the horde of the city's vagrants.

But Mathewar spent little time worrying about him. As they drew closer to Pergodi he began to think about Angarred. What would she say when he told her what had happened to him? Some women, like Iltarra, were drawn to power, but Angarred wasn't like that, thank all the Godkings. She would not leave him because his power had gone. She would probably feel sorry for him; he thought her pity might be even harder to bear.

One night he watched by the light of the half moon as Nim ate the food he had set out for him. "Thank you," Nim said softly, and Mathewar said, "You're welcome."

# TEN

olgar entered Pergodi Castle warily. A man wearing the double-tower emblem on his surcoat came up to him and bowed. "What would you like, my lord Polgar? Your father is in one of the council rooms, with King Jerret."

He didn't want to see his father, not just yet. He motioned to the chests and packs his servants carried and said, "I'd like this baggage put in my rooms, all except the pack I'm carrying—I'll take that myself. And do you know where my brother Cullen is?"

The man bowed again. "Right away, milord. Cullen is in his apartments, I believe."

Other servants, some of them Bound Folk, came forward to take his things. The ones who hadn't been bound seemed surprised by the weight; Polgar had stolen as much from the mines as he thought he could get away with. He had no idea what plans his father had for him, and it was good to have something in reserve, something of his own.

He walked up the stairs to his apartment, his shorter leg aching after the journey. When he got to his rooms he untied his bag and took out something wrapped snugly in cloth. Then he went to the elaborately carved wall across the room and pressed a carved rose.

A section of the wall swung open, revealing a cupboard. He put the package inside, then closed the door and made certain the latch had caught.

The servants came with his baggage. He asked for hot water for a bath, but before it was delivered he fell on the bed and slept for several hours.

When he woke he put on fresh clothes and left his apartment. Lord Annin Damazue appeared noiselessly beside him as soon as the door closed. "I'd like to speak to my brother alone, please," Polgar said.

Annin bowed. "Very well," he said. Something glinted in his eyes as he raised his head, a strange combination of ambition and fear; he probably wondered what his status would be now that they had reached the castle.

Two years ago, when the Harus had begun to rise at Jerret's court, Annin had befriended Polgar. Polgar knew, of course, that this friendship was at least partly because of the power his family held, but he felt certain that Annin also enjoyed his company. Why else would he have attached himself to the least powerful of the Harus, why wouldn't he have simply joined Drustig's circle, or Cullen's?

When Noldeth had ordered Polgar to the north, Polgar had asked Annin to come with him. He had been terrified of creating Bound Folk; he had even given Annin the power of the crown and watched him as he performed the binding, until he thought he could bear to do it himself.

They had had a good deal of fun together; they had done anything they wanted, like children staying up late and eating sweets. They had built their city like two boys playing at war, though with real houses and real soldiers. Now, they both knew, their friendship would change. Lord Noldeth held all the power here, and he disapproved of Annin's frivolity.

Polgar knocked at Cullen's door. "Who is it?" Cullen called out.

"Polgar."

The door opened. The two brothers stood for a moment, facing each other awkwardly. Then Cullen said, "Come in, come in," and led the way into his rooms.

They sat. "So," Polgar said, "Jerret pardoned you after all."

"You knew he would," Cullen said.

"Yes, I suppose I did."

They fell silent. Cullen crossed his legs. Polgar did not want to raise the subject he had come to discuss; he thought that if Cullen said nothing about it he would simply go to his rooms, leaving everything unsaid. He could not bear it if his brother called him a coward; it was bad enough hearing the word from his father.

"Did you bring the—Father's—" Cullen said.

"Yes, I did. Listen, Cullen, I . . . the Bound Folk . . ."

"The Bound Folk, yes. Did you come to hate them as much as I do?"

"Yes," Polgar said, relieved. His words came faster. "I never wanted to . . . It's very difficult, creating them. They scream, they cry, they swear they'll do anything for you if you just let them go. I even had to have Lord Damazue help me—I couldn't do it by myself."

"It's their eyes that bother me," Cullen said. "I can't stand to look into their eyes."

"Yes," Polgar said. "Do you know anything about the Gossek?" He went on without waiting for Cullen's answer. "I saw a lot of them in the cave—the Karedek army captured a good many and sent them to me to be bound. They don't believe in the Godkings, you know. Well, they believe in Marfan and Mathona, but then they think there are more gods underground, Tashtery and Lammergil. And these gods—they're the exact opposite of Marfan and Mathona. They're even supposed to stand upside down, at the same spots where Marfan and Mathona are standing right side up. And they—they punish you. If you've done wrong in this life they devise punishment for you in the next. Fire, sometimes, or thirst, or—well, they're very inventive. And I got to wondering what their punishment would be for me."

"Punishment?" Cullen said. "Oh, for the love of the Godkings, you don't believe this nonsense, do you? None of these gods and goddesses exist."

"No, I don't believe it," Polgar said slowly. "But I got to thinking—well, I wondered when I realized that binding people was wrong. Father says that these people are criminals, and anyway we need them for the mines and the army. But in the end I—I couldn't stand it anymore. I was never so happy as when I got your letter, telling me to come south."

"It isn't wrong, Polgar. Anyway, we need them. We need the army."

"Maybe. But I wanted to tell you—I just wanted to say that it's the most difficult, the most horrible work I ever did. To warn you."

Cullen leaned forward, hesitated, and then spoke quickly. "I wanted to ask you . . . I was wondering about—about the women. What they'll do."

"They'll do whatever you want them to." Polgar frowned, remembering the nights when he and Annin had arranged for one woman after another to visit their rooms. But he couldn't tell Cullen about the feeling of revulsion he'd had afterward; his father and brothers already thought of him as less than manly, and this would only confirm it in their eyes.

Cullen said nothing for a while, no doubt thinking, as Polgar had thought once, of an endless parade of women. Polgar cast about for another subject. "How's Drustig these days?"

Cullen frowned. "He—our spies told us that he's waging his own war in the north. In Goss."

"In Goss? Why?"

"I don't know. Maybe he wants to march through Goss and into Karededin. Maybe he thinks he deserves to be king here, since he's the oldest." Cullen hesitated. "But that's not the worst of it. The spies said he has some sort of weapon, something that makes men go mad. That turns everything to chaos."

"What kind of weapon?"

"I don't know. I don't know of anything that can do that. Father might, I think—I saw a strange look in his eyes when we heard about Drustig—but he denied it when I asked him. But if Drustig goes on, if he reaches into Karededin, I might have to create more Bound Folk to use against him. And that frightens me more than anything."

The door opened and Lord Noldeth came in without knocking. "There you two are," he said. "I want to transfer the Bound Folk to Cullen tomorrow. I have to hold Jerret's hand in the morning, but we can do it in the afternoon. Polgar, you didn't forget to bring what I told you, did you?" He said it as though he fully expected Polgar to have forgotten, as though Polgar had disappointed him many times in the past.

"No, Father," Polgar said.

"Good. And you're sure you have it safe?"

"Of course."

"All right, then."

Noldeth left. The two brothers were silent for a while. "Welcome home," Cullen said wryly.

Everyone talked about Polgar's return to the castle and his family; Angarred heard the news by evening. She began to worry. Mathewar had gone north to learn more about the Binder, but if the Binder was no longer there, then Mathewar should have started south as well. He had left in the middle of Spring, and it was only a few days until Summer.

A long time ago a friend had shown her passageways hidden in the walls of the castle. There were holes in the passageways at eye level, overlooking banquet halls and audience chambers and the apartments of important people. Early the next morning she went into an empty room and pressed a latch on the inside of the fireplace, and a section of the wall rolled outward, revealing a dark hall beyond.

She took one of the castle's torches and went inside, closing the wall after her, then headed in the direction of the Harus' wing. She knew they had been given rooms near the king, but she could not find them no matter how hard she tried. Perhaps their rooms had no spy holes. That would be unfortunate, she thought.

She wondered especially where Iltarra had got to. Her distrust of Iltarra had grown after the supper with Noldeth; the woman had seemed too eager to support her father, too ready with easy questions for him. Don't sattery addicts start drinking again? she remembered Iltarra saying—and that was after the woman had tried to flirt with Mathewar.

The walls made a sharp turn and she came to Jerret's part of the castle. A light shone farther down the hall and she went toward it and put her eye to the hole.

Jerret sat on a throne, gazing out over a long line of petitioners. He seemed too small for the throne, a child who had climbed up to his father's chair. Next to him sat Lord Noldeth, on a chair only slightly lower than Jerret's.

Most of the people in line said nothing, too awed by the Audience Chamber to speak. Light shone through the stained-glass windows behind Jerret and Noldeth, coloring them in red and purple. The floor was black and white checkered marble, with the king's seal, the two-towered castle, inlaid upon it. Thick fur covered the thrones, white for Jerret and black for Noldeth.

A man came forward, a farmer by the look of him. Some of the people had written down their grievances or carried petitions signed by the folks in their village, but this man had brought nothing; probably he could not read or write.

He spoke to Jerret, his voice too low and far away for her to hear. When he finished, Jerret looked at Noldeth. Noldeth leaned over and whispered in Jerret's ear, and Jerret nodded and turned back to the petitioner.

Angarred nearly groaned aloud. Jerret said something to the farmer. The farmer frowned and started to reply, but Noldeth waved his hand and two guards came forward, ready to march the man outside the castle walls.

The farmer turned and left on his own. From where they sat Jerret and Noldeth could not see his expression, but Angarred could, and she wondered how many dissatisfied people like him there were, how many folks throughout the realm who hated Noldeth. And how many of them had gone on to hate Jerret as well?

A short time later Noldeth began to cough loudly, cutting off whatever the woman in front of him was saying. When he stopped he turned and said something to Jerret. "Our audience is over," Jerret called out, though he had not finished with the woman, and the line of people after her reached to the chamber door and probably beyond. "We will be here next week."

The line broke up. Some folks stood for a moment, single petitioners, and husbands and wives, and groups from the same trade or the same quarter of the city. A few grumbled quietly but most said nothing, looking angry or frustrated or confused. The guards cleared a path to the door for Jerret and Noldeth.

Everyone left after that. Angarred headed back to the room with the fireplace, profoundly disturbed by what she had seen. She would have to get Jerret alone somehow, tell him how dangerous the Harus were. . . . She opened the door in the wall and then went outside into the hallway.

She heard footsteps and looked up to see Jerret and Noldeth coming toward her, followed by a good many guards. "Lady Angarred," Jerret said. "Hello."

Noldeth stopped; so did Jerret and the guards. "Hello, Lady Angarred," Noldeth said. "I was just thinking about that delightful supper we had together. Do you remember?"

"What do you want?" Angarred said.

"Some politeness, for one thing," Noldeth said. "Jerret said he would like us to get along. But for another, do you remember that I ventured a few truths about Mathewar, and that you wouldn't hear a word against him? Where is Mathewar, by the way?"

Angarred said nothing.

"Don't worry, he'll probably turn up," Noldeth said. "But I wanted to ask you a question. I said you were a witch at that supper, and as I recall you never defended yourself, though you tried to defend your husband. I do think Jerret has a right to know what kinds of people he has at his court—so I have to wonder why you never replied to my accusation."

"Why should I have?" she said. "I am a witch."

She held his gaze with a look as full of threat and power as she could make it. He looked back, saying nothing. Finally he glanced away.

"Good day, Jerret," she said, and continued down the corridor. Noldeth began to cough; she heard the sounds diminishing as she went.

She felt a wicked glee at winning the petty contest with him. That soon faded, though, and her misgivings returned, stronger than ever. "He'll probably turn up," Noldeth had said about Mathewar. Did he know more than he was saying?

Why hadn't Mathewar come back? She sensed that something had happened to him, something terrible. Was this Clear Sight, that moment of knowledge that came upon magicians unexpectedly? Or was she worrying about nothing?

———

That afternoon Cullen went to his father's rooms. Polgar was already there, along with Noldeth and one of the Bound Folk. On a table in front of him Noldeth had placed a velvet cloth the color of blood; on top of this rested a skull and half of a crown.

"Stand over there," Noldeth said with no preamble to Cullen, indicating the other side of the table. "Polgar, go stand next to him." He nodded to the bound man. "You stay on this side, with me," he said.

When everyone had arranged themselves Noldeth looked at each of them in turn. "Are we ready?" he asked.

No, Cullen thought. He wished he were brave enough to glance at Polgar, who would know how he felt.

"All right," Noldeth said. He placed the crown on the skull and turned to the bound man. "Whom do you serve?" he asked.

"I serve the one who wears the crown," the man said. He spoke flatly, without emotion, like a dead man who had been magicked to talk.

Noldeth nodded to Polgar. Polgar took the crown from the skull and placed it on his head. "Who wears the crown?" Noldeth said.

"Lord Polgar Haru wears the crown," the man said.

Noldeth looked at Cullen. Cullen reached out and lifted the crown from his brother's head. His hands trembled; he tried to still them but could not. He set the crown on his head.

"On the right side," his father said.

For a moment he did not understand; his father might have been speaking in old Gossek. Then he realized he had put the crown on the wrong side of his head, and he moved it.

"Who wears the crown?" Noldeth said.

"Lord Cullen Haru wears the crown."

A door seemed to open, somewhere in his mind. All the realms spread out before him, unrolling like a map. He saw the level fields and pastures of Karededin, the mountains on the border with Goss. There were the great mines, and there the Gossek valleys folded in among the hills. After them came the fog-shrouded land of Ou, uneasy with old magic. Out to sea lay the small islands of Finbar, where another man thought he would be king.

He felt connected to the bound man across the table, and through him to every bound person in Pergodi, in Karededin, in the world.

He knew how to order them, how to create them. He could make them do whatever he wanted.

Power thrilled along the lines linking him to the Bound Folk. He had more mastery than any man in the world, more than any king or magician or warrior. He would be king. He would be more than king, the mightiest man who had ever lived. The vision that unfolded before him took his breath away.

His father was saying something. He forced himself back to the room. "Who wears the crown?" Noldeth asked.

"I, Lord Cullen Haru, wear the crown," he said.

The bound man stepped around the table and stood next to him. "What do you command, Lord Cullen Haru?" he asked.

He could not think of anything, despite the vast panorama he had seen. "You have to tell him to do something," Polgar said. For some reason he was smiling, and Cullen wondered why he had been so eager to give up the crown. Perhaps it was as his father had always said; Polgar was a coward.

"You have to give them an order," Polgar said again. "Otherwise they won't follow you."

"Bow to me," Cullen said.

The bound man bowed. Cullen shuddered with pleasure.

"All right," Noldeth said.

Noldeth looked at Cullen proudly; before today he had only ever looked at Drustig like that. For the first time in a life of small snubs and dismissals Cullen felt he had his father's love and respect, and the feeling buoyed him like nothing else, even more than the servitude of the Bound Folk.

Cullen lifted the crown from his head. A pressure eased; he realized only now how heavy it had been. The right side of his head started to ache.

"The crown is yours, Cullen," Noldeth said. "If you want to create more Bound Folk, you put it on, look at the person you want to bind, and say, 'Thou art now bound to me.' Don't wear it unless you're creating Bound Folk—they'll obey you without it. Keep it somewhere safe."

Cullen turned the half crown over and over in his hands. It was made of strong metal, a deep black that seemed to swallow light, reflecting nothing. Spikes rose from the base, with white pearls at the points. The pearls shone against the darkness; for a moment they looked like eyes, watching him. He forced the thought away.

"Where—where did you get this?" he asked his father.

"From Ou," Noldeth said. "There's still a lot of wild magic there. When I found it—that was the beginning of our family's rise in the world, our ability to influence people and events. You might get the crown of Karededin one of these days, Cullen, but that's your true crown, though you'll never be able to wear it in public."

"What happened to the other half?"

"I don't know," his father said. He began to cough, on and on, as though by an act of will he had put his illness off until after the ceremony. Blood flecked the table in front of him, the skull, and the velvet cloth.


Cullen spent the next few days in his rooms, seeing how far his power extended over the Bound Folk. At first he gave them simple commands, telling them to fetch things and clean his belongings and comb his hair. By the third day he ran out of useful chores and he ordered them to sing for him, to declaim poetry, to skip in a circle.

There were a few women among them, and he watched as they capered around his room. He remembered Polgar's prudery, how he had not wanted to talk about the women. And yet he himself was reluctant to order one of them into his bed. It was those eyes, those dead eyes staring up at him. He could extinguish the lamps and close the curtains, but he would still know, he would see them in his mind . . .

He clapped his hands to banish his thoughts. The Bound Folk turned toward him. "Stop!" he said. "Stand on your heads!"

They moved clumsily to obey, some of them spilling back down to the floor. A loud outcry came from the king's part of the castle.

He rushed out the door and headed toward Jerret's apartments. His father and some others stood huddled around the door to one of the rooms.

"What is it?" he asked.

"Someone's dead, I think," a woman said.

The crowd made a space for him. A man in the room lay facedown at his table, a tray of food pushed to one side.

"Who is he?" Cullen asked.

A servant turned the man over. All the color had drained from his face; even his lips were white. "Chargad," Jerret said.

Cullen hadn't seen the boy before. Now he noticed that Jerret seemed frightened, that he could not even bring himself to look at the man but kept his head down and glanced at him through a thicket of hair.

"Who's Chargad?" Cullen asked.

"The—my steward," Jerret said. He turned his signet ring nervously around his finger.

"How did he die?" someone asked. "Was he poisoned?"

A horrible thought occurred to Cullen. He remembered supper with that dreadful woman, the witch, and the accusations she had made against his father, that he had ordered the witnesses to Jerret's ceremony killed. Had Chargad been one of the witnesses?

He couldn't ask Jerret, not with his father right there. But why else would Jerret look so afraid?

His father had given control of the Bound Folk over to him, though. Could Noldeth have kept some of the Bound for himself, men who continued to follow his orders? Were people being killed so that he, Cullen, could be king?

The thought made him uneasy. He had nothing against Chargad, yet the man might have gone to his death because of him. And there was that other man, the one from Finbar that Angarred had mentioned, someone he didn't even know. He looked around for his father. Noldeth gazed back at him, expressionless.

Cullen hurried back to his rooms, wondering who could answer all his newfound questions. The witch? No, the idea was ridiculous.

Could he talk to Polgar? But Polgar could do nothing; he was even more terrified of their father. No, he would have to confront the old man himself. Later, though, he thought. Not now.

He opened his door and saw the Bound Folk still on their heads. "Stand up, you fools!" he said. The Bound Folk rose to their feet, their faces impassive.

# E L E V E N

Hartil gave Brangwin some old clothes that had belonged to his son; they were too short, but Brangwin didn't care. Then the old man told him where he might find some horses running wild, horses whose owners had been seized by the Bound Folk.

"I thank you," Brangwin said. "I wish that I could be a prince in truth, so that I might reward you as you deserve."

"Your presence in my house is reward enough," Hartil said. It was an old form of politeness, but the farmer seemed to mean it.

The horses were where Hartil had said they would be. He captured one of them without trouble, an easygoing mare who would do anything for him as long as they stopped regularly for grass and water.

He rode south and east, toward Aspen Valley. He hunted every few days, living off the land like the soldier he had been. Sometimes he even felt happy. He had no duties; no one counted on him to do the impossible. No one even knew where he was.

He whistled "Irru's Ride" as he went, and then, when he felt certain he was alone, he essayed the words. "Oh, he rode away, and he rode away, and he rode from night till morn," he sang. They said he had a good singing voice, back at the castle. "And he never knew if he'd e'er return, and oh, his heart was torn."

He thought about his old life in the castle, how they used to mark the Dark Day. Folks believed that on that day, the Winter solstice, the two gods of the heavens and the two gods of the underworld met in a place outside of earthly realms, outside of time, and there exchanged some of the dead in their charge. Those who had been placed wrongly in Marfan and Mathona's realm, or who had shown a tendency toward sin over the year, were given over to Tashtery and Lammergil, and the gods of the underworld likewise delivered some of their people into Marfan and Mathona's care.

It was an inauspicious day: no one worked, and any task started that day would be doomed to failure. No one ventured outside lest they see the newly exchanged dead, thin as air and clothed in tattered gray. Brangwin and his brother and sisters terrified each other with stories about Tashtery's kingdom, while outside the castle the wind whistled like the souls of the damned.

As an adult he found the Dark Day horribly tedious. But when he was a boy he couldn't imagine anything more wonderful: no lessons, no work, nothing at all expected of him.

It was odd, he thought, that he should be remembering wind and rain and snow, when one bright sun followed another like a necklace of yellow beads. But the feeling of being at liberty, of having nothing to do, was the same. Like the gods, he felt free of the bonds of space and time, if only for a short moment.

The road began to rise and fall over soft hills covered with grass. He saw the sturdy sheep and goats of Goss, and the clever dogs that could turn whole herds in an instant. Folks passed him on stout furry-footed ponies and nodded and spoke in old Gossek. He answered them as best he could; he had forgotten a good deal.

The hills grew steeper and closer together, the valleys narrower. Lakes shone out of some of the valleys, the mountains reflected in their depths like drowned lands. Stone villages clustered together on the hillsides.

People here knew him and hailed him as Prince Brangwin. A few wanted to stop and talk, but he said nothing and rode on. They would hear his ill news soon enough.

As he came nearer to Aspen Valley he finally turned his mind to his responsibilities, to how he would spend the days left to him. One army or the other would find them within a few short months, and in that time he would have to learn how to die. He wondered if he could. And what would he tell Madaroc and Lirden and all the others, the people who depended on him?

One morning he saw wisps of smoke rising up beyond the next mountain. He urged the placid mare forward, smiling for the first time in a long while.

Just before they topped the mountain he felt a stirring of unease. It was a pleasantly warm day; Summer had begun sometime on his journey. Why would anyone light a fire? A part of him urged him to stop, to turn away from the mountain and ride as fast and as far as the mare could take him.

He pushed his misgivings aside and rode on. And there, from the top of the mountain, he saw what he had dreaded. Fire had ravaged the town. Everything had burned to the ground, leaving only blackened wood and ash. Ruins lay jumbled together; for a while he failed to recognize anything, and even hoped that he might have come to the wrong place. That large foundation over there had to be the meeting hall, though, and those fallen beams near it were probably from his cousin's cottage. And there—he lifted his eyes—there were the fields, the sides of the hills they had leveled and planted with such hard work. All gone now, all burned. Smoke rose from the charred wood to the sky.

His horse continued unguided into the valley. He smelled a thick reek of burning meat, saw what looked like toys in ragged clothes lying near the ruins. Crows pecked at the clothing, and now he saw more of them above the village, circling in the smoke.

He choked and dropped from his horse. For a moment he remembered his earlier madness and he struggled against it. He was the prince, the last remaining member of the royal family. But what was a prince if there were no people left to govern?

No—he would be no one. It felt good to be no one, to let all his burdens fall to the ground. No duties, no obligations, nothing to worry about ever again.

A red haze obscured his sight, and he turned and ran. "Tash-teeer-reee! Tash-teeer-reee!" a madil-bird cried.

————

Caireddin dressed carefully and studied herself in the mirror. Her mother had said that Drustig would come again today, that he might even ask for her hand. Caireddin didn't know how she felt about him, but she wanted him to like her—no, to be dazzled by her. She had not even gone to the tavern with her friends, so that she might be rested and alert when she met him.

She had heard the latest news from Tarkennin and the others: all the Harus had been pardoned save for Drustig. She wondered how he would explain that, and she grinned to think she held some advantage over him.

A knock came at the door. Shorry went to answer it, and she heard Drustig's steps along with the servant's as they headed down the hall. She fastened her mother's necklace, made of hammered gold and plump red rubies, a gift from King Tezue, then went to the room where her mother entertained visitors. Her heart beat loudly in her ears.

Lady Efcharren was there already, sitting regally in one of the room's many chairs. Caireddin and Drustig took seats near her. "Good day, ladies," Drustig said.

"Good day," Caireddin said. Her mouth was dry.

Drustig did not seem to hear her. "The war goes well," he said, showing them his crazed grin. "I knew it would, of course. I have magic on my side, and that makes victory certain."

"What sort of magic?" Caireddin asked.

Drustig looked at her for the first time and grinned again. "Don't worry about that, milady," he said. "I'll pursue the war. Your task is to provide me with legitimacy in the eyes of the Karedek, and to look beautiful."

Caireddin glanced at her mother. Was this a proposal? Drustig seemed to say he wanted her as his wife, but he had not asked her consent—he had simply taken it for granted that she would agree. Caireddin thought of herself as the least romantic of women, but even she had hoped for something more, some declaration of love perhaps.

"Excuse me, milord," she said. "I've heard rumors that the rest of your family has been called back to Karededin."

Anger flashed in Drustig's eyes, like lightning in a blue sky. A vein beat in the pale skin at his temple. "Yes, they were, and very smug and important they were about it too. I'll show them, though. Jerret's favor means nothing if Jerret dies—and my father says he's very ill. I'll take the crown then. I'm the oldest, I deserve it. I was promised it."

He made an effort to calm himself. "But I told you not to concern yourself with these things. I'll take care of everything—you're to do nothing until we arrive at Karededin and you take the queen's throne."

"I—I don't understand," Caireddin said. "I hadn't planned to go to Karededin."

Drustig took a breath. "Please forgive me, Princess Caireddin. I am so filled with plans for my future—for our future—that I thought I'd told you all of this already. I was in Goss to test the—the magical object, and now things are in readiness. When little Jerret dies my troops will sweep down to Karededin and wrest the crown from my brother Cullen." He nodded to her. "And of course all of this depends on you, my princess. You would give me legitimacy, as I said." Like Caireddin, he suddenly seemed to realize that there were rituals attendant on an event such as this one. He turned his intense gaze on her; for a moment he seemed to see to the core of her soul. "I would be honored if you would consent to be my queen."

A vast future opened before her, a life away from the endless cold and fog of Ou. Away from her mother and her petty plans, her hideously cluttered house. She would ride to war at Drustig's side, she would see his magic triumph over his brother Cullen. And then she would sit on the throne next to him, queen of Karededin. It sounded like something from an ancient ballad.

Did she want to spend her life with Drustig, though? Tarkennin had said he was mad, and certainly he didn't seem the steadiest of men. But then who wanted a steady man, a drudge content with whatever life gave him? She had never known anyone with Drustig's vision.

"Think it over," Drustig said. He stood. "I'll need an answer soon, though—as I said, Jerret doesn't have much time."

"Very well, milord," Caireddin said.

"I have things to see to," Drustig said. "Good day." He headed for the door abruptly, before Efcharren could call for Shorry to lead him out. As he passed the last suit of armor it lowered its arm with an eerie soundlessness, its sword pointed directly at his heart.

"Tashtery's fire!" he said, jumping back.

"Don't worry," Efcharren said. "It always does that. It belonged to some mad ancestor of Tezue's—I think it's cursed."

He swore again and left.

The two women sat for a moment, stunned by the whirlwind of his visit. Finally Efcharren said, "You know, I can't remember the last time that suit of armor pointed its sword at anyone."

"So you lied to him," Caireddin said. "I thought so."

"I wasn't lying," her mother said. "I was being polite. There's a difference. Anyway, you did right not to answer him right away. Think it over, let him worry about your decision."

"I wasn't trying to worry him. I truly don't know what answer to give."

"Do you want to marry him? There's always Cullen—either one could become king after Jerret dies."

"But—but they're not from the royal family," Caireddin said. As soon as she said the words she realized that she barely cared where they came from; she had merely asked the first question that surfaced from her confusion.

"The royal family!" Efcharren said scornfully. Caireddin expected another of her stories about King Tezue, but the other woman surprised her. "Do you truly believe that Tezue, that Rodarren and Jerret, are descended from Marfan and Mathona? Someone in the distant past took the throne of Karededin by force, and then made up all this folderol about gods."

Caireddin nodded. "I heard a disturbing story about Drustig, though." She told her mother what Tarkennin had said, that all the Harus had been pardoned but him.

"There *is* a disturbing air about him, you're right about that," Efcharren said. She laughed. "Holy Godkings, we agree about something! This is truly a remarkable day."

"I must be wrong, then," Caireddin said, laughing as well.

"Well, think it over," Efcharren said. "You have a few days to make your decision, after all. But remember that the man you choose will gain legitimacy simply by being married to you. And that means more people will follow him, and fight for him as well. Your choice could decide a war, and a dynasty."

Caireddin nodded and walked slowly to her room, barely listening to her. Could she make a life with Drustig? She closed the door and lay on her bed. Did she want to marry him?

Noldeth and Cullen hurried through Pergodi Castle. Polgar limped behind them, breathing hard.

Noldeth was speaking, but Cullen barely heard him. Instead he glanced around him as they went, noting improvements he would make if he were king. Those threadbare tapestries looked as if they had been there since Marfan's day; he could commission new ones, perhaps some scenes of the Harus riding to battle. And the windows there—surely they didn't need to be that narrow; no one had loosed an arrow from the castle since the city of Pergodi had grown up around it. He could widen them, bring some light inside, clear out the must.

They were meeting King Jerret, for another day of tedious tasks that needed to be seen to; Noldeth wanted his sons to learn the workings of the castle. Cullen forced himself to pay attention to his father, who was saying something about Dobrennin, the under-steward. Should he be promoted to steward? Would he be sympathetic to the Harus' cause?

Noldeth stopped suddenly. The others stopped with him. They had come to Iltarra's apartments. Noldeth raised his hand for silence, then thrust open her door.

Iltarra and Annin Damazue lay unmoving on the floor by the hearth, their arms and legs entwined. He was naked; she wore only her pearls. Iltarra turned to the door, still half asleep. Shock appeared on her face; she reached for the pile of clothes nearby and sat up quickly.

"Iltarra!" Noldeth said. "What do you think you're doing here?"

"I might ask you the same thing," Iltarra said. She struggled into the first piece of clothing that came to hand; it proved to be Annin's shirt. "These are my rooms, after all."

"Don't be a fool!" Noldeth said. "You know what I told you—how dare you disobey me? And you, sir"—he turned to Annin—"you will leave these rooms immediately."

"Surely you'll allow me to put on my clothes first," Annin said. "Sir."

Cullen tensed; he knew what happened to people who spoke so insolently to his father. "Annin, don't—" Polgar said.

"Naked or clothed, I don't care," Noldeth said. "Just go." He began to cough. He took out a handkerchief speckled with dried blood and pressed it to his mouth.

Annin pulled on his trousers and went to the door. "Don't worry, Polgar," he said, slapping him lightly on the back. "I'm not afraid of your father."

"You should be," Polgar said. He had intended it only for Annin's ears, but Cullen heard it, and so, probably, did Noldeth.

Someone came up to them as Annin left. "Noldeth!" Jerret said. "That's where you are. I've been waiting . . ."

No one thought to close the door. Jerret peered inside and saw Iltarra in Annin's shirt, then turned and watched as Annin, half naked, walked down the hall. "Iltarra," he said, "I thought that we—that you—"

"I'm sorry you had to see this, milord," Noldeth said. "If you'll leave us a moment I'll talk to my daughter, see if I can knock some sense into her head."

Jerret nodded. He began to walk away slowly, then turned back once to look at Iltarra. His face held nothing but hurt and betrayal; it looked bruised. Then he hurried down the hall.

Noldeth closed the door behind them. "Are we alone here?" he asked. "Or do you have other lovers hiding somewhere in your rooms?"

"Don't be ridiculous," Iltarra said.

"Why did you disobey me?" Noldeth said. "Jerret would do anything for you, anything at all. He was about to make you queen of Karededin—your children would be kings and queens, and you a god. What in the name of all the Godkings are you doing with this useless, jumped-up . . . I don't even know what he is."

"He's not jumped-up, for one thing," Iltarra said. "He comes from one of the oldest families in Karededin. The Damazues."

"Answer my question," Noldeth said. He coughed again and dropped into one of Iltarra's chairs. Cullen and Polgar sat near him but Iltarra continued to stand. Annin's shirt came down to the middle of her thighs.

"Jerret's a boy," Iltarra said. "I needed someone I could talk to. Someone older, cleverer."

"You needed!" Noldeth said. "What about me? Everything I've done was for you and your brothers—and in one instant of selfishness you've destroyed it all. You've betrayed me and everything I've worked for."

"Well, I didn't expect Jerret to join us. Or you, for that matter."

"Silence!" Noldeth said. Cullen flinched despite himself. "You think this is all very amusing, don't you? But I told you what would happen if you defied me. You'll never be queen now."

To Cullen's amazement Iltarra laughed. "Good," she said. "I don't want to marry Jerret anyway."

"Do you think that's the end of it, that you're free to do what you want? That I'd let you get away with this—this disobedience? I'll blacken your name to Jerret until he hates you more than he's ever hated anyone. Exile will be the best you can hope for."

"Go ahead," Iltarra said, but she looked uncertain now. "Jerret still loves me. We'll see which one of us he trusts more."

Instead of answering her Noldeth turned to Cullen. "Do you understand what I meant now?" he said. "A good player has to think of every possibility. I told you she might do something foolish, didn't I? Fortunately I still have some moves left to me." He looked at Iltarra. "I gave the crown to Cullen, but I can take it back if I want."

Cullen gasped. Would he bind his own daughter? No—he was bluffing, he had to be.

"You wouldn't dare," Iltarra said.

"Do you think so?"

Iltarra spun to face her brothers. "Cullen, you wouldn't give him the crown, would you? Not if he wants to bind your own sister."

"Father would never do that to you, Iltarra," Cullen said.

"That's not what I asked, is it? Look at you two, terrified to say a word against him. At least that was one thing you could say for Drustig—he wasn't a coward like the rest of you."

"No, Cullen knows how to obey his father," Noldeth said. "Not like my other children, it seems. I did warn you, Iltarra. You've forfeited my support, my influence. I said you won't be queen, and I mean it. I'm making Cullen the next king of Karededin."

"What!" Iltarra said.

Cullen began to smile. He had done it. He had waited out his dazzling brother, and his beautiful sister, and now he would be king. His father was looking at him, seeing him for the first time, understanding his worth.

Noldeth began to cough again. Iltarra looked from Cullen to her father and back. "You want to be king, do you?" she said to Cullen. She seemed almost sorry for him; he couldn't understand why. "Do you know what that means? How many people do you think Father's killed so far, in his eagerness to put one of us on the throne? Jerret read me a letter he got from Lord Ezlin today—one of Ezlin's friends died suddenly, no one knows why. Oh, and what a coincidence—the friend was a witness when Jerret proclaimed Ezlin his heir. And there was another letter a month ago, while you were gone. A man named Lord Aglar fell off a boat, it seems. A man who just happened to be a witness for Ezlin's claim."

"Enough—" Noldeth began. His coughing fit overtook him.

"And of course the steward just died, poor Chargad," Iltarra said. "Another witness. He's killing them off one by one."

Cullen thought of Chargad's death, the pale man facedown beside the food that had probably poisoned him. Well, but Cullen had killed people in war, good people too, some of them, folks who loved their parents and worshiped the Godkings. Sometimes people had to die; it was unfortunate, but that was the way things were.

Anyway, he didn't want to think of Chargad. Right now he just wanted to savor the idea of being king. He felt the deep pleasure of mastery, as if he had put on the crown of binding again, but this time he was holding everyone to his will, all the men and women in the world.

"That's not the worst of it," Iltarra said. "He has to kill Jerret too, for you to become king. And he'll do it—him or one of his Bound Folk."

Noldeth struggled to say something. "He told me Jerret might go quietly," Cullen said.

"You're so stupid, Cullen," she said. "Did you truly think Jerret would just pack up his things and wave farewell and ride off to the countryside? A popular king is dangerous if he's left alive—he's a symbol for the people, someone who will rally them against a usurper. And he can have heirs too, heirs who will grow up to challenge you. Jerret could have a dozen children, easily—he's young enough, and certainly capable enough. I can testify to that last, if you like."

"Don't listen to her," Noldeth said. "She'll tell you anything to get what she wants." He turned to Iltarra. "Say nothing to Jerret, do you hear me? Nothing at all about my plans. Oh, and I'll want my pearls back."

Iltarra put her hand to the string of pearls. "You gave them to me, before you left. They're mine."

"Yes, and now I want them back."

For the first time she looked frightened of their father. She had been very young—only five or six—when Drustig had challenged Noldeth and the beatings had stopped. Still, she knew enough to be afraid of Noldeth's rages.

"You said I could have them if I convinced Jerret to bring you back," Iltarra said, her voice shaking. "And I did that, I got him to change his mind. You can't—"

"Give them to me, Iltarra," Noldeth said. "Remember, I can still use the crown."

She took the necklace off slowly and handed it to her father. "Thank you," Noldeth said. "Let's go, Cullen, Polgar. Jerret's still waiting for us." He stood heavily and left.

Cullen followed him down the hall, thinking about his sudden change of fortune. Iltarra and Annin, Jerret dying, Noldeth's plans for him . . .

Suddenly he wanted to celebrate. They passed an attractive bound woman sweeping the floors. He let his father and Polgar go on ahead of him, then dropped back and ordered her to his rooms. She would be there waiting for him, he knew, however long their meeting with Jerret took.

# TWELVE

Two days later Mathewar walked into Pergodi Castle at dusk, passing courtiers and petitioners and servants. He was tired, and dusty from the road, and his knapsack seemed to grow heavier with every step. He wanted nothing more than to find Angarred and then sleep for a long time.

Polgar was probably already here, he thought; Polgar and Annin had ridden on ahead while he was still walking back to the stables to get his horse. He wondered what mischief the Harus had worked in his absence.

He turned down several corridors and headed through a dim gallery. Far at the end he thought he saw Angarred, and his heart lifted. They sometimes knew when the other would be arriving—but did that still hold true, now that his magic had left him?

She came toward him and held him. Her red and gold hair seemed to shine in the gloomy light. "What's the matter?" she asked.

She tensed and looked over his shoulder. He followed her gaze. A knot of men came toward them. "It's the Harus, with Jerret," she whispered. "He invited them back. Lord Noldeth's made it clear he doesn't like me."

"No, I imagine he wouldn't," he said softly.

"Mathewar!" Jerret said, breaking from his bodyguards to embrace him.

"Hello, Jerret," Mathewar said.

"Look at this!" Polgar said, coming up to Mathewar. "You are who you said you are."

Jerret looked from Mathewar to Polgar and back again. "What does he mean?" he asked.

"He thought to make me one of the Bound Folk," Mathewar said.

Beside him he heard Angarred say, "Oh, holy Godkings . . ."

"No!" Jerret said.

"I'm afraid he did," Mathewar said. "I have to talk to you, Jerret. Now would be best, or we can—"

"He isn't creating Bound Folk any longer," Noldeth said.

The true enemy, Mathewar thought. "Who is, then?" he asked.

"Do you see, Jerret?" Noldeth said. "It's as I told you—this man and his wife are envious of my position, and take every opportunity to slander me. You know the truth, that we swore never to make any Bound Folk ever again. But do you think he'll ever believe me?"

"Should I?" Mathewar asked.

He had tried to use his commanding voice, but it sounded no different from his regular speech. The commanding voice wouldn't work on Noldeth anyway, he thought; the man's sense of himself was too strong.

"It is customary to give a person the benefit of the doubt," Noldeth said. "Especially if you have no evidence."

"Ah, but I do have evidence. That's why I went north."

"Really? What is it?"

"That's for Jerret's ears alone."

"Do you see how hostile he is?" Noldeth said. "And you can't say I didn't give him a chance, that I didn't—"

"Jerret," Mathewar said. They all looked at him. Perhaps he could still command with his voice; probably, though, they had just heard his thinly concealed anger. "When can you receive me?"

Jerret looked at Noldeth. "I suppose we could spare a few moments now," Noldeth said.

"I'll see Jerret alone," Mathewar said.

No one said anything for a long moment. Mathewar had the sense that they were fighting for Jerret's soul, like the strange gods in the stories the northerners told. Jerret twisted his ring around his finger.

"I'll talk to Mathewar," Jerret said finally. He turned to Noldeth and said, as if placating him, "I'll just be a few minutes."

They headed out of the gallery, Mathewar still carrying the knapsack with him. "Remember what I told you about him," Noldeth called after them.

"What did he tell you?" Mathewar asked.

"That—that you drink sattery," Jerret said.

I've underestimated them, Mathewar thought. I knew they were deceitful, I just never realized how deceitful. "I did drink sattery," he said, as evenly as he could. "It was fourteen years ago, though."

"Why didn't you tell me?"

"I don't like to talk about it. It was a very stupid thing to do."

They found an unused room holding a table and a few chairs. The bodyguards tried to follow Jerret inside, but Jerret shook his head and the men took up positions at the door. Mathewar closed the door behind them, though he didn't put it past Noldeth to listen at the other side. Or to order one of his spies to listen; Noldeth seemed to have collected a good deal of information about him already.

"Can I ask you something?" Jerret said once they sat down.

"Of course."

"Can I—" He looked up at Mathewar through his uncut hair. "Can I have someone killed?"

"Well," Mathewar said, "that depends on who you want to kill. And why."

"His name's Annin Damazue." Mathewar raised an eyebrow. "He—he bedded Iltarra. Still beds her, I think. She won't talk to me—she's been very distant. I can't ask Noldeth about killing Annin, because Iltarra's his daughter—"

That family *has* been busy since I left, Mathewar thought. "No, I'm afraid not," he said. "You can only kill someone who broke the law."

"But—but there have been other kings who killed people they didn't like—"

"Yes, and they shouldn't have. Do you remember the oath you swore when you became king, to uphold the realm's justice? That means justice for everyone, high and low, rich and poor. Friends and enemies."

"But isn't it treason? What he's doing?"

"It would be if you were married to her. For now, though, she's answerable only to her father."

Jerret looked thoughtful at that. Then he frowned, and Mathewar knew he had decided not to broach the matter with Noldeth. "What if Annin broke the law?"

Mathewar tried not to smile. "We'll discuss it then," he said.

"You're always telling me things I can't do," Jerret said.

"You seem to have found out what you can do on your own. And is that what you think being a king is—doing whatever you want? It's tremendously difficult work. I'm always amazed at the number of people who want to do it." He hesitated. How much of a parent should he be to Jerret, this boy who had lost his own parents at such an early age? "I'm sorry to hear about Iltarra."

"Do you think she'll come back?" Jerret asked.

"I don't know, Jerret, I'm sorry. But you're young yet—there will be dozens of women wanting to marry you."

"But none of them like Iltarra. I'll never love anyone like her."

"You will, though. In time it will even hurt less."

Jerret scowled; like anyone who had been brought low by a first love, Mathewar knew, he felt certain he would suffer from her memory for the rest of his life.

"Do you want to hear what I learned in the north?" Mathewar asked.

Jerret nodded, not very enthusiastically. Mathewar told him about the Bound Folk, about the deserted cities and overgrown fields; he explained how he had freed one of the Half-bound. The boy began to pay attention when Mathewar described his imprisonment and his audience with Polgar, though probably because it was an exciting story and not for anything it told him about the state of his realm.

"But Noldeth said he's stopped creating the Bound Folk," Jerret said when he had finished. "So everything's fine now, isn't it?"

"What about the people he's already bound, though?" Mathewar said. "Shouldn't they be freed?"

He watched as the boy worked the problem out for himself. "Noldeth said they were criminals," Jerret said.

"They tried to bind *me*, Jerret. And I saw thousands of them. Are they all criminals, then?"

"Well, they made a mistake with you. But Noldeth said—"

"What were their crimes? Were they serious enough to merit such a harsh punishment? Could all those people have committed crimes that dreadful?"

"I don't know," Jerret said angrily. "Stop asking me all these questions. Noldeth knows, and I trust him. Why do you dislike him?"

"I don't dislike him," Mathewar said. It was the first lie he had told the boy. "I wonder about him. Why does he need so many slaves? What did they all do, to be made into Bound Folk?"

"Why don't you ask him?"

"I doubt he'll answer me. He doesn't seem to like me very much."

Jerret was silent a moment. "I have to uphold justice for these people too, is that what you mean?"

"Yes," Mathewar said. He tried not to show how much he approved of Jerret's answer; it would only embarrass the boy. "Exactly."

"All right, then, I'll ask him. But he's telling the truth. You'll see."

"I'd like that. And could you ask him something else? I'm curious to know how he bound all these people. Polgar said he had some sort of magical object, some device—I'd very much like to see it, to learn about it. It should be in the College, or at least studied by the masters."

"All right," Jerret said again.

"Good," Mathewar said. "I suppose that's it, unless there's something more you want to tell me."

Jerret hesitated. The boy had something else on his mind, then, Mathewar was certain of it. "No," Jerret said finally.

Mathewar reached for Jerret's thoughts, then nearly cursed aloud. When would he get out of the habit of using magic? When did people who had lost an arm stop trying to reach for things?

"Can I—can I talk to you again, if I want?" Jerret asked.

"Of course," Mathewar said. "Whenever you like."

They left the room together. Angarred had waited for them, and Jerret's bodyguards, but not, thankfully, Noldeth and the rest of the family. He and Angarred walked up the stairs and into their apartments, talking as they went.

At the apartment he finally dropped his knapsack and lay back wearily in one of the chairs while Angarred told him what she had seen and done in the past few weeks. He felt horrified to hear about Aglar's death and the attack on Jerret's friend; he had left Pergodi thinking she would be safe. Then other emotions overtook him: relief that she was unharmed, and amazement at her resourcefulness.

When she finished he told her his tale, complete but for the loss of his magic; he didn't think he was ready for that. Now it was her turn to be appalled, at his capture and his near binding.

"Why didn't you use magic to escape?" she asked.

He pretended not to hear her. "I wonder what Jerret was holding back," he said.

"I can guess," she said. "Chargad Steward died—and there are rumors that he was poisoned. The Harus might have killed another witness."

"Ah," he said. "No wonder he's worried. But I would have just blamed the Harus if he'd mentioned it, and he wouldn't have wanted that."

"What do we do now?" she said.

"I don't know," he said. "And there are other problems as well— we should get back to the children, for example. And the new term at the College will start in Autumn, and I need to be there before then."

"You aren't going to leave Jerret to the mercy of that—that—"

"No, of course not. But some of the masters would get up to all sorts of mischief if I wasn't there. And we both have classes to teach . . ."

"My classes aren't that important. Why don't I stay here?"

"And get into fights with Bound Folk?"

The moment he said it he knew it was unworthy. She had been right to defend Jerret's friend; he knew that. It was his bitterness speaking, bitterness he hadn't even realized he had. Why did she still have her magic when he had lost his?

"There's something wrong, isn't there?" she asked. "I knew it the moment I saw you."

He had wanted a fight, he realized—and she would not give it to him. He had to match her decency with his own.

"You did," he said. He took a deep breath. "When I freed Nim—when I—after I freed Nim I couldn't work magic."

"Oh!" she said. She put her hand to her mouth. "Oh, Matte. That's horrible."

"Please, Anne,*" he said. "I don't want pity. I couldn't bear it."

"What do you want, then?"

"I think—right now I think I want to sleep."

"Well, can I sleep with you?"

He smiled, the first time in a very long while. "I'd like that. But did you have supper? Aren't you hungry?"

"Oh, I don't care about that. I missed you so much, Matte—you were gone for so long—"

"I missed you too."

They stood and held each other. Then they went to bed and lay down, Angarred nestled against him. Perhaps, he thought before he fell asleep, things weren't as hopeless as they seemed.

Cullen headed back to his rooms after visiting his father. Noldeth's cough had grown worse—as if, Cullen thought, Iltarra's disobedience had weakened him further.

A familiar figure came toward him, a tall, thin woman with white hair. Lady Dubbish loved the life of the court, and to gossip about what she had learned; although she was at least sixty she didn't seem to understand that she might hurt people with her indiscretions. She had seen Cullen and was hurrying now, her eyes alight. He braced himself for whatever she might say.

"Lord Cullen!" she said. "It's good to see you."

"Good to see you too," he said. He expected her to ask about his exile, about Ou, but she seemed too full of her news for politeness.

"You must be relieved about Iltarra," she said.

"Why do you say that?" Cullen asked, surprised.

She bent her chin toward her chest, a habitual gesture, then stared up at him with her bright blue eyes. She looked like some rare bird.

*Anne: pronounced with two syllables—"An-neh"

"Well, it looks as though she's finally settling down," she said. "She seems very happy with Lord Annin."

"I know very little about my sister's doings, I'm afraid."

"She was—well—a bit wild while you were gone. No one really knew what she'd do next. Jerret seemed to fancy her, but then she began to flirt with Lord Ezlin . . ."

"Lord Ezlin?" he asked.

"Yes, you know. The man from the Finbar Islands, the one Jerret made his heir. I suppose he'll be very disappointed when he hears of Iltarra's new conquest."

Why was she telling him this? He didn't care what Iltarra got up to—all he asked of her was that she stay away from Jerret and leave the way to the throne open for him. Well, but the old lady was like a fountain, pouring out her gossip indiscriminately.

He realized she was still speaking. ". . . Lady Melleth. No, of course you haven't heard about that—you've been away. She and her husband had a terrible argument, right there in the Great Hall where anyone could hear them. I hear she's forbidden him her bed."

He remembered Lady Melleth, with her full mouth and green eyes. She always seemed to look down on him and his family; he had felt like a boorish commoner in her presence. Suddenly he wondered how she would treat him when he was king, and he smiled to himself.

They spoke for a while longer and he left, his mind full of fancies about Lady Melleth. It was good to be back in Pergodi, to see and be seen, to be—very soon now—the most powerful man at court. He should cultivate Lady Dubbish; he would need to know all about his subjects. For every useless piece of information, like her story of Iltarra and Ezlin—

He cursed. Iltarra and Ezlin—his father would have seen the implications immediately. No wonder Iltarra hadn't cared about Jerret—she had Ezlin, Jerret's heir. When Jerret died Ezlin would return to claim the throne—and Iltarra would be waiting for him.

He began to run. When he reached Iltarra's room he wrenched open the door without knocking. His sister sat by a window, reading something.

She looked up at him. "I would have thought you'd have learned to knock by now," she said. "Or don't you remember what happened the last time you came in here without my permission?"

He had no time for her mockery. "What are you and Ezlin planning, Iltarra?"

"Ezlin?"

"Yes. Did you think I wouldn't hear about it? You bedded him while we were gone."

"No, I didn't."

"I don't believe you. He's Jerret's heir, isn't he? You and he are plotting together to take the throne after Jerret dies."

She shrugged. "Believe what you like. I enjoyed teasing him, that's all. I teased a lot of people—Mathewar, for example—"

"The magician? What did you and he get up to?"

"Nothing, Cullen, I just told you. I'm not interested in either of them."

"Is that true? If you're lying I'll—"

"You'll what? Turn me into one of the Bound Folk?"

He sank into a chair, still panting from his run. "Tell me the truth, Cullen, since we're being honest with each other," Iltarra said. "What would you do if Father asked you for the crown? If he said, I'd like to turn your sister into a lump of mindless meat, can I borrow the crown for a moment? You'd give it to him, wouldn't you?"

"Of course I wouldn't," Cullen said.

"I wish you'd told him so. I wish you would stand up to him for once, you and Polgar."

"How can I stand up to him? What reason would I give for denying him?"

"Oh, for the love of the Godkings," Iltarra said. "You're twenty-six years old, you don't have to find excuses like a child. And what's wrong with saying that you don't want your sister bound? Why are you still afraid of him? He's an old man—he can't beat you anymore."

It was a good question, Cullen thought. Why did he still cower before his father? Why did he think of Noldeth as impossibly tall, and himself as a puny child? Noldeth was weak, he would die soon, and still Cullen couldn't bring himself to oppose him.

"I'll tell you what," Iltarra said, looking hard at him. "Let's swear to protect each other. You and me and Polgar, all of us. Jerret might not die, you know—even our father might find a conscience before the end. If you become king you'll help me, and if I get back in Jerret's favor I'll help you. And none of us will use the crown against the others."

"Are you going back to Jerret?"

"No, of course not."

"I don't understand. I don't know what you're planning. Why did you leave Jerret for Annin? Jerret's the king, for Marfan's sake."

"Because I love him."

He stared at her, and she laughed. "You've never been in love, have you?" she said. "Love has absolutely no place in your calculations. That's why I can tell you that I'll never bed Jerret, or Ezlin, or anyone at all besides Annin. When Father told me I'd never be queen all I felt was relief. I've found something better than anything he ever planned for me." She looked down at the piece of paper in her lap. "This is a poem Annin wrote. I'm reading it for about the thirtieth time, even though I've memorized it by now. You don't understand that, do you?"

"No."

"So what do you think? Will you swear?"

"If you swear to do what our father told you. Don't talk to Jerret about any of this. Help me if I become king."

She sighed. "I don't know. I did get to like Jerret, even if I don't want to marry him."

Cullen felt a rising anger. Why did she have to argue about everything? Why didn't she obey their father like the rest of them? Lady Dubbish had been right—she had grown too free while they had been in exile. She needed to be controlled somehow, needed to see that it was in her interest to keep Jerret ignorant. It would be too drastic to bind her, but . . .

Would it, though? If leaving her free meant that he would never become king? He held the ultimate weapon, the crown; he did not have to promise her anything at all.

Once again he smiled his secret smile. Finally, for the first time in his life, he held the upper hand.

"What are you going to do?" he asked.

She seemed to read something in his expression. "All right," she said finally. "All right. If you promise not to use the crown against me, I swear I won't talk to Jerret, and I'll help you if you become king." She shook her head. "Poor boy."

"Good."

"What about you?" Iltarra said. "Don't you feel sorry for Jerret?"

"I don't think about it," Cullen said.

A few days later Mathewar left the castle. He headed down the hill and into the city; he wanted to be alone for a while. Angarred had said she wouldn't pity him but she did anyway, though she tried to hide it. And he tried not to become angry with her but he did anyway, and both of them felt miserable a good deal of the time.

He wanted as well to see what the mood in Pergodi was like, how the people felt about the Harus. But instead of talking to the Pergodek or looking around him, he found himself wandering the streets and thinking about magic.

Almost all the people walking past him—almost all the people in the world—had no magic at all. None of them could work the transformations he had, or know the joy of getting the world to change according to your desire; they could not even make a fire or call up light in the darkness. Somehow they had gotten through life without that ability, though he couldn't imagine how. Somehow he would have to learn to live without it as well.

He reminded himself for the hundredth time not to give in to self-pity. Things might not be as grim as they seemed. He might find something in the library at the College to help him, or perhaps Tobrin . . .

He raised his head and saw Nim coming toward him. "Hello, Nim," he said.

The boy looked startled, but he didn't run away. "Hello," he said. He looked worse than he had in the prison. He had lost weight on the road, and was now so gaunt his clothes seemed to hang on him, as if he were made of tree branches instead of flesh and bones. He had deep shadows under his eyes, and someone had given him a bad cut on his lower lip.

"Are you all right?" Mathewar asked. "Here—would you like

some food?" He gestured to a stall by the side of the road selling eel pies.

"I'm fine," Nim said.

They had both been changed, he thought, but Nim's transformation had been even more violent than his own. The boy had been forced to learn too many things in too short a time; it was no wonder he failed at the simplest tasks. Mathewar reached into the purse at his side and drew out a few silver coins.

"Here," he said. Nim took them without seeming to acknowledge them. "If you need more come up to the castle and ask for me. And when I leave I'll tell someone to look out for you."

"Where are you going?" Nim asked.

"Back to the College. Don't worry, I won't ask you to come with me."

"When?"

"I don't know. I'll look for you before I go. Where are you staying?"

"Nowhere."

He should have known. "I'll find you." He nodded at the coins in Nim's hand. "Get some lodging. And eat some food, for the Healer's sake."

Nim turned and ran. Mathewar watched him and then headed back to the castle; it was growing late. He didn't know if he had made any progress at all with the boy. Nim had stayed and talked, had even asked questions, but once again he had fled before Mathewar could learn very much about him. He wondered if Nim would truly visit him at the castle or would continue to live on the streets.

Long shadows stretched out in front of the castle by the time he made it back. Angarred waited for him at the main door, looking excited. "Good news," she said. She spoke quietly, as if afraid to be overheard.

"What is it?"

"Hush. Lord Noldeth's taken to his bed. He's dying."

The castle seemed unnaturally silent. They ate in the Lesser Dining Hall, the only people seated at the great expanse of the table. Out in the halls the servants and courtiers talked in low voices and went about their business as quietly as they could.

"Where is everyone?" Mathewar said. "They can't all be at his bedside."

"Waiting to be summoned, I suppose," Angarred said. "I heard he hasn't even called his children to him yet."

"I wonder what he's doing."

"It doesn't matter, though, does it? He has only a day or so to work mischief, and then Jerret will be free of him."

"What about his children?"

"What about them? They seem very weak compared to their father—they can't possibly influence Jerret as much. Have you ever heard Cullen say anything at all?"

Mathewar laughed. "No, I don't think I have. And I got the feeling Polgar was afraid of his father, that he only bound people because Noldeth wanted him to. There's still Iltarra, I suppose."

"She doesn't seem interested in Jerret, though," Angarred said. Iltarra had made no secret of her new lover.

"Yes, and that's very odd. Why did she give up the chance to be queen?"

"Do you think we should stay on after Noldeth dies, then?"

"I don't know. Let's see if Jerret needs us."

A servant—not one of the Bound Folk—came in with pears and apples for dessert. She scowled at them as she cleared away their plates. Perhaps, Mathewar thought, she had overheard their conversation and felt they had not been respectful enough to Noldeth, or to the occasion. He knew that Noldeth had spies everywhere.

Well, as Angarred said, it didn't matter. The man would die soon, and their service here would be ended. They finished their meal and headed through the hushed stairs and hallways to their rooms.

# THIRTEEN

In the dead of night Noldeth called his sons to his room. His curtains were closed and the lamps doused; the only light came from the hearth-fire and the candles flickering in the corners, turning everything to wavering shadows. The air smelled heavily of wax and perfume, but a foul odor of sickness and blood wafted out over the room every so often and then disappeared.

Cullen sat next to Polgar by their father's bed and waited for him to gather the breath he needed to talk. His blankets were specked with blood.

"I don't have much time," Noldeth said, sitting with difficulty and leaning against the wall. "I'll come straight to the point. Of the witnesses to Jerret's ceremony making Ezlin his heir, only three remain alive. And Iltarra, of course, but she won't say anything against us. One of the three is Jerret's friend Talethe. He's a very clever lad—he suddenly decided to spend some time in the country, apparently, at his family's estate. We can assume he knows the danger of coming back to Pergodi, and that he won't be much of a threat to us."

So Iltarra was right, then, Cullen thought. His father had seen to it that the witnesses were killed. He wasn't even very surprised; he had known it already in some part of his mind.

"The other two witnesses, unfortunately, are that sorcerer and his wife the witch. I would have seen to them eventually, but I can't trust the two of you to do it. You'll have to discredit them, make it seem as though nothing they say can be trusted. You've heard me do this often enough. The sorcerer drinks sattery, his wife—"

"He hasn't had any sattery for a long time," Cullen said.

"I have very little time, as I said," Noldeth said. "That means no interruptions. Anyway, what's that to us? A lie that's told often enough becomes the truth."

A coughing fit shook him; the coughs sounded deeper and lasted longer than ever before. Cullen looked at Polgar, but his brother's face showed nothing.

Noldeth took another breath. "You probably won't have to worry about those two—they'll have to go back to the College soon. And once they're out of the way all that remains is to kill Jerret."

"I thought you said there might be another way," Cullen said. "That Jerret—"

"No interruptions, I said!" Anger flashed in Noldeth's eyes; for a moment, sick as he was, he looked like the tyrant of Cullen's childhood. Cullen cringed.

Noldeth made an obvious effort to calm himself. "As it turns out, there is no other way," he said. "I didn't think there would be. So. Which one of you is brave enough to do it?"

Cullen could barely think. He understood now that Jerret had to be killed; otherwise how could he himself become king? But he had thought it would be done cleanly, without any effort on his part, without even his awareness. How could his father ask this of him? Jerret had been his friend, had admired him, given him gifts . . .

"Oh, for the Godkings' sake," Noldeth said. "Drustig would have done it immediately, without a single question. You're both cowards—even Iltarra's braver than you are. Now—which one of you wants my good opinion? Who wants to spend his life knowing that he has the respect of his father, that he fulfilled his father's dying wish?"

Neither of them said anything. This time Cullen could not look at Polgar, and he sensed that Polgar too had not moved since his father's question. The rotting smell came into the room again, as if Noldeth had started to decay before his death.

"Why can't someone else do it?" Cullen asked. "What about the Bound Folk, or—or one of your spies?"

"Because I want you to, that's why," Noldeth said. "Because you've disappointed me all your lives, and I'm giving you one last chance to make it up to me. To prove that you can be king. And don't think to say yes and then not do it, because I'll come back and haunt you if you do."

"Does that mean—do you mean that if I don't do it I won't be king?"

"Unfortunately I'll have to carry out my plans no matter what you decide," Noldeth said. "I will not be a nobody in the Celestial Court when I die. My son will be king."

So that was why Noldeth had wanted to be king so badly, and why he had pushed his sons so hard after he had fallen ill. Even in his confusion Cullen marveled at how little he had known his father. Noldeth had never been at all religious, had never, as far as Cullen knew, even gone to a Godhouse on holy days.

It made a strange sense, though. Noldeth had started life as a carpenter and would have known what it was like to be treated as an inferior. In the Celestial Court a man or a woman had the same status they had in life; Noldeth as he was now would be lower than the kings of the Court, and probably others as well. But if one of his sons were king he would be raised high, nearly as high as if he had taken the throne himself.

Of course Noldeth had also wanted to be king for its own sake. As far back as Cullen could remember he had talked about all he would do and order and possess when he ruled Karededin.

"If Jerret isn't dead a week after I die, one of the Bound Folk will kill him," Noldeth said. "Of course that would be the coward's way out, but that's about all I've come to expect from you children." He paused, then said softly, "What are you thinking, Cullen? Are you thinking that you'll have to spend the rest of your life knowing you failed me? That if it's at all possible I'll come down from the Court and curse you until you wished you were dead?"

The fire in the hearth had gone out, Cullen saw; he felt dreadfully cold. He made one last desperate effort. He tried to imagine himself handing Jerret a poisoned cup or challenging him to a duel or telling one of the Bound Folk to kill the king. He saw Jerret's face in front of him, at first innocent and then terribly hurt by Cullen's treachery.

Noldeth lay back in the bed. "Very well," he said. "My children have failed me one last time."

"I'll do it," Polgar said.

Noldeth sat up, as startled as Cullen was. He might have thought Cullen able to kill someone, but clearly he had never expected anything from Polgar. Polgar had always infuriated him when they were children; he seemed to think that Polgar's limp was the boy's own fault.

The surprise left his face quickly and he smiled. "My boy!" he said. "It's too bad you can't be king and not your spineless brother, but unfortunately he's the oldest now that Drustig's gone. Now listen closely—I have some final instructions.

"Of course you know to get him alone, somewhere no one will see you, not even Bound Folk. I won't tell you what to do when you actually come to it—you'll know what's best for you. But you must be sure to get his signet ring, and to tell everyone that he proclaimed Cullen king with his last breath. And try to see that your feckless brother marries that bit of tail in Ou, what was her name?" No one said anything. Noldeth waved his hand. "You know the one I mean, Tezue's bastard. She'll give him legitimacy in the eyes of the people, and when he dies his statue will be placed in the Hall of the Standing Kings."

He lay down and closed his eyes. He looked paler than ever, nearly transparent. A blue vein stood out sharply on his forehead. Was he dead? Could they risk checking for a breath?

He opened his eyes. Cullen tried not to show his alarm. "And have Cullen give your sister to someone of rank," his father said to Polgar. "Make certain that she has high position and wealth. She did disobey me at the end but she managed to bring us back from Ou, and she deserves a reward for that. And this will buy her silence— she'll never say anything about Ezlin and the ceremony if she's well taken care of."

His eyes closed again. In the shadows his nose looked as sharp as a blade. He murmured something; his breath smelled rancid. Cullen and Polgar bent near him. What would he say at the end? Would he finally show some affection, or at least forgive them for not measuring up to his impossible standards?

"Thank you, Polgar," he said, straining to speak. "I'll die knowing I have one fine child to succeed me, that my life wasn't in vain. Here on my deathbed I give you all my esteem, all my love."

He murmured again. They drew closer. "A little more time," he said. "A little more time and I would have been king."

His head lolled back. The strain left his face, and they knew he was dead.

Cullen left quickly. He could not bring himself to speak to his brother, or to take care of the many things that needed to be done after his father's death. He went to his rooms and closed the door, breathing hard, trying to get the stench of the room out of his nostrils.

Why had Polgar agreed to kill Jerret? Was he that desperate for Noldeth's approval? Did he think to redeem himself after a lifetime of their father's scorn?

Was Polgar more courageous than he was? No, he couldn't be. Polgar had been a coward all his life; he couldn't even bind people without someone there to hold his hand.

Anyway, it was wrong to kill, especially to kill a king. He, Cullen, was the brave one; he had fought back against his father, had refused to act immorally and against the law, even though he stood to gain the kingship by it.

He felt virtuous for a moment, but then his familiar thoughts returned. He wanted to be king; he had spent the last week thinking of nothing else. And he would be king anyway, no matter what he did.

He thought of their father, giving Polgar his love. He had wanted that too, he realized, wanted it desperately. How could Polgar have mustered the courage?

He couldn't think. He left his apartments and went to search for a bound woman he could take to his room.

Toward morning the bells tolled for Noldeth's passing. When they went for breakfast Angarred and Mathewar found the castle even more muted than before, and some people in the corridors wept openly.

It took them until late afternoon to find Jerret. They finally caught up with him in the steward's office, planning Noldeth's funeral with Cullen, Polgar, and Iltarra.

Jerret wore mourning clothes of two colors, red and gold. Everything went by two, according to the religious, and Noldeth would now be reunited with his wife in the Celestial Court; the two colors were a reminder of this. Angarred marveled at how Jerret strictly kept to the custom; even his shoes were red.

They had arrived in the middle of an argument between Jerret and the steward. The steward, wearing the heavy chain of office, was their old guide Dobrennin, who had succeeded Chargad. The office had a table and a good many chairs, but the boy and the man stood a few inches apart, the white-haired steward looking down at Jerret's uncut hair. Noldeth's children stood too, saying nothing.

Jerret wanted Noldeth to have a king's funeral, to rest in the Hall of the Standing Kings until the religious took him on his final journey to the Celestial Court. Dobrennin explained firmly that this was impossible, that Noldeth had not been a king.

Finally Jerret seemed to realize that he would not get his way on this. He looked up and acknowledged Angarred and Mathewar. His eyes were red, and he seemed about to start crying again at any moment.

"You can honor him some other way," Angarred said.

"I will," Jerret said. "I'll give him the most lavish funeral in the history of Karededin."

Dear Godkings, Angarred thought, remembering the plundered treasury. "Listen, Jerret," she said. "We want to talk to you. When will you be free?"

"Right now, if you like," Jerret said. "Just for a few minutes, though—Cullen and Polgar are helping me plan Noldeth's funeral."

The surviving Harus did not look terribly helpful. They did not even look like people in mourning; none of them wore clothes of two colors like Jerret's. They stood together in a group, slightly away from Jerret and the steward. Cullen stared at the floor, and when he glanced up he seemed to be waiting for some catastrophe. But he at least was easy to read; Polgar and Iltarra had no expression at all.

Angarred glanced at Mathewar. It would be far better to talk to

Jerret alone; there were things that could not be said in front of the Harus. Well, they would have to make the best of it.

"Did you ever ask Lord Noldeth about freeing the Bound Folk?" Mathewar asked.

"No," Jerret said. He seemed about to cry again at the mention of Noldeth. "I didn't have time. And I don't have a lot of time now, with the funeral—"

"They should be freed, Jerret," Mathewar said. "Find out what you can, after the funeral if you have to. Perhaps Polgar or Cullen can tell you something."

He looked at the Harus. They looked away. He said nothing for a long moment, and finally Cullen turned to him, and then Iltarra. From where she stood Angarred couldn't see their full expressions, but it seemed to her that Cullen looked guilty about something; she wondered what it was.

"And I'll look in the library when I get home, see what I can discover," Mathewar said. "We should be going home in any case. Do you still need us here? I know you were worried about the Bound Folk, but now that Noldeth's gone . . ."

"I'll be fine by myself," Jerret said. He tried to look brave, but it was clear he had not yet learned what bravery was. Still, he had lost the expression of terror they had seen several times before.

"Are you sure?" Angarred asked Jerret. "Is there anything you want to talk to us about?"

Jerret shook his head. "Can you come to the funeral?" he asked.

"That depends on when our ship leaves," Angarred said, fervently hoping that they would be able to avoid it.

"I'd like it if you did," Jerret said.

"Well, we should say good-bye now, just in case we can't," Angarred said. "Thank you so much for your hospitality. We'll come back next year, if we can."

"Write if you need us," Mathewar said. "Or send for us—we'll come whenever you like. And I'll choose some court magicians for you as soon as I get back."

"Noldeth said—Noldeth said I don't need court magicians," Jerret said. "That they have hidden plans and wouldn't be completely loyal to me. That they could trick me."

"What plans would those be?" Mathewar said softly. Only Angarred, of everyone in the room, knew how angry he was.

"Well, you know." Jerret stopped. He seemed to realize he had of-
fended Mathewar, and that if he went on he would only give further
offense. "The—the College's."

"I assure you the College has no desire to govern. Magicians
might not agree with your plans, but they would do it openly—they
would have no secrets from you."

Jerret looked about to object to the magicians again. Angarred
moved forward quickly to embrace him. He hugged her awkwardly,
like her own sons, like any adolescent boy. He held out his hand to
Mathewar, but Mathewar hugged him firmly.

"Good fortune, Jerret," Mathewar said. "The Spinner watch over
you, and the Navigator guide you."

"Good-bye," he said. He looked briefly confused, and then he returned to planning Noldeth's funeral.

"Cullen still has a perfect record," Angarred said when they had
gone far enough from the steward's office not to be overheard.
"Once again he said absolutely nothing. I wonder what he was so
worried about, though."

"So do I," Mathewar said. "And I wonder why Iltarra was ignoring Jerret, and what Polgar was thinking behind that mask, and
whether the rumors are true and Noldeth poisoned the last steward . . ."

"Do you want to stay here after all?"

Mathewar shook his head. "He needs to make his own decisions,
with no one telling him what to do. Now that Noldeth's gone he
might learn how to be a king. And I can send him some court
magicians—he didn't actually refuse, thanks to you."

"I have to say I wouldn't mind going home," Angarred said. "We
have our own children to look after."

"True," Mathewar said. They headed to the stables to get their
horses, and then to the port to find out when the next ship left for
the College.

Two days later Cullen stood at his window and watched the magician
and his witch leave the castle. He felt a sickly excitement. Polgar

hadn't killed Jerret yet, but he was probably only waiting until those two went home.

A good many clerks had come up to him in the past few days, asking him about the petty details of his father's funeral—and each time he expected to hear that Jerret was dead. How would they tell him? "King Jerret is dead, and has named you his heir." "King Jerret is dead. Your brother wants to see you as soon as possible." He played with possible phrases, and his own reactions—shock, of course, and sorrow, and then a certain authority and regal bearing. He had practiced this before the mirror but could never get the expression he wanted. Any one of his family looked more like a king than he did—even that pup Jerret carried it off better.

He stared out the window and thought about what he would do when he became king. The law said that only the king was allowed to wear more than three colors at a time, and he had seen Jerret preening in multihued fashions: the sleeves slashed to show other colors underneath, each trouser leg dyed differently. It would be wonderful to wear something like that.

And he would get a horse faster than Drustig's, and larger rooms, warmer rooms, each with its own hearth. He would tell the kitchen what to cook, his favorite foods for days in a row if he wanted. A softer bed. A bigger bed.

Women, of course—Lady Melleth, for one. He would have to marry, but surely he could find a beautiful princess somewhere in the world. At that he remembered his father talking about marriage to Tezue's daughter in Ou, and sudden guilt washed through him. He reminded himself that his father was dead, that he didn't have to listen to him anymore, but the guilt remained.

Well, he could have women before he married, and even after. Any number of them would want to bed the king.

He turned away from the window and paced the floor. When would it start? When would Polgar do what he had promised? Was he the coward everyone thought him to be? What if he changed his mind, forswore himself? Several times Cullen had tried to talk to him, and each time he felt the same nervous excitement and had to turn away.

But the wait was growing intolerable. He woke at night from confused dreams, and suddenly Jerret's face was before him, and he remembered that the boy would be killed—had already been killed, maybe. It seemed impossible that anyone would do such a thing, and he wanted to leap from his bed and alert the watch, stop Polgar, warn Jerret, scream from the highest tower of the castle. He would force himself to breathe slowly, to calm down. It would be done, and that would be an end to it.

But when? Polgar had only four more days to act. He wondered if he could stand to wait that long.

# FOURTEEN

Brangwin was addressing the pigs in the forest. "The old Gossek word for 'honor' is *awith,*" he said. "It has the same root as 'heritage,' which is *awthi,* and 'story,' *awthu.* You might wonder why this is, since on the face of it these things would seem to have very little in common."

The pigs continued rooting for acorns. Brangwin took their grunts for interest and went on with his speech.

"You see, the honor of every man is bound up with the deeds of his ancestors, and this is true especially of the king. The king has a man whose only duty is to sing about his ancestors and their history up to the present. He does this at formal meals, and on occasions of state, and of course at the king's coronation and the birth of an heir. And he is called the *awithi,* which as you can see has the same root as all the other words we're discussing. You might call him a herald, but there's no exact translation into Karedek. Karedek, as you know, is a language of people without honor, treacherous sorcerers, and would not have any such concept."

One of the pigs studied him with small, clever eyes. A prize student, Brangwin thought, probably someone who hated the Karedek as much as he did. He began to speak to this pig directly. "A Gossek king derives his honor from all the worthy ancestors who went be-

fore him. If these ancestors are forgotten, the king's honor goes with
them. Worse, the king's own history disappears. He is less than he
once was—he becomes no king at all but an ordinary person. Did I
mention that 'history' derives from the same root?"

Brangwin paused. This next part of the lecture would be difficult.
There was no sound in the forest but the soft snuffling of the pigs and
the cry of a few distant birds. "When the Karedek fired—when the
Gossek castle burned, the *awithi* burned with it. So did his apprentice,
the *awithiku,* the man to whom he was teaching his store of knowledge.
Every schoolchild knows the long lists of kings, of course, and a good
many of them can give the history, but the *awithi*'s recitation is very
long, and so complicated that only he and his apprentice know it. It is
sacred, consecrated to the gods. And—and now no one alive knows it.
So the old kings—it's as if these kings no longer exist. That they—"

He took a deep breath and started again. "The foul Karedek did
worse than steal our land—they took our kings, our honor, our history. Our kings are lost. And so a prince, for example, a prince of
Goss . . ."

He could not continue. He slid to the forest floor and put his head
on his knees and his arms around his legs. A few of the pigs looked
up at him and then went back to foraging for food. He smelled a
deep loam and wondered where it came from, if someone had been
remiss in cleaning out the classroom.

Your students are waiting, he told himself. You have to finish your
lecture. He watched as the students turned into pigs, and he knew he
was going mad.


Mathewar had gone to the hold of the ship to practice magic. He lit
one of the lanterns, illuminating a small circle of light. Chests and
bags and bolts of cloth came forward out of the dark, their bulky
shadows wavering behind them; beyond that the hold stretched out
into the dim distance. He smelled spices and oranges and wood and
hay, and a moldering scent over everything. He was alone and unob-
served and in near darkness, all of which suited him perfectly.

He spoke the words to create a light. Nothing happened, and he
tried again. It will come back, he told himself, trying to banish the
despair that settled over him with every failed effort. It will.

A voice called out, so faint he thought he might have imagined it. Then someone screamed. Mathewar ran up to the deck. In the confusion he made out only that their ship had been boarded, and that these new men were drawing their daggers and looking for something.

He searched quickly for Angarred and saw her standing at the bow. He tried to make his way to her but more of the pirates came on board and blocked his way. Now he could see the attacking ship, close to their own. A pirate threw a grappling hook over their rails and started to climb.

"There he is!" someone shouted.

Several of the pirates headed toward him. He glanced around the deck, spoke a spell to unwind a coil of rope and tangle it at their feet. Nothing happened. He cursed loudly.

At the edge of his vision he saw Angarred flow into her leopard shape and leap toward him. Pirates and crew members scattered out of her way. Some of the crew had drawn their own daggers and were fighting the invaders; at least one man lay on the deck, dead or wounded.

"We want the magician only!" someone called. "Give us the magician and we'll go away!"

Who had shouted? He could make out nothing in all the confusion. Angarred had nearly reached him. He picked up the fallen man's dagger. Another man appeared out of the chaos. Mathewar turned to face him and struck the dagger from his hand.

Most of the pirates were converging around him and Angarred. "Kill the witch if you have to!" the same voice shouted. "The leopard. Take the magician alive!"

Angarred snarled and bounded toward one of the men. Everyone backed away; the fighting stopped briefly. Her claws raked the man's chest, and he screamed loudly and tried to get away. Angarred growled and prepared to leap again.

A spear came from nowhere and pierced her chest. She looked down at it. Her rear legs failed and her hindquarters dropped to the deck; she seemed to be moving very slowly, almost deliberately. Her front legs buckled and she fell. Her paws scrabbled at the deck as she tried to stand; then, as more blood spilled from the wound, her movements slowed. She shifted into her human shape and lay motionless.

The spear still protruded from her chest; the same blood trail dripped to the floor.

"Angarred!" Mathewar said. He struggled toward her, heedless of the daggers.

With Angarred down the battle began again. The two forces engaged, neither gaining the advantage. But the pirates, as they had said, wanted only him; they formed up and shoved their way past the crew, getting closer.

Then he lost track of the battle and could only concentrate on the man before him, tall, heavily bearded, from Takeke probably. The man had a sword, longer than Mathewar's dagger, but Mathewar managed to get inside the man's reach and wound him, how badly he had no idea. They parried awhile, and he saw a red stain appear on the other man's shirt and blossom outward. The man began to falter, then turned and ran.

He looked frantically for Angarred. Fighting men swarmed between them, blocking her. He tried to shoulder past them. Something hit his head, and he fell.

A day after Noldeth's funeral Cullen left his rooms and headed out into the castle, looking for the bound seamstress who was making his new colorful trousers. Iltarra came toward him in the corridor. He cursed; he had seen enough of his family at the funeral.

"Hello, Brother," Iltarra said.

"Hello."

"A fine send-off for our father yesterday, don't you think?" Iltarra said. "Better than he deserved, anyway."

"Iltarra!" Cullen said. He glanced around, looking uneasily for Jerret. He always seemed to be looking for Jerret these days. For that matter, where was Annin? He'd thought Annin and Iltarra were inseparable.

"Oh, don't play the good son with me, Cullen," Iltarra said. "He made our lives miserable and you know it. But you're free of him now—you don't have to worry about him ever again."

"That's true enough," Cullen said.

"Listen, I wanted to ask you a few things," Iltarra said. "I wonder if I could have my pearls back, the ones Father took from me."

Now he understood. This was no coincidental meeting; Iltarra wanted something, as always. Love had not made her any less greedy.

Still, why shouldn't he give her the pearls? "I suppose so, if you can find them," he said.

"They're in his room somewhere, I'm sure. Probably in the cabinet he built. Do you want to go look?"

When Jerret had given the Harus an entire wing of the castle, Noldeth had gone to each of the rooms and built a secret compartment. It was the only time Cullen could remember him using the skills he had learned as a carpenter.

Now he thought he wanted nothing to do with anything of his father's. Still, Iltarra was heading toward Noldeth's apartments, and he found himself following her.

Once inside Noldeth's rooms they went straight to his bedroom, then to a carved section of the wall. Cullen realized he was holding his breath. What secrets of Noldeth's would they discover? Iltarra pressed one of the wooden roses, and the door swung open.

They looked inside eagerly. There was nothing there.

Cullen let out his breath in a nervous laugh. "I might have guessed," he said.

Iltarra reached into the cabinet and felt the bare walls. "I know how our father thinks," she said. Something gave, and she pressed it harder. "Here."

The wall opened, revealing another compartment. She reached inside. "Hah!" she said, a small sound of triumph. She took out the strand of pearls.

"Is there anything else there?" Cullen asked.

"No, just the necklace."

Cullen felt inside the compartment anyway, but Iltarra had been speaking the truth; the compartment was empty.

She dropped the necklace over her head, then shook her hair to free it. "Why are you so fond of those pearls anyway?" Cullen asked.

"I just like them. And Father gave them to me—he had no right to take them back."

Cullen headed toward the door, eager to leave his father's rooms. Now he noticed that the room had been tidied and the bed made; the bloodstained pillow and blanket were gone. Still, he thought he could smell the odor of Noldeth's last illness.

Iltarra stopped in the front room. Servants had made an effort to clean this room too, but piles of papers—decrees and letters, maps and notes—still lay on the desk. "I wonder what these are," Iltarra said, paging through them.

"Let's go, for the Godkings' sake," Cullen said. The room was lit only by the windows; there were shadows in every corner. He hurried to the front door.

Iltarra ran to keep up with him. "Wait, there's one more thing," she said. "What are you going to do with Cherwith Province?"

"That was Drustig's land, wasn't it? I thought I'd keep it for myself."

"Why?" Iltarra said. They were out in the corridor now, and she lowered her voice. "You'll have the whole country soon enough. What's one province to you? And I know Father told you to look after me, see that I'm taken care of."

"I want it—that's what it is to me. Anyway, I've already given you the pearls. Don't be greedy."

"Do you want Cherwith Castle, is that it?" Iltarra laughed. "Are you going to pretend to an ancient lineage, use the Cherwith banner and arms like Drustig did?"

He knew why he wouldn't give the province to Iltarra, but he was not about to tell her. All during his childhood his father had compared him to others, and especially to Drustig. Drustig rode better, and fought with a sword better, and wore his clothes with more flair . . . Well, no one would ever compare him to Drustig again. He would be the king, the highest in the land, beyond compare. And he would have everything Drustig once had, everything his father had praised and his brother had flaunted in his face.

Iltarra laughed again. "Do you know what they say about Drustig? If you ask him his name you can almost hear him say 'Harue,' with just the slight hint of an 'e' at the end."

Cullen laughed with her.

"Poor Drustig—he always wanted so badly to belong to the old nobility," Iltarra said. "Do you remember when we were children, and he wanted to play at being king?"

"I remember he wanted you to be the jester, and then when you actually made a joke about him he hit you."

"That's nothing—after that he wanted me to be a chambermaid."

"Yes, well, I was supposed to be his horse."

"And he made a banner, and you told him that if he wanted to be true to the family his emblem should be a hammer, since Father had been a carpenter."

"He hit *me* then, I remember that."

A messenger approached them. Still laughing, Cullen turned to face him. "King Jerret is dead, my liege," the messenger said. "Your brother Polgar was with him at the end. Jerret named you his heir, and he wanted to give you this."

The messenger knelt and held out Jerret's signet ring. Cullen took it, feeling a shock of horror run through him. He turned to Iltarra, knowing she could read every emotion that roiled thought him: terror, and confusion over what to do now, and guilt. Especially guilt.

He went to his rooms without saying good-bye, then sat and stared at nothing. He knew he should be working—planning Jerret's funeral and his own coronation, consolidating power—but he had no idea how to do any of these things, especially the last. His father might have told Drustig how to be king, but the old man had never gotten around to teaching him.

He had not been king for an hour yet, and already he felt everything slipping away. Who would follow him, or obey his orders? Why in the name of the Godkings should they? He was nothing, nobody, just the son of an upstart commoner.

He looked at the signet ring. It was made of ancient gold and had worn away over the years; he could barely make out the castle with two towers etched on its surface. All the kings had used this emblem, clear back to Marfan if you believed the stories. Who was he to take it now, a man who had no royal blood at all in his veins?

The ring had been sized for Jerret and looked far too small for him. He scowled at the obvious meaning—even the ring did not think he deserved to rule—and pushed it down over the flesh on his little finger.

He found himself studying the carved wall across the room. Inside his cabinet was the half crown Noldeth had given him. There was no reason to worry, really; with the crown he could make anyone do anything he liked.

He stood, intending to take out the crown. But he felt a strange reluctance to touch it, even to see it.

Someone knocked loudly at the door. "Who is it?" Cullen asked.

"Dobrennin, my liege."

Who in the name of the Orator was Dobrennin? He sat and tried to compose himself. "Come in," he said.

An instant later he realized he shouldn't have said anything; anyone could be waiting behind that door, an assassin, perhaps. A tall, lean man came inside, and Cullen recognized him as the new steward. A memory of Chargad lying dead rose in his mind, and he forced it away.

Dobrennin knelt before him, then stood. "We have a great deal to plan, my liege," he said. "First the Godking Jerret's funeral, and then your coronation."

Relief swept over him. Of course other people would be helping him; of course he would not have to do everything himself. He could do no work at all if he wanted, if he found the right people.

"Your brother Lord Polgar has kindly offered to speak to the religious about Jerret's First Journey," Dobrennin said.

Cullen barely heard him. He felt a great weight lift off his shoulders. It would be easier than he had thought to be king. He might not even need his father's crown.

As it turned out, Cullen's coronation came before Jerret's funeral; the religious needed a week to carve Jerret's statue for the Hall of the Standing Kings. Cullen enjoyed the elaborate ceremony making him king, the rich panoply of nobles standing before him as he knelt and a religious set the crown on his head.

There had been some problems with the religious; the blood of Marfan and Mathona did not run in his veins and they had not wanted to proclaim him king. Polgar had managed to talk them around, telling them that Cullen had arranged to marry Lady Caireddin.

It was amazing how useful Polgar turned out to be; Cullen had never guessed he could be so competent. He had worked hard, seeing to dozens of details large and small. He had insisted on a closed coffin instead of a bier at the funeral, for example, so that Cullen would not have to look at the boy-king during the ceremony; and somehow he had convinced the religious to go along with this as well.

Cullen did not enjoy the funeral as much as the coronation. He did not go down into the city, where the common folk lined the streets to watch the procession pass with Jerret's coffin; instead he joined other nobles at the front of the castle and waited for the procession to come to him. Finally the religious rode into the castle courtyard and set down the coffin. Folks who had followed them through the city talked about the somber crowds they had seen, perhaps thousands of people, some of them weeping openly at the tragic death of the young king.

The religious began to chant, and everyone quieted. They sang the names of all the kings and queens who had gone before Jerret, and at the end they sang out Jerret's new name—Gerret, like his father—the indication that the dead king had changed utterly from his earthly form.

Cullen listened for Jerret's attribute. The boy had hardly done anything; what attribute could they possibly give him? "The Hunter," the religious sang out.

And what attribute would they give him, Cullen? What great deeds would he do as king? He felt excitement at the thought.

He was one of the pallbearers, of course. When the chant came to an end he helped pick up the coffin. It felt horribly light, and for the first time that day Cullen realized fully the enormity of what they had done. Jerret had been so young; they had cut off all the rest of his years, all the things he might have learned and done as king.

Some people pointed to him and Cullen realized he was crying. He wiped his eyes on his sleeve ostentatiously, hoping they had continued watching as the grief seemed to overwhelm him.

The pallbearers carried the coffin into the Hall and set it down. The religious lit the torch at the base of Jerret's new statue. The statue looked incongruous, almost ridiculous, Cullen thought—the boy stood as tall as the other kings, three times the size of a human, holding a hunter's spear.

Opposite him was another statue, this one of a girl around Jerret's age. The religious had married some poor child off to Jerret after he

died; they had had to, to keep the line of queens marching even with
the line of kings. She would have wealth and a high position, Cullen
knew, but she could never marry another man, never start a family.
Most important to Cullen, she would be kept away from any real
power in the castle.

When the torch burned as red as the others the religious picked up
the coffin again and carried it to the graveyard at the back of the castle. They would bury the boy there, then return to the Hall and sing
a new chant, this one stating that the Bearer had come for Jerret, that
he had continued his journey to the Celestial Court.

In the meantime the rest of the people were supposed to praise
Jerret, to talk about his accomplishments as king. Cullen overheard a
few of the nobles discuss the justice he had meted out; his great
learning, amazing in a boy his age: all the usual lies people spoke at a
funeral.

Mostly, though, the people simply talked about how young Jerret
had been, how sad it was that he had died so suddenly. A brown-
haired boy about Jerret's age stood in a corner, tears running down
his face. He looked familiar, but Cullen could not remember where
he had seen him before.

One after another the nobles in the Hall came over and tried to
engage him in conversation. Usually he would have enjoyed their
deference, their nervousness, but today they only wanted to discuss
Jerret, and he had to become fairly rude to get them to go away.

He forced his mind away from Jerret and thought of everything
he had to do: the petitions, the council meetings. Perhaps he could
get Dobrennin Steward to listen to petitions; the man had shown
himself to be wonderfully efficient, and the folks with petitions were
so horribly insistent, all of them whining about their petty problems.
The council meetings were different: he enjoyed telling his councilors what to do.

He wished the ceremony would end; he had some ideas about the
war with Goss he wanted to try out. He turned to the man next to
him. "I've never been to as many funerals as I have this week," he
said.

The man's expression changed; he looked puzzled and disgusted at
the same time. Cullen thought over what he had said and realized

how he must have sounded. "I mean," he said carefully, "I have a good deal to do. But I'm glad to be able to pay tribute to my father and King Jerret."

"King Gerret now," the man said.

Cullen took close note of the man, and vowed he would not survive long in his court.

Finally the religious returned. The torches at the base of the statues gave off an acrid smoke, drying his mouth. Cullen left the Hall early and went to the Council Chamber.

# FIFTEEN

Lord Talethe Tolgarred, fifteen years old, wiped his eyes and looked around for Lord Cullen. He couldn't see him anywhere; the man must have slipped out sometime before the end of the funeral. What now? He tried to find Chargad Steward in the press of people, but he too seemed to have gone.

The crowd parted and he saw someone wearing the steward's chain: an old man with a straight back, definitely not Chargad. The keys at his belt rang softly as he walked. Had Chargad died? So much seemed to have happened in the short time he had been gone.

He pushed his way through toward the man. "Excuse me," he said. "Are you the steward?"

"Dobrennin Steward," the man said, bowing.

"I need—I need to talk to Lord Cullen," Talethe said. "It's urgent."

The steward regarded him doubtfully. "King Cullen receives petitioners next week, my lord," he said. "You might come back then."

"It's important," Talethe said. "I can't wait a week. I was a friend of Jerret's. My name is Talethe Tolgarred—"

Dobrennin studied him again. His expression softened, catching Talethe's urgency, perhaps, or just taking pity on him. "Come with me," he said. "I'll see what I can do. Though he's in a foul mood these days—be careful what you say to him."

Talethe followed the steward through the maze of castle corridors, finally coming to a hall of rooms he had never seen. Dobrennin stopped at one of the doors and knocked.

"Who is it?" someone called out.

"Dobrennin Steward."

They heard a sigh from beyond the door. "What do you want? I'm busy here."

"Someone wants to talk to you," Dobrennin said. "He says it's important."

"What about?"

"He says he was a friend of King Jerret's—"

"For the Godkings' sake, open the door," Cullen said. "I can't hear you from out there."

Cullen stood behind a large table, maps spread out in front of him. A few bodyguards watched from the corners. The king looked up as they came in. For a moment he seemed to recognize Talethe, and something like fear showed in his eyes. Then he nodded to each of them, his face bland, and Talethe thought he must have imagined the earlier expression.

The vast distance of the table stretched between them. Talethe bowed, lowering himself the proper distance required for a king. "What is it?" Cullen said. "I've a great deal to do, as you can see."

Talethe rose. "My name is Talethe Tolgarred," he said. "I'm—I was—a friend of Jerret's. I've been at my family's estate, but I felt I had to come to Jerret's First Journey."

"Yes, yes, hurry up," Cullen said.

Talethe took a deep breath. "Jerret had a ceremony where he proclaimed an heir. I was one of the witnesses. Lord Ezlin Ertig, that's who he wanted to succeed him. And so when I got to Pergodi I was surprised to see that you had assumed the crown."

" 'Assumed'?" Cullen said. "What exactly are you implying?"

"N-nothing."

"I hope so, for your sake. What you've said has a whiff of treason about it."

"No, I didn't mean—I just wanted to tell you. In case you didn't know."

"You can take it for granted that I know everything that happens

in my realm. Jerret may have proclaimed this foreigner with the out-
landish name his heir, but after that, on his deathbed, he chose me as
his successor. Not that I need to explain myself to you. You can go
now."

"But Jerret said—"

"Dobrennin," Cullen said.

The steward moved forward and took Talethe's arm. For a moment Talethe thought to shake him off; then he calmed and allowed
Dobrennin to lead him out.

Dobrennin took him a little ways down the hall, then let him go.
"That was dangerous, my lord," he said, very quietly.

Talethe realized he was trembling. "I—I had no idea," he said. He
heard the fear in his voice. "I thought—I truly thought—"

"You thought Cullen had simply made a mistake," Dobrennin
said.

"Yes. I'm a fool, the worst sort of country rustic. I thought I just
had to tell him the truth and he would apologize, invite Lord Ezlin to
Pergodi, proclaim him the true king." He laughed bitterly.

"You must be very careful, my lord," Dobrennin said. "Do you
know what happened to my predecessor?"

"No."

"He died suddenly after supper."

"Poisoned?" Their voices had grown lower and lower, and they
glanced up and down the hall often to see if anyone was coming.

"I don't know. I know enough not to speculate, though. And
remember—he was another witness to Jerret's proclamation."

"How—how did Jerret die? They just said it was sudden—"

"I don't speculate on that either. Lord Polgar saw him die, and
then brought a doctor in to look at him, or so he said. The doctor
couldn't explain it. It wasn't poison, I don't think—all his food was
tasted. Did you know him well?"

The question nearly made him cry again. He remembered them as
children, exploring the castle, going to dances and masques that only
Jerret had been invited to, spying on Rodarren's council meetings and
dinners of state. He remembered Jerret's marvelous toys, made of
gold and silver and spattered with jewels. They had grown apart as
they grew older, though. He suspected that Noldeth kept them sepa-

rate, and the suspicion grew to a certainty when Jerret exiled the Harus and began talking to him again.

"I loved him," Talethe said. "I have to see that his last wish is carried out."

"You have to do no such thing," Dobrennin said. "You have no idea of the danger you're in. My best advice is to go back to your estate and stay there."

"But he stole—Cullen stole—"

"Hush," Dobrennin said urgently. "You don't know that for certain. Jerret might have decided on a new heir."

A servant headed toward them down the hallway. "Good day, Lord Talethe," Dobrennin said firmly. "The Navigator guide you on your journey." He lowered his voice again. "I can't do anything for you, do you understand? I don't like Cullen either, but he's the king, and my master. Go."

Talethe hesitated for a moment. He was unused to conspiracy; he wanted to talk longer to Dobrennin, unburden himself to someone who understood. And surely there was no need to whisper in front of servants. Of course they gossiped, Talethe knew that much, but only among themselves.

As the servant came closer Dobrennin's expression changed, became blank. He reminded Talethe of the sinister Bound Folk he had seen around the castle. "Good day," Talethe said.

He wandered through the castle awhile until he found the front entrance, then went to the stables for his horse. He could no longer use his family's apartment at the castle, that much was certain. He would have to take a room at an inn.

What a feebleminded idiot he had been, though. He remembered saying farewell to his parents and riding blithely toward Pergodi, and his face burned with embarrassment. His parents had been busy with the estate and had told him he was old enough to go on his own. He hadn't said anything to them about talking to Cullen; he had considered that such a simple errand it wasn't even worth mentioning. He had just said he was going to Jerret's First Journey. If someone killed him, he thought now, they would never know why.

But he felt certain Jerret had not made Cullen his heir. Jerret would have called all the witnesses back and held another ceremony if he had. At the very least he would have told them that he'd changed his mind.

No, Cullen had stolen the crown. Jerret had told him all about the Harus: how they had risen against him, how he had had to banish them. "I'm making Ezlin my heir," Jerret had said. "I love the Harus, and they taught me a lot, but I don't know if I can trust them."

Talethe got his horse and rode down the hill. What should he do now? Go back to his estate, as Dobrennin had suggested? Go to the Finbar Islands, talk to Lord Ezlin?

No—if he wanted to stand up for Jerret, for Lord Ezlin, he would have to stay in Pergodi. There were other witnesses, after all; he could feel them out, see if they thought the way he did.

Lady Angarred, for example. As a child growing up at court he had heard stories about her, how she had come to Pergodi, bringing little but the clothes on her back, to see justice done for her father. She had succeeded, and she had known even less about the court than he did.

Well, but she had the advantage of being a magician. He remembered how she had turned into a leopard when the bound man attacked him, and he thought how helpful it would be if he could do that. There were a few people he would like to rend to pieces, for Jerret's sake.

The next day he went back to the castle. Courtiers and clerks, guards and servants and Bound Folk clattered through the halls, and once again he realized how little he knew about the workings of the court. He had never visited Pergodi without his parents before, and they had always known which courtiers to flatter, which officials to bribe.

After a bit of searching he found the Great Hall, where the courtiers usually gathered. He gave his name to the chamberlain; the man announced him and he went inside.

The room shone with color; he had to wait a moment, to let his eyes adjust after the dimness of the corridors. Tiles and tapestries, mosaics and carvings covered every inch of the walls, each from a different era and placed with no regard for what hung next to it. Candles glittered blue and green and gold; light poured in from long windows set under the ceiling.

Dozens of courtiers stood around on the carpeted floor, talking and laughing, arrayed in bright colors. It had been barely a week since Jerret's death, Talethe thought bitterly, and already people had stopped dressing in mourning; nearly everyone wore three colors, the most they were allowed under the law.

For a moment Talethe couldn't see anyone he knew; then he spotted Dobrennin Steward heading toward one of the courtiers, holding a piece of paper in his hand. He at least still kept to the customs of mourning; he was dressed in green and black. "Dobrennin!" Talethe said, pleased to see a familiar face.

Dobrennin nodded politely and continued walking. Of course, Talethe thought. They would have to be careful not to let anyone know they had talked.

Talethe watched as Dobrennin went up to Lady Iltarra and gave her the message. She read it and frowned, then showed it to the man at her side. Even Talethe knew that this was Lord Annin; that much gossip had made it to the country.

Well, Lady Iltarra had been one of the witnesses. He made his way toward her through the throng. "Lady Iltarra," he said, bowing.

"Princess Iltarra," she said.

She was no princess, any more than Cullen was king. The title gave her reason to support Cullen instead of Ezlin, he realized; with Cullen off the throne she would go back to being only a lady.

Jerret had liked her, though. He could see why; she was very beautiful. Perhaps she still felt something for Jerret as well, would back him against her brother.

"Of course—I'm sorry," he said. He bowed lower, the proper distance required for a princess. He held the bow a little longer than necessary, needing the time to hide his thoughts and plan what he would say. Would she help him or not?

"Princess Iltarra," he said, rising. "I'd like to ask you something."

"Go ahead."

"I wonder—well, do you remember the ceremony where King Jerret made Lord Ezlin his heir?"

Iltarra smiled, very faintly; it seemed an odd response to his question. "Yes."

"Shouldn't Lord Ezlin be king, then?" Talethe asked.

Iltarra continued to smile. The row of pearls at her neck seemed to smile as well. "I'm afraid your news is long out-of-date," Iltarra said. "Jerret changed his mind and chose Cullen instead."

"There were other witnesses to the ceremony, though," he said, trying not to quail in the face of her certainty. "The steward, for example."

Iltarra sighed. "Talethe," she said. "You're a good lad, but you shouldn't meddle in things that don't concern you. Chargad Steward is dead."

"Well, what about Lady Angarred and First Master Mathewar?"

Iltarra glanced at the piece of paper she held and said nothing. The silence went on so long that he finally said, "What do they say?"

She held out the note Dobrennin had given her. "We just heard," she said. "Their ship was boarded by pirates and they were kidnapped."

He stared at the piece of paper, horrified. He had not known Mathewar and Angarred well, but he had liked them, what little he had seen of them. And Chargad's death and their kidnapping could not be a coincidence.

He went on; if he was going to be an idiot he might as well play the role until the end. "Well, there are still witnesses in Finbar," he said.

"Talethe, please, listen to me," Iltarra said. "Those witnesses are dead too. Things happen to people who champion Ezlin—he's a very unlucky person, it seems. Go back to your estate, raise your goats or whatever it is you have there, and don't speak of this matter again." She turned away from him, back to Annin.

Talethe headed to the door, trying not to run. He might be an innocent, he thought, but he knew a threat when he heard one. There was nothing more he could do here; he should take everyone's advice and go home.

Over a week later Cullen sat at a council meeting, looking down at his maps. It had been Polgar's idea to invade Goss in the first place, he remembered. At the time he thought Polgar had suggested it so that he could go north, away from their father. It was a good idea, though, no matter who said it; riches continued to flow south toward Karededin. Had he underestimated his brother all these years?

He looked around the table at his councilors. Lord Enlandin nodded at him, indicating he had something to say. Old Enlandin had served four rulers: Tezue, Rodarren, Jerret, and now Cullen. He had disappeared a year into Jerret's reign; Noldeth had sent all the councilors away save himself. After Jerret's First Journey, though, Enlandin had approached Cullen and asked about his council, and Cullen, who hadn't given the matter any thought, had been relieved to take on someone with so much experience.

Now Cullen inclined his head toward the old man graciously. "My liege, I've had some disturbing news," Enlandin said. He consulted a piece of paper in front of him. "It seems Lord"—he looked back at the paper—"Lord Ezlin Ertig, is it? At any rate, news has reached Finbar of Jerret's death, and this Lord Ezlin believes that Jerret made him heir to the throne. He has a signed document to prove it, he says, as well as some witnesses."

Cullen felt rage build within him. What had that impertinent whelp Talethe been doing? Had he been spreading rumors about him throughout the castle?

"I think you'll find there's no basis to this upstart's claim," he said, forcing himself to sound calm. "Anyone can forge a document. And I'd be very surprised if he can produce witnesses."

"That's not the worst of it, though, my liege," Enlandin said. "Our spies say Lord Ezlin is raising an army. He's thinking of invading Karededin and taking the throne."

"Is he?" Cullen said, furious now. "I'll show him what happens to people who rise up against the rightful king. We'll burn his ships to the waterline if he tries to land here, teach his army to swim."

"Yes, my liege," Enlandin said. "Unfortunately, we might not have enough men. Most of our troops are in Goss. And we've heard rumors that Drustig wants to claim the throne of Karededin as well."

Cullen slammed his hand down on the table. "Rumors and reports, is that all you're good for? Why can't you tell me anything for certain? Where are these troops, how many are there, when are they going to invade? And then come up with a plan to take care of them. Do I have to do everything?"

He remembered telling them only last week that he didn't want them giving him ideas, that he would do the thinking in council. He told himself to forget that he had ever said that, and the words disappeared into some murky part of his mind.

"Do you want us to call up more men, my lord?" someone asked.

Cullen looked at this new man. Finally, a sensible suggestion. Who in Marfan's name was he, though? Enlandin had brought him to the council meeting, along with some others he thought would serve Cullen well. "What's your name?"

"Lord Sorle, sir."

Of course—how could he have forgotten? Sorle was an old soldier, a commander in the War of All the Realms. Cullen had been twelve during the war, wishing desperately he could ride with a company of soldiers and fight the invaders. He had had to content himself by listening to the names and deeds of those who had fought. Sorle, he remembered, had been one of the heroes; they had sung ballads about him afterward.

"Yes, of course I want more men, Sorle," Cullen said. "What do you think—that I plan to meet this army with nothing but castle guards? See to it."

Sorle nodded. The council secretary wrote something down.

"Well, that's enough for today," Cullen said, standing. "We'll meet again tomorrow. And I expect to hear something besides vague gossip and stories. Good day."

The counselors looked at each other, open mouthed. Cullen nearly laughed. He strode to the door and left them.

He went to his room again, the only place he could be free from those prattling idiots, and thought about what they had said. It was worse than they realized, he knew. Drustig had some sort of weapon, something that drove men mad. Cullen had heard from several of the bound spies his father had used, and they all said the same thing: no one could stand against this weapon, whatever it was. Everyone who came near it bolted away in terror; even the emotionless Bound Folk failed to stand their ground.

He stood and went to the wall his father had built, then pressed the carved rose. The door to the cabinet swung open. He took out the half crown and turned it over and over in his hands. The pearls caught the light and glimmered. He could have an army great enough to defeat the entire world, if only he could bring himself to make more Bound Folk.

And then there was that horrible little meddler Talethe. He never should have talked to the boy; when he'd realized who he was in the Council Chamber he'd felt a terrible jolt run through him, as if he'd been kicked by a horse unaware.

Iltarra had told him Talethe had been asking questions in the Great Hall as well. What was he to do with the boy? Kill him, maybe, but Cullen shrank from the idea. Lock him up in the dungeons? But that wouldn't silence him; he could still talk to his guards and fellow prisoners, and sooner or later . . .

Perhaps he could get Polgar to kill him; Polgar had shown a talent in that line. Perhaps Cullen simply needed to say that he found the boy troublesome, and the next day Talethe would be gone, disappeared.

He had not talked to Polgar since their father's death, though. Almost everything lay unspoken between them; Cullen did not even know how Jerret had died. He had thought his brother would head back to the mines, but the man had stayed on, limping around the castle, going about his mysterious business. What did Polgar want? Would he try to blackmail him about Jerret's death?

The crown shone. The pearls were so white they seemed almost blue. They looked like eyes, a dozen eyes, watching him. His father's eyes. "This is your true crown, my son," his father said.

He dropped the crown and stepped back in shock. It rang loudly on the wooden floor. Who had spoken? Not his father, not now; he had finally won free of the old man.

He shuddered. He put the crown back in the cabinet as quickly as he could, and slammed the door.

# SIXTEEN

Things swirled around him, first lights and patterns and then roads and trees, animals and rooms. Mathewar tried to concentrate but could not hold any thought for very long. Where was he? Sometimes the room or forest would sway—was he still on the ship? Then this world too would burst apart, and he would be somewhere else, and then somewhere else again.

His head hurt and he could barely see out of one eye, and sometimes he remembered a fall. And something terrible had happened, but he shied away from thinking about it and hid himself in the shifting shapes around him.

Sometimes a man would come in to look at him, someone with black hair and blue eyes and long lashes. He knew this had to be one of the Harus, but which one? A few times he remembered that there was another son, a man who had been sent into exile, but then this thought too would disappear, as if someone tore it from his mind as cleanly as tearing paper.

Once he thought he saw him plainly, a man with a wild grin and a half a crown on the left side of his head. But this seemed so odd it had to be another illusion.

Then finally his surroundings came clear; for a moment he felt as if he were waking up from a fever. He sat in a bare room on a straw pallet. Someone had laid a spell on the door to prevent him from opening it by magic, and when he realized this he knew he had to remember something about magic, but this too was so unpleasant he forced his thoughts away.

If the man he saw was Drustig then he might be in Ou. But Ou was a good distance from Karededin, something like five hundred miles. Had he been delirious for that long? Or was Drustig in Karededin? No—he couldn't be, he had been exiled . . .

Drustig came into the room, almost as if Mathewar's thoughts had called him up. He wore the half crown on his head. The room spun. Mathewar concentrated on one coherent thought and finally managed to say, "What do you want, Lord Drustig?"

Drustig looked surprised, as if he hadn't even expected that much from his prisoner.

"Is my wife . . ." The thought floated away. Mathewar tried again. "Is my wife still alive?"

"Well," Drustig said. "That's one of the things we're going to talk about, you and I."

The black pearls on the crown seemed to swallow light; even the crown itself, made of some sort of white metal, looked dulled. Mathewar gazed at the pearls. They wrenched him away from the present, enveloped him in their darkness.

Angarred woke. She was lying in her human shape, she saw, and a vast pain radiated out from above her right breast. And she was in a cage, something that roused her to a fury as great as the leopard's would have been.

She tried to sit, but the pain cut through her and she fell back, panting. What had happened? Men had attacked the ship; they had gone after Mathewar and she had tried to protect him.

Mathewar. Where was he? She remembered a man shouting that he wanted Mathewar but not her, that they could kill her if they liked. At least Mathewar was alive, she thought. Probably alive, anyway. But what in the Healer's name did they want with him?

Her memories jumbled together, with no hint of where or when they had happened. They had been on a ship, sailing even at night when the moon gave enough light. And they had been on land, probably later, and she had lain in a wagon, jerking awake whenever they hit a rock or hole in the road. How far had they traveled, though? And in which direction?

The children. She sat up quickly, and the pain shuddered through her again. She had written to Atte before they left, telling the children that they would be home soon. What would they think when she and Mathewar failed to arrive?

In the days that followed she had realized that the man on the ship had been right: he had no use for her; they had captured her only to keep her from defending Mathewar. Once a day two guards came down a hallway and threw food into her cage as if she were an animal in truth, cooked meat several days old. They stood far away from the bars, careful to keep out of reach of her claws. She couldn't hurt them, though; she had no energy for transformation. She would wait until they left, not wanting them to see how weak she was, then crawl slowly toward the food.

She saw no one the rest of the day. She slept a good deal, and sometimes when she woke she found a bowl of dirty water nearby; she would take it with trembling hands and drink it down in a gulp. The rest of the time she lay on the cold wooden floor and went through her litany of questions. Where was she? Who had captured them? Most important of all, what did they want with Mathewar?

She had to escape, she knew, had to find out what had happened to him. Sometimes when she grew furious at her helplessness she would try to sit up or move her arm, biting her lip at the pain.

Every day she had pressed the clinging strands of a spiderweb to her wound. Now, looking at the wound for the dozenth time, she thought that she might have healed a little. She flexed her arm and nearly cried out, tried again and winced. But she could not wait any longer; the children were probably frantic, and the Godkings alone knew what they were doing to Mathewar.

She flowed into her leopard shape. The leopard eyed the bars and then stood up, growling, her long tail twitching. The pain faded. Angarred had noticed this before, that animals could ignore their injuries for a while, that their intense focus allowed them to concentrate on one thing only.

She shifted back to human and waited, trying to be as patient as a leopard watching her prey.

Time did not exist in the shadows; Mathewar could have been there an hour or a day or a century. He thought that Drustig had gone away and come back, but perhaps only an instant had passed between the time the man sat down and the time he asked his next question.

"I heard you freed one of the Bound Folk," Drustig said. "How did you do it?"

Mathewar nearly laughed with relief. "You don't need force for that," he said. "I—"

"Don't talk," Drustig said. "I'll take the answer from your mind."

The shadows swirled out over him, and once again he fell into darkness. Strange shapes glimmered before him: trees with brass leaves, animals with stars for eyes. He lost his way among the illusions, and he struggled to remember Drustig's question. The Bound Folk. Freeing the Bound Folk.

Suddenly Drustig invaded his mind. He broke through the walls shielding his thoughts as easily as if they weren't there and pulled apart layer after layer of memory. Each new assault hit with more power than the last, until his mind began to sear with pain. He struggled against the other man, but Drustig pressed on relentlessly, tearing through his mind, ripping into thought after thought.

The Bound Folk, Mathewar thought desperately. Take the memory of freeing the Bound Folk.

He felt rather than heard Drustig laugh. It was an insane laugh, as lost to reason as the world Drustig had taken him to. He knew then that Drustig no longer cared about the Bound Folk. His wandering attention had been caught by other things, pretty trifles, and he would go on and on looking for more.

Finally Drustig paused. He had found something that interested him; Mathewar did not know whether to be relieved or worried.

"The Stone," Drustig said. "Yes, I remember now. You were the last to have the Stone of Tobrin, and then it disappeared. If I had it I could certainly defeat my brother. Where is it, I wonder?"

Mathewar did not move. He could not allow Drustig to learn anything about the Stone. He used what concentration he had left to hide his knowledge from the other man.

Drustig began to rake his mind again. He came closer to Mathewar's knowledge of the Stone, and Mathewar sought another memory quickly, something important to divert him. The birth of his first child, Atte. Drustig moved away again.

A long time later Drustig stopped. Mathewar spun dizzily back to reality, or what he hoped was reality. His left eye saw only blurry shapes; his right eye saw Drustig, the half crown still on his head.

"I don't know anything about the Stone," he said. He was covered in sweat.

"Don't you?" Drustig said. "What if I told you I would give you your wife for the knowledge?"

"Would—would you?" Mathewar asked.

"I might," Drustig said. "Then again, she might be dead."

Mathewar had no strength left to hide his horror. Drustig laughed loudly at his expression.

Drustig stood. "Well, I have to leave you now," he said.

Once again the black pearls drew Mathewar's gaze, and the shadows swam forward, drowning him. "No," he said weakly. "Please don't . . ."

Drustig laughed, and the blackness surrounded him again.

Days passed. Drustig came back often and roamed through Mathewar's mind, plucking memories. Here he was as a young student coming to the College, here the day he met his first wife Embre, here the time he tried to free Nim. Mathewar watched him helplessly, adrift in years.

And here was Embre's death. Too late Mathewar realized that he should have tried to hide that. Drustig laughed. "Two wives dead, is it?" he said. "Someone's cursed you, it looks like."

Was that true? It felt true. But he could not hold on to any idea for long. Drustig's thoughts ran through him like swords. He took apart that memory and studied the next: Mathewar's first taste of sattery, after Embre died.

The warm drink flowed through him, reached every part of him. He felt the great peace of sattery, the sense that nothing mattered, nothing hurt, that everything was good and right. The pain of Drustig's invasion disappeared. For the first time in a very long time his muscles relaxed.

Why was Drustig allowing him this brief calm? He couldn't work it out, couldn't think. That was another effect of sattery: chains of logic corroded and fell apart; thoughts floated alone, unconnected.

Some time later—he had no idea how long—Drustig tore that memory away. The loss of sattery felt more painful than anything that had gone before, and he cried out.

Drustig laughed. The sound fell through him like a rain of glass shards. Drustig was mad, he knew. And now he realized that he too would go mad soon. He would come to forget which thoughts were Drustig's and which were his; they would be two insane people with one deranged laugh between them.

He thought Drustig went away after that. The shadows returned, but this time horrors hid within them. He caught half glimpses of skeletons, walking pieces of darkness, men with flesh dripping from their bones.

When he thought at all he felt mostly despair. Drustig's remark that he might be cursed continued to haunt him. It must be true, he thought; how else to explain the deaths of both his wives?

He came awake from a dream a few hours later, some nightmare he forgot as soon as he tried to recall it. A light glowed in the darkness. Who was in the room with him? He sat up quickly, terrified.

The light was his own, he realized, and for a brief moment he felt elation. Drustig's invasion of his mind had somehow forced his magic to return.

The triumph faded as quickly as it had come. He had created a light; well, so could any first-year student. What good would a light do against Drustig? And he didn't even have control over it; it had appeared while he slept. At the College the students made fun of their fellows who worked beginning magic while asleep; it was considered babyish, like wetting the bed.

Well, he thought grimly, I am a student. I'll have to learn everything over again. He tried to make the light bigger, to move it, but nothing happened.

There was something odd about the light, something wrong. If

Drustig had caused his magic to return, then perhaps it was tainted, insane. He had heard stories of crazed magicians, men whose deepest nightmares had escaped into the light of day. Did he want a magic that had been so corrupted? Worse, if he had gone mad, how would he know?

Then Drustig began to take his mind apart again, and the light skittered away crazily and went out.

He had more moments of clarity after that. He worked on his magic, slowly relearning the most basic teachings, all the while fighting against the pain in his head and the fantastical horrors that lurked within the darkness. He became convinced his magic had changed, though he didn't know in what ways. But he could not stop; he returned to it as he had returned to sattery all those years ago.

Every so often Drustig invaded his mind and his thoughts burst apart into a hundred pieces, but he grimly put them together again and went on. Sometimes Drustig was in the room with him when this happened, though more often the grating laugh appeared out of nowhere. Even if he escaped, he thought, he would hear that laugh to the end of his days. But he felt less and less certain that he would ever leave this room.

He came back over and over again to what Drustig had said, that someone had cursed him. He spent long periods of time, hours perhaps, trying to remember whether Angarred had been stabbed on her right or left side. If the spear had missed her heart she might still be alive. He could never answer the question to his satisfaction, and the uncertainty enraged him as much as anything Drustig did. But he hid his confusion from Drustig; he was learning to conceal his thoughts behind other, less dangerous memories.

One day he awoke, or found his way out of the darkness—the two had come to seem almost the same thing—to see Drustig sitting in front of him, calmly shredding his memories. All his fury and frustration overcame him, and he thrust into Drustig's mind and ordered him to stand. Drustig stood. Mathewar told him to open the door. The other man turned and walked to the door, then reached out for the latch. . . .

Drustig stopped and turned back. He laughed briefly. "Getting better, are we?" he said, or thought. He straightened the half crown on his head, and Mathewar's thoughts flew apart.

Things rustled and chittered in the darkness, terrifying things. He could see nothing, while all around him the sounds grew louder. All the fearful animals of his childhood returned: snakes and spiders, biting insects you couldn't see until they were upon you . . .

Someone cried out like a child needing comfort. A moment later Mathewar realized the sound had come from him. He screamed again, and Drustig laughed.

He had attacked too soon, he thought sometime later. He had not been strong enough. And now Drustig knew that his magic was returning, and would be ready. He had made too many mistakes, stupid mistakes.

"What would you give to see your wife again?" Drustig's voice came toward him out of the darkness. "Would you tell me where the Stone is?"

He hadn't known Drustig was in the room. He tried to concentrate, and managed to see the other man with his right eye. "To see her?" he asked. "To see her dead, you mean?"

"Very clever," Drustig said dryly. "No, to see her alive and well."

"Is she alive?"

"Tell me about the Stone."

"Tell me about my wife."

"You'll have to trust me," Drustig said.

Mathewar laughed with despair. His laughter went on and on. He sounded like Drustig, and after a long while he managed to stop.

More time passed. He thought about giving Drustig information in exchange for Angarred. The idea didn't seem so terrible. Drustig would turn all the world insane, but at least he would have his wife . . .

He came back to himself in his room. Light shone through a high window; he saw it with his right eye, and something else, a haze of color, with his left. He closed his right eye and found himself in a forest, the branches blurred to a filigree of green. Then that changed to a room where people walked in and out, and then a blue sea and a shoal of silver fishes.

It didn't seem strange that he saw something different with each eye; it was another of Drustig's illusions, or evidence that his magic had been contaminated by the other man. He opened both eyes and saw fish swimming along the far wall.

For some reason the thought of left and right reminded him of Drustig's terrible crown. There was something important there, something he needed to remember. . . .

He almost knew the answer; he could feel it, tantalizingly out of reach. Then the shadows flowed outward again, covering the confused picture before him. He struggled to hold on to his thought. He had always had an instinct for the right paths to take in the study of magic, and he knew that the crown was important, that it held the key to . . . The key to what? He couldn't remember.

Mathewar came awake to see Lord Drustig sitting before him. "Tell me where the Stone is," Drustig said.

He raked again through Mathewar's mind. "Ah, this is interesting," Drustig said. "Who is this old man? Is he a magician?"

Mathewar hurried to hide that memory behind something else, giving up another precious part of his life to Drustig, this one the day he married Angarred. "Angarred, yes," Drustig said. "Tell me where the Stone is and I'll return her to you."

A flock of birds flew across Drustig's face. Mathewar closed his left eye, then his right. He felt so tired. Why not? Why not tell Drustig about . . .

He stopped, horrified. His heart came awake, beating fast. He had almost let slip the magician's name.

"Yes, his name," Drustig said. "Who is he? Why is he important to you?"

Drustig followed the thought through Mathewar's mind, slicing through other memories put in his way to distract him. Mathewar felt the other man's eagerness, his excitement. If he gave that information up to Drustig he was lost; he would have nothing to trade for Angarred's life. Drustig laughed.

Mathewar sat very still, barely breathing. Then suddenly he stood and flung his arm at Drustig's crown, thrusting it past a crowd of people that had just appeared between them. The crown flew off and rang against the floor.

Drustig scrabbled for it. Mathewar ran to the door and opened it; as he had hoped Drustig had not bothered to lock it. He hurried down a hallway, saw guards at the far end, and turned back. He rushed past his room, caught a quick glimpse of Drustig setting the crown back on his head. Then more rooms, their doors closed. Was Angarred here somewhere?

People headed toward him and he looked around frantically for a place to hide. No, they weren't people but more phantoms, appearing out of one wall and walking through another. Perhaps the first guards he had seen had been illusions as well. He tried closing his bad eye but it took too much effort; he opened it and continued to run.

Down some stairs. Through a forest that had magically grown up on the landing. Past more cells, looking wildly for Angarred. More stairs, and more guards.

He moved quietly back up the stairs and studied the guards. There were four of them, two on either side of an open door, their lances upright.

They appeared to be real. He watched them a while longer, then created a light at the opposite end of the corridor. One of them saw it first and motioned to his fellows.

He tried adding the sound of an explosion. The blast was not as satisfying as he had hoped but he grinned, pleased that the ability had come back to him. The guards rushed toward the noise. He ran out the door and into daylight.

He stopped. He bent over and put his hands on his knees, trying to catch his breath. Where was he? He had come out of a great castle. Green grass stretched out all around it, and beyond that he thought he could make out a hedge of some sort enclosing the grounds. He felt horribly exposed, and the guards would certainly return soon.

He started to run again, slower than before, expecting to feel an arrow between his shoulder blades at any moment. After a while he felt as if he had been running forever, but the hedge came no closer. Perhaps it was another illusion; perhaps the grass went on to the next kingdom. He heard Drustig's laugh, and hopelessness enveloped him. It was as he'd thought; he would never break free of it.

Finally he reached the hedge, made of sharp briars. He pushed through it quickly, scratching himself on his exposed face and hands, then looked back through the brambles at the castle.

Jerret had given Drustig several castles. This couldn't be Karededin, though; Drustig had been exiled. Wind gusted past him, far too cold for Karededin in Summer. Was he in Ou, then?

What about Angarred? He watched a huge ship, sail bellying, run in a nonexistent wind before the castle. He wanted desperately to be inside, blinding guards with blasts of light, finding Drustig and forcing him to tell the truth.

But if he went back he would almost certainly be captured. He could not possibly stand against Drustig's crown; he would be forced to give up what he knew and then be killed. He needed to get help and return later when he was rested.

There was a gate in the hedge some distance away from where he stood. Guards stood in front of it and a road led out from it, heading toward the next town. He walked in a great arc around the guards and started down the road.

# SEVENTEEN

Guards came and flung meat into Angarred's cage. She held her side and groaned.

They flinched, as if she had made some terrifying animal noise. "Please," she said weakly. "I can't move. Could you bring the food closer?"

They looked at her and then each other, fear and suspicion evident in their eyes. "Please," she said again. "I'd like to eat just once more before . . ."

"She's dying," one of them said.

"Should we tell—"

"Probably. Do you want to—" The guard gestured toward the cage.

She lay back, her eyes nearly closed. She heard the key in the lock and the scrape of iron hinges, and she forced herself to stay still. The guard came closer; she saw his blurred shape through her lashes.

She changed into the leopard and stood. The man backed away. She growled and sprang for him. The leopard smelled his fear and wanted to close for the kill, but the part of her that was still human held herself in check. The man rushed for the door, and he and his fellow guard hurried down the hallway.

She followed. She kept the leopard shape, to run faster. The guards went up a flight of stairs. The leopard started after them, enraged and excited by the chase, but she forced herself away and down the stairs.

She continued down until she came to a door, guards standing to either side. The guards saw her; their scent changed suddenly to sharp fear and they scattered out of the way. The smell thrilled her, but she turned away from them and hurried out the door. One of them threw a lance after her; it bounced harmlessly off her side and fell away.

The pain dragged her down a little, but she hurried as fast as she could, passing fields and stands of trees, roads and rivers. All her senses had sharpened; everything seemed clearer, but simpler as well, her thoughts pared down to simply running. She heard birds singing, and insects buzzing in the grass, sometimes a horse clopping over the road. Farmers called to one another in the fields, though she no longer understood the language they used. They smelled like danger; so did the stenches of the towns she passed, and she gave them all a wide berth.

Her wound reopened. She slowed and began to limp, then ran on three legs. Still the leopard did not stop; her only concern was that someone might find the blood spoor and follow it.

She started to feel hunger in addition to the pain; she had not eaten since yesterday. She looked around for something skittering through the fields, a rabbit or squirrel. A small, nearly forgotten voice told her to stop, to become the other animal, the pale, hairless, vulnerable one that went on two feet. She halted reluctantly and was about to change when the same voice reminded her to hide herself first.

She went within a grove of trees and shifted. Her bones lengthened, her muzzle shrank, her fur disappeared. She rose on two legs and became Angarred again. The stark clarity of the land around her faded away, sounds grew dim, smells vanished; she felt muddled, weak.

She looked down at the wound. Blood soaked half her shirt. Shock ran through her and her sight wavered; she had to sit until the faintness passed. The leopard was far stronger, she knew, and had more endurance. She should never have run so far and so fast. She found a hidden spot among the trees and lay down, intending to rest for a few minutes.

Darkness covered the land when she woke; past the trees she could see only stars and a half moon smudged by clouds, looking like a watery reflection of itself. How long had she been asleep?

She tried to sit and gasped at the pain; she felt as if she were being pierced anew by swords. She lay back and waited for the stabbing to fade. Now that she had returned to her own shape other, more complicated questions came to her. Who wanted Mathewar captured, and why? How could she find him when she herself was lost? The guard had wanted to tell someone about her, she remembered, and she wished he had finished his sentence, gone on to mention a name.

The air had a chill bite to it, and the ground was uncomfortably cold. The place did not feel like Karededin; even the smell was wrong. Where was she?

She felt enormously tired, unable to think. She struggled against her weariness, but finally her eyes closed and she fell back asleep.

When she woke next it was day. The smell of nearby water had tantalized her when she had been the leopard, and she set off in search of the river, gritting her teeth at each step. She drank deeply and washed the blood from her side. The wound had closed, she saw, relieved. She started walking down a small path along the river.

Several times she grew impatient and wanted to change into the leopard, but she held herself back. The leopard would think of nothing but the joy of running, of feeling the wind ruffling her fur. She needed to be careful, to pace herself and keep an eye on her injury.

She ate the berries she found and stopped often to sip from the river. The road widened as the day wore on, and she thought she must be coming to a town. The pain at her side had grown during the day; she pushed herself harder, hoping to reach a place where she could find food and help.

Rocks filled the river now, and the current became noisier, chuckling to itself. She crossed a great wooden bridge, and as she came to the other side she smelled the brine and seaweed of the ocean. Where in all the realms had she come to?

The town was far smaller than she had expected, just a few houses and a tavern at the edge of the sea. The sun started to set over the water. Fog drifted in through the roads and over the houses, blanketing everything in white. Sometimes it seemed to twine itself into shapes, splendid white horses or pale, lost men and women.

The fog brought a chill with it. The cold pierced the gash at her side, and she began to shiver. She ran the last few yards to the tavern, ignoring the pain.

The tavern was dim and close, walled and beamed in dark wood. It smelled strongly of beer. She made her way through the gloom to the taverner behind the bar.

A woman stood in front of the bar, holding several drinks in her hands. She turned, and Angarred gasped.

"Rodarren!" she said. "What are you doing here?" A horrible thought came to her, and she said, "Am I dead?"

"I'm not—" the woman said. Angarred didn't hear the rest; she closed her eyes and slid to the floor.

Iltarra stopped Cullen on his way to the council meeting. "I saw Talethe again, down in the streets," she said.

For a moment Cullen's anger was so great he couldn't speak. He had warned Talethe weeks ago—why was that sneak still in Pergodi? What mischief was he working? "I thought you told him to go home," he said.

"I did, and so did Dobrennin," Iltarra said. "The Godkings know what he's still doing here."

"What's he saying? Is he talking about Lord Ezlin?"

Iltarra shrugged. "I don't know—I didn't stop to find out."

Cullen turned to one of his bodyguards. "Go down to the city and get me Lord Talethe Tolgarred," he said.

The bodyguard bowed and left. "What are you going to do with the poor boy?" Iltarra asked. "No one pays any attention to him, after all."

"He's spreading treason, Iltarra. And there are always dissatisfied folks who will listen to anyone speaking against the king."

"I hope you don't hurt him too much, Brother," Iltarra said. "I thought he was sweet."

Cullen left her and continued to the Council Chamber. He felt raw fury again, at Talethe, who had clearly stayed on to stir up the populace when Lord Ezlin landed; at Ezlin himself; at Iltarra, who had not even tried to help her own brother, who had selfishly narrowed her world down to herself and Annin. He wanted to hit something.

His whole family seemed to have turned against him, in fact: Drustig, who was about to invade; and Polgar, who wouldn't go home, who might blackmail him over Jerret; and Iltarra, who didn't understand what had to be done with traitors. He could trust no one.

He strode angrily into the Council Chamber. The councilors sat ranged around the table; they stood as he came in.

When they sat back down Cullen said, "What do we do about this lout Ezlin? Is he going to invade?"

"We think so, my liege," Lord Enlandin said.

"When?"

"We don't know that. We—"

"What do you mean, you don't know?"

"Our spies haven't been able to get close to him. Ezlin's grown very careful—it seems that some of his men have died mysteriously, and he thinks Karededin is responsible."

"Never mind that. When do you think he'll invade?"

Enlandin studied a piece of paper, probably afraid to meet Cullen's eyes. What a pack of cowards I've been saddled with, Cullen thought. "He's certainly had enough time to raise troops," Enlandin said. "And if he waits too long it will be Autumn, and the storms will prevent him from sailing. He might come any day, I'm afraid."

"Are we ready to defeat him?"

"We called up all the eligible men in Pergodi and the neighboring towns, as you told us. Our army should be far larger than his." Enlandin paused a moment. "Unfortunately, we haven't had time to fully train the new men."

Cullen glared at him. Why, why did they persist in finding excuses?

"Still, even untrained, they should be enough to defeat the Finbarek," Lord Sorle said.

"Excellent," Cullen said. "Now what do we do about Drustig?"

No one said anything; apparently they hadn't expected this question. "Bring back the troops from Goss," Sorle said.

"According to the reports, though, there are fewer soldiers than we thought, in the mines and in Goss," Enlandin said. "They're mostly Bound Folk up there, and the Bound Folk wear out quickly from hard work. Also, if we bring most of your men south, there won't be enough to continue the war in Goss." He hurried on. "There's good news there, though, my liege. The rebels haven't attacked in a while—it's possible their leader is dead."

"Good," Cullen said again.

"Then should we assume we won't hear from the rebels again?" Enlandin asked. "Do you want to order the troops in Goss to move south, to Pergodi?"

"Yes, let's do that."

"How many?"

Cullen thought of what he had heard about Drustig, the reports of men fleeing in terror. "All of them."

"All of them, my liege?" Enlandin looked up in surprise. "But we need men to stand against Drustig, if he invades from the north. If there's no one to stop him—"

Cullen thought of Drustig again. He needed to have as many troops around him as possible in order to feel safe, an unbreachable ring surrounding Pergodi. What was the middle of the country to him? They could fend for themselves.

"I'm the king," he said. "I don't have to explain my actions to you."

"Of course, my liege," Enlandin said.

"There is one difficulty, though, milord," Lord Sorle said. "As my fellow councilor mentioned, most of the troops in Goss are Bound Folk. Someone needs to go there and order them back, and they won't listen to anyone but . . ." He trailed off. Noldeth had controlled the Bound Folk, but no one knew who had charge of them since Noldeth had died.

It was a good question, Cullen thought. He couldn't go; he had just started tasting the delights of kingship. Anyway, he needed to be here, to meet Ezlin's troops.

"My brother Polgar will ride north," he said. He felt pleased with the answer; it solved the problem of the Bound Folk, and it meant that Polgar would finally leave the capital and whatever mischief he was planning.

But he would have to take out the crown and perform another ritual, giving Polgar control of the Bound Folk once more. He could share control, he knew that; Polgar had done it with Annin. But he didn't trust his brother, especially with an army at his back. What if he had plotted with Ezlin, or Drustig? He turned to Lord Sorle. "And you'll go with him, see to it that he doesn't make any mistakes."

"Very well, my liege," Sorle said. "May I suggest that you start building their quarters now?"

"Of course," Cullen said.

"What if they don't come in time?" Enlandin asked. "Or if Ezlin and Drustig invade together?"

"I need more troops," Cullen said sourly. "I know. You're like a singer who knows only one song, Lord Enlandin. What are you telling me, then? Do you think we should just surrender, is that it? I told you I didn't want reports—I wanted plans. Or have all of you forgotten how to think?"

No one spoke. "By the Warrior, I've never seen so many simpletons. I can pull men off the street who have better ideas."

"Perhaps you can turn the new men into Bound Folk," Sorle said. "That way they won't need as much training."

Cullen's heart beat wildly, erratically. His thoughts careened out of control; he had to race after them to catch up. He couldn't make more Bound Folk. He couldn't tell the councilors that—they would think him weak. He needed trained men, men who would follow orders. He could put on the crown, it would be simple . . .

"All right," he said, standing. "That's enough for today."

He hurried back to his apartments. He could feel himself trembling, and he hoped he did not meet anyone in the corridors; he was certain he looked terrible.

Once inside his room he went to his secret cabinet and took out the crown. The pearls seemed bluer. No, they couldn't be—it was an illusion. They were looking at him, though. He thought of his father's blue eyes, as vast and empty as the sky.

"Put on the crown, my son," his father said.

The voice didn't startle him this time; he had half expected it. "No," he said. "I'm not going to create more Bound Folk. I haven't killed, and I haven't enslaved anyone—my conscience is clean."

"That's a nice distinction to make," his father's voice said. "How many folks were killed because of you?"

"Silence! Go away! I won't listen!"

"I just want to help you," his father said. "The crown will solve all your problems, you know that. You can make a vast army, conquer the whole world if you want to."

"Go away. You're not here—I imagined you."

"Go on—wear the crown. Take up your heritage."

He raised shaking hands to his head. Then he dropped them, threw the crown into the cabinet, and slammed the door.

The next day Cullen's bodyguard came to his apartments and told him they had found Talethe. "Where is he?" Cullen asked.

"In the dungeons, my liege."

"Bring him to me."

"Here?" the guard asked. Prisoners were usually interrogated in the dungeons, or by lords in the Council Chamber.

"Here, yes," Cullen said. Why did people insist on questioning him, as if he were some sort of prisoner himself?

The man bowed and left him. Cullen paced his rooms. It seemed a long time before the bodyguard came back, but finally Cullen heard a knock at his door. "Come," he said.

The guard entered, holding tight to Talethe's arm with one hand. "Good," Cullen said. "Now leave us."

"You mean—you want to be alone with the prisoner?"

Cullen sighed. "Yes. Wait outside with the other guards."

The man seemed about to ask something else, but Cullen stared at him and he left.

He studied Talethe for a moment. The boy looked terribly ordinary; he had brown hair, brown eyes, a sharp chin, and a sharper nose. Cullen had never really paid much attention to him at court. Now, though, his features stood out starkly. He was thinner and paler; he seemed to have caught some illness in the brief time he had been in the dungeons. He hugged himself as though he felt cold, though Cullen kept his apartment comfortably warm.

"So, my boy," Cullen said. "Why haven't you taken everyone's advice and left Pergodi?"

Talethe chewed on his lip. It looked raw and ragged, as if he had bitten it continually since he'd been arrested. "I—I don't know, my liege," he said. "I will, I promise you."

"You don't know?" Cullen said. He shook his head, incredulous. "I'll tell you why, then. Because you want to help Lord Ezlin when he invades."

"Is Lord Ezlin going to invade?" Talethe said.

He sounded amazed. For a moment Cullen hesitated; the boy had truly not known. He could not possibly be part of a conspiracy working for Ezlin.

No, Talethe was play-acting, he had to be. Why else had he stayed on? Cullen went to his hidden cabinet and took out the crown.

"Very good, my son," his father's voice said.

"Don't talk to me!" Cullen said, angry. "I'll do this on my own, with no help from you."

Talethe looked startled, clearly wondering why Cullen was speaking to the air. Cullen felt a moment's dread. He must be mad, then; no one else heard the voice. He pushed that thought aside to worry about later, after he finished his business here.

"Do you know what this is?" he asked, showing Talethe the crown. "Do you know what the Bound Folk are?"

Understanding showed in Talethe's face. He backed away.

"Why so frightened, my boy?" Cullen asked softly.

"I—I've heard rumors."

"Ah. What have you heard?"

"That you can create Bound Folk. That Lord Noldeth gave you the power."

Cullen smiled. "Perhaps I can. Tell me what you know, otherwise . . ." He looked at the crown in his hands.

"I don't know why I stayed. Honestly. I thought—I was waiting for something to happen . . ."

"Like what? What did you want to happen?"

Talethe went even paler. "Something. I don't know. Things happen in the city. You know."

"You were looking for someone you could talk to. Another traitor."

Talethe said nothing.

"You're too honest, that's your problem," Cullen said. "You've

never learned court etiquette, court manners. You spent your childhood playing with little Jerret, the second most important person in
the realm, and you never thought about what would happen to you
without his protection. No one fawns over you anymore, is that
right? No one pays attention to anything you say. Those people in
the Great Hall would have eaten you alive."

"I—I don't want to be fawned over—"

"Of course you do. Everyone does. I do—that's why I worked so
hard to become king. That's why all of Ezlin's witnesses died, one by
one."

Talethe gasped. "You did kill them!"

"I didn't, no. Other people did, people who wanted to make me
king."

"I'll tell—I'll tell—" Talethe looked around wildly.

"Who? Who will you tell? Everyone in the castle is loyal to me.
You still don't understand, do you? Why do you think I confessed to
you?"

Cullen lifted the crown to his head. His hands were steady, he noticed, pleased. He could do this. Talethe deserved it. No one spoke
against him, no one.

With only the slightest hesitation he said, "Thou art now bound
to me."

Talethe's eyes turned blank; he looked as if he were dead. Cullen
shuddered with disgust. He tried to keep his expression unconcerned, then realized that he didn't have to show his usual mask; it
was as if there were no one with him in the room. He fell back into
a chair.

Talethe hadn't moved. Cullen tried to think. "Go to the
seneschal," he said. "Ask him to find you a place with the servants,
and do whatever he says."

Talethe said nothing. He headed toward the door, walking with
that unnatural gait they all used.

"I'm proud of you, my son," his father said.

"Silence!" Cullen said. He threw the crown into the cabinet; it
clanged loudly against the wall.

# EIGHTEEN

A ngarred woke in one of the strangest rooms she had ever seen. She lay in a canopied bed so large it nearly filled all the available space. Furniture crowded around it: unmatched chairs sitting one on top of the other, reaching nearly to the ceiling; chests piled against the walls; clothes and dishes stacked haphazardly.

The sun shone in through the windows. She stirred and felt the injury at her side, but the pain seemed less than before. She glanced down and saw that someone had wrapped it in clean linen.

A woman came into the room. She was stout and middle-aged; she wore well-made clothing and her fine brown hair was gathered into a loose bun. "Where am I?" Angarred said. "I saw—I thought I saw Rodarren. The queen that was."

"That was my daughter," the woman said. She seemed to puff up as she said it, like a proud hen.

"Your daughter?"

"Yes," the woman said. "I'm Lady Efcharren, and she is Lady Caireddin. King Tezue was her father."

"So the rumors are true!" Angarred said. "But this can't be Karededin—Tezue would never have allowed you to stay as long as there were legitimate heirs."

"No—this is Ou."

"Ou," Angarred said. She lay back in the great bed, wondering how many days she had traveled, all unknowing. She knew little about Ou, only that it lay a long way north from Karededin.

"She'll be queen of Karededin someday, if the Godkings are good to us," Lady Efcharren said. "She's had offers already from Lords Drustig and Cullen."

"No, how can that be? Jerret is king, and his heirs will be king or queen after him."

"Jerret is very ill, my dear."

"Is he?" Angarred sat up, wincing at the pain. "He was fine when I left. Who told you he was ill? Was it the Harus?"

Lady Efcharren nodded, unruffled. "Lord Noldeth told us himself," she said.

"Lord Noldeth is dead," Angarred said pointedly.

"That's too bad—I'm sorry to hear it. But it doesn't change anything—my daughter will still marry one of his sons."

"I wouldn't be so quick to marry your daughter off to any of them. Drustig is banished, and the other two are simpletons."

Efcharren shrugged, clearly uninterested in Angarred's advice. "But who are you, my dear?" she asked. "How do you know so much about the Harus?"

"I'm Lady Angarred Hashan," she said.

The other woman's eyes widened at the title. "But what in the name of the Spinner happened to you? My daughter and her friends had to carry you from the tavern."

"We were kidnapped. My husband and I. We were sailing away from Pergodi, and pirates attacked our ship."

"Where is Lord Hashan, then?"

Lord Hashan was her father, a man who had moldered away in his decaying hall and then died. Then she understood. "My husband is Mathewar Tobrin," she said.

Efcharren started. "A magician!"

"Yes."

"We don't think highly of magicians in Ou, Lady Angarred. There's wild magic everywhere, and meddling with it is far too dangerous. You shouldn't have even been abroad at night in the fog."

All the more reason to study it, Angarred thought. Aloud she said, "I don't know where he is. The pirates said they wanted him, not me—I don't know why."

"Oh, dear," Efcharren said. "Well, I'm afraid you're far too weak to go looking for him now."

"Do you know someone—anyone around here who might have wanted to kidnap him?"

"No, I don't. I'm sorry."

Angarred wondered if that was true. If Drustig had come courting Efcharren's daughter then perhaps he lived nearby. Still, she couldn't show suspicion of her hostess, especially while she lay in that hostess's comfortable bed.

"Get some rest, and we'll see how you feel in the morning," Efcharren said. "Are you hungry? Would you like something to eat?"

To her surprise Angarred found that she would. "Yes, please."

Efcharren left, and a while later a servant came into the room with a bowl of soup. It had been made of odds and ends of leftover food; she tasted beef and mutton and the faintest hint of eel. It was surprisingly delicious, though; she ate it all, and then settled back to sleep.

She spent a number of days in Efcharren's house. She weaned herself from soup and began to eat meat and fish; they tasted wonderful after the spoiled food in the cage. Otherwise she slept; sometimes she talked to Lady Efcharren, whose belief in her daughter's bright future never wavered.

She wrote letters to Atte, which Efcharren gave to traders passing through. The traders took them reluctantly, unable to promise they would be delivered; Karededin was unsettled, they said, and war could come at any time. But when she asked Efcharren who the traders thought would war with Karededin the other woman didn't know; she simply shrugged and said, "I suppose it's all because Jerret's so ill."

Once the daughter herself came into her room. Even though Angarred knew who the girl was she felt startled to see her; Caireddin looked so much like a younger Rodarren, one whose face had never been scarred by a crazed cousin.

"Hello," Angarred said. She sat up; her shoulder ached, but far less than before.

"Hello," Caireddin said. "Is it true you lived in Pergodi?"

Angarred smelled the tang of the tavern coming from the girl. And now she noticed that Caireddin wore men's clothing, fops' clothing, and carried a dagger at her waist, and stood with one hand on her hip, in the pose of the gallants in Pergodi. She had thought, from Efcharren's talk, that Caireddin was cosseted and pampered, that Efcharren hid her away like a precious legacy.

"Yes, I did," she said.

"I'll be there soon, I suppose," Caireddin said.

Caireddin had come to ask about Pergodi, Angarred saw, but she did not want to give away how little she knew. She reminded Angarred of herself at that age, nervously pretending to worldliness, so pig-ignorant the courtiers had taken her for an idiot. But this realization did not bring a feeling of closeness with the other woman; instead Angarred found herself recoiling from her. Had she ever been that obvious, that unsophisticated?

"I'm marrying some king or other," Caireddin said. "Drustig or Cullen."

"Listen, Caireddin," Angarred said. "You shouldn't have anything to do with the Harus. They're horrible people, greedy, ambitious. Anyway, neither one of those men will ever rule Karededin. Jerret's the rightful king."

"They say Jerret will die soon," Caireddin said, sounding unconcerned.

"Your mother said the same thing. It isn't true, though."

"That's what I heard."

"Lord Noldeth doesn't—"

Caireddin looked up at a sudden noise. Angarred heard the sound of horses drawing wagons, and over it the ringing of a myriad small bells. Caireddin ran to the window.

"Travelers!" she said. Lady Efcharren came into the room at that moment, and Caireddin turned to her and said, "We have to go to them, ask them where Lady Angarred's husband is."

"I doubt she can walk so far," Efcharren said.

"What are Travelers?" Angarred asked.

"Thieves and scoundrels," Efcharren said.

"They'll tell your fortune," Caireddin said. Her affectations disappeared; she seemed excited as a child.

Angarred could not help but catch some of her enthusiasm. "I'd love to see them," she said. "But I think your mother's right—I can't walk all that way."

"We'll invite them in," Caireddin said.

"Never!" her mother said. "The Godkings know what they'll steal."

"And how would you tell if they had?" Caireddin said, looking around at the crowded room. "I'll tell you what—I'll bring one of them in, and watch him every step of the way."

"Very well," Efcharren said. "But there had better be nothing missing afterward."

Caireddin ran out of the room. "I'll have to leave you to it," Efcharren said. "My position does not allow me to talk to them."

Efcharren left, and a moment later Angarred heard two sets of footsteps coming up the stairs. Caireddin rushed into the room, barely missing a tower of chairs. A man came in behind her. He wore women's clothing, a skirt and blouse and a necklace of cheap gems and beads.

Angarred blinked, but Caireddin seemed to see nothing unusual in the man's garb. The girl and the man set to work dislodging two chairs from one of the stacks, then sat opposite each other.

Caireddin handed him several coins. "What dost thou wish to know?" he asked.

He spoke like someone from the Forest of Tiranon, Angarred thought, the wild wood near the College. A good many magicians came from Tiranon; Mathewar had been born there, and the forest folk lived in villages built in vast clearings. But as he continued to talk to Caireddin she realized that his accent sounded wrong, that he was affecting it to appear more knowing. She hadn't truly thought that anything would come of talking to a fortune-teller, but she felt disappointed nonetheless.

"Who will I marry?" Caireddin asked.

"Hast three choices," the Traveler said. "One is—"

"Three?" Caireddin said. "No, there are only two."

Angarred expected the man to change his prediction, but to her surprise he did not back down. "Three choices, I tell thee. One is to the right, one to the left, and the last is—"

"In the middle, I suppose," Caireddin said wearily. She seemed to have already lost patience with the man's vague phrases.

"In the middle?" He stopped, as if to consider what she had said. "No—he is nowhere. Neither one. Or both of them, I suppose."

"And you think I should take the third, I'll bet," Caireddin said. "That's what all the tales say, and you've probably heard the same tales I have."

"I don't think you should do anything," the man said. "For myself, I would take the third man, but you will do what you will do."

"How interesting," Caireddin said. Her tone stated clearly that she had finished with him. "Lady Angarred here has a question as well."

After the man's disappointing response to Caireddin, Angarred did not want to ask him anything. He turned to her, and for the first time she noticed his unusual eyes, green, with shards of gold radiating out from the center. His eyelashes, thick and dark, only emphasized the remarkable color. The rest of his features—brown hair, a straight nose, thin lips—were ordinary, overshadowed by the blaze of his eyes. Without thinking about it, her eyes fixed on his, she asked, "Is my husband still alive?"

"Yes," he said.

"Yes?" she asked. "That's all?"

"That's all."

"But where is he?"

"That I don't know."

"How do you know he's alive, then?"

"How? I don't know that either."

"Someone from the Forest of Tiranon would say 'aye,' actually," she said, allowing her disgust at his play-acting to show. "Not 'yes.'"

"Would they? I'll have to remember that."

"So you admit you're a fraud."

"I admit no such thing. Anyone is free to speak in any accent they like."

"I can report you to the College of Magicians, you know. My

husband is Mathewar Tobrin, the First Master at the College—you may have heard of him."

"Indeed I have."

"They take a dim view of using feigned magic for trickery."

He widened his astonishing eyes. "I haven't tried to trick you," he said. He had dropped the accent, she noticed. "I tell the truth as best I can."

"Your best isn't very good, then," she said. "Even I could have made up something better to tell Lady Caireddin."

"Ah," he said. "But would yours be the truth?"

She felt weary suddenly. "Never mind," she said, lying back in the bed. "What do I owe you for this—this performance?"

"Nothing," he said. "My lady Caireddin has paid for everything. Fare thee well, ladies."

"I'm sorry," Caireddin said when he had gone. "Their fortunes are usually better than this, all about wonderful adventures and romances."

"I didn't expect much, to be honest," Angarred said. "Do they all dress like that?"

"Yes. But if you ask them they'll say their clothes aren't strange at all, that half the people in the world wear them."

"Why do they do it, though?"

"They don't say."

"But why—"

Efcharren cried out from downstairs. "Caireddin, you feather-brain!" she shouted. "You said you'd watch him. He took my silver vase!"

Caireddin laughed. "Which one?" she called back.

# NINETEEN

Mathewar looked up and saw a village ahead. He felt weak, and he continued to see trees and towers and castles where none existed, and he wanted desperately to stop and rest. But he stayed on the road, trying to get as far away from Drustig as he could before dark.

The sun had started to set by the time he reached the next village. He walked through the cobbled streets, the smell of supper wafting out to him from the houses. Suddenly he felt ravenous. In the distance he saw a tavern, the Owl and Fiddle. He hurried toward it and went inside.

The tavern was half full. He made his way toward the taverner at the opposite end, distracted by a sudden flurry of snow coming down between them. The taverner, a large woman wiping down the bar, glanced up at him and then went back to her work. "What would you like, sir?" she asked.

He had felt disoriented all day, as if the land he walked through was another illusion, or some trick of Drustig's. "I—I'm looking for my wife," he said.

"I'm flattered, but I'm already married," the taverner said.

Mathewar smiled, the first time in days, or even weeks. "No, I mean—it's a long story. Can you tell me what place this is? What country?"

She looked up again, startled, and seemed to truly see him for the first time. "Tashtery's fire, man, what happened to you?" she asked. "You look terrible."

He started to stammer out some explanation. She turned away, toward a young woman talking to some folks around a table. "Aragall!" she called. "Come here. Where's your mirror?"

Aragall came over to the bar, holding an empty tray. "Well, I don't carry it with me," she said.

"I'd have thought you'd want to—you look at it so often," the taverner said.

"It's in my room."

"Well, don't just stand there gabbing—go get it."

Aragall started up the stairs to the next floor. "My daughter," the taverner said. "She's getting married in a week."

"Congratulations," Mathewar said.

"Don't talk, man. Sit down. I'm Eddish, by the way."

Mathewar pulled out a chair and sat. The part of his mind that still seemed to work warned him not to give his real name, in case Drustig came to hear it. "I'm Therry," he said.

"Good day, Therry," Eddish said. "What did you mean when you asked what country this is? No, don't talk, try to relax. This is Ou."

He leaned back in the chair and stretched out his legs. He'd thought so, but he hadn't wanted to believe it.

"There she is," Eddish said. "What took you so long?"

"It was a few minutes, Mother," the girl said. She took a fragment of a mirror from her apron pocket and handed it to him.

The illusions had stopped for a moment, thankfully. He looked into the mirror cautiously, then tried not to gasp. His left eye had filmed over like an old man's, and there was still a bruise, now fading, on his cheek. His face was dirty, and some of his hair had come loose from its tie and fell in clumps to his shoulders.

"I was—my wife and I were captured," he said. He began the tale, then stopped when he came to the part with Drustig.

"Don't worry, I know who it was you saw," Eddish said. "We've

had our own problems with Drustig the Half-crowned ever since he
came here. What did he want with you?"

"I'm still not sure," Mathewar said. He had decided not to tell
anyone he was a magician; that news would almost certainly be re-
layed to Drustig. "He just wanted to look through my mind, I think."

"You need some beer," Eddish said. "And some supper, and a
room for a few days. Our rooms are only a half a swan a night."

"I—I don't have any money," Mathewar said.

Eddish frowned; clearly she wasn't the sort to give away something
for nothing. "I can work, though," he said. "I can fix things, or wash
glasses, or—or anything."

"You'll need someone after I'm gone, Mother," Aragall said.

Eddish studied him. He didn't look as if he could lift a glass, let
alone wash it, he knew. "That's true, I will," she said finally. "And the
back fence needs mending. I'll give you supper and a room for tonight and take it out of your wages. And tomorrow Aragall can show
you around."

After supper she led him upstairs to a small clean room. The room
contained nothing but a bed and a chest, but it looked as beautiful as
the Celestial Court to him. He fell on the bed and slept deeply, without dreams.

The work at the tavern proved to be easy, requiring little thought.
He mended the fence; he tried to bind a strengthening spell into it as
he worked but did not think he had succeeded. He washed dishes and
glasses and wiped down tables. After a while he got to know the customers and greeted them by name, farmers and their wives mostly,
and their children and dogs.

In the morning, before the tavern opened, he practiced his magic
in his room. Then he went downstairs to the empty tavern and tried
more binding spells for the benches and tables and barrel staves. He
felt himself growing a little more adept each day, though perhaps he
only imagined it.

As he became stronger, though, so did the corruption he had felt,
Drustig's imprint. The illusions crowded him most often after he had
worked some magic, another gift from Drustig. He tried to banish
them, or at least keep them under control, but often enough phantoms would come between him and the tavern's customers, forcing

him to stop what he was doing, giving him a reputation for absent-mindedness.

He worried about Angarred constantly, but he knew he had not yet regained enough of his magic to help her. Still, he felt horribly impatient; almost every moment he wanted to drop everything, rush out the door, and run back to the castle.

And he worried about his children as well. He wrote letters to Atte, though the traders he gave them to could not promise to deliver them. Something was happening in Karededin, or would happen, they said, perhaps a full-scale war. But when he pressed them for information they could only give him rumors: Jerret was ill, was dead, Drustig had invaded, a rebel leader had taken control of Goss.

One night he woke hearing a scream, and realized an instant later that the scream had been his. He had had a confused dream, lost once again among Drustig's phantoms and illusions. And at the end of it he had heard a hideous crazed laugh, Drustig's laugh.

Suddenly he felt a terrible certainty that Drustig was in the room with him. He sat and created a light quickly, but it was too dim, it did not penetrate into all the darkened corners. He spoke a few words and it grew brighter.

The light doubled, and doubled again. The room filled with floating stars and candles. He looked at them in despair. Had he done this? Was he still too weak for most magics? Or was this more evidence of Drustig's evil, had he been contaminated beyond saving?

Then he remembered, and closed his left eye. The glittering points disappeared; only the light he had created remained. Some sanity returned, and he understood that Drustig could not possibly be here with him. He could see into all the corners now; they were bright and bare, with no shadows.

He closed his eyes and slipped back into sleep. Drustig's laugh sounded through his dreams.

The next day, his day off, he wandered through the crooked lanes of the village. He came to the apothecary's, and he lingered for a long time across the street, staring at the front door. He had only to walk inside, he knew, and the owner would sell him sattery, enough for days of bliss. And why not, after all? He had started drinking sattery when his first wife died; he had been plagued with bad dreams then as well. Now his second wife was probably dead. Wasn't that a good enough reason to begin again?

He turned away and headed back toward the tavern. Maybe later, he thought. Not today.

One day, a week and a half after he had started working at the tavern, the door opened and two strangers came inside. Although they were clearly men they were dressed in women's clothing, skirts and blouses and kerchiefs. One had a beard; the other wore a cheap necklace and some bracelets. Conversation stopped slowly as everyone turned to look at them.

"Fortunes?" the one with the necklace said. "Dost thou want thy fortune told?"

"Outside!" Eddish said. "I've told you and told you—I don't want any of you Travelers in here. Now get out!"

Mathewar stood behind the bar washing up. He looked at Eddish in surprise; he had never seen her so angry. Other people were standing and moving toward the two men, their menace clear in the way they walked. "You heard her," one man said. "Out!"

Folks around them murmured in agreement. Silver flickered; someone pulled out a knife. Surely Eddish would do something now, Mathewar thought, but she simply stood behind the bar, her plump arms folded.

The outsiders raised their hands, trying to placate the mob. "We want to tell thy fortunes, nothing more," the bearded one said. The man with the knife moved closer.

Mathewar put down a mug and headed out into the crowd, then spoke a few quiet words. The knife took on the seeming of a fish and flopped over in the man's hand. The man dropped it in surprise.

A few people laughed. "Is that all you've got?" a man asked.

"Mine's longer than that, at least."

"And probably not so gray, either."

More folks laughed. Mathewar could not hold the illusion long; the fish returned to a knife when no one was looking. He snatched it up and put it behind the bar.

The two men took advantage of the distraction to slip outside. Some moments passed, and then a few people rose as casually as they could and followed them.

Mathewar watched with interest. These men were hated, but enough people wanted their fortunes told to make it worth their while to come here. Could they really tell fortunes? Were they magicians? They spoke with the accent of the Forest of Tiranon. Intrigued, he left his dirty dishes and went outside.

The night had grown dark; at first he could see nothing but stars. Then he noticed several bulky shapes in the distance, illuminated by faint light. As he went closer he saw that the light came from lanterns at the front of three caravans. The two strange men sat in the lanterns' glow, their legs crossed under their long skirts. A customer from the tavern sat in front of each of them, trying to get comfortable on the ground, listening intently. Another man stood a few feet away, shifting from foot to foot, waiting his turn.

Mathewar stood behind him. The man scowled; clearly he didn't want anyone to know he was there.

The folks from the tavern, a man and a woman, got up at the same time and walked away. As the woman passed Mathewar saw that there was something odd about her face, though in the dim light he could not make it out. The man looked furtive but pleased with himself, as if he had heard something promising.

Mathewar sat in front of the man with the necklace. "What dost thou want to know?" the man asked.

Mathewar realized, disappointed, that his accent was false. He decided to stay despite that; he had not expected much to begin with.

"Is my wife still alive?" Mathewar said.

"I don't know," the man said. "What does she look like?"

"Aren't you supposed to tell me that?"

"She's your wife, man."

"Thy wife."

"What?"

"People with that accent say 'thy wife.'"

"That's right," the man said. "I'm always forgetting that. Are you from the Forest of Tiranon?"

"Yes." He sighed and got to his feet. "Well, I thank you. I should be heading back now. How much do I owe you?"

"What did you do here, Reti?" the bearded man said, turning to-

ward his friend. His own customer was gone. "Have you got us involved with a magician?"

"You *are* a magician, aren't you?" Reti said, looking at Mathewar
with new interest. "You changed that knife into a fish, back in the
tavern."

"Yes," Mathewar said, leaning against the caravan.

"I knew it!" Reti's friend said. "See what you did, Reti? He could
report us to the College."

"What I did? He could have come to you just as easily, Remi.
Anyway, he helped us—we were nearly killed in that tavern—"

"It's clear you're not magicians, in any case," Mathewar said.

"Well, to be honest—"

"That is, some folks might call us—"

"But to be strictly truthful, we would have to say—"

"We would have to say no. We're not."

Mathewar laughed. He couldn't help but like these men, rogues
though they might be. "You can't really tell fortunes, then," he said.

"Of course we tell fortunes," Reti said. "We just told some tonight."

"If you're asking if they come true, though—"

"Well, perhaps with a bit more practice—"

"Anyway, people seem happy with what we tell them. We like to
think of ourselves as performing a service."

"Bringing hope into humdrum lives."

"Keeping folks from despair."

"And you have no idea if my wife is alive or not," Mathewar said.

"I might, though," Reti said. "Tell me what she looks like."

Mathewar sighed. "Long hair, red and gold. Blue eyes. A bit
shorter than me."

"I saw her!" Reti said. "I told her fortune. Where was it . . . ?"

"You saw her?" Mathewar asked. "Where? How was she?"

"I don't remember. I don't remember any of it, except that she
had beautiful hair."

Mathewar felt fresh hope, though he tried to quell it. Angarred *did*
have beautiful hair. "Was she injured?" he said.

Reti shook his head. "Maybe. Maybe she was. I'll tell you what.
We're just about to head to our camp for Autumn—we can go back

the same way we came, visit the villages we missed on the way out. You can come with us—maybe something on the road will remind me."

"And in exchange you can teach us the accent of Tiranon," Remi said.

"I don't know if I should," Mathewar said.

"Ah," Reti said. "Morals." He said the word as if Mathewar had expressed an odd preference for some trifle, quails' eggs or velvet shoes.

Should he go? Reti's remark was such a thin thread to hang his hope from. "Why should I trust you?" he asked. "You pretend to be from the Forest, pretend to tell fortunes . . ."

"I swear I'm telling the truth," Reti said. "By the Moon."

"The Moon, which takes a different shape every night," Mathewar said. "As do your stories, I suspect."

"It's our highest oath," Remi said.

For the first time he heard a seriousness in the other man's voice. And he sensed more: that in this case at least they were telling the truth, or most of it. There was something about the Travelers, something more than they showed the world . . . If nothing else, they had aroused his curiosity.

"All right, I'll go with you," he said. "I have to say good-bye to the taverner first—I'll be right back."

"Good," Reti said. He introduced himself and the other man, his brother. "What's your name?" he asked.

"Mathewar," he said, and then felt startled; he hadn't intended to give his real name.

Eddish hailed him when he went inside the tavern. "I still need these dishes washed, you know," she said.

"Listen, I need to tell you—" he said. A great hoard of jewels appeared in front of him, glinting in some phantom light, and he had to concentrate to make out the taverner's face.

"Yes? If it's something to do with those scoundrels, those Travelers, I don't want to hear it. I'm perfectly willing to pretend you went outside to piss, or to meet a friend."

"No, I wanted to talk to them. And they said—"

"Never mind what they said. It's all lies, and malicious lies at that."

Most of the folks in the tavern were watching them now, all but a few who had looked away, pretending disinterest. The woman who had had her fortune told turned toward the door, as if to say she wanted nothing to do with such an unsavory subject.

"Why do you dislike them so much?" Mathewar asked.

"Why?" Once again Eddish's good-natured face contorted with anger. "Just look at them. Wearing women's clothing, for one thing. You can't tell me that's natural. And they tell lies to people, build people's hopes up and then leave, so they're far away when all the pleasant dreams come crashing down. And they steal things—they even steal children, or so I've heard. No, the best thing is to have nothing to do with them."

"I'm afraid I can't do that," Mathewar said, looking at her levelly. "I'm going with them."

"Going with them! You're joking, aren't you? No, I see you're not. Well, get out, then. And don't ask for your wages this week, because you won't get them."

"They said they could help me—"

"Help you! Rob you and throw you out on the road, more likely."

"Just as you have," Mathewar said.

The taverner opened and closed her mouth, for once at a loss for words. "Good-bye," Mathewar said.

He went upstairs and got his few coins. Then he headed back through the tavern and the crowd of people, all of them staring openly at him now.

Reti and Remi waited for him at the caravans. Eddish must have spoken loud enough for them to have heard every word, Mathewar realized. "Come with us," Reti said.

They climbed the stairs to one of the caravans and went inside. Painted tin lanterns hung from the ceiling and were placed on every surface that could hold them; after the darkness outside the light seemed dazzling. The furniture was brightly colored, mostly green but red and yellow and orange as well.

An old woman sat at a table. "This is Mathewar Tobrin," Reti said to her. "He saved our lives in the tavern. And this is our grand-mother, Kizi."

Folks went in and out of the caravan, talking and laughing: small children, a few older people, the children again. "Sit down, sit down," Reti said to Mathewar during a rare lull.

Finally the parade came to a halt, and the two men sat across the table from him. Now that he had light enough to see he noticed that all three of them had remarkable eyes, green streaked with gold.

Kizi reached for a red and orange bottle on the table. She poured three glasses of some colorless liquid, then held the bottle up to Mathewar, a question in her eyes. Mathewar shook his head.

The three raised their glasses. "May we be forgiven," the grandmother said.

"Forgiven," the other two responded.

They drank. Reti shuddered slightly, and Remi blinked; only the grandmother seemed unaffected.

"All right," Kizi said. "Now tell me how it went."

"Good, very good," Reti said. Mathewar looked at him in surprise. "We told a man he would find love soon—so of course he will look at every woman he meets in a different light. And we reminded a woman of the Romance of Charrad, and perhaps she will remember that story and realize that good men do not beat their wives."

The old woman nodded. "Bruises?" she said.

"Oh, yes. Even on her face—she looked terrible."

As the brothers talked Mathewar saw that he had been right; there was more to the Travelers than most people understood. "Well," said Kizi when they had finally finished, "enough of this for tonight. How much did you get, boys?"

Reti and Remi untied the purses from their skirts and poured them out. Coins rolled and spun on the table.

"Good, good," Kizi said. She gathered up the coins and made them disappear into a pocket in her skirts.

Reti grinned at Mathewar. "And you were starting to think we do all this for noble reasons," he said.

"Why do you do it?" Mathewar asked.

"Ah. It's not time to ask that yet."

In the next few days the caravans headed south, following branches off the main road to small towns and villages. Mathewar, impatient, wanted to force them to keep to the road, but he knew that he could not say anything, that their livelihood depended on these little places.

Reti and Remi went out in the evenings to tell fortunes and nearly always returned with money for Kizi; returned, too, with evidence of the villagers' hostility, cut lips and bloody noses. Once Remi showed his grandmother a long gash on his forearm, and they sat at the table while she treated it with a foul-smelling salve.

"Why in the name of the Healer do you go out there when you know they hate you?" Mathewar asked.

"They don't all hate us," Remi said. He jerked his arm away from Kizi. "Ah, Mathona's milk, be careful!"

"They seem to."

"We could have used you there, it's true," Remi said. "I would have dearly liked to see that knife turn into a fish."

He noticed that Remi did not answer the question. But as the days passed he watched closely, and he learned a few things on his own. The family traveled together in the three bright green caravans. They carried a good deal with them, most of it vividly colored, rugs and hangings and beads and lanterns, tables and chairs and beds. The caravan where they ate, the first one Mathewar had seen, held a brazier over which they cooked their food. They fed it wood when they stopped for the night and doused it carefully when they started again in the morning.

A lot of people filled the caravans too: the grandmother, a grandfather who slept most of the time and rarely left his caravan, Remi's wife and their two children. Most of them had Remi's and Reti's green-gold eyes, which seemed to have remained constant from generation to generation. The grandfather and Remi's boy dressed in shirts and breeches; only the two brothers wore women's clothing.

Once Mathewar asked them if they had taken him on to make eight passengers, an even number, since odd numbers were considered unlucky. Reti studied him awhile and then said, "We don't believe that here." But when Mathewar asked him what he did believe he changed the subject with his usual deftness.

They hadn't invited him along for money, that much was certain. Despite his protests they would not let him pay for anything from his small store of coins.

During the long trips the adults played cards or sang or practiced fortune-telling with each other, and the children ran from one caravan to another, involved in their own games. One evening thick fog and mist rolled in from the sea, and that night Reti and Remi stayed inside the caravans. The fog was haunted with magic, they told Mathewar, and he could feel that this was no mere superstition, that something strange and wild was abroad that night.

That evening Reti and Remi told the children stories, odd, enigmatic tales about the long history of the Travelers. In these stories they used a different name for themselves, one that Mathewar never heard from any of the villagers they visited: the Forsaken.

Mathewar still had terrible dreams filled with Drustig's laughter; he would find himself in the caravan, sitting upright, his heart pounding. He never knew if he screamed aloud or not; he thought he did, but Reti and the grandparents, who slept in the same caravan, would do no more than stir and turn over when he woke.

He got up early, usually, but the family was almost always up before him, making breakfast, working out some silly piece of fortune-telling, packing up before they moved on.

One morning, just as he reached the caravan with the stove and food, he heard Remi's and Reti's voices from inside. It was a serious conversation, with none of their usual bantering, and at one point Mathewar thought he heard his name.

He stopped just outside the door and listened. He felt a little guilty for eavesdropping, but he told himself that they had not been completely honest with him either. And why would they want to talk about him?

"Did you tell him yet, Brother?" Remi said.

"No," Reti said.

"Will you tell him at all? Or wait until we get there?"

"I don't know. I suppose I'll see what happens."

"You're right—trust in Mathona and seize the chance she gives you. But be careful."

"Don't worry, I will."

Footsteps headed toward him. Mathewar pretended to reach for the door just as Remi opened it. He stood aside for the other man and then went in.

Who was Reti going to tell, and what would he tell him? Had the brothers heard something about Angarred? But if they had, why hadn't they said anything? They knew how desperate he was for word of her.

He headed toward a cooling pot of porridge on the stove. No, there was no reason to suspect they knew anything, and even if they did they wouldn't hide it from him. He had woven an entire tapestry of a story from two fraying threads, a possible mention of his name and an enigmatic conversation.

Someone moved at the corner of his eye, deep within the caravan. It was Drustig; Drustig had come for him. He turned quickly and saw the dull gleam of the silver crown.

No, it was only Reti, getting out a bowl. He had forgotten the other man was still in the caravan. "Good morning," Reti said.

"Good morning," Mathewar said, trying to keep his voice steady.

# TWENTY

athewar spent his time working on magic in his caravan, especially when the brothers were out fortune-telling. He
felt himself improving—very slowly, but he thought he might someday regain most of what he had lost. But as he grew stronger so did
the strange visions, despite his attempts to banish them.

Now he made a light, then a few more, then made them spin. He
allowed himself to remember the last season, when he had been
mired in gloom, when he had thought he would feel the same un-
happiness until the end of his days. For the first time he had really
considered all those people who had no magic, had marveled that
they could live that way.

He gave thanks to the Healer, or whatever gods had helped him,
that he would not be like them after all, that his life once again held
excitement and knowledge and delight in his abilities. He knew now
that he would keep working on his magic no matter how defiled it
had become, and he prayed that Drustig had not harmed him irrevocably.

At mid-afternoon he heard horses and looked out the caravan
door. Remi and Reti had returned early.

"Come with us," Reti called, dismounting.

His usual lightheartedness had gone; he sounded as if he brought ill news. "What's happened?" Mathewar asked.

"I'll tell you when we're all together," Reti said.

Remi got Kizi, and they went into the kitchen. What was wrong? Had they found Angarred?

They sat at the table. Remi brought out the bottle of spirits, which Mathewar had learned was called Mathona's Tears. "What is it?" the old woman asked.

"Bad news, I'm afraid," Remi said. "King Jerret's dead."

"What!" Mathewar said. "No. No, he can't be!"

"We heard it from a trader," Reti said. "They've mostly left Karededin—they say there will be a war, maybe several."

"Who—who's the king?" Mathewar asked.

"Cullen," Reti said.

"Cullen!" Mathewar said. "That lack-witted, spineless idiot!"

Remi and Reti exchanged glances. They seemed taken aback, and he realized that he had never told them how close he was to the king, how well he knew the politics of the castle. They did not even know his position at the College, only that he was a magician. "How—how did Jerret die?"

"It was sudden," Reti said. "No one knows why. They say he proclaimed Cullen his heir before he died."

"They murdered him, then," Mathewar said, sitting back heavily.

"That's what some are saying. But no one dares speak out against the Harus, especially Cullen. They say the Harus know how to take away a person's will, turn them into slaves."

"Yes," Mathewar said. "I should never have left Pergodi. I shouldn't have left Jerret to the care of those—those bloodthirsty vipers. I should have known."

"How could you have?" Reti said softly.

Mathewar looked at him. "Because that's what magicians do," he said, matching Reti's tone. "It's all my fault. If I hadn't left Pergodi I could have saved Jerret, and Angarred would still be alive—"

"You don't know she's dead."

"I know. I did everything wrong. I should never have freed Nim—"

"Who's Nim?" Reti asked.

"Never mind," Mathewar said. "What about this war you mentioned? Is Lord Ezlin going to fight for his inheritance?"

Remi looked at his brother again, one eyebrow raised in surprise, then poured glasses of Mathona's Tears for himself and Reti and his grandmother. For the first time Mathewar accepted one as well.

"Lord Ezlin, yes," Remi said finally. "The war might have started already—the news was fairly old. And it looks as if Lord Drustig might fight Cullen as well."

"Drustig? Why? What claim does he have?"

"Anyone can go to war," Reti said. "He doesn't need a claim." He lifted his glass. "May we be forgiven," he said, and the others repeated, "Forgiven."

Mathewar, who felt as if he needed forgiveness more than anyone there, said nothing, but raised the glass to his lips and drank. It tasted horrible, like an apothecary's failed experiment. His eyes teared, and he wiped them with his sleeve.

After a moment, though, he felt a warmth that spread out to every part of him. It reminded him of sattery, though it was nowhere near as strong; still, for the first time in fourteen years he knew something like the same blissful peace. He knew, too, that the stuff was a mortal danger to him, but he ignored that and took another sip.

"What is Cullen like?" Remi asked.

"You know, I've never heard him speak," Mathewar said. "He always seemed to exist in his father's shadow. I suppose he'll come into his own now that Noldeth's dead—and the Godkings help us when he does."

"He could be nothing like his father, though," Remi said.

Mathewar shook his head. "Jerret died after Lord Noldeth did. Someone in that family killed him, and Cullen was the one who benefited most by his death."

They continued to talk and drink, but Mathewar said little. Should he return to Pergodi? Things had unraveled so far there he didn't see how he could help. He could try to expose Cullen as a murderer— but then who would succeed him? Ezlin, possibly, but from what Mathewar had seen of the man he thought he'd make a dreadful king. And with Cullen gone Drustig would make a play for the throne, and Mathewar did not see how he or anyone else could prevent it.

And leaving Ou would mean giving up his quest for Angarred. What if Drustig had her, what if even now he was putting on his terrible crown and tearing apart her mind? She knew nearly as much as Mathewar did about the Stone, and he didn't think she could hold out as long. Worst of all, if he left he would be giving in to that part of him that was certain she was dead.

It was all too complicated. Drustig might be on his way to Karededin, leaving Angarred in Ou. Should he stay then? He lifted his glass and saw that it was empty, and he reached for the bottle of Mathona's Tears.

"You shouldn't drink too much of that," Reti said.

"You're right," Mathewar said. "Sattery's much better. Quicker, too."

Reti said nothing. Mathewar had noticed that the Travelers rarely came out and said anything directly; they preferred to speak in vague hints and oracular phrases. Reti might tell him some obscure story, the point of which not even he understood, but he would let Mathewar drink himself into a stupor if he wanted. At the moment he wanted that very much.

He was responsible for Jerret's death, whatever Remi and Reti said. He should never have trusted the Harus; even with their head loped off they stayed alive, working their malice like some evil snake out of legend. Pictures of Jerret rose before him; he had no idea if they were illusions or effects of the drink or a reminder of his guilt, but he thought it didn't much matter.

Once again he saw Jerret's delighted face as he worked little magics for the boy. Jerret at Rodarren's funeral, his expression stern as he practiced being a king. Jerret tangled in the Harus' net, confused, not knowing where to place his trust, trying desperately to do a job no one had prepared him for.

He saw Angarred at the funeral too, standing next to Jerret, comforting him after he had lost his mother. Then images of Angarred crowded out Jerret, what seemed like hundreds of them, jumbled memories of their life together.

He had failed her too, failed her not once but over and over. He'd been unable to save her from Drustig, and unable to rescue her once Drustig had her. And hadn't that been the case with his first wife,

Embre, as well? He'd thought he could stand against the most powerful magician in all the realms, and then, when she'd been taken from him, he'd frittered away his time, waited until it was too late and she was already dead.

He had been too arrogant then, he knew that. But he'd thought that Embre's death had taught him something. He had learned nothing, though; he'd only repeated every one of his mistakes. There was a word for someone who ignored all the lessons of his past: fool.

He remembered what Drustig had said, that he was under a curse. It must be true, he thought. He had performed all the same actions as before, one after the other, working as blindly as a bound man.

Someone spoke. He looked up; Remi's wife Neri held out some skewered meat on a plate. The rest of the Travelers had come into the caravan when he wasn't looking, crowding around the table—or were they an illusion? He closed his bad eye but they did not go away.

He took the plate. The meat sizzled and dripped. He reached for the bottle of Mathona's Tears but it was empty.

"You haven't spoken all evening," someone said.

He glanced up and saw rows of books in a candlelit library. Beyond them he could just make out Reti. What had he said?

"No," Mathewar said finally. The flames of imaginary candles moved dizzily.

"Why not?"

"Must I speak?" he said. Everything seemed to be spinning now; he tried to ignore it. "Anyway, you and your brother are far more silent than I am." He almost said "silenter"; he forced himself to pay attention.

"Nonsense. We're constantly telling stories—you must have heard us."

"Your stories are filled with silence. They are what silence would sound like. They are riddled with riddles. Why do the Travelers tell fortunes?"

"It's not the right time to ask that."

"No, but maybe it's the right time to answer it."

Reti laughed. "You think like us," he said.

"I don't know if that's a compliment or not," Mathewar said.

Reti laughed again. "Very well," he said. "I'll tell you a story."

Everyone around the table quieted; stories, especially their own histories, had an importance to the Travelers Mathewar didn't completely understand.

"Once, long ago," Reti said, "when all the plates were silver and all the cups were gold, our mother Mathona had a lover. This was not Marfan but another, a man whose name has not been remembered but who is known only as the Bridegroom.

"Mathona and Marfan were at odds in those days. Mathona taught the people how to plant and to harvest, and how to herd animals. Marfan taught them how to build and to measure, how to count the passing of the days. And so the people who followed Marfan began to build houses and then towns and then cities, crowding in together with those who believed as they did. And those who followed Mathona lived among the fields and pastures and forests, and they planted their crops and herded their animals.

"We, of course, our people, supported Mathona. In those days we did not travel but were farmers and herders, and we distrusted those who lived in cities. We did not build much, though we became famous for our blacksmiths. But even our blacksmiths did not work for the builders in the city, did not fashion hammers or saws. They made only plows and horseshoes and other things that the followers of Mathona would need.

"Mathona and the Bridegroom were very much in love and wanted to wed. But Marfan wanted Mathona for himself, and he hated the Bridegroom. So Mathona and her lover chose a secret place, a clearing in the woods, in which to get married, and they invited only a few of their friends from among the animals and people.

"But someone betrayed Mathona to Marfan. Someone told him about the clearing in the woods. He went there, and he hid until the ceremony nearly ended, and then he burst into the clearing and killed the Bridegroom with his sword. And he and his men took Mathona captive, and he carried her off to be his wife.

"And so ever since we have been severed from our mother Mathona. And ever since, because of the great wrong we did her, we have wandered the world telling fortunes."

"But—" Mathewar said. The spinning had stopped, thank all the Godkings, but he felt that he had missed something. Either that, or

Reti had left out the most important part of the story. "I don't understand. What wrong did you do?"

Reti said nothing. Identical eyes around the table regarded him, green and broken gold. One of Remi's children giggled. This part must be traditional, he thought, and the children had already guessed or been told the answer.

"One of the Travelers told Marfan where the wedding would be," Mathewar said. "That was the wrong you did."

The children laughed. Clearly they had given this answer as well, and it had been wrong.

Kizi looked at him gravely, as if his life depended on solving the riddle. In his confusion he thought somehow that it did. He closed his eyes briefly. He wanted desperately to pass the test, though he didn't know why Reti's good opinion mattered to him. "One of your blacksmiths made the sword," he said finally.

Reti looked surprised, gratifyingly so. "Yes," he said.

"But I still don't understand. He didn't make the sword to kill the Bridegroom, did he?"

"No."

"Did he sell it to Marfan?"

"Of course not. None of the Forsaken would have dealings with him. No, he sold it to someone, who sold it to another, who sold it to Marfan."

Mathewar shook his head, then immediately regretted the sudden movement. He felt almost completely baffled now. Was this more of the Travelers' nonsense, or was he just too drunk to understand? Had Reti merely exchanged one set of riddles for another?

"But then you're blameless," he said. "Guiltless. Innocent as air. How dare she impose penance, impose punishment, make you tell fortunes and go out in women's clothing—"

"Is this women's clothing?" Remi said, looking down at his skirt and his hairy legs sticking out past the hem. "You said this was the latest fashion in Pergodi, Reti."

"That's what they told me," Reti said. "What, do you think they were wrong?"

"I think they might have lied to you, Brother."

The children giggled. Reti said something, then Remi; then one of them said, "It isn't penance. It's worship."

That made no sense whatsoever. Mathewar gave up trying to understand. He lost some time then; when he next looked around the Travelers were singing in an eerie minor key about the Moon. The song held sorrow and joy in equal measure: sorrow for their lost home, and joy in serving the Goddess they loved.

He knew nothing more until he woke the next day, somehow miraculously in his own blankets. He remembered fragments of the night before and understood that Reti had wanted to teach him something, but the only thing he had learned was that drinking too much Mathona's Tears brought a head-splitting ache the next morning.

That afternoon Reti invited Mathewar to go with him into the next village. "Why?" he asked. "Am I supposed to learn something from this too?"

"You might," Reti said.

"That's almost an answer, by the Orator. What is it I'm supposed to learn, then?"

Reti busied himself hitching a horse to a caravan, the one he and Mathewar usually slept in. Then he sat up front, indicating to Mathewar that he should join him. "Where's your brother?" Mathewar asked, but Reti said nothing.

They traveled the main road for a while. Neither of them spoke; the bells of the caravan jingled loudly in the silence. The air was crisp, warm for Ou; he had to squint against the sun, which seemed far too bright. The bells seemed to have set up house inside his head. He had felt the same after drinking sattery, and he marveled at how his life had come around in a perfect circle: two dead wives, uncounted nights of drinking.

But it had only been one night this time. He wanted more Mathona's Tears, but he could not bring himself to ask Reti. No, what he really wanted was sattery.

They passed a man on a horse who scowled at them, and another who made gestures Mathewar thought were intended to ward off evil. The raw hatred brought back all his unanswered questions of the night before and he said, "You never did tell me why you go out in the world and tell fortunes. You said last night—I thought you said it was worship, not penance."

"Worship, yes. Mother Mathona does not punish or impose penance. This is how we become closer to her. We dress in women's clothing because she is a woman, and we tell fortunes because that is how we spread our beliefs. We are forbidden to preach by the religious, who hold that Marfan is the most important of the gods."

"But you said you're severed from her," Mathewar said. "Isn't that a punishment?"

"We severed ourselves. We uprooted ourselves from the soil, from her body. We saw the great wrong we did her, and so we decided to travel the world and spread her teachings. But it's not penance. We've forsaken her only to worship her better."

"I still don't understand," Mathewar said. He was being too blunt, he knew, unable to match Reti's subtlety, but he didn't care anymore. "I don't see anyone learning from you. People don't worship her more than Marfan, or even as much."

"Are you sure? Her presence is felt in all sorts of ways. I've heard that the First Master at the College has invited girls to learn magic, for example."

Mathewar tried not to look startled. Did they know who he was after all?

"Once a seed has sprouted you cannot push it back under the ground," Reti said. "We will see more of Mathona in the days to come, I think. Marfan teaches knowledge, but Mathona teaches wisdom. Marfan teaches law, but Mathona teaches . . . not misrule exactly but joyfulness, lack of restrictions. She is the Moon, the mutable Moon, the quicksilver trickster Moon."

He recognized Reti's words from last night's song. Just then the other man turned the caravan down a small winding street. They passed widely spaced houses, too few to be called a village, then stopped near a small but ornate house. Reti stepped down. "Come," he said.

Mathewar got out and studied the house doubtfully. It seemed too fussy, too cluttered, with enough towers and balconies and cupolas and trimming for a place twice its size.

Reti knocked on the door. Just before it opened Mathewar's mistrust returned, bringing with it all his suspicions of the Travelers. Where had Reti brought him? Was Drustig here, had they sold him out to Drustig?

The door opened a crack, and a stout middle-aged woman peered out at them. "You!" she said to Reti. "Don't think I'm letting you in my house again. And who is this one?" She looked at Mathewar. "Why aren't you wearing the same masquerade as your friend here?"

"He has his own odd customs," Reti said. "Anyway, we don't want to come in. Can we talk to your guest?"

"You stole a vase the last time you were here," the woman said. "Don't try to deny it. Maybe if you give it back—"

Suddenly Reti held a large richly decorated silver vase. It was not magic—at least Mathewar didn't think it was. "Here," Reti said. He handed it to the woman and went past her into the house.

"Wait—this isn't mine . . ." the woman called after him.

"Hello," Reti said to someone in the dim recesses of the hallway.

"Hello," said a familiar voice.

Mathewar went inside after him, barely able to believe what he had heard. Angarred stood there. He ran to her and held her tightly. She made a small noise and he let her go quickly.

"Did I hurt you? Are you all right? What are you doing here?"

"I'm fine," she said. "What about you? What are you doing with Travelers?"

"Traveling with them," he said, and laughed for sheer happiness.

A young woman stepped out of the gloom. She looked astonishingly like Rodarren, but he put that mystery aside to concentrate on Angarred. She seemed pale, even in the dark hallway, and too thin.

"Holy Godkings," she said. "What happened to your eye?" She touched his cheek softly, and he tried not to flinch.

He looked up to see Reti standing just inside the door, grinning at them. "You knew she was here all along, didn't you?" Mathewar said.

"Go talk to her," Reti said. "You have a lot to say to each other."

"I have a lot to say to you too, it seems. Why didn't you tell me she was here? That she was alive?"

"Come on, Matte," Angarred said. "Tell me where you've been, what you've been doing. You can talk to him later."

"And he won't give me any answers then either, I'll wager." He turned to Reti. "Does this amuse you? Was my life, and Angarred's— was it all a joke? Did you and your brother have some good laughs about us?"

Reti shook his head. "It wasn't a joke," he said.

"No—jokes are supposed to be funny."

"Come on," Angarred said. "Please." She took his hand and led him deeper into the house.

He couldn't think about Reti now. He followed Angarred into a room smelling of mold and filled with rugs and furniture and suits of armor, and they sat in two of the many chairs.

They talked for a long time, interrupting each other, stammering in their desire to mention everything. In their eagerness they could not keep to a strict chronology, so that Mathewar talked about the Travelers before he described how he had met them; and Angarred explained about Caireddin's claim to the throne before telling him how she had come to live in Lady Efcharren's house.

When he told her about Drustig and his half crown she gasped. "Drustig!" she said. "So that's who imprisoned us. What did he want from you?"

"I don't think even he knew. He wanted whatever knowledge I had, I suppose, anything he could use against his brother."

"How did he know we would be that ship?"

"I'm sure he has spies in the castle. He might have told them to capture us if they ever got the chance."

"Caireddin wants to marry him, you know."

"She does? Why?"

"Her mother's ambitious for her. For some reason she thinks Drustig will be king."

She hadn't yet heard about Jerret, Mathewar realized. He dreaded telling her.

"Angarred," he said. "There's bad news, I'm afraid. The traders say—they say that Jerret is dead."

"Oh, no!" Angarred said. She put her hand to her mouth. "No, he can't be. The Harus killed him, didn't they?"

"I think so," Mathewar said. He repeated what Reti and Remi had told him. "It's my fault. If I hadn't left him—"

"We both left him."

"Yes, but—"

"It's not your fault. You can't see everything."

Why did everyone insist he was not responsible? He had killed Jerret, almost as surely as if he had put a knife to his throat.

"You warned him about the Harus," she went on. "What else could you have done? You don't—with your magic gone—"

"Oh," he said. "I didn't tell you. I can work some magic again."

She looked puzzled, clearly wondering why he wasn't more excited. "But that's wonderful!" she said.

Was it? How much of his magic had been poisoned by Drustig? Should he tell her about the visions?

As if thinking about them had called them up, he saw a pack of silver wolves pad silently through Efcharren's visiting room, snow falling all around them. "It is wonderful, yes," he said. He could barely glimpse her face through the whiteness of the illusion.

He and Angarred talked a little more. He said nothing about the wolves, and after a while they went away. Finally their stories met at the front door of Lady Efcharren's house. Angarred leaned forward and kissed him softly. "What do we do now?" she asked.

"I have to go back to Karededin," he said. "Though I don't see what I could possibly do there."

"*We* have to go back," she said.

"Are you well enough?"

"That's funny, coming from you. You probably can't even see out of that eye."

Oh, I can see, all right, he thought. Not anything in front of me, though.

"Anyway, what about the children?" Angarred said. "I wrote letters—"

"So did I. But the traders said—"

"—that Karededin is too unsettled," she said. "They didn't think the letters would get through. Atte must be terribly worried about us."

"Well, we can't leave today," he said. "We'll go tomorrow."

Lady Efcharren came into the room, holding the vase Reti had given her. "This is much nicer than the one he stole," she said. She placed it on a table already crowded with vases. "I did try to give it back, but he didn't seem to want it. It would look good here, don't you think?"

"Lady Efcharren," Angarred said. "You've been so good to me I hate to ask for another favor, but . . . Could you possibly let my husband stay here for a night?"

Efcharren seemed to see Mathewar for the first time. "He's the magician, isn't he?" she said doubtfully.

"I'm afraid so," Mathewar said, trying to look as harmless as possible.

He must have succeeded, because Efcharren said, "Well, all right." She returned to studying her arrangement of vases. "I had no idea I had so many," she said.

# TWENTY-ONE

Mathewar slept without nightmares, and woke late to see golden blocks of sun coming in through the windows. He turned to Angarred and held her lightly. I could stay right here forever, he thought. Let Karededin take care of itself.

They rose even later, dressed, and went downstairs. Shorry had breakfast ready for them. She served them at an enormous round table with one claw-footed leg; it barely fit the room it was in and they had to rearrange the heavy leather chairs to sit down.

Halfway through their meal of bread and herring a knock came at the front door. Shorry hurried to answer it.

"Is Princess Caireddin home?" a man asked.

Even before Mathewar recognized the voice he felt himself tense. "It's Drustig," he said quietly.

"Yes, she is," Shorry said. "Come with me."

Drustig's and Shorry's footsteps came closer, heading down the hallway toward them. They stood, ready to summon whatever powers they could against the lord. The footsteps turned away, growing fainter. Drustig and Shorry had gone through a door, probably into the strange room Mathewar had seen earlier, filled with the cast-offs of kings.

"What if he comes here?" Angarred whispered. "Maybe Efcharren wants to serve him breakfast. There's no way out except past him."

They heard more voices: Shorry fetching the two women, Caireddin heading downstairs, Efcharren coming out to meet her. Then, as the two ladies joined Drustig, these sounds faded too.

"I'd give a lot to know what they're saying," Mathewar said. "I'm curious about that crown."

"You're not going to listen at the door, are you?" Angarred said. "You more than anyone should know how dangerous he is."

He shook his head. "No," he said. "I thought I'd go inside."

"What!"

"Hush—they'll hear you. I'll disguise myself—I can be a servant, waiting on Lady Efcharren."

"And you think she'll just accept you? A servant she's never seen before? You know how she feels about magic."

"What did I do before I met you?" Mathewar said, smiling. "I must have walked without thinking into a thousand perils. It's a wonder I didn't get killed."

"It is," Angarred said. "I'm going with you."

He knew better than to argue. "All right," he said. "I'll turn you into a servant as well."

Once creating disguises had been easy; now, like everything else, it came slowly, painfully. He spoke some words. Nothing happened for a moment, and he felt a familiar despair settle over him.

Then Angarred changed. Her dress turned shabby and plain, like Shorry's, and her hair appeared to be tucked up under a cap; a few dull strands streaked with gray fell to her shoulders. Her face grew lined, care-worn, filled with worry about the household.

He changed himself as well, and they set off. Instantly he felt weary, like an ancient retainer worn out from a lifetime of service. He found himself stooping as he walked. A glamour was not a true change but an illusion; still, someone who was transformed became caught in the net of deception and began to think and act like their disguise. But he had had to make himself and Angarred older, to ensure that Drustig did not recognize them.

They passed the kitchen, then came to Efcharren's visiting room and went inside. Drustig was saying something, and both the women laughed. Efcharren turned and saw the two of them; she stepped back, startled.

Mathewar bowed. "I was wondering if milady needed anything more from us," he said. He bowed to Caireddin. "My princess."

Efcharren recovered quickly. "We do, actually," she said. "Go to the kitchen, please, and help Shorry bring out the food."

He bowed again, and Angarred curtsied. As he looked up he saw Caireddin try not to smile. She knew who they were, then, and she thought the whole thing a great joke.

They left the room and headed down the hallway, trying to hurry, pushing forward against the faltering pace of their disguises. "How did you know she wouldn't say anything?" Angarred whispered.

"I didn't, really. I thought she might want to appear to have more servants than just Shorry, for one thing. And she wouldn't want to look confused in front of Drustig."

They went inside the hot kitchen. Shorry was arranging something on a tray, her back toward them. "Here, we'll take that for you," Mathewar said.

Shorry turned quickly. "Who—" she said, nearly unable to get the word out. "Who are you? Stay back—don't come any closer or I'll scream."

She rapped against the wall twice, an even number for protection. It seemed a strange gesture to make, so far from the Godkings, and Mathewar wondered if Lady Efcharren had brought Shorry along from Karededin. "Don't worry," he said, slipping into the quick speech of the Pergodek. "We're just some people Efcharren hired, to help with the work. We can take those trays."

Shorry seemed reassured, as well as grateful for the help. She handed him the tray. "You can get that one," she said to Angarred, pointing to a platter holding three cups and a flagon of wine.

Drustig and the two women had taken seats by the time they returned. "King Jerret is dead, milady," Drustig said. "My wretched brother Cullen usurped the throne that should rightfully be mine."

Mathewar moved among them with his tray. Drustig helped himself to two meat pies, then put one whole into his mouth and talked around it. "I've stopped fighting in Goss," Drustig said. "Everything went as planned there—I'm ready to press on to Karededin. And I have a great many men, all of them ready to flock to my banner. It's time to meet my brother in the field."

Angarred set down a glass for each of them. Drustig began to talk about troop strength, food stores, weapons. Mathewar tried to remember it all, but his mind moved more and more sluggishly as he grew closer to the old man he impersonated. He needed to memorize everything, though, needed to tell King Jerret . . . No, not Jerret, what was he thinking . . .

"Here—what are you doing?" Drustig said suddenly.

Mathewar looked up, alarmed. Drustig grasped Angarred by the wrist; wine from the flagon slopped over onto the table. "You serve Princess Caireddin first, do you hear? She has royal blood, more royal blood than you'll ever see again."

"Yes, milord," Angarred said. She mopped the wine with a piece of cloth from her tray, her head bent over her work.

Drustig continued to study her. Mathewar held his breath. "Very well, then," Drustig said. He twisted her arm and then dropped it.

Angarred poured the last of the wine into Lady Efcharren's glass. "I'll go back to the kitchen, see if there's anything else," she whispered to Mathewar. "You stay here."

He nodded and slipped into a spot against the wall, between two great wardrobes. Drustig seemed to have forgotten him; he was talking to Caireddin now, his face alight with excitement.

Drustig went to one knee before Caireddin. "And I cannot think of anyone more worthy to share my journey to Karededin, to work at my side, to sit next to me as I rule. To fill me with inspiration. I know I am unworthy of your lineage and beauty—that even if I held the throne I would be unworthy—but—"

Caireddin looked at Drustig with admiration, almost worship. Mathewar knew from what Angarred told him that the girl only pretended to cynicism, that she had adopted her pose to protect herself against her mother's ambition and her burdensome heritage. Now he saw how thin her pretense was, how much she craved love and attention.

Still, Drustig would be the worst possible choice. He would have to talk to her before they left, tell her some things about the Harus.

Angarred came back with another laden tray and went toward the three of them. Suddenly a suit of armor stepped out from the wall, blocking her way. She jumped back. One arm lowered with eerie soundlessness, until the sword it held pointed directly at her. A bell sounded. A voice came from within the helmet:

"Beware the falling of the sword
  Beware the dulling of your sight
  At the tolling of the bell
  Those you fear will come to light."

Drustig stood and roared like a wounded bear. "What's he saying? What light? Where?"

Angarred dropped the tray and ran for the door. Mathewar followed, speaking quickly as they went, trying frantically to shed their disguises. They reached the front door of the house and burst through it, panting.

They hurried to the road. Mathewar looked back and saw Drustig at the open door, heard him cry out as he pounded after them.

He could not undo his illusion. Perhaps he was not yet strong enough; perhaps he still thought too much like the old servant. "Hurry!" he said to Angarred as they ran, breathing hard. "Change shape!"

"I can't!" she said. She was pressing her hand to her wound, a look of pain on her face. She slowed. "You have to—"

He said a few last words and felt the semblance fall away from him like a heavy cloak. He looked back again. Drustig was gaining on them; he could not hope to outrun such a young man no matter what his shape. "Change!" he said again.

She needed a moment to transform, he knew, needed to reach for the shape within her. He thought he could almost hear Drustig hurrying behind them, closing the distance between them. He remembered the half crown, the moments of insanity as his mind grew closer to Drustig's, and he thought he might rather be killed than go through it all again.

They rounded a bend in the road. Ahead of them stood a green caravan. For a moment he thought it was a phantasm, one of the hallucinations he saw with his bad eye. He closed his eye as he ran but it did not go away.

They rushed toward it. Reti waved to him from the front. "Hurry!" he called.

Reti! he thought. I never wanted to see that man again, not him or his family or his wretched caravan.

He had no choice, though. They ran for the open side door. Mathewar jumped inside, then reached out and pulled Angarred up next to him. The caravan began to move; the door banged against the outside wall a few times before Mathewar managed to close it. Bells rang out shrilly.

He leaned against the wall and tried to catch his breath. Through a small window he could see Drustig standing on the road, shouting after them.

"Are you all right?" Angarred asked after a moment.

"I'm far too old for this," he said.

Caireddin watched Drustig run from the room, and continued to stare at the door after he had gone. "That was Angarred, wasn't it?" Efcharren said. "And her husband, that magician?"

Caireddin turned to her mother slowly. She felt suspended, unable to move until Drustig returned and the drama played itself out. Everything depended on what he said when he came back. If he asked about Angarred and Mathewar she would know he was still thinking of himself, that his sole interest in her was her lineage. But if he continued his proposal . . .

"Why did the suit of armor move just then?" Efcharren asked.

"I don't know, Mother," Caireddin said, irritably. "It's mad, you said so yourself."

It seemed a long time before Drustig strode through the door, though probably only a few minutes had passed. He went quickly to kneel in front of her.

"You must forgive me, my lady," he said. "Those—those rude louts interrupted a moment I hoped you would remember forever. Now all I can say is that I am entranced by your beauty, and would think myself the most fortunate man alive if you would consent to take me as your husband."

His vivid blue eyes shone like jewels. She shivered at his intensity. He actually thought her beautiful, though her mirror told a different story.

"I won't lie to you, my princess," Drustig said. "It's a huge gamble—but I think you're brave enough to take it, to wager everything. It will be a great adventure, if nothing else—makers will write songs about us for hundreds—thousands—of years to come. But it's a gamble I think we'll win, especially with my—with what I found in Ou. We will sweep through Karededin, and when my brother is vanquished you will take the throne that belongs to you by right."

"Yes," she said, breathing the word. Then, louder, "Yes, I would love to travel with you. To be your wife."

"Wonderful." He stood. "You won't regret this, I promise you. I have to attend to my men for a while, but I'll come for you the day after tomorrow. Be ready to travel, my lady. To travel, and to see marvels you have never seen before."

He went to the door, then turned back. "Oh, one more thing," he said. "Those servants of yours. Who were they? Why did the armor warn me against them?"

"Lady Angarred and her husband—" Efcharren said.

"The magician!" Drustig said. He stalked back and forth, glancing out the door and then returning. "What were they doing in your house, and in disguise? Were you helping them spy on me?"

"No," Efcharren said. "No, my lord. I don't know why they disguised themselves. They—"

"You don't know? That's hard to believe, milady. You accepted them as your servants easily enough."

"I—I didn't realize—"

Once again Drustig seemed to calm himself. "Well, never mind. You didn't know that they're enemies of mine, and dangerous fugitives besides. If they come back you'll hold them for me, won't you?"

"Yes, of course," Efcharren said.

"Good day, then," Drustig said.

Her mother went to the front door with Drustig, speaking softly as if gentling a wild animal. Caireddin barely noticed them. She was thinking of Drustig's words, that she would see marvels. What would that be like? She couldn't imagine.

She felt hot, flushed. She wanted to leave immediately, this moment, to ride far away from Ou and her cramped, useless life.

Efcharren came back into the room. "Well," she said. "It looks as if my little girl is getting married. Are you certain this is what you want?"

Was it? Was this trembling, this excitement, love? She remembered Tarkennin saying that Drustig was completely mad, remembered the flaring of anger she had seen in the lord's eyes.

No—she loved him, she truly did. He was the only person who understood her, who recognized the restless, caged feeling that made her want to lash out and destroy something. Who understood it and more than matched it: after all, he planned to overthrow a king.

"Of course," she said.

"Come along, then," her mother said. "We have a great deal to do. What kind of dress would you like to be married in?"

Mathewar and Angarred sat amid the rugs and blankets and pillows of the caravan. Mathewar had not given much consideration to the Travelers; he had thought he was done with them. But now, as they left the pocket-sized village and headed down the main road, he remembered again how they had played with him and Angarred, how he had spent an agonizing week thinking she was dead.

He had learned several ways to keep his anger in check, and had in turn taught these disciplines to his students. This was necessary; magicians who acted irrationally were dangerous to themselves and others. He called on these methods to calm himself, but it took him a good while before he no longer wanted to blast Reti to ashes. And even after that he continued to think of ways to terrify the man, to keep him from interfering ever again.

When the caravan had gone a good distance away from the house Reti stopped and came back to join them. "What did you stay for?" Mathewar asked, standing.

"Matte!" Angarred said. She turned to Reti. "Thank you—you saved our lives."

"Thank you, yes," Mathewar said. "Now tell me why you didn't leave yesterday."

"I thought you might be in danger," Reti said.

"All right," Mathewar said. He had been leaning against a wall, his arms crossed. Now he stepped forward and stood close to Reti. "We need to stop somewhere, get some horses."

"I'm going back to the camp," Reti said. "I'll help you find horses tomorrow, if you like."

"We need them now," Mathewar said, using his compelling voice. "We have to leave as soon as possible. A murderer sits on the throne of Karededin, and a madman is coming to challenge him."

"Yes, we understand this," Reti said. "We're going to discuss it, see what we want to do."

"You mean the Travelers?"

"The Forsaken, yes."

"What can you possibly do? Steal their vases?"

"We've been talking about this for a while now," Reti said, ignoring him. "We think that the time is ripe for us to go to Karededin. That Mathona's teachings might fall on fertile soil there."

Mathewar wondered briefly when they had had this discussion; he had never heard a whisper of it. And what else hadn't he known? He had thought he'd shared in the Travelers' lives, but apparently they had kept him outside, their secrets hidden from him.

"And you can't take us to get horses," he said.

"There isn't anywhere on the way," Reti said.

"I'll have to take your word for that, I suppose," Mathewar said.

"Matte!" Angarred said again.

Reti bade them farewell and headed up front, and the caravan began to move again.

"Why in the name of the Orator were you so rude to him?" Angarred asked.

"Why are you so polite?" Mathewar asked. "They knew where we were, both of us, knew we were looking for each other, and they didn't bother to tell us. I spent a week thinking you might be dead, all because of them."

"That *was* strange," she said. "I'm just so glad they found you I'd forgive them anything, I suppose. But why didn't they tell you where I was?"

"I have no idea. They want to teach people, show them the error of their ways, though what business it is of theirs I don't know."

"What do you mean? How do they teach people?"

He described the things he had seen them do, told her why, for example, they had stolen Lady Efcharren's vase. "I'm certain they wanted me to learn something from all this, but I'm afraid I disappointed them—I have no idea what it could be."

She hesitated a moment, then said, "I think I know."

"Do you? What is it?"

"Promise you won't get angry first."

"Of course I won't."

"Well, I think—well, things come easily to you. You learned magic quickly, and then you became the king's magician, and then First Master . . . Well, you haven't had too many setbacks in your life."

"What!" he said.

"You said you wouldn't get angry."

"I'm not angry. But how can you say . . . My first wife died, for Mathona's sake. Surely you would call that a setback. At the very least."

"Yes, of course. But that's what I'm saying—you didn't know how to respond to tragedy. It was as if you just gave up, you avoided thinking about it. You withdrew into sattery—"

"A doctor gave it to me—"

"All right. But you blamed yourself—"

"Because it was my fault—"

"And when you thought I was dead you blamed yourself for that too, didn't you? And you told me you thought Jerret's death was your fault."

"And that shows me avoiding tragedy, or whatever it was you said? It shows just the opposite—that I take responsibility for my failures."

"But you weren't responsible."

"I was, though. If I'd stayed in Karededin I could have saved Jerret from the Harus."

"How could you have known he was in danger?"

She sounded like Reti. "I should have. That's what magicians do. If I hadn't freed Nim, if I could have seen clearly—"

"You did what you thought best. But for the first time in a long time you were wrong, you made a mistake. And you're not used to it. You think you can't fail like other people."

"Don't be ridiculous—"

"Tell me you didn't think of sattery when you heard Jerret had died. Or when you thought I was dead."

"Of course I didn't." He spoke the lie without thinking; in the heat of the argument he had forgotten that she often knew his thoughts. "And even if I did, I don't see what that proves. I think about it every day, sometimes every hour."

"All right," she said. She sat back against the wall of the caravan. "I don't know what to tell you, then. I thought that the Travelers might be teaching you humility, how to accept failure. That when you take responsibility for everything it's a form of arrogance, because you think no one can make things right but you. I must be wrong, though."

She was; she had to be. He had failed before, and hadn't wrapped himself in the comfort of sattery. He remembered the night he had drunk glass after glass of Mathona's Tears, and he put that out of his mind, to think about later.

"What did they hope to teach you, then?" he asked.

"Nothing, I think. They didn't seem to think very much about me."

"So you're perfect, is that what you're telling me?"

"No, of course not. They just cared more about you, I think."

He said nothing. In the silence they heard the horse's hooves and the jingling of the bells.

They reached the Travelers' camp by late afternoon, just as Remi and Neri began to serve supper. Mathewar introduced Angarred to the rest of the family, and they all went into the kitchen caravan to eat. He felt uncomfortable; he had thought he would never see these people again and now here he was, accepting their hospitality once more.

The caravan smelled deliciously of roast goose. He ate very little, unwilling to take anything from them, but Angarred praised the food and accepted another helping from Neri.

They would talk and make plans after supper, probably. He decided to wait them out; if they intended to talk privately they would have to tell him outright to go away. But they surprised him, as they often did; after they passed around the bottle of Mathona's Tears Reti turned to him and asked if he wanted to stay.

Perversely, he decided not to. He and Angarred went outside and walked around the camp. The sun had set, leaving behind the chilly night of Ou. The waning moon shone above them. She did not want to argue, he saw, relieved, and neither one of them mentioned their earlier discussion.

"I have an idea about that half crown," he said. "Polgar said that his father put something on his head when he created Bound Folk. I wonder if it's the other half, if the two were once one. And now each has half the power, one to bind and one to loose."

"But how did it get broken in the first place?" Angarred asked.

"Perhaps it was used in the Sorcerers' Wars, and then broken to diminish its power," he said. "And if the two joined together again they might create something very dreadful and very powerful, something no one's seen since Tobrin's day."

"Wouldn't Tobrin have bound that power into the Stone?"

"He told me once that he never traveled beyond the mountains. He was very old at the end of the Wars, and probably tired from all the work he had done. And the magicians have always known that there are still powerful magics in Goss and Ou."

"But—either Drustig or Cullen will win the war. One of them will get the other half of the crown in spoils, and will almost certainly put the two together. And—"

"We'll have to stop them," he said. He smiled tiredly.

"How?"

"I haven't the faintest idea. But now you see why I'm so anxious to get back to Karededin."

The Travelers began to sing, their shivery voices calling to the moon.

The next day the Travelers brought them to a horse trader. It was only then that Mathewar realized he had very little money, barely enough to buy an ancient broken-down nag for each of them. He said nothing about this to the Travelers, but Reti sensed his dilemma somehow and offered to pay for their horses.

"No, thank you," Mathewar said. He nearly asked Reti where he had stolen the money but he restrained himself; there was no point in starting an argument now.

"What if I give you a loan?" Reti said.

"And how will we repay you?" Mathewar asked. "We'll probably never see you again."

"There have been stranger meetings."

"All right," Mathewar said, with ill grace.

He and Reti said a cold, polite farewell. Reti climbed to the front of the first caravan. "Look for us in Karededin!" he called to them.

"We will!" Angarred said. "Good-bye!"

They got a horse for each of them and headed south.

# TWENTY-TWO

After the excitement faded Caireddin realized, a little startled, that Drustig had not set a date for their wedding. When she mentioned this to her mother Efcharren said that of course they would marry before they left; she was so certain of it that she had already asked her friends and neighbors to the ceremony.

Caireddin wasn't so sure. What if Drustig decided to wait until he became king? Would he delay the wedding until Efcharren traveled all the way to Karededin?

She had another problem as well, but it was not one she could discuss with her mother. Would Drustig expect her to be a virgin? Her friends had frequently gone wenching, as they called it, and she had gone with them, finding a man to bed while they disappeared with their own female companions. She had not found as much pleasure in it as they had, though, and after a while she had stopped going; perhaps, she had thought, this was something men enjoyed more than women did. Still, she was more experienced than most brides. An ordinary man would mind, she thought, but surely Drustig, who could see into her very soul, would understand why she had done it.

Drustig blew into the household like a storm, his cloak trailing behind him like rain clouds. "Are you packed?" he said to Caireddin. "Let's go."

She glanced at her mother. "When—when are we getting married?" she asked.

"Married?" he said. "In Karededin, of course. The religious have to perform the ceremony, otherwise the people won't accept us as man and wife."

"But we'll wait for my mother to come, won't we?"

He frowned. Even in the short time she had known him she had learned his expressions, and she recognized this as a sign of impending anger. "I can't think of that now," he said impatiently. "Come on, let's go. My men are waiting, and Karededin lies before us."

She looked at Efcharren again. "I'm coming with you," Efcharren said.

"Mother!" Caireddin said.

"That's impossible," Drustig said. "You'll just be in the way."

Efcharren studied him, her eyes level. Once again he seemed to realize he said the wrong thing. "I'm sorry, milady," he said. "I've grown too used to the rough manners of war. All soldiers are coarse, I'm afraid, and mine are even coarser than I am. So you see, an army camp is no place for a woman in your position—you would be appalled at what goes on there."

"I've seen worse," Efcharren said. "I'm coming with you."

"Yes, of course you have," Drustig said.

Caireddin glanced at him sharply. Was he referring to her mother's life before she became King Tezue's mistress? He returned her gaze, his eyes bland.

"If you're coming you'll have to hurry," he said. "My men are waiting, as I said."

Efcharren went up the stairs. Drustig frowned after her and said something too low for Caireddin to hear.

Her mother returned a moment later, wearing a simple shirt and trousers; Caireddin had never seen them before. She carried a traveling bag of fine leather. She seemed purposeful, no longer the dithering woman who could not even choose between two paintings.

"Are we ready then?" Drustig asked. He smiled, showing most of his teeth. "Good. Let's go."

Caireddin and Efcharren got their horses from the stable at the end of the street, and the three of them set off.

They stopped at an inn for the night, and met up with Drustig's forces the next day. The army stretched out as far as Caireddin could see, a vast sprawl, men cooking, singing, arguing, staging mock battles. There were women among them as well, all different sorts, seamstresses and laundresses and cooks and prostitutes. The great crowd of people and horses had churned up the ground beneath them, turning it to a uniform field of mud and dirt. It stank of the sewage of hundreds, maybe thousands, of people, and of horses and sweat and leather and cooked meat.

Men came and took their horses. "I'll have to leave you ladies and go talk to my commanders," Drustig said. "My tent is up that way, the biggest one. Go make yourselves comfortable, and I'll see you later."

They walked carefully through the mud. Men whistled at them and called out lewd suggestions, but they both ignored them.

They found the tent easily; it was by far the largest in the row, made of cloth in various colors, purple and gold, red and black. Efcharren stood for a while, studying it, and then said, "Four colors. In Karededin only the king is allowed to have more than three. He has some gall, your Drustig."

The tent was furnished in luxury, with tables made of fine wood and leather chairs and thick carpets. Two sleeping pallets, each covered with silk and furs, stood at either end of the tent.

"We'll have to get you a bed," Caireddin said to her mother.

"Not at all," Efcharren said. She bent to one of the pallets and in a few minutes had fixed up a soft nest of blankets. "I suppose he won't want to bed you until you're married."

Caireddin blushed, and turned away to hide it. She could be as coarse as any of her friends, but she found it almost impossible to talk to her mother about the dealings of men and women. The very fact that Efcharren knew so much about the subject, more than anyone Caireddin had ever met, filled her with intense embarrassment.

They waited for Drustig for what seemed like hours. A bell rang out over the camp. They peered out of the tent and saw a long line of people waiting for supper, each carrying a tin plate. Women at the front were ladling out something from a fat-bellied cauldron.

Caireddin wanted to join the line, but Efcharren felt certain that Drustig would take his supper with them. They stayed in the tent another hour, watching the line grow shorter. The smell from the cauldron—a greasy blend of vegetables and old meat—began to make them hungry. Finally they could not resist any longer; they found some plates and got in line.

"Look at this," the man in front of them said to his companion. "Are you ladies taken for the night?"

"I get the younger one," the other man said.

"The older one's not too bad, though."

"Yes, we're taken," Efcharren said coldly. "This is Drustig's intended wife, the daughter of King Tezue. Watch your mouth, or Drustig will close it for good."

"Drustig's wife?" The first man looked doubtfully at Caireddin. "I hadn't heard he was about to marry. What do you think—should we take them to our tents and show them some fun?"

"Better not," the second man said. "What if it's true?"

The first man laughed. "She wishes it were true! What would Drustig want with this—this mouse?"

"Still—" the second man said.

"All right, all right. We'll find some women with real meat on their bones."

The line shuffled forward. The men reached the front and turned their attention to the serving women. Someone dumped a watery mess on Caireddin's plate and then her mother's, and they hurried back to the tent.

They ate, then waited some more. Night came. Without discussing it Caireddin wrapped herself in the furs on the floor; her mother took the pallet. They slept.

They woke in the middle of the night. Drustig came into the tent, holding a bright lantern. Several men followed, laughing loudly at something. All of them smelled as if they had been drinking.

Light from the lantern fell on Caireddin. Drustig stepped back, as if he had forgotten she was there. "Who's this?" one of the men asked.

"Never mind," Drustig said. The men sat at one of the tables. Drustig unrolled some maps, and they talked and laughed until morning.

The entire camp packed up the next day, leaving the field strewn with chicken bones and horse dung and other garbage, and they headed south. The two women rode among the soldiers, ignoring their threats and jeers as best they could.

Each day seemed much like the one before it. The great apparatus of the army moved slowly, going ponderously past fields and orchards, towns and villages. They met almost no one on the roads—Drustig said that folks had heard rumors of his coming—but sometimes they saw farmers with a wagon-load of produce, or merchants carrying the latest shipments from the south. On some evenings a cold fog draped over the trees around them like fine cobwebs, and one day a white mist flowed through the road like a river. They stayed where they were that day, unable to see more than a foot in front of them. Drustig paced and cursed to his commanders, but the men refused to move, muttering about Ou's magic.

Caireddin rarely saw Drustig, who spent his time talking and planning with his officers. She understood, of course, that he was busy with important, weighty matters, but she could not help but wonder what had happened to that sympathy she had felt run between them. Could she have been so wrong about him? Perhaps he preferred men, or was uninterested in pleasure, or enjoyed war and fighting the way others enjoyed the delights of the bed.

She said nothing, though; she did not want to distract him from his responsibilities. It was Efcharren who finally said she had had enough; she was going to talk to Drustig and demand that they be treated better. "At the very least," she said, "we should have a servant to look after us. The Spinner knows what might happen to us among all these men."

"I don't know, Mother," Caireddin said uneasily. "He's very busy."

"Busy with what?" Efcharren asked. "Drinking and throwing dice?"

"With—with his plans," Caireddin said. "Plans for war."

"He should have it all worked out by now. And it's a good long while to Karededin—the ten minutes he spends talking to me can't possibly make a difference."

"Yes, but—but I don't want to make him angry."

"You can't go into a marriage thinking that way. If you don't stand up for yourself you've lost the battle before you start. You have to—"

"What do you mean, lost the battle? Marriage isn't a war."

"Oh, yes it is, and don't forget it. You want things, he wants things—and you have to make it clear to him that you won't back down. Otherwise everything will go his way, and what kind of life is that?"

"Marriage is based on love," Caireddin said.

Efcharren laughed scornfully.

"What do you know about it, anyway?" Caireddin said. "You've never even been married."

Two dull red spots appeared on Efcharren's cheeks. "Maybe not, but I've had more love than most wives," she said. "You listen to me—I know what I'm talking about. If you don't talk to Drustig I will."

"I wish you wouldn't."

"Wish for the sun to kiss you, and see what happens," Efcharren said.

She confronted Drustig when he came in with his friends that night, while Caireddin watched from her blankets and pretended to be asleep. "You can't treat a member of the royal family this way," Efcharren said. "If you don't respect her then none of your followers will. She's an investment, and she has to be protected like one. At the very least she should have a servant, or a guard."

Drustig laughed. "An investment, yes," he said. "But you're not, isn't that right? You're expendable." He laughed again, his eyes glittering coldly in the candlelight. "Let's go somewhere else," he said to his men. "This place has become a henhouse."

The next day, though, a soldier showed up at the tent and announced curtly that he would be their guard. He was an old man, one-eyed, his body pared down to ropes of muscle. He stood in front of the tent during the day, and went with them to get food at mealtimes, and he saw to it that they rode up at the front of the camp, with Drustig and his circle.

Caireddin and Efcharren both tried to talk to him, but he said nothing after that first introduction. It was as if, Caireddin thought, he regarded them as enemy captors. She couldn't blame him; serving as a guard for two women must be dreadfully boring after the things he had seen.

The train moved on. At some point they passed into Goss, but Caireddin only knew about it when she overheard Drustig talk to his men one night. "There are armies of Bound Folk in Goss," he said. "My contemptible brother Cullen sent them. Keep an eye out, and let me know if you see any. I'll blast them back to Karededin, give Cullen a taste of what I can do."

But they encountered no one as they went forward. Drustig paced, eager for a fight, and wondered aloud why Cullen had pulled back his troops, whether it was a trick or if his brother could truly be such a simpleton. And Caireddin had to admit she wouldn't mind some excitement; it seemed they passed the same trees and houses over and over again, the same birds hovering in the sky.

They saw no more of the unnatural mist, though; there was less magic in Goss than in Ou. They began to pass a few trees turning gold, and Caireddin realized that Autumn was coming. Clouds filled the sky, some days, and a cold wind blew.

One afternoon their scouts came riding back with news: they had seen an army camped over the next hill. "They're not Bound Folk, though," one of the scouts said. "I think they're what's left of the Gossek army fighting Karededin."

Drustig grinned. "They haven't heard the rest of the country's given up, I suppose," he said. "Well, they'll die as easily as Bound Folk."

"Shouldn't Caireddin move back, away from the fighting?" Efcharren asked.

"Not at all," Drustig said. "She'll be in no danger here, I promise you. And she can watch me triumph over my enemies."

He reached into his saddlebag and brought out what looked like a sickle or half moon. No, it was half a crown, Caireddin realized. He set it on his head and rode out before his men.

The "army" the scouts had reported was a ragtag group of men, maybe twenty of them. They dropped what they were doing and hurriedly faced Drustig's army, fumbling with their weapons. Drustig drew his sword and galloped toward them, his long black hair flowing out behind him.

Caireddin watched him, thrilled. He looked magnificent out there all alone, one man against an army.

He laughed loudly. Someone screamed, a harsh, strange sound in the quiet afternoon. Another fell to the ground and curled up into a ball, muttering to himself. A few men broke away and ran aimlessly down the road.

The first man kept screaming. His eyes were wide, as if he saw horrors he could not comprehend. Most of the others had gone, all but one who crawled on his hands and knees down the road, as slow as if he traveled over broken glass.

Drustig's horse reared. His sword flashed in the sunlight. The men cheered, and he rode back toward them, grinning.

"What—what was that?" Caireddin asked. "What did you do?"

"That was what will make me king of Karededin," Drustig said. "And make you queen beside me."

"But what was it? Why do you wear that crown?"

"What does it matter? The battle's won, and not one of my men killed."

Her excitement was beginning to turn sour in her stomach. She had expected to see great deeds, heroism, the stuff of ballads. Instead Drustig had turned all those men into fools and lunatics, without a single moment's danger to himself.

"It doesn't seem—" she began.

Suddenly Drustig looked back at the road. In his blind, panic-stricken flight one of the men had run straight into Drustig's army. Drustig laughed again and the man changed course abruptly and fell into the bushes by the side of the road.

"But how can you—" Caireddin said.

Drustig turned to her. Power flowed out from the crown and touched her mind. She was caught in a maelstrom with nothing to hold on to, everything a blur of sounds and shapes. She heard singing, and then a great many people shouting at her, and then the land itself blew away like a piece of paper in the wind. A voice called to her, telling her to flee, and she turned and turned, trying to get clear. . . .

She came back to herself slowly. Drustig's face hung before her, blotting out the sky, a second sun. "You were fortunate," he said. "That was only a small moment of what those men experienced. You will never question me again."

She said nothing. "What is it?" Efcharren asked. "What happened?" Caireddin shook her head.

A few hours later the sun began to set, and the army stopped and made camp. The guard escorted Caireddin and her mother to supper, then brought them to Drustig's tent and left them.

When she was certain they were alone Caireddin turned to her mother and said in a low voice, "I changed my mind. I don't want to marry Drustig."

"What happened to you out there today?" Efcharren asked.

"I saw something of his mind," Caireddin said. "He's cruel, and—and he enjoys it. He doesn't love me, or anyone else. He can't."

Efcharren sighed. "Did you truly think—" She shook her head, as if amazed at her daughter's innocence. "Well, it doesn't matter. We have to get away. We'll wait until night and then find our horses."

"Can't we just tell him? He can find someone else to marry. He isn't interested in me, anyway."

"Haven't you learned anything from me? He wants you for your lineage, your blood. That's all. If you tell him you're leaving he'll keep you locked up like a criminal. That's if you're fortunate—he might just kill you so no one else can have you."

Caireddin said nothing. She had thought of herself as a sophisticate, an observer of others' foibles, and here she was, enmeshed in a stupid trap of her own making. Her mother was right: she had frittered her days away, learning nothing.

They settled down to sleep. Caireddin thought she would stay awake for hours, but when she next opened her eyes she saw her mother looking out the tent flap, a triangle of darkness beyond.

"It's time," Efcharren whispered. "Let's go."

They packed their few belongings, wrapped themselves in their cloaks, and left as quietly as they could, heading toward the horse pickets. A sliver of moon shone out for a moment; then clouds returned, shutting it up again, and the only light came from tents and campfires. A few people still walked through the camp, carrying messages, heading toward assignations. Sentries paced in the distance.

It had rained during the day here, turning all the dirt to mud. Someone had set a few boards down, and they stepped from one to another carefully. They reached a grove of trees; the ground under it was nearly dry, and soldiers lay sprawled wherever they had come to rest. Caireddin nearly put her foot on one in the darkness and jumped back just in time.

When they came out from the trees they heard the muffled movements of the horses. They began to hurry. A loud crack sounded. Caireddin looked around wildly and saw that her mother had stepped on one of the boards and broken it. They stood still a long moment, holding their breath, but no one woke.

The moon gleamed fitfully. They reached the first of the horses just as the clouds returned.

"Fury," Caireddin called softly. "Fury."

Fury whickered. She ran toward him. He called again, catching her scent. He was truly the mildest of horses; she had named him as a joke. She had done everything as a joke, up until this moment. She reached him, put her arms around his neck.

"Going riding?" someone said.

It was Drustig. Impossibly, he stood there in the night, his eyes and teeth seeming to shine in the dark. "You're valuable, as your mother says," he said. "An investment. Don't you think I keep an eye on you?"

The guard, Caireddin thought. He must have stayed near the tent, watching us.

Efcharren moved out of the shadows. No, Caireddin thought. No, stay back, stay hidden. But Efcharren came forward until she stood next to her.

"And where did you think you were going, this fine night?" Drustig asked her.

Neither of them answered. Caireddin, with a thrill of fear, remembered the half crown. He wasn't wearing it; she looked at his hands but could not make out anything in the dark.

"Well, you won't do it again, by the Warrior," Drustig said. He reached for something at his side. Weakness flowed through her and her knees buckled; she nearly fell but managed to hold on to Fury. "No," she said. She had wanted to scream, but it came out as a whisper.

Drustig laughed. He raised his hand. Something gleamed, a long curved knife. In one quick movement he lifted the knife and slit Fury's throat.

The horse cried out. It was not like anything she had ever heard; it sounded like a scream of terror from everything that had ever lived and died. Fury tried to rear, kicked out, shrieked again. His eyes flashed. Blood poured from his neck; it looked black in the darkness.

The horse fell to the ground. The dreadful howl continued, though, on and on, and at last she realized that it was coming from her. She remembered her dagger finally and unsheathed it, then lashed out at Drustig, heedless of the knife.

Two men grabbed her from behind. One forced back her wrist, making her drop the dagger. A third man moved out of the shadows and took hold of Efcharren. "She has teeth, does she?" Drustig said. He bent and picked up the dagger. "Give me their bags."

The men stripped them of their bags and threw them to Drustig. He opened Efcharren's first and reached inside. "Well, well," he said, lifting out a handful of rings and coins and bracelets, their colors muted in the dim light. He tossed them up and down a few times. "Caireddin's dowry. I think I'll break with tradition and take it before the wedding."

He threw the bags back to the guards and moved down the line, stopping at Efcharren's horse Sugar. "And this is yours, isn't it?" he said pleasantly to Efcharren.

He raised the knife. Caireddin closed her eyes, but she could not block out the horse's terrible squeal. When she looked again Sugar lay slumped on the ground next to Fury.

"The other horses will be guarded from now on," Drustig said. "And if you try to leave I'll kill you both. Efcharren, I'll kill you second, so you can watch your daughter die."

# TWENTY-THREE

To Cullen's delight Lady Melleth had agreed to become his mistress. He spent a good deal of his time with her, ignoring his obligations; his last council meeting, where he had decided to send Polgar north, had been three weeks ago.

He was in bed with Melleth when a knock came at the door. "Go away," he called out. Melleth giggled.

"We've spotted ships from Finbar, my liege," Dobrennin Steward said. "They're a few days out from Karededin."

It was nearly Autumn; he had assumed the Finbarek had given up on the idea of war. "Why bother me about it now?" he said.

"We've engaged them in battle, sir," the steward said. "I'll let you know if they manage to land."

"Good, good," Cullen said.

Three days later Dobrennin knocked at the door again. This time Cullen was alone, planning a banquet and wondering what exotic foods would impress his new lover. "Come!" he said.

"We couldn't stop the Finbarek ships, my liege," the steward said. "They've reached Pergodi Harbor."

Cullen looked up from his desk. He hadn't given any thought to the attack from Finbar since Dobrennin told him about it, and now he felt a first tinge of fear. "Well, what are we doing about it?" he asked sharply.

"Our men are heading toward the harbor now," Dobrennin said.

Cullen stood and called for his body servant. "I'll need my armor and my sword," he said to the man. "Oh, and make certain the groom readies my horse, the new one. And I should—"

Lord Enlandin had entered behind Dobrennin. "With respect, my liege, you should not risk your life," Enlandin said. "It's far too dangerous. We need you here."

Cullen wanted desperately to be at the harbor, battling alongside his troops; fighting was the thing he knew best. No one had ever accused him of a lack of courage. But Enlandin was right; the king must be kept safe. Who would take charge of the country if he died? There was only Polgar.

"Your councilors are on the western balcony," the steward said. "You can see how the battle goes from there."

Cullen nodded and followed the two men. As he left his apartments the guards at the door moved into position behind him.

When they reached the balcony he saw that others besides the councilors had come out to watch the battle. There was Iltarra, with Lord Annin, of course, and Lady Dubbish, that incurable busybody, and another old courtier from Tezue's days, Lady Karanin.

Everyone stood when he came in, and Dobrennin ushered him to a chair at the front. He heard the rustle of fine clothes as the councilors and nobles took their seats after him.

What were they all doing here? Did they think the battle some sort of entertainment; were their days so tedious that they found blood and death exciting? Some of the nobles had even brought trays of cheese or sugared cakes to the balcony, and were eating between glances at the harbor.

Cullen turned back to look at his sister. She gazed out over the water impassively, ignoring him. For the most part he believed that she had fallen in love with Annin, but every so often he wondered if she and Ezlin had conspired against him. Why else had she tried to talk him out of binding Talethe? Did she hope for a victory for Finbar now, was she waiting for Lord Ezlin to ride heroically to the castle and sweep her in his arms? But Lord Annin was at her side as always, and he would be inconvenient, to say the least.

He looked out at the roofs and turrets and battlements of the castle tumbling down the hillside. Beyond them lay the city, and then the harbor. The ships, both Karedek and Finbarek, appeared tiny, like gnats fighting in a pool of water.

As he watched he became impatient again, and angry. It was bitterly strange that he should sit up here, out of danger, when the Harus, he and Noldeth and Drustig, had been famed for their prowess in battle. There hadn't been a major war in his lifetime, but he had fought in border skirmishes in Takeke and Goss, and he had ridden in Drustig's uprising against Jerret until Jerret's army had overcome them. A war was coming, though, either with Ezlin or with Drustig. He found himself looking forward to it, eager to show off his skill in battle. He would meet Drustig and overcome him, settling their rivalry once and for all.

Thinking about his brother reminded him of Polgar. Even Polgar was a decent soldier; he fought well on horseback, though he was useless if his horse fell. But Polgar had gone north, to fetch the troops of Bound Folk. Cullen counted to himself, working out the number of days it would take Polgar to get to the mines and come back. The man should have been here already if he hurried—what was he playing at? Perhaps it took longer to travel with a large group of men, even Bound Folk. Or was he deliberately slowing the journey?

The day wore on. He could see very little from the balcony, just that the positions of the ships changed slowly in relation to each other. Sometimes he couldn't even tell which ships were his and which belonged to Finbar.

He began to feel hungry, and he reached over and took one of Lady Dubbish's cakes. She glared at him with her bird's eyes and he smiled at her; surely she wouldn't dare argue with the king. She drew her chin in closer to her chest, and he took another cake, just to spite her.

As evening fell, Cullen sent Dobrennin to order the servants to bring supper. Soon after the steward had gone a few of the councilors began to murmur and point down to the water. Finally, Cullen saw, something was happening: one of the Karedek ships was slowly listing to the side, and a few of the Finbarek moved toward shore.

The sun blazed across the ocean as it set. In the last moments of the day the Finbarek loosed burning arrows and two Karedek ships burst into flame, shining on the water as if the sun had ignited them.

The rest of the Finbarek ships sailed to shore, and the battle moved to the harbor. Cullen tightened his fists in anger. What were they doing down there? If only he hadn't sent Sorle north with Polgar; the old soldier would have reduced the ships to kindling by now.

How had the Finbarek defeated his navy so easily? Enlandin had said that the new troops weren't ready for battle, but why hadn't the council anticipated this and started training them earlier?

He looked around the balcony for Enlandin and spotted him in the shadows at the back. Perhaps he would have him sent to the dungeons when this was over. The thought cheered him for a moment.

When he turned back to the port he could see nothing; everything was drowned in darkness. Then small lights sprang up; both sides were kindling fires against the cold. "I want someone at the harbor," he said without looking away. "And then come back here and tell me what's going on."

He did not hear anyone move, and he turned around quickly. Where was Dobrennin? Then he remembered that the steward had gone for supper. His gaze slid over Iltarra and Annin and settled on one of the councilors. "You," he said. "Move."

The councilor seemed about to argue, then changed his mind and hurried out. Cullen relaxed back into his chair. For a moment he had had the dreadful feeling that they had all gone, deserted him, thrown in their lot with the deceitful Finbarek.

The night grew chilly before the councilor returned. The servants came back with food and were sent away again, this time for cloaks and furs and lanterns. Finally the man hurried onto the balcony, panting, and bowed before him.

"My liege," the councilor said.

"Yes, yes, hurry up," Cullen said.

"The Finbarek hold the harbor, but the fighting has stopped for the night," the man said. "And a good many of our men are camped around them, waiting for dawn."

"Are there enough of them, do you think?"

The man hesitated. Cullen nearly hit him, but he began to speak again. "I don't know," he said. "I think so."

"You *think* so?"

"Y-yes, my liege."

Cullen sighed loudly. "Someone go down there and get me an accurate count, for the Warrior's sake," he said. Then, remembering the last time, he turned and nodded to his guards. Several of them saluted and headed out.

Cullen peered into the dark anxiously. It would take at least an hour before they came back and probably more—he had only dolts and donkeys to work with.

No one said anything for a long while. He looked down at the plate in his lap and realized he had eaten everything on it; he couldn't remember tasting anything. He handed it negligently to one of the councilors.

Stars shone brightly, reflecting the constellations of fires at the harbor. They could see the white sails and black hulls of the ships, rocking softly at the piers. There seemed to be more of them, Cullen thought. Probably some had come ashore after the Finbarek captured the harbor.

The guards returned. Their report was, if anything, more useless than the councilor's. One of them thought the Finbarek had more men, one had counted more Karedek, and two thought both sides were equal.

Where was that clod Polgar? Why hadn't he hurried? He had known his errand was urgent. Cullen stood and gathered his cloak around him. "I'm going to my rooms," he said. "I don't want to be disturbed."

"What if—" one of the councilors said.

"You heard me," Cullen said angrily. "No interruptions."

He strode from the balcony, his guards following. The councilors filed out after him, hurrying to get out of the cold.

Once inside his apartments he nodded to four of the guards. "I want you to go to the dungeons and bring me some prisoners," he said. "Young men, healthy ones."

When they left he took the half crown from the cabinet, quickly,

before he could change his mind. He held it and paced the apartment, wondering impatiently where the guards were. The night
would be over before he could finish his work.

"You should have started this sooner," his father said.

Cullen ignored him. A long time passed, and he thought his father
had finally gone away. Then the voice came again: "You might not
have enough time even now."

"Silence!" Cullen said. "I'm doing what you wanted—isn't that
good enough for you?"

"I just want to help," Noldeth said.

Cullen remembered that tone—aggrieved, as if he had only your
interests at heart, and you had failed him again.

Finally the guards came back. They stood before him, waiting
for orders, each of them holding firmly to one of the prisoners.
Cullen hesitated. Could he do this? But he had no choice; he
would lose the war if he didn't, and Karededin with it. He put on
the crown. "Yes," his father said. "Now you see. You see I'm
right."

The guards did not change expression; clearly they had not heard
the voice. He would think about that later, though. He looked at the
first man in line and said, "Thou art now bound to me. Go to the
harbor and help the Karedek soldiers against the enemy."

The man's face changed, became blank. The guards jerked back,
aghast. The newly made bound man walked with a steady, unnatural
gait to the door. The rest of the prisoners cried out and tried to pull
away, but Cullen continued down the row, making each of them
Bound Folk. When he finished he asked the guards for more men.

The guards grew more and more horrified as the night wore on,
until some were trembling uncontrollably and others would not
come into his room no matter how much he threatened them. And
the prisoners, too, began to beg and sob and cry out; they must have
realized what was happening when their fellows did not come back.
He began to use the guards only to fetch the prisoners, and set Bound
Folk to watch over the men once they were in his room.

By the time morning came he felt exhausted, and the right side of
his head hurt as if a weight had been dropped on it. He had not real-

ized how much work creating Bound Folk would be. He had sat down sometime during the night without noticing; now he took the crown off, rubbed his head, and closed his eyes.

When he woke the sun came through his windows; it was probably noon, or close to it. He stood quickly and hurried down the hall just as bells all over the city rang out for midday.

The councilors and nobles had gotten to the balcony before him. "Why didn't you wake me, you idiots?" he asked.

"You told us not to interrupt—"

"Never mind. Do any of you know how the battle's going, or should I get myself new advisors?"

"It looks as if we're winning," a man said. He spoke eagerly, as if pleased to have some good news. He pointed. "See? Some of the Finbarek ships are on fire, and those others are sailing away. And one of our men came to tell us we've driven the Finbarek back to the shoreline. We seem to have got . . ." He hesitated, his eager expression gone. "Some new men joined us during the night."

Cullen grinned at him. The man shrank back in his chair, understanding finally how the Karedek troops had gained the victory.

By evening it was over. Karedek soldiers marched into the castle with their prisoners, and Cullen moved to the Council Chamber to accommodate all of them. Lord Ezlin had been captured, he was pleased to see; he stood between two men, his normally florid face white and slack with terror.

"What do you think of your friend now?" Cullen asked Iltarra.

"I told you," she said. "He was never my friend."

"Iltarra!" Ezlin said, clearly astonished at her betrayal. "Can't you help me? Please, Iltarra—tell your brother not to kill me." He turned to Cullen and said quickly, "I renounce all claim to the Karedek throne, King Cullen. I'll go back to Finbar and never trouble you again. They'll pay a great ransom for me, anything you like."

Cullen smiled, enjoying the sight of the other man pleading before him. "Oh, I don't think I'll kill you now," he said.

"Thank you, my liege," Ezlin said. "Thank you. You won't regret—" He seemed to suddenly realize the full meaning of Cullen's

words. "What do you mean by 'now'? When will you—are you going to—"

"Take him to the dungeons," Cullen said, waving his hand.

The soldiers forced Ezlin away. He continued to cry out, to beseech Cullen. "Please, my lord. My liege. I'll pay anything, anything
you like. . . ."

His voice faded. "What are you going to do with him?" Iltarra
asked.

"I don't know yet," Cullen said. "Turn him into one of the
Bound Folk, maybe."

"Ah," she said. She left, Lord Annin trailing after her.

He watched her go. There seemed to be a great deal of meaning in
that one syllable, but, as always, he had no idea what she was thinking.
What did she feel toward Ezlin now? Why had she asked about his
fate if, as she said, there was nothing between them?

He looked over the rest of the prisoners but did not recognize any
of them. "Take these men's names, see if we can get a ransom for
them," he said. "Then send them to the dungeons as well."

Dobrennin Steward stood and brought over a pen, several sheets of
paper, and an ink pot. Cullen yawned; he'd had too little sleep last
night, and clerk's work always bored him. He could trust Dobrennin
to take care of the details. He stood and left the room.

Most work in the castle had stopped for some reason, and the boy was
the only one in the entire wing. He opened the door to one of the
apartments and carried his broom and rags inside, then started his
usual cleaning.

The mirror in the third bedroom caught his eye. He had seen it
many times—he couldn't remember how many—but now he walked
over and looked into it.

He saw a young man with hair cut so short it was difficult to tell
the color, though it might be brown. The eyes were brown too.

Who was he? He felt a sudden panic; his chest grew tight and he
could barely breathe. How could he not know his name?

He looked down at his hands. They were red and chapped, all the
nails broken. He could not remember seeing work-worn hands before; they looked as if they belonged to someone else.

The hands reminded him of something. He had an urgent errand, he had to talk to someone, to set something right . . .

The room around him started to grow dim. No, he thought in terror. Don't let me forget, please don't let me forget. I am . . . I am . . .

His eyes grew blank. He picked up his broom and began to sweep.

# TWENTY-FOUR

Polgar and Sorle returned five days after Cullen's victory over the Finbarek. Cullen had a moment of suspicion that Polgar might have planned it that way, but he put that thought aside. Sorle had kept an eye on his brother, and he trusted the man—for now, anyway.

The Bound Folk followed Polgar and Sorle into the courtyard. People watched from the roofs and windows of the castle, some amazed at the size of the army, some horrified by the sight of so many blank-eyed men marching in unison, singing their dull song to keep in step. A number of unbound men walked in the center, hemmed in by the rest of the regiment.

Cullen had been watching from one of the balconies; now he went down to meet them. "Hello, my brother," he said. "Lord Sorle."

He looked out over the army spread in front of him. From the ground there seemed to be more of them. Would he have to lead these men in battle? He had commanded men before, of course, but this would be very different, and he cursed his brother Drustig for forcing him into this position.

"We've built quarters for them on the jousting fields," he said. "This way."

He led them around to the new buildings. They had been thrown up hastily, with bad wood, and there were gaps in the roofs and walls. And now he saw that they were far too small; he hadn't had any idea of the size of the army Polgar would bring back.

"We'll put them to work building more," he said. "The Bound Folk are wonderful that way—they'll do anything you ask them. Eh, Brother?"

He nudged Polgar, hoping for some fellow feeling. With their father dead his brother was the only other person who had commanded Bound Folk, the only one who could understand the excitement mixed with dread that Cullen felt around them. And Polgar had created most of this army, far more than Cullen ever had. But his brother said nothing, just shaded his eyes and looked out over the vast throng.

What was he planning? Would he seize control of the army, try for the kingship like Drustig? He was the only brother so far who hadn't. Cullen would have to rebind these men, make certain they would obey only him.

"We brought a good many unbound young men to join your army," Sorle said. "You'll have to bind them as soon as possible."

Cullen nodded.

"And you'll need to feed them," Sorle said. "Some of them are half starved—there wasn't enough food for them along the way. And they'll need clothes, uniforms perhaps."

Now Cullen noticed that many of the Bound Folk looked ill, or far too thin. Most of them wore rags; several had no clothes at all, and sores or wounds festered along their bodies.

"Yes, of course," Cullen said. "Find someone to do that, would you, Sorle?"

Sorle nodded.

"If that's all I'll say good-bye," Polgar said. "It's been a long journey." He turned to go.

Cullen looked out over the Bound Folk. They were all his; they would do anything he asked. He shuddered.

Efcharren seemed to lose heart after the night they tried to escape. She knew what to do when a courtier sent a poem or a gift, Caireddin thought, or when he pretended to love another, but she

had never seen such brutality; it was out of her experience altogether.

They rode now in the baggage carts, or packed in with the turnips
and onions. At night they slept in a different, much smaller tent. Two
men guarded them wherever they went.

"Listen," Caireddin whispered one evening, "I have an idea. The
guards stand out at the front of the tent, isn't that right? All we have
to do is lift up the cloth at the back and we can escape."

Efcharren looked at her dully. "It's heavy," she said.

"Of course it's heavy," Caireddin said. "I didn't think this would
be easy. We have to leave, though. I can't marry him."

"You go."

"Oh, no. I'm not leaving you with that man." Caireddin thought
a moment. "Let's go tonight," she said. "It looks like it'll be overcast
again."

Her mother said nothing. But when Caireddin woke her that
night Efcharren joined her at the back flap of the tent. Caireddin
hadn't dared test it earlier, in case someone saw her; now when she
tried to lift it she saw that it weighed far too much for her alone.

"Help me," she whispered to Efcharren.

Efcharren pulled up on the cloth. Together they made a small gap
and put their heads through. Caireddin looked around quickly but
could see nothing in the enveloping dark. Was a guard standing a few
feet away, waiting for them? Was Drustig?

They pulled their weight forward with their elbows, wriggling in
the dirt to free their bodies. Finally they managed to stand. Mud covered both of them, and Efcharren's usually immaculate hair hung in
strands to her shoulders. Caireddin started to grin, then realized that
her mother would not find anything about their situation funny.

Efcharren moved toward the pickets again, but Caireddin pulled
her back. "They're guarding the horses now," she whispered.

"What will we do for horses, then?" Efcharren said.

Caireddin had been so impatient to get free she hadn't thought
that far ahead. "One thing at a time," she said.

They headed for the opposite side of the camp, toward a stand of
trees. A gray blanket of clouds covered the sky and she could see only
an arm's length in front of her—but that was good, it meant that

Drustig would be blind as well. She wondered if Drustig could see in the dark, like Tashtery in the Gossek and Ounek hell.

They passed under the shadow of the trees. Sheer darkness surrounded them now; they had to guide themselves by touch alone. She felt rough trunks and ragged leaves, and once she stepped on something soft and had to stifle a noise of disgust.

They hadn't entered a stand of trees, she thought a while later—this was a forest, with no end to it. Perhaps they could rest here, wait for daylight. An animal ran from them, rustling the undergrowth. Someone shouted, "Who's there?"

She stopped. Footsteps came toward them. Had they seen her? No, they couldn't have; they must have heard something. The steps moved closer.

She grabbed her mother's arm. "Run!" she whispered.

They hurried through the forest. A nearly full moon broke out from behind the trees and clouds, lighting a narrow path. Branches broke as they ran. Once her mother slid on a carpet of pine needles and went down. Once Caireddin found herself sprawled on the ground with no memory of what had happened; she had tripped on something, clearly, and the shock had driven it from her mind. Efcharren pulled her back up and she stood, ignoring dozens of aches.

After a while it seemed to her that they had run for hours. Sometimes they heard pursuing footsteps; a few times something scuttled or bounded away from them, some animal or other. She remembered Tarkennin saying that an animal in the forest was usually more afraid of you than you were of it. She hoped fervently that he was right, though she had no idea how he would know such a thing.

Finally her mother stopped, panting hard. Caireddin stopped as well. Once they had come to a halt she could not bring herself to move again, not if all Tashtery's legions were after her.

"They're gone," Efcharren said. "I think they've given up."

They listened awhile longer. The moon had set; by the light of the stars everything looked dull and vague. The silence felt excruciating; who knew who might be out there, waiting for them? She wanted to scream, to dare them to find her.

"There's no one there," Efcharren whispered.

"You're probably right," Caireddin said, risking a normal tone.

Nothing moved. They sat where they stood, in the middle of the trail. "What now?" Efcharren said. "We have no horses, no food, we don't know where we are . . ."

"No money," Caireddin said.

"Well, as to that . . ."

Efcharren lifted her shirt and tore out the hem, then held something out to Caireddin. She took it gingerly. A quick red light flashed across the gloom, like a spark from a fire. Her ruby necklace.

"I thought Drustig got everything," she said.

"I sewed this up before we left that first time," Efcharren said.

Caireddin laughed. An animal moved in the forest, going fast on four feet.

"Hush," her mother said.

She laughed again. What had seemed hopeless a moment ago might be possible; they might actually survive somehow. "Remember what I said," Efcharren said. "We don't have horses, or food—"

"It's all right," Caireddin said. "We'll get out of here."

"And where will we go? Drustig will send his men to watch the house." Efcharren sighed. "Look at us. Look at you, the daughter of kings . . ."

Her words reminded Caireddin of something. "We'll go to Pergodi, to Cullen," she said. "He wanted to marry me as well. And we'll tell him about Drustig's crown, his weapon—Cullen will want any information we can give him about his brother."

"Do you know how far it is to Karededin?" Efcharren asked. "It's hundreds of miles. And there are mountains on the border . . ."

Caireddin did not listen to the rest. She measured herself against the distance to Karededin, against the mountains. Could they do it? She hoped so, but she had no way of knowing: she had never been tested before.

They lay down on the hard ground and slept, and woke with the dawn.

Two days later nearly all her confidence was gone. They had deep scratches on their arms and faces, and their clothes hung in rags. Wildflowers and berries grew all around them but they had not eaten any; they did not know which ones were poisonous. The nights had been cold and full of the noises of animals, chirps and clicks and hoots, and once, horribly, they heard something howling, a lonely sound filled with anguish. Worst of all, they had not managed to find a way out of the forest. More than anything, more even than food, Caireddin longed for sight of an uninterrupted sky.

Efcharren stopped walking and dropped near a thicket of brambles. She ran her fingers over some berries; they were green, a strange, poisonous color. "I'm going to eat these," she said. "I'm so hungry I don't care anymore."

"Please don't," Caireddin said. "We'll get out soon, we'll find a town . . ."

"Will we? It seems to me we've been going in circles. I think I remember this hedge."

The hedge looked familiar to her too. She had tried to head south according to the position of the sun, but the trees had blocked the light and she had grown confused.

She took out her necklace and looked at the rubies, as thick as her little finger. It was probably the most valuable thing for a hundred miles, she thought bitterly, and at the same time it was completely worthless. You can't eat rubies, she thought. This seemed an important discovery, the answer to a thousand riddles, and she turned to her mother to share it with her.

"Look," Efcharren said softly.

"What? Where?"

"Hush. Over there. A man."

Now Caireddin could see him. He had long matted hair and filthy clothes; she had missed him because he had seemed a part of the forest. He appeared to be talking to himself, or perhaps to the trees.

"Should we ask him for help?" Efcharren said.

"He's crazy, Mother," Caireddin said. "He won't know anything. He probably doesn't even know who he is."

"Well, but we don't know anything either. And right now he's our only chance."

"What if he's dangerous?"

"He seems harmless to me."

Caireddin couldn't tell. She knew that her mother trusted men, trusted them overmuch perhaps; she had gained everything she had from men. "All right," she said. "We'll ask him. But be prepared to run."

An evil Karedek sorcerer had turned Brangwin's councilors into trees. He had to talk to them, though; they had to make plans for the coming battle. But he was having a good deal of trouble attracting their attention.

Trees whispered behind him and he turned quickly, wondering if some of them had finally broken free of the spell. But instead of his councilors he saw something completely unexpected. A woman.

She was beautiful, he thought, Mathona come down to earth. He stood transfixed. Then suddenly he remembered the sorcerer who plotted against him, and a terrible fear held him paralyzed for a moment. Was she an illusion too? Had the sorcerer sent her to weaken him?

Another woman, this one older, came behind her. He felt engulfed in confusion. Who was she? Who was the younger one, for that matter? She couldn't possibly be Mathona; he must have been mad to think so. He *was* mad.

"Hello," the first woman said. She smiled; the radiance of it nearly blinded him. "I wonder if you can help us. We seem to have gotten lost."

He squinted at her, trying to see through the light that surrounded her. His sorcerer enemy could not have made anything so fair. "Who are you?" he asked.

"My name is Lady Caireddin," the woman said. "And this is my mother, Lady Efcharren. We need someone to guide us out of this forest. Do you think you can help us? We can pay you."

She held out something, a handful of red. Berries, he thought. "Oh, we won't need to eat those. I can find you fish, and wild game—"

The two women glanced at each other. They looked puzzled; he had said something wrong, though he had no idea what it might have been. Finally the older one asked, "So you'll be our guide?"

He supposed he would—he had already offered to hunt for them. He nodded.

"What's your name?" the younger one—Caireddin—said.

What *was* his name? He had known it once, not too long ago. Brangwin. And with that a great deal came back to him. He had run away, had lived in the forest a long time: judging from the trees it had been nearly an entire season. He had been a prince of Goss once, but terrible things had happened to that country, things he didn't want to think about now.

He had taken too long with his answer; the women were looking at each other again. "Where do you want to go?" he asked.

"To Pergodi," Caireddin said.

Pergodi! The evil sorcerer lived there. No, there was no sorcerer; that had been part of his madness. But a dangerous magician did live in the capital—Mathewar, the man who had enslaved Goss. And Karededin was still his enemy; the minute he set foot in that country he would be captured and almost certainly killed.

Why did these women want to go there? He studied them, and to his surprise he realized that he knew them, he had met them before. Old Tezue's mistress and his illegitimate child, that's who they were. They had visited the Gossek court several years ago, and he had spent a tedious evening making polite conversation to them. Efcharren had wanted something, some political advantage, he couldn't remember what. Caireddin had been younger then, fourteen or fifteen, and nothing like the woman she had become.

Caireddin and her mother hadn't recognized him, though. He must have changed a great deal. He could go to Pergodi as the madman of the forest, perhaps even get close to Mathewar or King Jerret. He would be happy to kill either one of them.

"You don't have to take us all the way," Caireddin said. "We just want to get out of the forest."

"Perhaps you can take us over the mountains as well," Efcharren said.

He searched his mind for scraps from his old courtly life. "It would be an honor to accompany you ladies to Pergodi," he said.

"Thank you," Caireddin said. "What's your name?"

He couldn't give them his real name. He said the first thing that came to him, his cousin's nickname. "Daro."

Daro proved not to be as crazy as Caireddin and her mother had thought. He caught three fish with a rough spear he had probably made himself, then cooked them over a fire and served them with the berries Efcharren had wanted so badly. A few hours later he led them to the edge of the forest.

They spoke little that day, Efcharren because she did not usually speak to menials and Caireddin because she could not think of anything to say. The next morning Caireddin woke before anyone else and went out into a wide meadow to look for food. She found some more berries—what a lot of different berries there were!—and took a few to show Daro.

He was still asleep. She was starting to feel very hungry; she knelt beside him and shook his shoulder gently. In one swift uninterrupted movement he grabbed his spear and sat, and the next moment Caireddin found herself on the ground, the spear at her throat.

"Don't—" Caireddin said.

Daro had already moved back and set the spear down. "I'm very sorry, milady," he said.

She sat up and felt her throat carefully, but he did not seem to have pierced the skin. "I'm all right, I think," she said. "Are you—are you a soldier?"

He paused; he seemed to hesitate at every question they asked. "I was, yes," he said.

"Who did you fight for?"

Another hesitation, this one shorter. "For Goss," he said. "Against Karededin."

"Oh," she said. "Will it bother you to go to Karededin with us?"

As soon as she asked the question she wished she could call it back. Of course it would bother him—what did she think? "You don't have to come all the way," she said.

"I wouldn't mind seeing Karededin."

"Good."

"What about you, milady?" he asked. "What did you do?"

Without thinking she gave her usual answer. "Drank," she said. "Cheated at cards."

She couldn't open her mouth without sounding stupid, apparently.

Here was a man who had seen great hardship, who had fought a long and hopeless war and finally lost; he must think her impossibly frivolous, someone who had never done anything that mattered.

To her surprise, though, he seemed a little wistful. But the expression did not reach his eyes, which looked hard as stone. "How did you come to be wandering in the woods?" he asked.

"I ran away from my wedding," she said. Another frivolous answer, but she didn't want to tell him about Drustig. For one thing Drustig had invaded Goss; Daro might see anyone who knew him as the enemy. And she had a stronger reason as well: she did not want to admit how stupid she had been.

The sun rose above the horizon. She had not seen the sun whole for several days, only glimpses of it entangled in the trees; it had seemed trapped by the branches, caged. She watched now as the light grew clearer, and something lifted within her, as if she too were free now.

"Here we sit, and you had something you wanted to ask me," Daro said.

She had forgotten about the berries. She showed them to him and he said they were fit to eat, and they went to the meadow to gather more.

After their breakfast she and Efcharren went to a nearby stream to wash. When they returned to the camp they found that Daro had washed himself too, and had straightened out the tangles in his hair and beard as best he could.

They continued on. They reached a small town tucked against a river, and then a village large enough that Caireddin might hope to pass unnoticed. Daro helped her prise a stone from the necklace, while Efcharren looked on and clicked her tongue in regret.

When they finished, Caireddin set out into the village, searching for a pawnshop. Suby used to sell family heirlooms when he lost at cards and then buy them back when his luck changed; Caireddin had been in more of these places than she cared to remember. Efcharren followed her cautiously, looking startled by her daughter's expertise, and then astonished when she saw how well Caireddin haggled with the pawnbroker.

"We should go to another town for supplies," Daro said. "A young woman and her mother selling an expensive jewel is unusual enough, but pawnbrokers don't tend to gossip. But the longer we stay here the more people will come to hear of you. Including your betrothed, the man you ran away from."

He looked at her with the first sign of curiosity he had shown, but she said nothing.

They took the main road to the town, for the first time coming out in the open. Daro led them cautiously, studying trees and bends in the road for ambushes, glancing with suspicion at other travelers.

Caireddin felt exhausted. Her feet hurt from constant walking, and she longed for a horse; if they rode at least she would have different aching muscles to think about. Still, she saw the sense in what he said, and she followed wearily.

In the next town they bought bread and dried fruit, blankets, a tin for water, and several packs. Daro left them while they were examining horses; when he came back he wore a sword in a deerskin scabbard at his belt.

"I'll need a sword as well," Caireddin said. Drustig had taken her dagger along with everything else.

"Don't worry, milady," Daro said. "I'll protect you."

"Do you think I don't know how to use a sword?" Caireddin said. "I've fought in duels."

Once again she saw that wistful expression on his face, as if he longed to return to a more frivolous time. He said only, "It isn't that. No one should learn the arts of war except by necessity. If you start on that road you will never leave it, no matter what work you do in times of peace."

"I should think it's necessary now, don't you?" she said.

"Very well," he said, and they went to find a sword that would fit her.

# TWENTY-FIVE

With the horses Caireddin and her company were able to make better time. Their first day on the road they passed little but empty fields and ruined villages. Even more eerie were the villages that had been abandoned whole, the houses still standing, the crops growing. Dogs padded up and down the streets and chickens clucked in hen yards, waiting for masters who would never return.

"What—what happened to the people here?" Caireddin asked once.

"They became Bound Folk," he said.

Drustig had mentioned the Bound Folk as well. But when she pressed Daro for more he said nothing.

She wondered how well he knew the land, if he had seen these towns and villages while people still lived in them. That afternoon he stared at a tangle of briars, and it looked as if there were tears in his hard eyes. Then he turned away, and she thought she must have imagined it.

"What is it?" she asked.

"A hedge," he said.

"I know it's a hedge. You were looking at it now as if it meant something to you."

She hadn't expected an answer, but to her surprise he said, "It's called Briar Hedge, milady. There was a great battle here, with so many dead they could not be buried. The villagers nearby planted briars around the bodies so the wolves wouldn't dig them up."

"Oh," she said. She wanted to say more, to express her sympathy, but she could not find the words.

"You asked about the Bound Folk, milady," he said. "This—all of this is their work. The Binder in Karededin takes away their will, and then orders them to destroy the people of Goss. The Karedek are a cowardly folk, too cowardly to do their fighting themselves."

She realized something then. "So when you went into battle against the Karedek you—"

"We fought Bound Folk, yes."

"Can they be fought?"

"No."

A picture came to her, a great formation of soldiers, men who would not turn back for fear or because the battle was going against them. And when they died the Binder simply made more, and yet more, sending out wave after wave of them.

"Why did you do it, then?"

"Everyone asked me that. I don't know. Because the act was important, even if we died performing it."

She saw now what his life must have been like, a series of grim battles, fought out of a hatred of tyranny. Fought out of selflessness, with no hope of reward.

And the war had burned him to the bone, burned away all politeness and hypocrisy. He spoke honestly because he could not do otherwise. It was terrifying to be near such truthfulness, and she wondered what he thought of her, whether she found favor in that severe gaze.

"Who is the Binder?" she asked.

"I don't know," he said.

He rode on ahead of her; the gesture said as clearly as words that he no longer wanted to talk.

The next day, though, he was the one who started the conversation. "Why didn't you get married?" he asked.

"It was an arranged marriage," she said. There it was, her first lie. "I found I couldn't stand the man."

"You must be someone important then, milady."

"Not important enough to be called 'milady' all the way to Pergodi," she said. "My name's Caireddin. I'm, well, a minor piece in the game. But I have a good name—the man would have benefited a great deal from the marriage."

"Ah."

She felt shabby, hiding her identity from him. "I'm King Tezue's daughter, actually."

He didn't seem as surprised as he should have been. Well, probably her lineage made no difference to him—though she had heard that the Gossek set a great store by such things. "Who are your parents?" she asked.

"No one of importance. Anyway, I was the second son—I never expected to inherit anything."

"Was? Do you mean your brother died? I'm sorry to hear it."

"Yes, milady. Caireddin."

"Will you inherit now?"

"There's nothing to inherit. The entire country is destroyed, including my—my family's land."

"I'm sorry," she said again.

"Well," he said, clearly wanting to change the subject. "It's odd what you grow up to expect. I never thought I'd have much. But you—you must have known from the beginning that you had a great future."

She had never really considered it. "I don't remember a time when I didn't know I was someone important. People treated me differently, and my mother wouldn't let me forget who I was for a moment." She turned, but Efcharren was too far to hear her. "But, well, there's no shortage of queens in the world. No one needs me. I suppose I never expected much either."

"Are you going to Pergodi to get married?"

"I don't know," she said. "I'll have to see what happens." At least, she thought, that wasn't exactly a lie.

"Be careful, milady. The Karedek are treacherous. And they're greedy for power—they even study magic to get it."

They rode without speaking for a while. She warmed to him, glad that he trusted her enough to satisfy her curiosity. And for the first time she noticed how handsome he was beneath all the rags, his long, lean body, the sun shining on his newly washed hair. He rode expertly; he and the horse seemed almost one creature.

He began to whistle "Irru's Ride," and without thinking she sang the version her friends had taught her: "Oh, he rode away, and he rode away, and he rode from night till noon. And he never knew that she wasn't dead, 'cause he'd stabbed her with his spoon."

He stopped whistling and turned toward her in one swift motion. Tashtery's fire, she thought, she'd done it again—she'd only ridiculed the most important event in Gossek history.

Then he made an odd sound, a sort of bark. He barked again, and she realized to her amazement that he was laughing. He laughed harder, and she laughed with him, and soon they were both whooping like lunatics, unable to catch their breath. Efcharren came up beside them, her face composed save for a faint look of exasperation.

His hard expression returned soon enough. His face had changed remarkably when he laughed, though, and she thought that she would give another of her rubies for one of his smiles.

Later that day he stopped and stared back down the road they had traveled. She squinted and saw a line of people walking toward them. "Who are they?" she asked.

"Bound Folk," he said.

He must have eyes as sharp as an eagle's, she thought. "Shouldn't we—well—get away from them? Hide somewhere?"

"Do you see that woman in the line? The one with yellow hair?"

"No. Who is she?"

Instead of answering he galloped off to meet them. What in Tashtery's name was he doing? She wanted to call after him but was afraid of drawing the Bound Folk's attention.

The Bound Folk came closer. She could see them now, could see the yellow-haired woman Daro had mentioned. Daro dismounted and drew his sword and began to engage the man at the head of the line.

"What is he doing?" Efcharren asked.

"I have no idea," Caireddin said.

"Didn't he tell you?"

"No—he just rode off."

"Maybe we should leave him," Efcharren said nervously. The clang of sword on sword came toward them faintly. "Look—he's taking on a dozen people by himself. I told you he was mad."

"Let's wait a minute," Caireddin said.

Daro had already felled two men. Another moved forward; in the next moment this man dropped from his horse to the dirt road as well. "There were only three Bound Folk, it looks like," Caireddin said. "The rest are prisoners, I think."

She rode toward him. It was only in that moment that she remembered that she too had a sword, and had boasted about fighting a duel.

Daro walked over to the yellow-haired woman. He grasped her to him and held her, but she made a small noise and backed away, then showed him her hands, bound at the wrists by rope.

"Of course," Daro said. "I'm sorry." He began to slice the binding with his sword, leaving behind traces of blood from the dead as he cut. "What happened?" he asked. "How did you survive? Is my cousin—"

The woman shook her head. "Madaroc is dead. Our children too. They're all dead."

She said nothing more, and Daro went to work on the bindings of the other prisoners. They hadn't complained about waiting; they seemed resigned, with no will of their own.

"This is Lirden, my cousin's wife," Daro said, without turning away from the rope in front of him. "She escaped a great burning, the destruction of Aspen Valley. I never thought to see any of my family alive."

The prisoners began to mill around, rubbing at their wrists where the ropes had cut into their skin. "What will you do now?" Daro asked Lirden.

"I don't know," she said. "They were taking us to—to the Binder. We were to be made into Bound Folk."

"I know," Daro said. "You're free now, though. Why don't you come with us? We're going to Pergodi."

"Pergodi!" Lirden said. Some liveliness had entered her blue eyes; Daro had shocked her. "But you hate the Karedek. What do you want with the people who killed your—"

"Hush," Daro said quickly. Who killed your what? Caireddin wondered. "I'm taking these women there—if you come along I can protect you as well. That is, if they agree. Lady Efcharren? Lady Caireddin?"

Caireddin tried not to scowl. Did she want this woman traveling with them? She had thought Daro alone and unencumbered; now it turned out he had at least one relative, and maybe a whole passel of them showing up later.

No, she was being ungenerous. "Of course she can come," Caireddin said.

Daro finished with the last prisoner. He wiped his sword on some grass to scour away the rest of the blood, then helped Lirden mount his horse and got on behind her.

"What do you want to do?" he asked the prisoners.

No one seemed to know. Most headed off in the opposite direction, away from Karededin; some stayed where they were, blinking as if unable to understand what had happened. None of them followed Daro to Pergodi.

Daro leaned forward and began to whisper into Lirden's ear. Caireddin felt a jolt of jealousy; her heart jumped and then began to beat quickly and heavily. What was he saying to her?

"Will you teach me to fight like that?" she asked him.

"If you like," he said, and then turned back to Lirden.

The next day she saw a line of mountains in the distance, a gray smudge on the horizon. At first she thought she imagined it, but when she pointed it out to Daro he nodded, looking worried.

"That's where the Binder's city is," he said. "We'll have to go around it somehow."

As they came closer to the mountains he grew more and more anxious. He had avoided talking to other people, but now he took to stopping travelers from the south and asking them questions about the road ahead.

What he heard appeared to satisfy him, though he seemed puzzled at the same time. "They say the Binder's city is abandoned, that he's gone to Pergodi," he said that night over their fire. "The entire main road is unprotected—anyone could sweep down and take the capi-tal."

Drustig had said something similar. But she couldn't tell him that, couldn't admit how much she knew about his enemy.

"Why were those Bound Folk taking us to see him, then?" Lirden asked.

Daro shrugged. "Perhaps they hadn't heard that he'd gone. Or perhaps they were told to bring prisoners to the Binder, and they continued to perform their task mindlessly, over and over." Lirden shuddered, and Daro went on quickly: "In that case you might have been released once you got to the city."

Lirden shuddered again. "Or they might have taken us all the way to Pergodi," she said.

The next day the land began to rise; they had reached the foothills. They said nothing as their horses began to climb.

They spent days riding over the mountain. The air grew clearer and colder as the path rose, and on the high peaks above them they could even see snow. They began to pass abandoned mine shafts, some dangerously close to the road, and they had to slow their pace to keep watch for them.

"The Binder didn't care where he built his mines, I suppose," Daro said. "It didn't matter to him how many people he lost."

"Who is the Binder?" Caireddin asked again.

"I don't know. Someone from Karededin—the king, maybe, or one of that horrible family he has advising him, Noldeth or Drustig—"

"Not Drustig," she said.

He turned to her quickly. "Why not?"

She cursed to herself. "Because he's been exiled. He hasn't been allowed back in Karededin."

"And how do you know that?"

His eyes seemed to look within her. And she had to match his honesty with her own; she wanted his approval that much.

"I told you I ran away from my wedding," she said. "It was Lord Drustig I was to marry."

"Why would you marry such an evil man?"

"I had no choice. He wanted to marry me. But I couldn't stand him—that's why I ran away."

"What is Drustig doing in Goss?"

"He wants to take Karededin, now that King Jerret is dead."

"Jerret is—is dead? Who rules in Karededin?"

"Cullen. Drustig's brother."

He thought a moment. "And you're going to Karededin to marry Cullen, I suppose."

How had he guessed? "You don't understand . . ." she began.

"Oh, I understand all I need to."

She grew angry. Who was this forest-dweller to judge her? "No, you don't. I'm King Tezue's daughter—with Jerret dead I'm the only living member of the royal family. There are very few people in the world I can marry. And I need Cullen to protect me against Drustig."

"They're a vile family, the Harus. They're like a tree that grows in poisoned soil—the fruit is of necessity poisoned. Cullen is just as evil as Drustig."

"He couldn't possibly be. Anyway, how do you know? Have you ever met him?"

"I don't need to. I know the Harus, I've seen what they've done in Goss. You're very innocent in some ways, milady. You learned too late what Drustig is capable of, and had to run away—are you certain you won't do the same with Cullen?"

"Innocent! At least I haven't hidden myself in a forest while the rest of the world goes by. At least I know who's king in Karededin."

"Innocent, yes. Have you ever seen Bound Folk?"

"Yes," she said, though she had only seen the men he had fought earlier. She lifted her chin defiantly. "But what does Cullen have to do with them? Why are you so certain he's the Binder?"

"With Jerret dead and Drustig in exile there are very few candidates. Cullen or his brother Polgar or their father Noldeth—"

"Lord Noldeth is dead as well," she said. She had wanted to show him how little he knew, but she realized too late she had only proved his point.

"Ah," he said. "So there are the two brothers, and the sorcerer Mathewar. And that's—"

"Mathewar! I met Mathewar. He's not the Binder."

"Where did you meet him?"

She sighed, tired of his suspicions. "In Ou. But Drustig hates him, for one thing. And I met his wife, and she certainly wasn't the sort to marry the Binder."

"His wife the witch."

"Oh, think what you like!" she said. The man had a thousand enemies, it seemed—and as Cullen's future wife she had probably just joined the list. She felt a sudden panic as a thought came to her. "Are you going to leave us now?"

"No. I promised to take you to Pergodi, and I will."

She marveled at his sense of honor. He seemed incapable of bending, of compromise; it was no wonder he had gone mad.

"Thank you," she said.

For the rest of the journey through the mountains he spoke to her and Efcharren only when necessary, his tone polite, unobjectionable. For her part she had begun to watch him, curious now that he had stopped talking with her. He had begun to teach her swordwork in the evenings, and she felt a delight she couldn't name at seeing the corded muscles on his arms stand out, at the way he could talk and fight at the same time, effortlessly. She asked him questions about Goss then, but he would not break from his lessons to answer her.

She felt that she had been judged and found wanting. He probably thought her interested only in riches and power; perhaps he expected her to offer herself to every king in every realm until she found one to marry her.

She did not offer him more explanations, though. She told herself she didn't care what he thought. She had failed the test of truthfulness—well, no one else could pass it, no one but him. People had to live in the messy world, had to compromise and make allowances and give in occasionally.

The path led them between two peaks and then down the other side of the mountain. At the base of the mountain they saw a closed gate in the midst of a wall made of red stone. They turned to skirt the wall; it seemed to take hours.

On the other side they found two great dragon towers with another gate between them, this one open. Daro moved forward cautiously and looked inside. "You should see this, milady," he said.

She guided her horse next to him reluctantly. A deserted city spread out before her, larger than any place she had ever seen. Buildings clustered together haphazardly, some in ruins, some unfinished, some topped with shining turrets and towers and domes. These last looked like castles, but there were half a dozen, at least—how many kings had lived there? Tall towers reared up over the buildings, and great statues of kings and queens and birds; they seemed about to call out to their fellows halfway across the city. Fires burned out of control in some quarters; and a few men and women wandered the streets, looking lost.

"The Binder's city, milady," Daro said. "What kind of person would build a place like this?"

She said nothing, and continued down the road.

# TWENTY-SIX

A few days later Angarred and Mathewar climbed the same road over the mountains. "Do you know what worries me?" Mathewar said. "It's almost certain that Drustig would win any battle between him and his brother. Cullen has the Bound Folk and could create more, but Drustig could turn them all into madmen, scatter them across the realm. And Drustig—"

"I know. He terrifies me, and all I know of him is what you told me. He doesn't care what other people think, doesn't care whether what he does is right or wrong. . . ."

"I don't think he knows the difference," Mathewar said. "Or even that there is a difference. I can still hear his mocking laugh . . ." He shook his head. "I would love to talk to Tobrin right now. He couldn't possibly say this is none of his concern—if Drustig wins he'll turn Tobrin's mind inside out. And there's a good deal in that mind Drustig cannot be allowed to know."

"Do you have any idea where he is?"

Mathewar shrugged. "The Godkings know," he said. He looked around him at the deserted mines. "And what's Polgar doing now, I wonder? He had control of the Bound Folk, and then Noldeth told him to give it up to Cullen. He said he'd be happy if he never created more of them, but I wonder if that's true. People who have power don't usually give it up."

"Maybe Cullen and Polgar will kill each other," Angarred said, sounding hopeful. "No, that would leave the way open for Drustig."

The sun flared on the white peaks above them as it set. They stopped for the night. The sky turned rose and gold and copper; then the sun dipped below the mountains and a cold wind sprang up. They spread out the blankets they had found in abandoned houses and huddled close for warmth.

The next day they headed down the other side of the mountain. A few days after that they reached the opening to Polgar's cave. Mathewar created a light and took Angarred a little ways into it, showing her the curtains and icicles of stone, the blue river with its blind white fish.

She shivered. "Are you cold?" he asked.

"Let's go," she said. "This is a terrible place."

Mathewar had not had any bad dreams since he found Angarred. That night, though, perhaps because of the reminder of his near binding, he woke abruptly, his heart beating loudly. "What?" someone said. "What is it?"

He heard the grating laugh that followed him everywhere, the madman's laugh. He tried to stand, to scream. A face loomed out of the darkness, and on it he saw the half crown, and the stars winking behind it like sinister jewels.

He was adrift again, surrounded by chaos with no way out. Drustig's laugh beat against his mind like waves, bringing with it the denizens of madness: walking chairs, advancing toward him with their mouths open, showing rows of teeth; trees with their crowns planted in the earth and their roots in the air; the pale fish from the cave, grown to monstrous size. He heard the laughter again, and he realized that this time it was he who had made it, that he would soon be as insane as Drustig.

The voice came again. "What is it?"

Angarred was there, somewhere. He went toward her through the delirium, holding hard to the sound of her voice.

"You've caught my madness like an infection," Drustig said. "You'll never be free of it, no matter how far you run."

"No," he said feebly. "No, I'll never—"

More laughter. The boundaries between him and Drustig blurred; he could not tell the two of them apart, could not say which of them had laughed.

"It's all right," Angarred said.

The voice was closer. He headed toward it, following it back to the shores of sanity. Then he truly opened his eyes, and saw only the remains of their fire and the hanging stars above them. He caught Angarred's scent in the darkness and held her tightly.

"What did he do to you?" she asked, her head close to his.

He shook his head, though she could not see him in the dark, and said nothing.

The next morning they rode past the bizarre town Polgar had created. The dragon towers were empty, deserted, and the gates stood open. Mathewar risked a look through the gates but saw only a few people wandering aimlessly. Still, he felt a malevolent awareness, as if someone watched them, the dragons perhaps. He knew he was only remembering his imprisonment, that the guards and those above them were truly gone, but he and Angarred hurried away nonetheless.

When they reached the Karedek side of the mountains he noticed that Angarred looked paler, and that her hand strayed up frequently to her wound. "Are you all right?" he asked. "Do you want to stop for a while?"

"We can't stop," she said. "We have to get to Pergodi."

"We can if you have to."

She hesitated a moment and then said, "I think I might want to—to change my shape. I'll be stronger as the leopard."

"I suppose I could lead your horse," he said. He looked at her doubtfully. "You wouldn't want to eat it, would you?"

She laughed, then winced as the pain returned. "I'll try not to."

She dismounted and stood a moment, reaching within her for her other shape. An instant later she dropped to the ground and flowed seamlessly into the leopard. The horses jerked away at the strange, terrifying smell. By the time Mathewar calmed them the leopard had hidden herself in the cover along the road, as shy in her way as the horses.

Karededin looked worse than Goss: Polgar had taken more people from his own country. The mines lay open, unworked and surrounded by slag, and whole towns stood vacant, as if some great calamity had befallen them. They passed cows bellowing to be milked, their udders heavy, and crops withering in the fields, surrounded by weeds. In the orchards unharvested fruit lay rotting on the ground, clotted with flies, the air thick with their sweetish smell.

In the evenings, after Angarred returned to her human shape, they went into the abandoned houses looking for food and more blankets. The silence oppressed them, though, and they never stayed long.

Mathewar began to see evidence of the Bound Folk marching south: fields that had been stripped of crops, and piles of bones, the remains of cows or sheep. Fire had ravaged one town, leaving only the stone houses standing; probably it had gotten out of control and the Bound Folk had not stayed to put it out. The sharp smell of burning followed him for the rest of the day.

He rode faster, anxious to be away from the devastation. Sometimes a soft rustling came from the trees and bushes to his right, the leopard keeping pace with him; sometimes he slowed and looked for her tawny coloring within the green. He had another reason for hurrying: he wanted to see if Dorrish was safe, if he and his village had survived the hordes heading toward Pergodi.

There were people on the road now, though not nearly as many as on his first journey north. Angarred had to swing farther and farther away from the road to stay hidden; he worried about her until nightfall, when they met up again and she changed.

It was almost Autumn; early rain pelted them as they neared Hoy, heavy drops of water that seemed as weighted as stones. A chill wind blew from the mountains. He drew his cloak around him and pushed on, knowing the leopard could weather the storm better than he could.

He came to the fields surrounding Hoy at dusk, as the rain began to let up. There was just enough light to see that the crops had been ravaged, every last grain of wheat and rye taken. He continued through the near dark, filled with anxiety and dread.

A man carrying a spear stepped out of the gloom. "Stop there," he said.

"Who are you?" Mathewar asked.

"The gatekeeper," the man said. Another man with a spear joined him; they both looked grim, determined. "Get down from your horse. What's your business in Hoy?"

Mathewar dismounted. Something nudged his side, and he turned and saw the leopard. Her eyes shone like red coals, and she parted her lips in a near growl.

The second man pointed to her with his spear, unable to speak. "What's wrong?" the first man said.

The second man dropped his spear and ran. The first man finally spotted her; he began to back away slowly, gibbering. "Wh-wh-wh—" He threw his spear; it landed several yards from Angarred. Then he turned and ran after his fellow guard.

Angarred shifted back into her human shape. "Not very hospitable, were they?" she said. She grinned widely, showing her teeth, an expression more suited to the leopard's face than her own.

They continued on, coming to a wall that loomed over their heads. Mathewar counted back to the last time he had been in Hoy and realized, impressed, that they had built it in four months.

He went closer to examine it. Each stone fit snugly against its neighbors, with very little mortar between them. He could feel Dorrish's strengthening spells, good solid work without any of the flashiness young magicians were so fond of.

The wooden gates stood open; the guards must have been in too much of a hurry to close them. He and Angarred went through, and then he returned to pull the gates shut and drop the iron bar into place.

Despite the devastation to the crops the village looked much the same. They headed through the deserted streets, past the Cat and Stars, closed now, and on to Dorrish's house. He knocked on the door.

No one answered, though they could hear movement from within. He knocked again and called out, "Dorrish? It's Mathewar."

The door opened a crack and Dorrish looked out. Light spilled over them from inside the house. The two gatekeepers appeared out of the gloom, drawn by the illumination.

"Where's that cat?" the first gatekeeper said. He held his spear on Mathewar, his hands shaking.

"I don't know," Mathewar said. He made a show of looking around and seeing only Angarred.

"You saw it too, though, didn't you?"

"I did. It must have run off, though."

"All right." The man lowered the spear. "What's your name and your business in Hoy?"

"I'll vouch for him," Dorrish said from within the doorway.

The gatekeeper eyed Dorrish, looking unconvinced. "All right," he said finally, and then he and his fellow headed in the direction of the gate.

"Come in, come in," Dorrish said. Bergad peered out of the kitchen. "Sit down, please."

They sat at the table. The room was cold, with no fire in the grate. Dorrish had lost some weight, Mathewar saw, and his face had grown haggard. Worse, the eyes that had once looked around him with amazement now seemed guarded, suspicious of everything.

Bergad stayed in the kitchen, her eyes on Angarred, her expression filled with terror and amazement. Dorrish must have told her about Angarred, then, and she had worked out where the cat had gone.

The last time he had come here he had been a hero, Mathewar thought. This time he was a man with a familiar, perhaps a witch. Everyone in town would have heard about the leopard by dawn. Well, it couldn't be helped.

Bergad came into the room, carrying a tray with bread and cups of ale. She set it on the table, casting quick glances at Angarred, and returned to the kitchen.

"What's happened here?" Mathewar asked.

Dorrish sighed heavily. "What you've seen. The Bound Folk came through, hundreds and hundreds of them. They took all our crops, all the wood we had for Winter. They broke through the gate—there were so many of them we couldn't stop them. And then they—they rounded up the young men, as many as they could find, and took them along. I suppose they'll be turned into Bound Folk and will join Cullen's army when they get to Pergodi." He hesitated and then said, "I couldn't stop them. The villagers got very angry—they said they didn't know what good I was, or why they had given me this house, or had supported me all this time. I tried, truly I did, but I couldn't—I couldn't—"

"No one could," Mathewar said.

"I know that. They knew it too, probably. They wanted someone to blame, I think."

"Listen," Mathewar said. "I'm afraid there's more coming. Drustig is headed this way to fight with his brother."

Dorrish put his head in his hands. "There's nothing left for them to steal," he said. "It's all gone. And I've heard about Drustig, how cruel he is . . ."

"You have to warn the villagers. Tell them—I don't know, tell them to put some food aside for Drustig and then let him discover it. If he thinks that's all you have he might go away."

"What makes you think the villagers will listen to me?"

Mathewar remembered the doubt in the gatekeeper's eyes. "Is it that bad?"

Dorrish said nothing, but Mathewar saw his hopelessness. "You can come with us to Pergodi if you like," Mathewar said.

Dorrish sat up. "No, I'll stay here," he said. "I'll face Drustig along with everyone else."

"Are you sure?"

"Of course not. Who can be sure of anything in these times?"

It was a good answer, Mathewar thought. "Is there any news from Pergodi?" he asked.

"A lot of rumors. Someone attacked Karededin and was beaten back, though no one knows where the attack came from. A trader who came by yesterday said he'd heard it was the Finbar Islands."

Mathewar looked at Angarred. So Ezlin had come to claim his inheritance. "Have you heard anything of Lord Ezlin? Ezlin Ertig?"

Dorrish shook his head. He seemed to have no curiosity about Mathewar's question.

No one spoke for a long time. Bergad came into the room cautiously and said, "Would you like to stay here for the night? We have very little to offer, I'm afraid. . . ."

"No, thank you," Mathewar said. "We have to get to Pergodi."

"Of course," Bergad said.

They stood and made their farewells. They had eaten none of the bread, but this time Bergad did not reproach them.


Brangwin looked through the Baelish Gate, the northernmost gate leading into Pergodi. He had been dreading this, the true test of his disguise. His family had come to the city three years ago, visiting Queen Rodarren; surely someone he had met then would recognize him.

He had other reasons for hesitating as well. There were probably Bound Folk in Pergodi; they had all been heading south, after all. And he had grown unused to crowds, this last season in the forest. He thought of the battles he had fought, how he had hardened himself; that had been nothing compared to simply riding through a gate. He clenched his fists and urged his horse forward, and the three women followed.

They rode through the crowded streets and lanes of the city, passing craftsmen and beggars, markets and taverns, dead-eyed sattery addicts and bright, exotic Takekek speaking in a strange guttural tongue. Carts squealed by, farmers and fortune-tellers called out to them, bells rang. Once they had to press themselves against a wall as a line of religious walked by, two by two, chanting in low voices. He watched everything carefully, quickly, alert for danger.

He saw little evidence that the country was about to go to war; shops and stalls had remained open, and the people went about their business as always. After a while, though, he noticed that there were very few young men; they had all been called up for the army, probably.

And there were almost no Bound Folk. They must be in barracks somewhere, he thought, training against Drustig and his army.

At that moment he looked up and came face-to-face with a bound man sweeping the streets. He jerked back and pulled on the reins without thinking, and his horse stopped abruptly.

The women had gone on. He hurried to catch up with them.

"Do you see that hill there, in the middle of the city?" he asked Caireddin and Efcharren. "Pergodi Castle is at the top. I'll say my farewells now—I'm certain you can go on without my help."

"Wait," Caireddin said. She reached into her purse at her side, brought out a glittering handful of coins, and held it out to him.

"This—this is a fortune, milady," he said. "You can't have meant to give me all this."

"You saved our lives," she said. "We'd be wandering in the forest even now if you hadn't helped us."

He was still thinking of Rodarren, and now he saw that Caireddin looked a good deal like the dead queen. Both had deep dark eyes and an astonishing smile, a smile that seemed intended only for the person who had caught their attention.

With Rodarren this had looked like wisdom, but he could not tell if Caireddin would ever attain that serene dignity. She seemed a strange mix, one moment innocent, the next more worldly than even he had been. And yet she was only two years younger than he, eighteen to his twenty.

He wondered what she would think if she knew how they worked at cross-purposes: that she had come to Pergodi to marry the king, and he to kill him.

"Be careful, milady," he said without thinking.

She looked up at him, puzzled. "Why?"

"I still don't trust Cullen." He said this quietly, so no one on the crowded street would hear. "And when Drustig attacks you should flee—he has a weapon—"

"I know. I felt it."

"Did you? So did I."

Odd that they only learned this about each other now, as they were saying farewell. He wanted to ask her more, but just then Efcharren called, "Caireddin! Let's go—we should be there by supper."

"Do you—do you have a place to stay?" Caireddin asked.

"Don't worry—there are cheap inns near the Spiderweb Bridge."

"Good." She smiled—it was Rodarren's smile once again. "May Marfan and Mathona guide you."

He watched her go. For the first time in a long while he thought of poetry. How would he describe her? But all the phrases he thought of were dull and stale, used hundreds of times before. He had lost all his words in the forest.

It was just as well, though. She was here to marry Cullen, after all.

# TWENTY-SEVEN

Caireddin and her mother spent some time buying clothes fit for the court, then rode up the hill. They reached the castle an hour or so before the sun set. Caireddin wondered when they served supper here; she had grown very hungry. They rode through the courtyard and settled their horses, then went in through the main door.

She had never seen a building this vast. They walked through a maze of corridors, past what seemed like dozens of chambers. Why did they need all these great halls? she wondered. One for state business, one for dining, one for dancing . . .

Had she truly believed she could be queen of this domain? She felt as if they were mice, padding cautiously through a place designed for a different order of being altogether. Even Efcharren seemed daunted.

A lean, gray-haired man headed toward them, walking very straight. He wore a silver chain around his neck; a great bunch of keys jingled at his belt. "I wonder if you can help us," her mother said. "I'm Lady Efcharren, and this is my daughter, Lady Caireddin. We're looking for King Cullen."

The man nodded; he seemed to have heard of Caireddin. "I'm

Dobrennin Steward, milady," he said. "The king left orders not to be disturbed. Does he know you're here?"

"No, I'm afraid not."

"I'll tell you what, then. I'll get you both settled and go talk to him, and I'll come for you in an hour. Whatever happens you'll get supper then, I promise you."

He signaled to passing servants to take their bags. Two of the servants walked toward them with an unnatural, even gait, and as they came closer Caireddin saw with horror that they had dull, dead eyes. So these were the Bound Folk, the people Daro had fought; she understood his anger better now. But how could he be so certain that Cullen had had anything to do with them?

She and her mother followed the man through the castle. His feet seemed to make no sound on the tiled floor. "Who is he?" Caireddin whispered.

"The steward," Efcharren whispered back. "See his chain? That's the sign of his office."

They went past more rooms and galleries and chambers. Finally Dobrennin stopped and chose one of his keys. "Here you are, my ladies," he said, opening a door in front of him. "I hope you enjoy your stay in Pergodi. And if you need anything, please come to me." He bowed and left them.

They went inside. Efcharren walked through all three rooms of the apartment, nodding to herself. Caireddin followed. The furniture seemed a little worn but had once been very fine: beds covered in silk brocade, carved wooden chairs and chests, dim tapestries and carpets. There were two hearths, both empty now, and each room had windows that looked out to the west. The sun was setting over Pergodi; lights began to flicker in the windows and on the streets.

"Good, very good," Efcharren said.

"What is?" Caireddin asked.

"The rooms you're given say something about the respect in which you're held. This is very good for such short notice, but we should be moved somewhere grander soon."

A woman came with clean sheets and hot water, and stayed to build up the front fireplace and light some candles—not one of the Bound Folk, thank Marfan and Mathona. Efcharren watched with satisfaction. "Good," she said again when she had gone. "Though it would be better if we had our own servant."

They washed off the dirt from their journey and put on their new finery. A few moments later a knock came at the door, and a voice murmured, "Dobrennin Steward."

Efcharren opened the door. "The king would like to dine with you," Dobrennin said. "He's in the Lesser Banquet Hall. Follow me—and please remember how I take you, or it will be hard to find your way back."

Caireddin still felt dazed at her surroundings and paid no attention to the twists and turns along the way. They came to the banquet hall; the double doors stood open, and within the room about a dozen people in rich clothing sat around a great table. This is the *Lesser* Banquet Hall? she thought. Something smelled wonderful, meat heavy with spices.

The steward knocked. A man at the head of the table looked up. "Lady Efcharren and Lady Caireddin, my liege," the steward said.

The man at the table gestured to them to come in. As she went closer Caireddin recognized Cullen, the second of Lord Noldeth's sons. She had not paid much attention to him, enspelled as she had been by Drustig, and she saw again, disappointed, how ordinary he looked. Power had hovered over Drustig like lightning, but there was none of that excitement around Cullen.

Efcharren nudged her and dropped into a curtsy. Belatedly, she did the same.

Cullen remained seated. "Well, my lady," he said. "My ladies. This is truly a pleasant surprise. I planned to send for you both when my rule was secure here."

"We came to bring you news of your brother, Drustig," Efcharren said, rising. "He's moving south from Ou. He—"

"This is not a discussion for supper, surely," Cullen said.

"Of course, my liege," Efcharren said.

An awkward moment passed. Finally Cullen seemed to remember his manners and said, "Sit down, please. Anywhere."

Caireddin sat next to an older man at Cullen's side. "This is Lord Sorle," Cullen said, nodding to the man. "And here"—he indicated a woman across from him; she looked very like Drustig—"this is my sister, Princess Iltarra, and Lord Annin." They sat very close, deep in conversation. They looked up and nodded at Caireddin briefly, then Iltarra murmured something to Annin and he smiled and brushed his mouth across her cheek.

There were other people at the table, but Cullen didn't introduce them; instead he began to talk to Lord Sorle. An old man to Caireddin's left, on the other side of Efcharren, was saying something to the woman across the table from him. Farther down were other nobles, all of them dressed in brocade and silk and velvet, jewels at their ears and necks and fingers.

Someone moved in the far shadows of the room. Caireddin reached for her sword, then realized that of course she wouldn't be wearing it. Tashtery take this dress, she thought, and all formal clothes.

Several men came forward into the light. They wore an emblem on their chests, a castle with two towers. She had seen others with this uniform, and she realized, feeling foolish, that these must be the king's bodyguard. At least no one had noticed her confusion.

Servants brought out plates of roast boar. Caireddin ate quickly. When she finished she saw that the king was still talking to Lord Sorle and Iltarra to Annin. She took a long drink of a dusty red wine, then looked over at her mother. Efcharren shrugged.

Finally Iltarra glanced up. Caireddin seized her chance. "I didn't know the king had a sister, milady," she said. "Are there more in the family?"

"We have a brother, Polgar," Iltarra said. She wore a magnificent rope of pearls at her neck, Caireddin saw, with one pearl larger than the rest.

"Where is he?" Caireddin asked.

"He isn't seen much in public," Iltarra said. She had an odd smile, as if she expected Caireddin to understand something more from her words. Caireddin had no idea what it could be, though. Was Polgar somehow unfit for company? Mad, or hideously deformed?

Iltarra turned back to Annin. Caireddin looked around the table again, wondering why they had ever come to this dreadful place, these horribly rude people. The man on Efcharren's left murmured something; Caireddin caught the words ". . . marry King Cullen . . ." and she strained to hear more.

"Then it's fortunate for him that Lady Melleth couldn't be here today," the woman said. "I hear she's ill."

"Lady Dubbish!" the man said. He looked pointedly at Efcharren.

"Oh!" Lady Dubbish said. She leaned across the table as if to whisper something to the man, but her voice carried to Caireddin, and probably farther. "Well, perhaps someone should tell them that Cullen has a mistress." Her bright blue eyes shone.

"Remind me to show you my new horse tomorrow," the man said, clearly changing the subject. Lady Dubbish looked disappointed. "He's quite magnificent."

At last the uncomfortable meal ended. Cullen stood, followed by the others around the table. "May we speak to you later, my liege?" Efcharren asked.

"Of course," Cullen said. "Make an appointment with my steward."

"Where is he?" Efcharren asked.

"Oh, I don't know." He headed to the door, his guards falling in behind him.

They spent a long frustrating time searching for Dobrennin, an hour if the city bells were anything to go by. Finally they met someone who showed them to the steward's office.

Dobrennin found a place in the king's schedule for the day after next. Then they headed back to their apartment; to Caireddin's relief her mother had paid attention on their way to the banquet hall and found it easily.

As soon as Efcharren closed the door behind them Caireddin said, "I'm not going to marry Cullen. He's horrible. At the very least he should have paid some attention to his guests. The very least."

"I'm afraid you have no choice, Caireddin," her mother said.

"What do you mean? I don't care about marrying royalty—you're the one who wants to see me on the throne."

"It has nothing to do with me," Efcharren said heavily. "You're the only descendant of the Godkings, the only one left with royal blood in her veins. If you marry anyone but Cullen your children will be a constant threat to him. He'll probably kill you before he allows that to happen."

"But—" The walls seemed to close in around her. She felt trapped, as if she had been placed in one of those hideously small prison cages she had heard of. She began to pace back and forth. "But I don't *want* to marry him. Can't we run away, go somewhere? Why didn't you tell me this before we ever came here?"

"If you run away he'll find you, or he'll come to hear of you somehow. You're too well known to hide. And I didn't tell you because I thought you'd figured it out for yourself. You were the one who wanted to come here, after all."

"I can't marry him. I can't. He's a dreadful man."

"Did you think Tezue and I loved each other forever, like a God-king and his queen? He could be very difficult sometimes."

"Yes, but that was your choice. You wanted to be his mistress. And Cullen has a mistress too, did you hear? That horrible old woman said so."

"What if he does? A good many kings have had mistresses—you of all people should know that. But you'll be his wife, the one who goes with him to the banquets and tournaments and state visits. You don't know how often I wished I could be there with Tezue."

"Maybe he and that mistress will marry each other, and I can go home."

"That won't happen, Caireddin, you know that."

Caireddin stopped pacing and looked around her. "Where's my sword?" she asked.

"What—are you planning to kill him now?"

"No, I just want it. People could have me killed, as you said." She found her bag and lifted out the sword.

Efcharren headed toward the bedrooms. "You can't carry a sword in the castle, Caireddin," she said. "People will take it the wrong way."

The next day her mother led Caireddin to the Great Hall, the place where nobles met and talked; Efcharren told her she should learn courtly manners as soon as possible. They gave the chamberlain their names and he announced them, and they stepped into a hall as filled with color as a hoard of treasure.

All conversation came to a halt as the nobles turned to stare at them. Gossip about her had spread quickly; they headed toward her one by one, seeming to realize that they might be looking at their new queen.

A few were openly fawning, bowing and curtsying as if she were already Cullen's wife. They asked her the same questions over and over: how was her journey, how did she like the city, what did she think of Cullen?

Three or four people exclaimed over her "quaint" Ounek accent, until she thought she might almost prefer Cullen's rudeness. But slowly the tenor of the conversation changed. "I thought you ought to know," a sly-faced woman with elaborate curls whispered, her face close to Caireddin's. "The woman standing across the room—Lady Melleth—is the king's mistress."

Caireddin followed her gaze. Lady Melleth was very beautiful; she had light brown hair, also in curls, a full mouth, and tilted green eyes like a cat's. Caireddin smiled and nodded, and the other woman, cheated of the response she wanted, walked away without saying farewell.

After a few moments it seemed she had been there for hours. Silk and lace, feathers and flowers, ribbons and jewels swirled around her; she felt boxed in by clothing. The colors were too strong, the perfumes of the courtiers too rich; the soft-voiced conversations sounded like insects buzzing. She spoke the same answers so many times they lost their meaning; she felt like an idiot who had learned only three or four phrases. Her face became as stiff as her dress from smiling, and the bright windows and paintings and jewels began to hurt her eyes.

Another person bent close to her and pointed out Cullen's mistress, and then one more, both claiming to have Caireddin's best interests at heart. Caireddin said nothing to either of them. It was easy to seem dispassionate, she thought, if you didn't really care.

Finally, Lady Melleth herself glanced at her out of those exotic eyes. Suddenly Caireddin had had enough—of the meanness, the hypocrisy, the false flattery. She looked for her mother but did not see her anywhere. On impulse she left the room, went out to the stables, and got her horse.

She hiked up her dress and rode down the hill, heading for the city. She did not know what she wanted there: a game of cards, perhaps, or some convivial people to drink with. At the base of the hill she took a twisting road at random.

A while later she crossed one of Pergodi's bridges and saw that she had come to a neighborhood of rich folk. The houses here had gates and towers and arches and balconies; they sprawled down to the river's edge, each walled off from the next by a stone fence.

She turned to go back and realized she was lost. House after house stretched out before her; there seemed no way out of this cursed place. Perhaps she had wandered into Tashtery's hell. Finally, after a good many wrong turns, she found the river and followed it back to the bridge.

The bridge reminded her of something. Pergodi was called the City of Seven Bridges, and Daro had said that he could find cheap lodging at the Spiderweb Bridge. Certainly there was nothing cheap here; this could not be the bridge he had meant.

She asked several people for the way to the Spiderweb Bridge, and finally a man directed her out near the edge of the city, by the Tornish Gate. The bridge seemed made of cobwebs itself, light and airy, but it supported her weight and her horse's when she rode across.

Five or six inns crowded the street, leaning against each other. She went into one after another and asked for Daro or Lirden, but none of the innkeepers had heard of them. Finally it occurred to her that the Gossek might have given false names, and she began at the first inn again, this time with descriptions.

She had grown so discouraged that when the innkeeper started nodding she didn't understand him at first. "Yes, yes, they're here," the man said. "Upstairs. They have Gossek accents, like you said. Like yourself, in fact."

She headed up the stairs, marveling that someone could think Gossek and Ounek accents sounded alike, and knocked at the door. It was only then, standing with her hand raised, that she wondered what she wanted from Daro.

The door opened and Daro stood in front of her. She had forgotten how tall he was, and how lean; he didn't seem capable of pinning her to the ground, let alone fighting an army of Bound Folk. For a moment she felt his hand pushing her down once again, and excitement stirred within her.

"What do you want, milady?" Daro asked. "I've fulfilled my promise to you."

She felt as if she had been slapped. She forced herself to show nothing; she would give some excuse and leave. But Daro seemed to realize how impolite he had been. "I'm sorry for the discourtesy," he said. "You surprised me, I'm afraid. But why have you come to visit?"

"I was wondering if you could teach me more swordwork," she said.

He shook his head. "I'm afraid not. I will not do anything that might aid Cullen."

"Cullen! I hate Cullen! He thinks of nothing but himself and his own pleasure. He has a mistress, did you know that? And he's a fool—he won't listen to advice, he doesn't even seem to know there's a war coming . . ."

Daro leaned against the door frame and crossed his arms. He seemed to be smiling through the thicket of his beard. "You did warn me, I know," she said.

"I did," he said. He hadn't been smiling, she saw; he would not make fun of her. "But I still don't see what I can do for you."

"My mother says I have to marry Cullen. That he needs me because I'm Tezue's heir, and if I don't marry him he'll kill me."

He nodded. She wished he would say something, anything. "Did you know this would happen?" she asked.

"I guessed it."

"Why did everyone know but me? I never would have come to Pergodi if . . . Can you help me?"

Now he did smile, though it was weary, self-mocking. "What would you have me do, milady?" he asked gently. "I fought him, and I lost."

"Well, can you—I don't know—take me away from here?"

"Where? He'll only find you again."

"That's what my mother said. But I hate him—I can't marry him. I don't know what to do—if Cullen wasn't bad enough there's Drustig, and Drustig has that horrible crown and will probably win any war between them. And then I'll be handed over to him like a spoil of war. I swear to Tashtery I'll kill myself before I go back to him."

Daro seemed to hesitate for a long moment. Finally he said, very quietly, "If I tell you something would you swear to keep it secret?"

"Yes."

"Very well then. I came to Pergodi to kill Goss's enemies."

"You—you mean to kill—you want to kill Cullen?"

"Hush." He looked up and down the hallway, though there was no one there. "Goss's enemy is the king of Karededin, whoever he is. Jerret or Drustig or Cullen."

"Why are you telling me this? Can I help you?"

"You might. I need to be within the castle itself, to get close to Cullen somehow. I thought that I might pose as your servant."

"Of course. Of course you can." She laughed. "My mother was just saying that we could use a servant."

"Let me get my things, milady," he said.

He went inside and closed the door behind him. She wondered where Lirden was, if they shared the room, and then felt ashamed at her trivial thoughts. Surely she had more important things to worry about.

So Daro would be her servant. He had served them on the road to the capital as well, but she had thought of him as a leader then. She could not imagine him humbling himself, or standing quietly in the background; he seemed larger than that somehow, a man whose world encompassed greater things. She told herself not to be intimidated; he was only a common soldier, after all.

They headed toward the castle, Caireddin riding and Daro walking at her side. They said very little. Caireddin's excitement grew as they went; she had not realized how much she missed his truthfulness in the midst of all the court's hypocrisy. No, if she was sworn to truth she would have to admit to missing him for more than that. She glanced at him, admiring his easy strides, the way he towered above most of the Pergodek.

She wondered what in Tashtery's name she would tell her mother; she had the feeling that Efcharren had been glad to see Daro go. And surely she couldn't give away his true purpose.

When they got to the apartment Efcharren came out from her bedroom, talking all the while. "So there you are. I'd hoped to introduce you to more people, but I suppose you've had enough for—" She stopped when she saw Daro. "Who is this? It's the man from the forest, isn't it? What's he doing here? I thought he had his own lodgings."

"He's our new servant, Mother," Caireddin said.

"Surely not. He'd make a terrible servant."

"You said we needed one. And he needs the money."

Efcharren sighed. "Oh, very well." She turned to Daro. "You're to accompany us to the banquet hall in the evenings—there's no point in having a servant if no one knows about it. And I want you to see to it that our rooms are clean, and that we have hot baths waiting for us in the morning, and something to eat. . . . I'll give you other orders as I think of them. You do know where the servants' quarters are, I suppose?"

Caireddin had not given any thought to where Daro would stay. She looked at him quickly, but he simply nodded.

"And after supper you can teach me swordwork," she said.

"Yes, milady," he said.

Efcharren woke her the next day. "It's time for our audience with the king," she said. "Get dressed—in something suitable, please. Oh, and do something about your hair."

Dobrennin had given them directions to the Council Chamber. Efcharren knocked, and when no one answered she pushed the door open. Cullen sat behind a table, a great expanse of wood between him and the two women. Several maps lay spread out before him.

He looked up and frowned briefly, as if he was trying to place them. Then he smiled and said, "Come in, come in. What can I do for you?"

What ugly eyes he has, Caireddin thought. Small, and some muddy color between brown and gray. It's too bad he didn't inherit his family's looks.

"It's more a question of what we can do for you," Efcharren said. She looked pointedly at a chair on her side of the table, but Cullen did not ask them to sit. "My daughter Lady Caireddin and I were kidnapped by your brother Drustig and taken along with him on campaign. We managed to escape, but first we learned a good deal about him and his troops and weapons."

Caireddin marveled at how well her mother turned their story into one that would please Cullen. The king nodded. "Go on," he said.

"We learned he has a weapon—a kind of half crown—that causes terror and madness in his enemies," Efcharren said. "We saw him use it against some Gossek—it was formidable, my lord."

"Yes, yes," Cullen said. "We knew about this already. And never fear—I have something to counter it. He has a weapon to loose, but I have one to bind."

Caireddin could not imagine what he meant by that. Her mother looked puzzled as well. "I shouldn't worry about Drustig, my ladies," Cullen said. "We'll triumph over my treacherous brother, and then I'll proclaim Lady Caireddin my queen in front of all Karededin."

"We know more than that, my lord," Efcharren said. "We can tell you how many troops he has, what kinds of weapons . . ."

"We have spies to tell us this," Cullen said. He bent over his maps again. "I'm afraid I'll have to ask you to leave—I have a great deal to do here. You'll join me for supper once more, I hope?"

The audience seemed to have ended. Efcharren looked as if she wanted to say something, but then she curtsied and left the room. Caireddin followed.

"Do you see how horrible he is?" Caireddin said quietly, when they had gone some way down the hall. "He didn't even thank us, after all we went through. And he just assumed that I'd marry him, as if I'd look twice at an old toad like him."

"You will marry him," Efcharren said.

"No, I won't."

"Yes, you will," Efcharren said. "Come with me."

She led Caireddin through a maze of hallways. "What do you think he meant by that strange talk about weapons?" Caireddin asked. "One to loose and one to bind, something like that?"

"I have an idea," Efcharren said.

"You do? You seemed as confused as I was."

"Yes, but I remembered something later. I've seen these—these artifacts in Ou . . ."

"What about them?"

"I'll tell you when I'm certain," Efcharren said. "Look—you've managed to get me lost here. No, wait—here we are."

Despite her words, Caireddin didn't see that they had arrived anywhere. Efcharren made a few more turnings and began to walk faster.

Finally they came to a great hall. Huge statues stood to either side; red torches burned at their feet. Efcharren had told her about this place many times, but something about the vast room, the silence, the smoke from the torches, made her begin the tale again.

"This is the Hall of Standing Kings," Efcharren said. "Every king and queen who has ever lived is represented here, starting with Marfan and Mathona. Here is your father, King Tezue, and his queen, Chelenin. Dezue and Cherenin, they call them now." Surprisingly, her mother faced her rival Cherenin with equanimity, even some awe. "There's no one left of this great line except you. Cullen has to marry you—if he doesn't he tells every Karedek that ancestry counts for nothing, that all their previous kings were nobodies. And they won't stand for that—they'll rise up and overthrow him."

"Good. He's a terrible king." The words sounded louder than she intended; they seemed to echo off the walls.

"Hush. He'll imprison you before he lets that happen. Or kill you so the line dies out and no one can challenge him."

Caireddin studied the row of kings: the rough stone, the red wash of light from the torches. What would happen if Daro succeeded in killing Cullen? What if she simply didn't marry the man? She saw the religious shutting the doorways at either end, saw dust and cobwebs settling over everything. The people would come to forget this long and powerful line of kings and queens; they would begin a new count, with Cullen at the head of it. And finally they would even forget the Hall, and some child playing in the castle would discover it anew. . . .

Only because of her. She shuddered to think of the influence she had, of the countless beliefs and traditions she would change, and all because she refused a marriage.

Her mother saw the shudder. She seemed to think that it came from reverence, that Caireddin had learned the lesson she had intended, because she said, more gently, "All right. Let's go."

# TWENTY-EIGHT

ngarred and Mathewar arrived at the castle the next day. No one challenged them at the main door or while they walked through the halls to their rooms, but Angarred did not relax her watchfulness. There was no reason to think that Cullen would be any friendlier than his father had been.

"Is that—" Mathewar said.

Angarred looked up to see Cullen heading toward them, surrounded by bodyguards. A shiver of fear went through her, and she forced herself to remember him as she had last seen him, the charmless brother, the one who seemed to have no thoughts of his own. Still, he was the Binder now; she could not allow herself to forget that.

"If he speaks to us at least we'll learn what he sounds like," Mathewar said, and she laughed.

Cullen drew closer. "You!" he said. "I heard you were dead."

"We're quite alive, as you see, my lord," Mathewar said. He bowed. Angarred curtsied, a little late. "We'd like to talk to you."

"We heard you were kidnapped," Cullen said.

"Yes, by your brother Drustig."

"Drustig?" Cullen glanced from one of them to the other, a flicker of fear showing in his eyes. Then he looked away, staring down the hallway at nothing. "What did Drustig want with you?"

"I don't know, my lord. I suspect he wanted a magician."

"How do I know you're not still working for him? How did you get away?"

"We escaped—"

"Did you? Or did he let you go, so you could come to my court and spy for him?"

"Listen," Mathewar said, using his commanding voice. "We have to talk to you. We know things about Drustig, and what he's planning—"

For a moment Cullen seemed to pay attention. Then he shrugged and said, "Everyone wants to tell me about Drustig. Do you think I have no spies of my own?"

"Whatever your spies told you it wasn't enough. I saw him use a crown—"

"Oh, for the Warrior's sake. I know all about his crown. Now if you'll excuse me . . ." He turned away.

"My lord," Mathewar said. Cullen looked back. The fear had returned to his eyes. "You will speak to me, one way or another."

"Very well," Cullen said. "Very well. Come join us for supper. We eat in the Lesser Banquet Hall."

He left. "He wants to pretend we're nothing more than courtiers," Angarred said quietly.

"He wants to discredit us," Mathewar said, his eyes still on Cullen. "His father told him to."

Angarred looked at him quickly. "Did you take that from his mind?"

Mathewar nodded.

"Did you see anything else?"

"No. Perhaps fortunately—his mind is a morass. But we have to be watchful."

As they headed to the banquet hall that evening they saw Lady Efcharren and her daughter coming from the other direction, a servant following them. Angarred lifted her skirts and ran to greet them. "Lady Efcharren!" she called. "Caireddin!"

She was surprised at how delighted she felt to see them. Well, they weren't enemies, at least, and might even be allies.

"Angarred!" Caireddin said.

The servant looked shocked at the name; probably another one who had heard of her, Angarred thought. He moved behind his two mistresses until he stood in the shadows of the hallway.

She embraced Caireddin, the stiff fabric of their gowns rustling as they met. "It's good to see you," Caireddin said. "How are you?"

"Much better, thank you," Angarred said. "But what about you? What are you doing here? I thought you were marrying Drustig."

"I was," Caireddin said. She told her the story of their travels with Drustig, their escape, their decision to come to Pergodi. She seemed far different from the girl who had talked so blithely about marrying kings; she had had to grow up in a hurry. "But now my mother thinks I have to marry Cullen, and I—"

"Hush!" Efcharren said. "There are things you don't talk about here."

Angarred nodded to show Caireddin she understood, and they headed toward the banquet hall together, talking softly. The servant hung back, waiting for them.

Cullen scowled as they entered, and Angarred saw his thought as clearly as if he had spoken it aloud: he hadn't known that the two of them had met before, and now he worried that they might conspire against him.

She and Caireddin took seats next to each other, giggling. Iltarra was opposite her, deep in conversation with Lord Annin. Cullen sat at the head of the table, talking to a man she recognized as Lord Sorle. She knew a few other nobles there, that funny old woman Lady Dubbish, the old courtier Lord Enlandin. Enlandin had once been a toady to whoever was in power, a weak and silly man, but the events of the War of All the Realms, and his own growing experience through the years, had made him a seasoned councilor. Unfortunately, Angarred thought, it was Cullen he had chosen to advise.

Servants came through a far door carrying plates piled high with food. Iltarra looked up. "Mathewar!" she said. She smiled, as if she had only just noticed him. "Angarred. It's good to see you back safely. We heard you were captured by pirates."

"Drustig's pirates, milady," Mathewar said.

"Drustig!" she said. "What did he want from you?"

"I'm still not certain," Mathewar said. He turned to Cullen. "I'd like the king to hear my account first, at any rate. When can I see you?"

"Oh, we know all we need to know about Drustig," Cullen said.

"All, milord?" Mathewar said. "His weaponry? The terrible things he does on the field of battle?"

"Drustig," Iltarra said, ignoring his last comments. "I should have known. Only he would be so audacious, and so stupid." She sounded almost admiring.

The interruption allowed Cullen to return to the man at his side. "Who is the man with Lady Iltarra?" Angarred whispered to Caireddin. "I don't remember him from my time here."

"Lord Annin," Caireddin said, pitching her voice as low as Angarred's. "He and Iltarra weren't here yesterday. My mother was disappointed, for some reason."

Iltarra turned her look of admiration on Mathewar. "How in the name of the Godkings did you escape?" she asked.

"I wouldn't be disappointed if she never came here again," Angarred whispered to Caireddin.

Caireddin laughed loudly. Cullen frowned at her, and she quieted and turned back to her plate. "As I said, we'd like to tell our story to the king first," Mathewar said to Iltarra.

Caireddin finished eating, then leaned over to Angarred and whispered, "This is the fourth day in a row we've had boar. I think it's his favorite dish." She hesitated and then said, "I hate it."

Cullen lifted his mug, peered into it, and scowled. "Where are those cursed servants?" he said angrily. "Iltarra, you're closest to the sideboard—can you bring me some more wine?"

"I'll do it, milord," Efcharren said.

"I don't care who does it—just get me the wine."

Efcharren stood at the same time Iltarra did. Suddenly Efcharren stumbled and fell against the princess. She flung out a hand to steady herself and grabbed Iltarra's necklace instead.

Pearls spilled to the floor, flaring out for a brief moment like shooting stars. They scattered, bounced, rolled into corners, pattering like soft rain. "You stupid, clumsy woman!" Iltarra said.

"I'm terribly sorry, milady," Efcharren said. She got to her knees awkwardly. "Here, let me help you."

"Get away from them!" Iltarra said, kneeling next to Efcharren. "Just go away. You're never to come to another banquet again, do you hear?"

"Yes, milady." Efcharren held out a handful of pearls. "Here—I found these for you."

Iltarra snatched them away. She studied them closely, then dropped them on the table and continued searching. Efcharren stood with difficulty and went back to her seat.

Angarred watched with rising amusement as Iltarra scrabbled for her pearls. Other courtiers looked on as well; Lady Dubbish seemed to take particular note, as if she meant to tell the rest of the court what had happened. "There's one over there," Angarred said. "In the corner."

Iltarra turned to her furiously, then crawled to the corner. The servants came to clear the dishes away and Iltarra ordered them back to the kitchen. "Does anyone see any more?" she asked. She stood and brushed down her dress carefully.

"No, milady," Enlandin said. Lady Dubbish shook her head.

Iltarra looked at the pearls on the table. "One of them is missing," she said. "The largest one. It isn't here." She glared at Efcharren, barely able to contain her rage. "You stole it, didn't you? You know what it is, you found out somehow . . ."

"No, milady, I swear," Efcharren said.

"Search her," Iltarra said to the guards.

"No, please . . ."

"It's the only way to make certain she doesn't have it. No one else touched them."

Iltarra and Efcharren both looked at the king. "Please, milord, I beseech you . . ." Efcharren said.

"She stole my pearl, Cullen," Iltarra said. "She can't be allowed to get away with that."

"Oh, very well," Cullen said, turning to the guards. "Search her. Anything for a little peace. No, not here, you idiots! Take her away."

"I didn't take anything, I swear . . ." Efcharren said. The guards grasped her roughly and forced her out the door.

Angarred's enjoyment disappeared far quicker than it had come. Poor Efcharren, to be suspected like a criminal . . . But what if the woman really had stolen the pearl? Perhaps she had planned it; she was disappointed Iltarra hadn't been at the banquet the day before.

Everyone at the table waited until the guards came back. No one even pretended to eat; all of them watched the double doors intently, saying nothing.

Finally the guards stepped inside, thrusting Efcharren forward. "She doesn't have it, milord," one of them said.

"Then where is it?" Iltarra asked the guards. "Come on, you louts, help me look."

But though she and the guards searched for over an hour they found nothing. They were still poring over the floor, inch by inch, candles in their hands, when Angarred and Mathewar left.

Mathewar headed out from the apartment the next day; he wanted to see Cullen's army of Bound Folk. He went down a flight of stairs to another section of the castle and turned a corner. A boy stood farther down the corridor, dusting the sconces.

"Nim!" Mathewar called, hurrying down the hallway.

The boy looked up. To Mathewar's astonishment he smiled; his eyes, which had once looked like chips of cold dirty ice, now seemed warm, open. "How are you?" Mathewar asked.

"I'm fine," Nim said.

"Are you sure?"

"Of course." Nim lowered his voice, though there was no one in the corridor to hear them. "I've been very fortunate since you last saw me. I was given this job in the castle—and because I work for the king now I don't have to join the army. I have no desire to fight for Cullen and his pack of Bound Folk."

"No, I don't blame you," Mathewar said.

"I have to stay out of Cullen's way, though. He's been known to bind people when he thinks he doesn't have enough men. I've seen him wandering the castle with his guards, taking anyone who looks strong enough."

Nim certainly had reason to worry—he looked fleshed out, far healthier than before. "And you—why are you in Pergodi?" Nim asked. "I thought you were going back to the College."

"I want to talk to Cullen," Mathewar said. "See what he plans to do about Drustig."

"They can kill each other, for all I care."

"Yes, but who will rule then?"

Nim shrugged, unconcerned. "Someone will show up. They always do."

"Do you need anything?" Mathewar asked.

"No, I'm fine."

"Good, very good," Mathewar said. "I'm staying in the castle—if you want to talk to me just ask the steward where I am."

"All right," Nim said.

Mathewar continued down to the castle's main door, feeling hopeful; at least one thing in this dreadful city had turned out well. He had worried about Nim; in a way he had given the boy life, and he felt tenderly toward him, almost like a son. Though Nim still didn't seem to realize what he had done, and would never know how much he had sacrificed.

He sighed. He wished he could see his own sons, and his daughters as well.

He ran into an old friend next, a man who had a good deal of interesting information. Lord Ezlin Ertig, the man said, had been jailed but not yet turned into one of the Bound Folk. This was more good news; Ezlin could rule if Drustig and Cullen were somehow defeated.

But his optimism died when he saw Cullen's army. They had been quartered in barracks on the jousting field; as he came closer he saw men on the field drilling in rows, marching in chilling perfection. Beyond them stood the barracks, and he marveled at how much work Cullen, or Cullen's Bound Folk, had done in only a few months. Though the quarters had been thrown together clumsily; he could see cracks in the wooden walls.

An unbound man stopped him as he entered. "I'm here to inspect the troops," Mathewar said in his commanding voice, and the man nodded and stepped back.

The room was dim, the only light coming through gaps in the ceiling. Rows of pallets stretched out into the unseen distance. It reminded Mathewar of his own imprisonment, and his heart constricted with dread.

Men sat on their pallets without moving, without speaking, hundreds of them. The lack of noise was eerie; he found himself straining for the slightest sound: breathing, or the wind whistling through the cracks in the walls.

Could these men stand against Drustig? They were enough for a conventional battle, but he did not think they could face Drustig's half crown. He went back to the castle, feeling heartsick at what he had seen.

Efcharren didn't come to the banquet hall that evening. Angarred had just finished greeting Caireddin, and wondering whether Efcharren would ever be forgiven, when the king and his other guests arrived.

Cullen came through the double doors first. After him came a man wearing the castle emblem on his coat and carrying a small harp slung over his back.

Suddenly Caireddin's servant moved; he went down on his knee in one fluid motion and lowered his head. The folks at the door murmured, and the king turned back.

"What is he doing?" Cullen said, pulling the man savagely to his feet. "You bow to the king, you peasant, not his musician."

The servant bowed to Cullen and straightened. He stood impassively with his head lowered, his long unruly hair shadowing his face.

"He thinks the man is an *awithi,* my lord," Lord Sorle said.

"An *awithi*?" Cullen said. "What in the name of the Orator is that?"

"It's a sort of holy man they have in Goss," Sorle said. "He recites the king's lineage at important occasions."

Cullen looked suspiciously at Caireddin. "You didn't tell me your servant was Gossek," he said.

"We're from the north, my lord," Caireddin said. "We have only Gossek and Ounek servants."

"I should have known," Cullen said. "Look at that muck on his face." Most Karedek men were unable to grow beards.

Cullen dismissed the servant with a gesture. "One minute, my lord," Annin said.

"Yes, what?"

Annin took the servant's chin in his hand and forced his head up. "This man looks familiar."

"Surely you don't know any Gossek menials," Caireddin said, laughing a little.

"No, but I visited the royal family once," Annin said. "This is—"

The man broke away and ran down the corridor. "Seize him!" Cullen shouted to his guards.

The guards rushed after him. He ran quickly; he had nearly reached the corner, and the guards were far behind. Angarred found she was clenching her hands, hoping for some reason that he would get away. Caireddin made a soft noise in her throat.

One of the guards put a pipe to his lips and whistled shrilly. Other men came from around the corner, heading for the servant, trapping him between them. The lone man looked almost calmly from one group to the other, apparently weighing his chances, and then turned and ran toward the king's bodyguards. The guards advanced on him, their swords out.

"Tashtery, no," Caireddin whispered.

One of the guards fell back. Angarred saw the silver glint in the servant's hand; he had been carrying a hidden knife, against all the laws of the castle.

But now the servant began to retreat. The guards kept their long swords out, fixing a distance between themselves and the servant's knife. He thrust the knife forward several times, testing for a gap, but could not reach them. Little by little the two groups closed on him, pinching him in their vise.

One guard put his sword at the man's throat, and another wrenched his knife away. The rest surrounded him, bolder now, and dragged him back to stand before the king.

"Prince Brangwin," Lord Annin said. "That's who he is."

"What!" the king said.

"What?" Caireddin said, much softer.

"He's Prince Brangwin of the Gossek royal family, my lord," Annin said. "Perhaps the last of that lineage. Though why he walked into his enemies' arms is beyond me."

"Why did you?" Cullen asked.

Brangwin said nothing.

"Did you want to kill me?" Cullen asked.

Silence from Brangwin.

"I don't have time for this," Cullen said. "Take him to the dungeons and have him tortured. Find out what he's planning, if there are any more Gossek hiding in Pergodi." He laughed. "I'll have quite a collection, what with him and Lord Ezlin. A menagerie of monarchs. Put them next to each other—they can talk about lost chances."

"Milord—" Caireddin said.

"You aren't going to ask me for mercy, are you?" Cullen said. "He's the leader of my enemies—I can't possibly let him go."

"But he's harmless. He would never hurt you."

"No one's harmless. Everyone has plans and schemes, and because I'm the king they all plan and scheme against me. I can't trust anyone. You, milady—what was your part in all this?"

"Me?" Caireddin stepped back. "Nothing."

"Did you know who he was?"

"No. Of course not."

"Tell me now if you and he conspired together. I'll learn everything when he's tortured anyway."

"Please don't. He's a refugee, he has no plans, I swear it—"

"I warned you. One more plea on his behalf and I'll add you to my collection."

Caireddin said nothing.

"Say, 'Yes, my lord.'"

"Yes, my lord."

"Good. Now let's go have supper and listen to my musician. Rooting out treason makes me hungry."

"I'd like to go to my rooms, milord," Caireddin said.

"That would look very suspicious indeed, milady," Cullen said. "Guards, see that she stays here."

She glanced at Angarred wildly, and then the guards closed around her. She looked, Angarred thought, like a drowning swimmer in the last moment before going under. The king went into the hall, and everyone followed.

The next day Caireddin rode to the city and sold another ruby, then returned to the castle. The first person she approached told her how to find the dungeons. She headed down a flight of damp, chilly stairs. A man came toward her out of the gloom.

He was short and squat, with a pale face and pale hair. "What business do you have here, milady?" he asked.

"I'm looking for a certain man," she said. "A prisoner."

"The whereabouts of the prisoners are secret," the guard said.

"I'll pay anyone who leads me to him."

"How much?"

She named an amount that made him raise his pale eyebrows. "And the name of the prisoner?"

"Prince Brangwin."

"I'm afraid I don't know him, milady." He sounded genuinely disappointed.

"Do you know who does?" Caireddin asked. "I can pay generously for information."

"Wait here." He walked away into the shadows. Would he bring back a guide? Or would he gather his fellows and come back to rob her? She had dressed in a light cloak for the ride into the city, and now she shivered in the cold. She parted the cloak and grasped the hilt of her sword tightly. Somewhere water dripped monotonously to the floor.

Finally he came back with another guard. This man was his opposite—tall and skinny, with dark hair and eyes—but they looked somehow alike, brothers maybe, or cousins. Perhaps it was their shared pallor, a whiteness like a fish's belly.

"Come," the tall man said.

"One moment," she said. She poured coins into the first guard's upturned hands and then followed.

The prison corridors wound like a maze. She passed cells set into the white stone walls, and locked iron doors, and rooms where more pale men sat, watching over prisoners in hidden rooms farther in.

Torches shone for most of the way, but there were stretches of darkness where she had to put her hand out and feel the cold stone of the wall. She kept close tally of all the twists and turns, certain her guide would leave her at the end.

Finally the guide stopped. The prison had grown colder as they walked, and now it was as chilly as a Winter night in Ou. She peered through the bars of a cell and saw a man sitting on the ground, his head bowed over his knees. Long hair hid his face, but she knew him despite that. She paid the guard and walked toward the cell.

"Hello," she said. "Prince Brangwin."

Brangwin looked up and smiled wearily. He wore only the clothes he was captured in; he must have been freezing. "Caireddin," he said. "It's good to see you. I hope you understand why I couldn't tell you my real name."

"I suppose," Caireddin said. She sat on the floor and they moved closer, only the bars between them. Water seeped from the stones in the walls. "I told you who we were, though."

"I met you once, milady," he said. "You and your mother came to Goss a few years ago, and we sat at a banquet together. Do you remember?"

She looked at him. "I'm trying to imagine you without all that hair," she said.

He smiled. She felt delighted at his rare smiles; she thought she would do almost anything for another of them. "I remember you, though," he said. "You were—fifteen, I think."

"Tashtery, no," she said, laughing. "I was a bratty child then. I hope I didn't do anything too insulting."

"I don't think so." He hesitated. "You're very different now."

She could think of nothing to say to this. It made her bolder, though, and she reached her hand through the bars for his. They sat awhile like that, holding hands, saying nothing, as if to mention the contact between them would somehow break the spell.

"There's so much about you, about your life, that I don't know," she said. She went on quickly. "You don't have to tell me anything, though—I know you've been through—" Through what? A tragedy? It sounded so inadequate. "Through a good deal," she said feebly.

"There's very little to tell. The Karedek burned our castle, and nearly everyone in my family died. I was away, reciting poems to a woman I barely remember. Then the survivors came together, my cousin Madaroc and his wife Lirden and some others, and they made a life for themselves in a hidden valley. And then they died too, all but Lirden."

"And you fought Bound Folk. I've seen them now—they're horrible."

"Horrible, yes."

"And then you came up against Drustig."

"Yes. And it was his crown that made me mad."

"I felt Drustig's crown too. I've never met anyone else who did, though. The way the world seems to slip away from you, leaving you alone and terrified, with no one to help you . . ."

"Yes."

They said nothing for a while, aware of the bond between them, of the warmth of their hands. "That's why we ran away, my mother and I," she said. "I couldn't bear him after that."

"Why in Tashtery's name did you want to marry him?"

"I don't know. I had some romantic ideas, stupid ideas . . . It's very hard being Karedek royalty—there are so few of us. I can only marry certain people. And now it looks as if Cullen—as if I have to—I feel trapped, caged. No, I'm sorry—it's you who are caged. I can never talk to you without sounding foolish."

"You don't sound foolish at all. Though I have to warn you, milady—Caireddin—it's dangerous for you to be seen here."

"I had to know if you were all right. I'm sorry I couldn't save you from Cullen."

"You couldn't possibly have changed his mind. And it was brave of you to try—most people would have distanced themselves from me as quickly as possible."

"Is there anything I can do for you?"

"There is, yes. Could you talk to Lirden? She doesn't know what's happened to me—she must be frantic. Tell her to leave Pergodi immediately—it's no longer safe here. You'll have my gratitude forever."

"Of course."

"She's still at the inn. Do you remember where that is?"

She nodded.

He hesitated, his face uncertain. "There's one more thing," he said finally. "I've seen you talk to Mathewar at the king's banquets—"

"I told you before—I met him and his wife in Ou."

"He's a man fraught with peril, milady. A sorcerer. How do you know he didn't create the Bound Folk, or plan the invasion of Goss?"

"Because I know him," she said. She backed away from his intense gaze, letting go of his hand. "He'd never do anything like that."

"Have you seen any other magicians at the castle? Anyone else who could have worked these unholy magics?" Before she could answer he went on: "You're really very innocent in some ways, milady. You didn't understand Drustig's evil at first, remember. Or Cullen's."

"But Drustig—but he's nothing like Drustig or Cullen. Anyway, he has no influence at court. He's been asking for an audience with Cullen, but Cullen keeps putting him off."

"What does he want with Cullen?"

"To talk about the war, I think."

"Yes, that's another odd thing," Brangwin said. "Drustig can't be far away, but Cullen spends his days in frivolities—dining and hunting and listening to music. And yet Drustig has a weapon, a terrible weapon. . . ."

"My mother and I tried to tell Cullen about it, but he said he already knew."

"Well, maybe he does. Maybe he has a way to counter it—he seems very confident. But I think that Drustig is the more powerful, and that he will best his brother. I hate them equally, but I suppose Cullen is less evil than Drustig. If I were free—" He looked full of purpose, flayed down to one desire.

"What?"

He lowered his voice, though there was no one else in the corridor; as Caireddin had thought, the guard had long since left them. "I would kill them all, milady," he said. "Drustig and Cullen and Mathewar, all the men who destroyed my country."

She sat back, startled at his resolve. The cold of the floor had seeped into her bones, and she shifted awkwardly. "I should go now," she said. "I'll come back, I promise. And I'll talk to Lirden."

"Thank you, milady. And keep watch over them for me, Cullen and Mathewar. Tell me what they do."

"I will," Caireddin said.

After she left she got her horse and headed down to the city for the second time that day. At the inn she described Lirden to the innkeeper and was directed to the room next to Brangwin's. What did that mean, that they didn't share a room? She shook her head and knocked on the unpainted wooden door.

No one answered, though she heard someone moving inside. "It's Caireddin," she called out. "Your friend sent me."

The door opened. Lirden wore a brown skirt and green blouse, both simple and undecorated. She looked up and down the hallway, then finally swung the door wider and gestured Caireddin inside.

The room contained a chair and an iron cot. A tallow candle smoldered in a sconce. A few clothes were neatly folded and placed on top of the chair.

"We can sit on the bed, I suppose," Lirden said. "You said my friend—"

"Prince Brangwin," Caireddin said. "Yes."

Lirden drew in a sharp breath. "Does everyone know his name now?" she asked.

Once again Caireddin cursed herself for her gracelessness. If Brangwin's name had been discovered, the news she brought was almost certainly bad. She had hoped to tell Lirden about Brangwin's arrest gradually, but it seemed she had none of these people's talent for intrigue and disguises. "I'm afraid so," she said.

"Then what—what happened to him?" Lirden asked.

"He's in prison." Lirden bowed her head. "I managed to talk to him there, though," Caireddin went on, and Lirden looked at her, suddenly hopeful.

"How did you get into the prison? How are his spirits? What did he say to you? And how in Tashtery's name did Cullen learn who he was?"

Caireddin nearly laughed. "One question at a time, please. I bribed the guards to take me to him. He seems well, considering." She told the other woman about Brangwin's arrest, and finished by saying, "He said to tell you to leave Pergodi—that it's dangerous here."

Lirden stood and began to pace the stained wooden floor. "Is he well, truly? Not dispirited or unhappy? Or did he tell you to say that?"

"He . . ." Caireddin began, searching for the right words. "He didn't seem unhappy. He talked about what he'd do if he were free."

Lirden shook her head. "Amazing," she said.

"What do you mean? Why is that amazing?"

"Don't you know what they're going to do to him, milady? He's the king of Goss now, though no one's said it aloud. He can't be allowed to live. First Cullen will torture him, find out what he knows about Goss. He's probably already started. Then—"

"No. No, he hasn't been tortured."

"He wouldn't tell you if he had been. And after the torture Cullen will bind him and make him fight for his enemy, for Karededin. It's the thing he fears most. And if they don't bind him they'll kill him, and that would almost be better."

Caireddin said nothing. She hadn't thought beyond her visit, hadn't realized what he faced alone in his cell. No wonder he had desired revenge so strongly. "I'm sorry, milady," she said.

"Don't call me that," Lirden said fiercely. Caireddin heard a sob in her voice; she was changing the subject, seizing on trifles to avoid thinking about Brangwin's fate. "He told me who you are. I'm far lower in rank than you, milady."

For a moment Caireddin almost told her about the cage she found herself in, her only choices to marry the king or face death. She said nothing, though; as her mother would say, it was not a fit subject for outsiders.

Longing swept through her. If only she could be free, if she and Brangwin could run somewhere far away from kings and wars and politics . . . No, she couldn't think about that. It was no good dwelling on what she couldn't have.

"Do you love him?" she asked Lirden.

"Of course I do," Lirden said. "He's my king—and a good man."

The answer told her nothing, and she couldn't bring herself to ask again. Had they shared the small uncomfortable cot, barely big enough even for one person?

"I'm not leaving," Lirden said suddenly. "No one here knows who I am, or that I have anything to do with him. I'll bribe guards, just as you did, and I'll find some way to free him." She looked at Caireddin defiantly. Then her brave show collapsed, and she said, "Please don't tell him."

"I won't," Caireddin said. "But I think you should do what he says. People may have seen you together. Your prince knows about danger—listen to him, milady."

Lirden shook her head.

"All right, then," Caireddin said. "I'll tell you if I discover anything—and I hope you'll do the same for me. Do you have any money?"

"Yes. Thanks to your generosity."

"Then the blessings of Marfan and Mathona go with you."

"And you," Lirden said.

# TWENTY-NINE

E very supper, Angarred thought, brought some new surprise. That evening Annin was absent. Iltarra fidgeted restlessly all through the meal, bringing her hand up to her neck where the pearls used to be.

Annin stayed away the next evening as well. Had he left Iltarra? But he had seemed so in love with her.

Only Cullen appeared the same, unworried by war and change and magic. Sometimes Angarred thought that even he looked hectic, his eyes too bright, his cheeks too red—as though he lived in a fever dream, determined to hold to what he had until the fever overtook him and he died.

He continued to summon entertainers to his banquets, as if he thought that was a king's sole purpose. The second evening of Annin's absence he told them he had invited a pair of fortune-tellers.

Even with this announcement Angarred was unprepared for what happened next. The plates were taken away, the doors opened, and Reti and Remi walked into the room. They both wore skirts; Remi still had his beard and Reti his cheap beads and bracelets.

Mathewar exclaimed softly. "I know you!" Caireddin called out.

The brothers nodded to everyone blandly, as if they had never seen any of them before.

They took two empty chairs and placed them near the king. Mathewar turned away, pretending disinterest, and began to talk to Angarred.

Angarred could not help but overhear, though. "Some will rise and some will fall," Remi said to Cullen. "The high will rise above them all."

Cullen laughed, delighted, and slapped his hand against the table. "Do you hear that?" he said to the others. "I'm the highest, the king—and I'm going to rise even higher. Above everyone else, is that what you said?"

"Yes, milord," Remi said. "Above them all."

Remi continued to talk to Cullen, but Reti moved his chair near Mathewar. "Wouldst like us to tell thy future?" he asked.

"Can you tell my past?" Mathewar asked. "Why didn't you tell me you'd seen Angarred?"

"I think you know," Reti said.

"Stop talking to this wretch and tell me more," Cullen called to Reti. "Am I going to be victorious over that toad-eater Drustig?"

"Yes, come over here," Lady Dubbish said. "What do you see in my future?"

"We can only repeat what we've said before, milord," Remi said.

" 'Rise above them all,' " Cullen said, and laughed again.

"Milord," Mathewar said. Only Angarred, of everyone at the table, knew how angry he was. "Why do you listen to these deceivers? They tell you what you want to hear, nothing more."

"Who are you to tell me who to listen to?" Cullen asked. "You're supposed to be a magician, but I've heard precious little by way of prediction from you."

"I've asked to speak to you before, milord."

"You were filled with doom-laden prophecies, as I remember. Drustig's weapons, Drustig's power . . . Maybe if you told me something pleasing, like these men here, I would have granted you an audience."

"I have nothing pleasing to say to you, I'm afraid," Mathewar said. He stood and spoke a few words, and the doors slammed shut. "You are going to lose this war, and lose it badly, if you don't listen to me. It may already be too late."

Cullen stood and looked around wildly. "Guards!" he said. "Guards!"

The guards took a few steps toward Mathewar and then stopped, identical looks of terror on their faces. "I'll let you go when I'm finished," Mathewar said to them. He leaned forward, placing his palms on the table. "You say you know about Drustig's terrible weapon—"

"I do," Cullen said, sounding much less certain now. He did not meet Mathewar's gaze.

"Very well. But you've never experienced it, and I have. And I tell you that your troops won't stand against it, that no one can. They'll scatter before Drustig like sand." He paused. "But you have a weapon as well."

"Where did you hear that?" Cullen asked.

"Never mind. Your weapon and his belong together—they were broken apart years ago, during the Sorcerers' Wars. If I can study yours, milord, I might learn enough to stop his."

"I won't—no, you can't have it. I'm not even admitting I have a weapon. But if I did I'd never let you see it. How do I know you won't turn it against me?"

"You'll have to trust me."

Cullen laughed bitterly. "I don't trust anyone," he said. "Especially not you."

"Then you'll lose the war. It's as simple as that."

"No, I won't," Cullen said, growing bolder now. "I have the largest army Karededin has ever seen, all of them absolutely loyal to me. And I can always make—get more soldiers."

"Yes, I've seen your army," Mathewar said. "And I'll say it again—they'll never defeat Drustig."

"They will, by the Warrior. They'll overpower him and take his crown."

Mathewar shrugged and stepped back from the table. "If you believe that then I can't help you."

"I don't care if you believe me or not," Cullen said. "Well, we've had the talk you wanted. Now open the doors and let us out."

"I have one more question, milord," Mathewar said. His voice seemed to compel Cullen to look at him, though he did not pitch it any louder than before. "How did Jerret die?"

Cullen blanched. "I—it was very sudden. That's all I know."

"Indeed it was," Mathewar said. He said some words, and the doors swung open.

Folks looked at each other in confusion. Mathewar sat next to Angarred again. Reti said, "Farewell to you, fair lords, gentle ladies. We'll take our leave now."

"Now?" Cullen said. "You've hardly started. Tell this interfering magician that I'll defeat Drustig without his help. Tell him he's crazy."

"Well," Reti said. "I can't take him to task for that. We're crazy too."

"What about my future?" Iltarra asked.

"We've told you all we know," Reti said.

"You've told us nothing," Cullen said. "Don't think I'll pay you for this."

"Oh, we don't do it for pay," Reti said.

The brothers strode out of the room. "Why do you do it, then?" Cullen called after them. "To show off your wardrobes?" Iltarra giggled.

"I've met one of these men before," Caireddin said to Cullen. "He didn't tell me anything useful either."

"They're the worst fortune-tellers I've ever seen," Cullen said.

"It doesn't matter, milord," Caireddin said. "They told you the most important thing—that you'll triumph over your brother. There's nothing more to say after that."

"Yes, that's true," Cullen said, looking at Caireddin with new interest. "You're a very perceptive young woman."

Angarred blinked at Caireddin in surprise. Why in the name of all the Godkings was she toadying to Cullen? She hated the man.

Caireddin moved to the chair Remi had vacated. She bent her head toward Cullen, and a moment later the king laughed loudly.

"I don't understand any of this," Angarred murmured to Mathewar.

"Nor do I," Mathewar said.

Without discussing it they stood and headed for the door, leaving Cullen and Caireddin deep in conversation.

The next day Caireddin went into the dungeons again. She paid her bribe to the guard at the foot of the stairs, then headed through the cold corridors to Brangwin's cell.

She didn't completely understand why she had talked to Cullen the night before. She was tired, she knew that much, tired of fighting Cullen and her mother and her fate. If she threw her lot in with Brangwin she would face even more hardship; he would have to escape, and then battle the combined might of Cullen's forces to regain his kingdom. . . .

And Brangwin was a terribly difficult man. He seemed to carry his long sorrowful history with him like a heavy sack; she was not allowed to forget for one moment that he had enemies everywhere. Cullen and Drustig and even Mathewar—his grudges multiplied, with no end in sight.

It seemed easier just to give in. Even the fortune-tellers had said Cullen would triumph. And Cullen wasn't as ugly as she had first thought—no beauty, but then she couldn't really expect more.

She reached the cell. "Caireddin," Brangwin said, smiling. "It's good to see you."

She felt immediately guilty for her thoughts, and for her conversation with Cullen the evening before. And she remembered what Lirden had said, that he might at any moment be turned into one of the Bound Folk. Who was she to judge him?

"Here," she said, handing him some beef wrapped in linen she had brought from the kitchen. "I thought you might want this."

Brangwin unwrapped the cloth and smiled again. "Thank you," he said. "Though the sight of you nourishes me more than any food." He set the cloth down. "Tell me—did you see Lirden? How is she?"

"She's worried about you, but otherwise she seems fine."

"Good. And is she leaving Pergodi?"

"I suppose so," Caireddin said, feeling little guilt at the lie. Lirden's movements were her own business.

"What else is happening up in the world? Has Cullen done anything to prepare for war?"

She told him about the Travelers, and Mathewar's anger at the king, everything except her talk with Cullen at the end. "That's odd, about Mathewar," he said. "He's the poisoned root, the cause of the evil growing here, the man who supplies Cullen with Bound Folk. And yet the king won't even speak to him."

There it was again—more of Brangwin's obsessions. She tried not to sigh. "I still don't think Mathewar created the Bound Folk. He said Cullen has a weapon, something like what Drustig has. I think that's how Cullen makes more of them."

She stopped as an idea came to her, and then another, and yet another, until finally she thought she understood everything. "He said Drustig's crown, and whatever Cullen has, he said they were one thing and then broke apart. So Cullen probably has half a crown too. And Cullen said Drustig has something to loose, but he has something to bind—so it's probably his crown that creates the Bound Folk. Yes, and then Mathewar wanted to study it but Cullen wouldn't let him—Cullen said he didn't want Mathewar turning it against him."

"Of course not," Brangwin said. "I'd be careful around that sorcerer too."

This time she did sigh. "But don't you see? Mathewar has nothing to do with the Bound Folk."

"Maybe," Brangwin said. "But I still don't trust him."

You don't trust anyone, she wanted to say. Instead she talked to him for a few moments more and then escaped upstairs, to the light of day.

Mathewar walked toward the castle's entrance, intending to pay another visit to the barracks. Something was about to happen, he thought; he had felt restless for days. He turned a corner and found himself face-to-face with Reti.

"You," he said. "I thought you had nothing more to say to us."

"We don't," Reti said. "But it's very comfortable in the castle."

"Of course it is. A good many valuables, for one thing. Is that the game you're playing? I've never known you to curry favor with kings before."

"We don't work that way, you know that. Think about what we said."

"'The high will rise . . .'" Mathewar said. "Are you saying there's someone higher than Cullen? But who?"

"It's not time to answer that question," Reti said.

"No, of course not. But because of what you said Cullen thinks he'll best his brother—"

"Which makes him overconfident—"

"And Caireddin wants to marry him, probably because she thinks he'll triumph—"

"She's free to make her own decisions—"

"You have an answer for everything, don't you?"

"No. Sometimes we don't even have the questions."

"You've had one question for a while now. Why didn't you tell me where Angarred was?"

"I told you," Reti said. "You already know the answer to that."

Mathewar said nothing. He had noticed that insight did not usually come all at once, in the form of blinding light, that most realizations happened slowly, a new belief gradually replacing the old. During the journey south to Karededin he had thought about what Angarred had said about responsibility, and now he realized, somewhat to his surprise, that he had come to agree with her: he'd had no way of knowing that Jerret would die.

It was still true that his arrogance had caused his first wife's death, at least partly. But he had paid for that in grief and repentance, and would pay still in years to come. He could not keep viewing everything through the bleak colors of Embre's death.

It was that same arrogance, he saw now, that made him think the fate of the realm rested on his shoulders, that caused him to blame himself for everything that went wrong. He hated to admit it to Reti, though. And he disapproved of the Travelers' methods, the way they played on emotions and expectations.

"Tell me something," he said. "You don't think I had any responsibility for what happened to Jerret. Or for Angarred, when I thought she was dead." Reti nodded. "But here you are, the Forsaken, believing you caused the Bridegroom's death, when you had nothing whatever to do with it."

"I suppose you could see it that way."

"Don't you feel any need to be consistent?"

"Not really. We're crazy, I told you that."

Mathewar laughed in spite of himself. He tried to summon his anger against these rogues one more time. "Is that why you told me the Bridegroom's story that night? Because you wanted me to start thinking about responsibility?"

"Yes."

"But why do you interfere in people's lives like this? You can do a great deal of damage."

"We do it for Mother Mathona," Reti said.

There was nothing Mathewar could say to that. But he had more questions, and it looked to be a long conversation; he went to a flight of stairs and sat down. Reti sat next to him, stretching his hairy legs so that they stuck out from the bottom of his skirt.

"All right," Mathewar said. "But if you know anything that might help us overcome Drustig, or get rid of Cullen, you should tell me. This isn't a game. The fate of all the realms rests on this war—and I have a feeling Drustig is near, very near, that the war could come as soon as tomorrow."

Reti nodded. "We have that feeling too."

"Are you able to predict things, then? How did you know there was someone above Cullen?"

"We can predict a little. Usually not enough to do any good."

"What else do you see?"

"Nothing. Truly."

"Why are you telling me so much? What happened to all your enigmas and ambiguities, your slippery stories?"

"I don't know. I suppose I think of you as one of us. Very few people have ever solved the Bridegroom's Riddle."

Mathewar had nearly forgotten the question at the end of Reti's story. He had known it was a kind of test, but not how important it had been.

"And no one's ever solved it drunk," Reti said.

"I wasn't drunk," Mathewar said reflexively.

"How long ago were you a sattery addict?"

"What? How do you know about that?"

"You said something about it. When you were—"

"When I was drunk. All right. Fourteen years ago. And yes, I sometimes used to lie about it without thinking." He looked at Reti. "You're a very dangerous man. In fact, you remind me of a man named Tobrin, someone else I'd like to question."

"Who's Tobrin?"

"A powerful magician. He knows something about all this, but he won't help us. He says he doesn't want to interfere."

"Can I tell you a story?" Reti asked.

"You've been telling me one long story since I met you, I think," Mathewar said, but he was smiling.

"Once, long ago," Reti said, "when all the plates were silver and all the cups were gold, there was a man who picked up a book by a Master and became fascinated with his teachings. This first man, the Student, read everything he could by the Master, and studied his books over and over, and talked to everyone who had ever met him. Finally, though, he thought that he would only truly understand the Master's teachings if he could see him and talk to him for himself.

"So the Student sold everything he had except his books and set off on his journey. He had heard that the Master lived at the other end of the continent, so he rode hundreds and hundreds of miles to the west. He passed through a great many perils, and was nearly killed a number of times, but those adventures don't come into this story. Then, finally, he reached his destination, and he was told that while he was on his journey the Master had moved a long distance away, to a city in the south.

"So the Student packed up his books again and set off for the south. And once again he passed through a great many perils, and was nearly killed a number of times. And then finally, after years and years of traveling, he reached the city where the Master lived. He arrived very late at night, and he found a room at an inn and waited for morning.

"He was too impatient to sleep, intoxicated by the thought that in the morning he would see the wisest and holiest man in the world. He stayed up reading through the books he had collected. At first he did this to remind himself of the Master's teachings, so that he would not be shamed when he met him. After a while, though, he saw that there was more in these books than he had ever conceived, and he re-alized that he had not read some of them for a long time. He read on and on, reaching insight after insight. And then finally, in the dead of night, he gave a great cry of understanding. Then he went downstairs, saddled his horse, and headed for home."

"That's the Student's Riddle, I suppose," Mathewar said.

"Yes," Reti said, looking at him intently.

"Don't worry, I can guess the answer," Mathewar said. "It's a lot easier than the first one, thank the Godkings. A man should be his own master, and not look to another for wisdom."

Reti said nothing.

"But my problem with Tobrin is very different. I need knowledge from him, not wisdom—knowledge of magic. He could overcome both of these brothers, I'm certain of it."

"Very well," Reti said. "I wish you good fortune, then."

"And you," Mathewar said.

He continued on to the main entrance. He couldn't rid himself of his sense of foreboding, and the fact that Reti felt it too made him doubly anxious. His illusions returned; they crowded the corridors of the castle, stronger than ever. Stars brightened into candles, candles blossomed into trees. Colors swirled before him, noblewomen's dresses, a drift of leaves. Finally they overwhelmed everything else, and he gave up his attempt to visit the barracks and returned to the apartment.

He was able to attend the king's banquet, but he went to bed shortly afterward. He dreamed of a great army, and at its head a rider wearing half a crown. The white metal of the crown shone so brightly it cast the man and horse into shadow—or perhaps there was no one there, there was only a crown working evil without awareness. The land changed as the man rode forward, fraying, falling into pieces, turning to chaos behind him.

He screamed. The crown seemed to sense him and moved toward him, obliterating the sky.

He screamed again. It turned into a shrill laugh that went on and on, though he tried desperately to stop it. The rider laughed in response. The sounds joined, until he couldn't tell which of them was laughing. Suddenly he had the terrible fear that it was his face beneath the crown, that he and the rider were the same. He flailed out, trying to get away, but his arms were caught.

"Hush," someone said. "It's all right. Hush."

"No!" he shouted. "No!"

"Wake up," the voice said.

He knew the voice, though he couldn't remember whose it was. He understood that it promised rescue, though. He headed toward it through the changing land.

He opened his eyes. He had created a light during his nightmare, and by its illumination he could see Angarred. She held him close.

He looked beyond her. Chairs lay scattered across the room, their arms and backs broken off; a chest missing its lid had overturned, spilling out clothes.

"Holy Godkings," he said. Magicians were not supposed to be able to cast difficult spells while asleep; at least, he had never heard of anyone doing so. Was this more of Drustig's poisonous legacy? "I'm sorry, I didn't mean . . ."

"It's all right," she said again.

They held each other, each of them, Mathewar knew, thinking the same thing. The two armies would clash soon, but the outcome would be bad, whatever it was; neither Cullen nor Drustig would rule wisely. And he and Angarred, and all their friends, all the great city of Pergodi, would be crushed as if between two rocks. They would all pass through pain and terror, and for what? What would be changed by the coming war?

All he had left to him was this brief comfort in the dark. He wanted to tell her his dream, but a great weariness overtook him. "You always come to rescue me," he said. His voice felt raw from screaming. "No matter where I go."

The next day scouts galloped into the courtyard and ran up the stairs to the Council Chamber. Drustig's troops had come at last.

# THIRTY

This time Cullen made ready for battle; he would be leading the Bound Folk, who could not act without his orders. He preferred an army that would do his bidding without question, Mathewar knew; only Lord Sorle and Lord Annin and a few other unbound men would march with him from the castle.

Despite this, Mathewar and Angarred prepared to follow them. Mathewar did not intend to leave such an important battle to Cullen.

Caireddin, who had come to visit Angarred with her mother, asked if she could join them. Lady Efcharren said with asperity that she would stay in the castle, that under no circumstances could the heir to the royal family be risked in battle. To Mathewar's surprise Caireddin nodded, accepting her mother's orders with no argument.

Mathewar and Angarred got their horses and mounted, then watched as the Bound Folk filed past the courtyard gate. They were a grotesque army, moving in absolute unison, singing the same monotonous song. They came on and on; Mathewar thought there were a few thousand of them, at least. He and Angarred rode out at the end, and no one turned to look at them.

The army marched along a main road toward the Baelish Gate.

People lined the road, but instead of cheering they stood silent, their expressions showing fear and awe and dread.

The army passed through the gate and headed north. They stopped only once, at midday, to eat hard tasteless bread and relieve themselves, then continued on. An hour later Cullen rode down the line shouting orders. Mathewar could not hear what he said, but he saw that the other man was enjoying himself despite the danger. He realized that Cullen had always wanted to fight a great battle, that it was only in warfare that he felt happy. Whatever else folks said about the new king, they could certainly not call him a coward.

When he finished speaking the troops began to push forward, a few of them trampling others in their hurry. They strung out in a precise line across several low hills, entirely blocking the main road. Divided up this way there seemed to be fewer of them, and Mathewar remembered uneasily what Caireddin had said about the size of Drustig's army.

Mathewar and Angarred moved their mounts back behind the line. The Bound Folk were quiet now, all their concentration on the road. A horde of men came toward them, shouting and laughing.

For a quick moment Mathewar noticed the contrasts between the two. The Bound Folk were silent, unmoving, orderly, the men they faced loud, dirty, violent. Then the armies collided and he saw nothing but confusion, brief clashes, horses screaming, people falling.

Metal clanged on metal. Someone shouted in triumph and then fell to the ground, pierced by an arrow he never saw. A man pushed past several soldiers and took an ax stroke meant for his fellow. Five or six folks from both sides slipped away from the fighting and ran off down the hillsides.

A sword flashed in the sun. It was Drustig's, his horse rearing above the fray, his sword arm upraised, the half crown upon his head. He was too far away to be heard, but somehow his mocking laughter shrilled out across the battlefield and the fighting halted for a moment. Mathewar shivered in the bright sunlight.

Drustig and his men pressed ahead. Some Bound Folk ran from the hideous laughter; others stood without moving, stupefied. More and more slipped from Cullen's command, and another wave of

Drustig's men surged forward, shouting nonsense, reveling in the slaughter.

Cullen rode back and forth, speaking a soft command to the men who had broken away. They struggled back from their lunacy and returned to their regiments, then drew up in ordered lines and turned to face Drustig again.

Cullen had not had his crown as long as Drustig, Mathewar thought; he probably needed time to learn how to command an entire army. And as Mathewar watched he realized that Cullen could only bind a few men at a time, while Drustig could cast his madness over hundreds. However hard Cullen worked, he would always be too slow.

More crazed laughter sounded, a grating noise like sword scraping sword. The Bound Folk's newly formed line collapsed, and the fighting broke into chaotic skirmishes. A group of Drustig's men pushed forward through Cullen's troops at the weakest point.

Several men ran toward Mathewar. He looked quickly for Angarred but did not see her. When he turned back the men were nearly upon him. He called up the spells he had learned at the College. Illusion made him a giant crowned with radiance, and sheer light played around his sword.

Drustig's men fell back from him in alarm. He urged his horse forward and the men scattered. Then someone laughed, a sound like screaming. Drustig's head and half crown filled the sky and he wanted to run, to ride away down the hill and back to the castle and lock himself behind sturdy doors twice-barred with iron.

The laughter stopped. He braced himself against it and looked around for Angarred. It came again, wave after wave of it. His horse, maddened now, galloped flat out away from the field. He struggled to control it; it reared and he fell hard to the ground.

He stood with difficulty. The laughter had stopped, but he could still hear it clanging in his head, driving away all reason. He searched frantically for Angarred. His earlier idea, that he could somehow reach Drustig and take the crown, seemed a child's dream; he could do nothing here.

He ran back to where he had last seen her. She was gone. He

turned around wildly. He saw a picture as if it were happening in front of him: she and Drustig sitting in a room, Drustig raking through her mind.

He looked down and saw her. She had the dazed expression of the other mad soldiers, and somehow he knew that she had tried to change her shape and forgotten how.

He bent to lift her up. Her eyes still did not focus; she stared straight ahead at something only she saw. He spotted her horse a few feet away, and he slung her arm over his shoulder and led her toward it. She fell against him, a dead weight.

He tried to help her mount, but in the end he had to throw her over the horse like a sack of grain. He got on behind her, holding her. The horse galloped away from the fighting. Someone laughed behind them, a shriek like metal being shaped on a wheel, but it was fainter and easier to resist. Angarred moaned.

"It's all right," he said. "It's all right."

As he left the battle he saw Cullen rebinding those around him, building a defensive wall made entirely of Bound Folk. But his men were succumbing to insanity in the hundreds, as if to a plague.

Mathewar didn't care. He wanted Angarred in the castle and safe; he would think of what to do after that.

He hadn't been aware of time passing on the battlefield and was surprised to see the light dimming as he reached the courtyard. He put Angarred's arm over his shoulder again and helped her walk to the entrance. She had done this for him once, long ago; the memory gave him hope.

Finally they came to the apartment. He opened the door and settled her on the bed inside. Her eyes were blank, vacant as the sky, and he knew she was wandering through Drustig's land of shapes and shadows.

He held her hand and whispered her name several times, trying to call her back. He reached out for her mind but could feel nothing, not even the presence of another life. He spoke her name again, growing desperate now.

Sometime later he created a light and stood wearily, then went searching for a servant who could bring her food from the kitchen. But she would not eat, just turned her face away restlessly when he pressed her. He sat next to her on the bed, keeping long vigil in case she woke. Illusions played against walls when he looked up, but he ignored them.

Cullen slept poorly in his tent, waking several times in the night. Incredibly, he might lose this war; Drustig might beat him once again. Everything had gone so well—Drustig's exile, his father choosing him as heir, Jerret's death—that he thought he had been blessed by the Godkings, that the Spinner had at last seen his worth and woven him a glorious fate. He had refused to think about reverses, had not listened to anyone who said the war would go badly.

He woke fully as the sun leaked in through the seams of his tent. He could not allow Drustig to triumph; he would have to make more Bound Folk. But where would he get them? He had taken nearly all the men in the city.

He stood and stretched. Prince Brangwin, he thought. Lord Ezlin. But he did not want to bind them, at least not just yet; he enjoyed having his enemies in his power. Anyway, they were only two men; he needed many more than that.

He went to his pack for his crown. He had had a strange dream in the night, that someone had come in past all the guards and rifled through his things. The dream was disappearing now, turning to smoke, but he thought the thief had even put on the crown, had turned to him and . . .

No, no one could have possibly gotten into his tent. But the ropes of his pack seemed tied differently. Surely he would not have made a knot that simple?

He thrust the pack open and raked through it, feeling the silk and brocade of his clothes. He turned it upside down and shook everything out, trying not to think about how light it was. Even after he had dumped everything on the floor he ran his hands around the inside, frantically searching for the hard metal crown, then pawed through the clothes on the floor.

The crown was gone. It had not been a dream. He would die at the hands of his brother, as he had always feared.

He sat on the bed and began to shiver. He pulled up his knees and hugged his legs to him, trying desperately to think what to do next.

Who had stolen the crown? Did Drustig have it, did he have both of them now? He could almost see the thief's face. The man had turned toward him and said . . .

His tremors grew stronger. There was no way out. Drustig's men would overrun his; he would die today.

A knock came at the door. Mathewar felt dread even before he came fully awake. Who would be calling so late? Had Drustig won the war already? Then he saw the sun coming in through the windows and he realized that it was morning; he had somehow managed to sleep leaning against the wall.

He tried to see the person's mind but could not, could only get an impression of someone he trusted. Cautiously, he opened the door and went outside.

Caireddin stood in the hallway. He saw her shock and he wondered how he looked to her, drawn and haggard and filthy from battle. He ran his fingers through his tangled hair. "Did you see King Cullen?" she asked. "How is he?"

"We did, for a moment," Mathewar said. Why, he wondered again, had this otherwise sensible woman fallen for Cullen? Did she want to be queen that badly? "We had to leave, though. Angarred was touched by Drustig's crown."

"Oh!" Caireddin said, bringing her hand to her mouth. "Oh, Tashtery, no."

At least she still cared for someone besides Cullen. He had been too harsh, he saw, and he tried to soften the rest of the news. "I don't know if you should hope for too much. When I left Drustig's forces seemed to be winning."

"Cullen stopped Drustig's forces at the city walls," she said. "That's what folks said at supper, anyway."

"Then you know more than I do, milady." Mathewar shook his head. "I hadn't expected him to last the night. Drustig was turning all his troops to madmen."

"Cullen made enough Bound Folk to defend the city. Some folks in the castle are even saying he might overcome Drustig."

"I wish that were true. You've never experienced the madness he spreads, have you?"

"I have, actually. Just for a while—he wanted me to stop arguing."

He hesitated, unwilling to ask the question he needed answered. "Do you know—did the soldiers he attacked ever recover?"

"I don't know," she said. "We never stayed long enough to see. Wait—yes, at least one of them did. Brangwin, the man we traveled with."

"The prince of Goss?" Mathewar asked. She flinched a little at the name spoken openly, then nodded. "That's something, anyway."

"Please, we have to do something," Caireddin said. "Cullen's a far better king that Drustig would ever be—you have to help him."

"I can ride out with him again, but I don't see what I can do. I might as well stay here with Angarred."

"But Drustig will probably kill Angarred if he wins. You too."

Mathewar said nothing. He knew Caireddin was right; he could not stay in the castle, much as he wanted to. If Drustig became king he might destroy Karededin just because it amused him.

"I'll look after Angarred," Caireddin said.

"What can you do for her?" Mathewar asked.

She looked startled at his bluntness. "What can you?" she asked.

"I don't know," he said. He felt horribly torn. What if she died while he was gone? What if she woke and asked for him? He had to decide; the day's fighting must have already begun. No, he knew what he had to do; he was just putting it off to stay longer with Angarred.

Someone ran limping down the hall toward his rooms. Polgar.

"Mathewar," Polgar said, panting. "I—I have something for you." He reached into a bag on his back and brought out a half crown. Black, with white pearls: Cullen's.

"Where did you get this?" Mathewar asked.

"Stole it. Hurry—he probably knows it's missing. Put it on."

"Put it—" He took the crown and turned it over and over in his hands. He couldn't just put it on. Magical objects like this one could be dangerous; they had to be treated with caution, studied and tested and researched in old books.

"Quickly!" Polgar said, glancing up and down the hall.

"What do you want me to do with it?" Mathewar said.

"I don't know! Free the Bound Folk, stop the war. Stop Drustig."

Mathewar nearly laughed in despair. How could he hope to do any of that? He had very little idea of what the crown's powers were; Polgar might have asked him to establish the Celestial Court on earth while he was at it.

"I'm done with creating Bound Folk," Polgar said. "Done with doing dirty work for my father or my brother. It's time the crown went to someone who understands magic."

Polgar's stand against his family moved Mathewar more than anything else the man had said. Without stopping to think any longer he set the crown on his head, on the right side since Drustig had worn his on the left.

All sounds faded. The Black Crown yearned toward the White, and he saw Drustig fighting on the battlefield. He heard the madman's laugh and he quailed. Then he continued on, groping toward Drustig's mind.

Caireddin turned to Polgar. "Why did you steal from the king?" she asked. "That crown is the only chance he has of winning the war."

Polgar looked surprised at her anger. But in stealing the crown Polgar had aided the enemy, and that was treason; she could not let him get away with that.

"Because I don't want my brother to make more Bound Folk," he said. "When I was the Binder I saw what an abomination it is to take away a person's will. It becomes easier and easier, you know—soon you're binding someone just because he disagreed with you, or you don't like his looks. Our family never should have had the crown. It should go to someone who knows about magic."

"Yes, but—but Drustig has a crown as well. Cullen will lose without his own weapon. And Cullen has to be king."

Polgar looked at her, puzzled, probably wondering why she supported Cullen so strongly. She couldn't tell him, though; she couldn't even explain it to herself. When she thought of Cullen it wasn't as the Binder, the man who had proved so disastrous for Karededin; instead she saw him as his office, a vague presence surrounded by the aura and panoply of kingship.

"Maybe Mathewar can do something about Drustig," Polgar said.

"And he might be able to free the Bound Folk—he said he did it once."

Mathewar fell suddenly against the wall. His eyes were dull, the color of a flat gray sea, and he swayed, as if he might drop to the floor at any moment. "He's under the spell of the crown," Polgar said. "We have to bring him inside, get him comfortable. Quickly!"

Polgar propped Mathewar up with his shoulder and led him into the first room of the apartment. Caireddin ran farther in, looking for a blanket. She stopped when she came to the bedroom. Angarred lay still as an effigy on a tomb, her hair like live fire next to her pale face. Two effigies, she and Mathewar, Caireddin thought.

Caireddin pulled a blanket off the bed, apologizing to the other woman as she did so, and hurried back to Polgar. Together they spread the blanket on the floor and laid Mathewar on top of it.

The pearls on the crown looked like Iltarra's great pearl, Caireddin thought, the one that had disappeared. A horrible idea came to her, and she studied the crown intently. No, she thought, even my mother would not do something so vile. But Efcharren was capable of a great deal; Caireddin had never discovered any limit to her ambition.

"Look," Polgar whispered. "His eyes are moving. The crown didn't bind him, thank the Godkings."

Caireddin nodded; Mathewar did not have the blank gaze of the Bound Folk. "What's happening?" she asked. "Where is he?"

"I don't know."

They both looked at the magician. His eyes roved restlessly, never stopping. What did he see?

A noise brought her out of her thoughts, someone running loudly down the hallway. Cullen, Caireddin thought in alarm. She rushed to the door, and Polgar followed.

But she saw only an old man, though he ran quicker than any old man she had ever known. No, he was a boy; the white hair had confused her.

"Nim," Polgar said.

"Do you know him?" she asked.

The boy raised a sword. He was nearly upon them before she realized he intended to fight them. She drew her own sword and they clashed together.

"Annin bound him," Polgar said, over the clang of swords. "I'll go find him, tell him to call his boy off."

Caireddin risked a quick glance at Polgar. He had no sword. "Annin's with Cullen," she said. "Everyone's gone. Get Prince Brangwin. In the prison. Bribe the guards. Hurry!"

Polgar ran down the hall as fast as he could. As he went she remembered that Angarred had a sword he could have used. But could he fight? How well? He had seemed anxious to get away; perhaps this was the best way he could help.

Polgar hurried down four flights of stairs to the dungeons. His bad leg hurt, and he had to stop several times to catch his breath. Once in the prison itself he didn't need to bribe anyone; all the guards knew what the Haru family looked like and were eager to help him. He had gotten into Cullen's tent the same way; there were advantages to having a famous face.

As soon as he made clear what he wanted several guards appeared to take him farther into the maze of corridors. "Here we are," a guard said, stopping before one of the cages.

The first person he saw there was not Brangwin but a woman standing by the bars of the cage. She wore a heavy fleece–lined cloak against the cold. She glanced at him as he came forward; her blue eyes caught the light of one of the torches and turned luminous, like rare undersea fish.

He turned to the man in the prison cell. "Prince Brangwin?" he said.

"Yes," the man said. "Who are you?"

"Lord Polgar. I—"

"Polgar?" Brangwin said. His voice held anger and hatred and fear. "Are you going to bind me now?"

"No," Polgar said quickly. "I want to release you. We need your help."

"What makes you think I'll help you?"

"Brangwin!" the woman said.

Polgar turned to her. "Who are you?" he asked.

"My name is Lirden Servant, milord," she said. "I come here sometimes to talk to a fellow Gossek."

"Tell him he has to come with me," Polgar said. "I don't have time to argue."

"You're the Binder, aren't you?" Brangwin said. "You killed my family, laid waste my land, turned my people into slaves. As I said before, why should I help you?"

"I was for a while, yes," Polgar said. "No longer."

"And you think that absolves you? 'I was a monster, but I stopped'—is that what you're saying?"

"I'm saying that if anything absolves me it will be what I'm doing now. I stole the Binder's crown from my brother, and I'm trying to free the people we enslaved with it. I gave it to a man who once freed one of the bound, but he's under attack. If you want to fight against Cullen, against binding, you'll come with me."

"What happens after I defend this man? Will you imprison me again?"

Polgar sighed. "What happens after? I have no idea. Everything will be changed. If we both live, and if I can do it, I'll see that you're released."

"Good of you," Brangwin said. "Considering it was your family took away my freedom."

"We can sort out our differences later," Polgar said. "Here—Caireddin's your friend, isn't she? She's the one who asked for you—she needs your help."

"Caireddin? Why didn't you say so?"

Polgar motioned to the guards to open the cage. "I didn't think I'd have so much trouble talking you into freedom," he said.

They hurried through the dungeons. The cold had penetrated Polgar's bad leg, and he was soon forced to drop back. He called the guards over to him and gave them directions.

Lirden walked next to him. "You have to forgive him, milord," she said. "He's lost all his battles—he's very bitter. But he's a good man, really."

"I'll try to keep that in mind," Polgar said, attempting a smile. He felt frozen by the cold, though, and he was afraid it looked more like a grimace.

---

Caireddin turned her attention back to the boy. He knew very little about swordwork, she saw, but he was taller and stronger, with a greater reach. She tried a feint Brangwin had taught her but he ignored it; he had the same crazed intensity of the other Bound Folk and he continued on toward her despite her tries to deflect him.

She used his unwavering obsession against him and managed to slip around and come at him from the side. She scored a long gash down his arm; he seemed not to notice, though, and continued on, driving her back into the apartment. She could not win out over him, she realized. He would not stop until he was at the point of death. She could only hold him back and pray he made a mistake.

After a while he began to push her to one side of the room, closer to Mathewar. But what did he want with the magician? No, what did Annin want? The crown?

Nim forced her back, step by step. She heard only her harsh breath and the ring of sword on sword. She grew frantic. When would Brangwin come?

Someone appeared at the door. She nearly relaxed her guard in her relief. But it was only the fortune-teller, Reti.

"What—" he said. He looked around him, seeming to take everything in. "What can I do?"

"Get Angarred's sword," Caireddin said. "In the bedroom. Hurry!"

The man ran off and returned with the sword. He held the hilt with both hands and swung it toward Nim like a man chopping at a tree. He knew nothing about swordwork, she realized, and her heart sank.

"Never mind," she said, panting. "Get Brangwin, someone who can fight."

He didn't hear, or deliberately ignored her. He swept his sword around again. The air beneath it made it lift; he didn't even know enough to correct for that, the first thing every fighter learned. He slashed the sword back as if playing with it, seeing what it would do, and managed somehow to connect with Nim's sword and push it to the side.

Nim turned on him. Reti jumped away. Nim sliced through his

skirt, and Reti somersaulted out of his reach. The trick would have stopped anyone else out of sheer surprise, but Nim continued on relentlessly.

Nim had his back to Caireddin now. She danced around him and thrust hard through his side. He pulled away without slowing, leaving her sword half covered in blood. Die, she thought fiercely. Why don't you die?

Reti swung again. The arc of his sword ended far to the right, leaving him open. Nim moved forward for the final thrust, but somehow Reti capered nimbly away from him. Nim followed, but too slowly.

Caireddin struck him near the first wound she had made. He turned toward her sluggishly. She aimed as Brangwin had taught her, and pierced his heart.

He fell. She stepped away, shuddering; she had never truly connected swordwork and death. Blackness rose before her, and she nearly fainted. She leaned on her sword like a cane and breathed hard, forcing the blackness away.

She looked at the body sprawled out unmoving on the floor and shuddered again at what she had done. Mathewar lay behind him, looking as dead as Nim. No, his eyes still moved. What was he seeing? Why did Annin want him dead? Had he discovered something important, or was he trapped in madness?

Brangwin hurried through the door. "What happened?" he asked. "Are you hurt?"

She could barely draw breath to answer him. "No," she said. "No, I'm all right. One of the Bound Folk attacked—"

Brangwin's eyes narrowed. "Mathewar," he said. He bent and lifted Nim's sword and headed toward the magician.

# THIRTY-ONE

athewar went toward Drustig. In the strange dreamworld in which he moved he saw the other man as a great half crown, spread out across the sky like an arc of bone, the pearls above him black stars. Drustig's face was shadowed; only his eyes peered out from the darkness, their vivid blue nearly as black as the pearls.

From his height he could see the clash of armies beneath him. One group of soldiers were lined up into neat rows and ranks; they marched with precision toward the other side and then broke apart at the shock of meeting, their minds torn by fear and madness. Other men swarmed about in confusion, unable in their terror to find a way off the battlefield, and were mowed down. Cullen sat in his tent, trembling, as Drustig's army came closer.

Mathewar called on the strength of his own crown. He had order on his side, and rational thought. He reached out and felt a vast connection to the Bound Folk, like strings of a net running between him and hundreds of people, thousands. His control stretched all the way to the mines between Karededin and Goss, and then farther still. He had never held such power. He understood Cullen, then, and Drustig, and he felt amazed that Polgar had let go of it so easily.

Some of the strings had been torn by Drustig, he saw, and a few cut loose completely. Some folks had been bound by Noldeth, some by Polgar or Cullen; even Annin had enslaved a few.

Could he free them? But he had other things to do first. He gave a command, and as one they formed into regiments again and headed toward Drustig's army.

Drustig laughed wildly. The Bound Folk halted; some ran, others stood where they were, still as a Godking's statue. Some hurried in circles or worked at tasks only they saw, caught in waves of insanity.

Mathewar quailed, waiting for the madness to engulf him. But Cullen's crown and the distance between them seemed to protect him. He felt once again for his connection to Cullen's army.

He moved within their minds and found only confusion. He saw them wandering through borderless realms, looking frantically for a way out but meeting only nightmares. One man ran screaming, certain his hair was on fire. Another saw himself surrounded by enormous green cats with moons for eyes. A third found himself in a treasury; he knelt and pawed through roots and mud, seeing coins, crowns, legendary swords with rubies and topazes on their hilts.

Drustig's army ran forward, calling foul names, brandishing swords, axes, and clubs. The maniac laughter came again. Order, Mathewar thought. Precision. He used the power of the crown to take the sound and turn it, softening the jagged scream, changing some notes to create a dull melody. Another shriek came, and another, each louder and more discordant, and each returned to Drustig controlled, made understandable.

Through it all something pulled at him. He realized, horrified, that the Black Crown had not stopped calling to the White, that they yearned toward each other like a magnet drawing iron. He held himself back, trying as best he could to resist the great undertow, but the two crowns continued to reach for one another. The pull was like some great force of nature, the drag of tides or the turning of the seasons.

He had to keep them apart, though; he could not risk falling under the White Crown's spell. He tried to focus. Once more he took the chaotic sounds Drustig hurled at him and changed them into something more orderly.

He fought against Drustig this way for a long time; how long, he had no idea. His changes grew simpler, drearier, his responses unthinking. He wrapped himself in routine, monotony, a familiar back and forth. His songs slipped down to two notes, and then one.

He came to himself with a jolt. He was becoming one of the Bound Folk: the binder binding himself. He saw, horrified, that the Bound Folk had moved farther from his control: they stood without guidance or volition, milling around in confusion and terror. Drustig's horde surged forward despite the lack of resistance, hewing with swords and axes, shouting with cruel glee. Drustig's laughter unfurled like a flag over the battlefield.

Cullen had probably used some phrase to keep the Bound Folk in check, Mathewar thought. The crown still held an imprint of Cullen's hopes and fears and memories, and he reached for the knowledge. There it was: "Thou art now bound to me," he said, or thought, first to one man and then the next.

It was too slow; Drustig would cut all the ties in a single instant. He felt for the connection again and saw how he could combine the phrase with a spell, and bring them all under control at once.

He worked quickly, first binding them and then ordering them back into the field. They moved in a body, slowly at first, then at a fast walk. At the same time he worked intently to soften the mad laughter and keep the two crowns apart. He felt stretched to the limit, as if he were carrying a dozen unwieldy things at once, and he did not see how he could continue. Sooner or later he would drop something, and they would all come falling down.

The army of Bound Folk hurried forward now, nearly running. Cullen came out of his tent, holding his sword; the tie he still felt to the Folk seemed to have called him.

To Drustig's troops it must have seemed as if the men were coming back to life. Drustig's shining crown faded as Mathewar's power grew. His unruly troops dropped back. Drustig tried to laugh, but Mathewar forced the order of the Black Crown on him.

His soldiers retreated farther, then began to run. Drustig glanced behind him, then turned back to Cullen and the advancing Bound Folk. Fear appeared in his eyes.

He ran. The closest of the Bound Folk hurried forward to surround him. "Get rope," Mathewar told them. "Tie him so he can't escape."

Several of the Bound Folk brought rope out of their packs and secured him tightly. Cullen walked toward his brother.

With the battle over the pull of the Black Crown toward the White became even stronger. Suddenly Mathewar understood something: the power of the crown had become corrupted with its breaking. If the two halves joined, the crown would be restored to its power, to the purpose for which it had been fashioned. He had to make it whole again.

With this realization came sheer terror. He would have to take the White Crown, deliberately place himself under its influence, and then somehow, from the depth of madness, find a way to forge the two together.

He looked for Bound Folk to bring the crown to the castle. But while he was distracted Cullen had reached Drustig. "Did you think you'd become king?" Cullen said. "You can't defeat me—I have the Spinner on my side, and she looks out for me. Anyway, our father declared me the heir."

Drustig laughed. Cullen and the Bound Folk dropped back, and Drustig's troops paused in their flight. Mathewar reached out quickly to the nearest of the Bound Folk, and the man swung his sword at Drustig's crown. The crown fell to the dirt.

Drustig and Cullen watched it fall, but neither made a move toward it. Cullen came forward again.

"You lost," he said. His voice grew shrill; his sword trembled between them. "You lost, finally you lost. I have everything you ever wanted, crowns, women, riches, power. That woman from Ou, Caireddin—she's in love with me. And our father approved of me. He's proud of me, his faithful son. Me, and not you."

"Poor Father," Drustig said. "No one but you and Polgar, the weaklings, left at home. Well, he did the best he could with such poor material. But I was his first choice, you know that. If I hadn't been exiled—"

"Silence!" Cullen said. "I won here, not you."

"Did you? You'll never live up to my example, not if you rule for a hundred years. You couldn't even win this war on your own—I felt someone helping you. No matter what you do, you'll always wonder if I would have done it better."

Cullen stepped closer. Drustig didn't care if he died, Mathewar saw; perhaps the power of the crown had burned his mind. Mathewar's terror returned. Had Drustig been insane before he wore the crown, or had the crown made him so?

Cullen seemed to listen to someone. And Mathewar, who wore Cullen's crown now, watched as the illusion came into focus, feeling chilled: Lord Noldeth, praising Cullen's deeds. Another one driven mad by the crown.

"You see?" Cullen said. "You see? Father approves of the work I did here."

"Does he?" Drustig asked.

The vision faded as Cullen's uncertainty returned. Maddened, Cullen took another step forward. Mathewar understood an instant too late. Before he could react Cullen plunged his sword into Drustig's throat.

Drustig fell to the ground. Mathewar quickly ordered two of the Bound Folk to take Drustig's crown. But Cullen dove for it first, and as the Bound Folk came closer he stared at them, his power over them diminished but not entirely gone. He stood and held the crown over his head but then seemed to change his mind; even he felt afraid of its power.

"Let's go back," he said. "We'll tell the folks at the castle about our victory."

"What about Drustig?" someone asked. "Shouldn't we bury him? And the other dead as well?"

"Yes, yes, some of you stay here and do that," Cullen said impatiently. "Oh, and make certain he's dead." He turned back to his tent, carrying the crown proudly before him.

Mathewar watched him leave. Should he order more Bound Folk to take the crown from him? Did Cullen have enough power to stop him? He didn't think so, but he would almost certainly have to kill Cullen to get it, and that would cause more bloodshed, maybe even a civil war. And what if Cullen put it on to defend himself?

But Cullen was heading to the castle on his own. Mathewar could decide what to do when he got there. At that he felt the same jolt of fear as before; he would have to fight a king, and then descend into madness.

"No!" Caireddin said. "Don't go near him!"

Brangwin looked at her. She could not possibly stop him, he knew. And the man he had long sought lay before him, insensate, helpless; he would never have another chance like this. "He's my enemy," he said, not moving the sword from Mathewar.

"He's not your enemy," she said. "He's doing something— something important for Karededin. See, he has the crown on his head . . ."

"Yes, I see. I told you he creates Bound Folk."

"He doesn't! Cullen's the Binder, and Polgar was before him."

"Polgar was what?" Polgar said, coming into the room with Lirden.

"Tell him Mathewar never bound anyone," Caireddin said.

"Why should I believe anything Polgar says?" Brangwin said.

"I don't know," Polgar said wearily. "Because I'm telling you the truth, perhaps. I told you, he freed someone once. And with the crown he might be able to free them all."

"Is that what he's doing?" Brangwin asked.

"I don't know. I think so."

"He's not creating Bound Folk," someone said. Brangwin turned to him quickly and saw a man dressed in women's clothing, a Traveler. "I swear it by the Moon. He hates the very idea of them. Whatever he's doing, it's tremendously difficult. He needs us to keep watch over him."

Brangwin shook his head. No one he knew had ever trusted Travelers; they were widely thought to lie, to steal, to kidnap children. Why should he believe this man?

"What if you're wrong?" Caireddin said.

"What?" he said.

"You're the most honorable man I know," she said. "But it's easy to be honorable when you're certain who the enemy is. The Bound Folk attacked your country, and you had to defend it—there was no question there. But what if you're wrong about Mathewar? How can you know what honor demands if you don't have the whole truth? Is it honorable to kill an innocent man?"

Could she be right? What had once seemed so plain lay broken into a thousand pieces, each with its own truth. Goss had been assailed by so many that he couldn't even say who the real enemy was. "In Pergodi there's no end to perplexity," they said in Goss, when they talked about Karedek intrigue and double-dealing.

"I don't know," he said. "I don't know who to trust."

"Trust me, then," she said.

He lowered his sword. To his amazement he found that he did trust her, beyond logic, beyond everything he had learned. There was a connection between them; he had felt it even on the road to Karededin. It had weakened since then, but it had not entirely disappeared.

"Well, then, why did you ask me here?" he said. "You say you want to defend Mathewar, but against what?"

"We did need your help," Caireddin said. She stopped and looked at Nim. Her first death, he thought. He understood a good deal then.

"Lord Annin bound this man," Polgar said. "I let Annin use the crown sometimes—he enjoyed finding out its powers. He discovered he could bind people to do just one thing—the rest of the time they would think they were free, but when something happened or they were given a command they did Annin's bidding. I think he told this man to attack Mathewar if he put on the crown."

"But why would Annin do that?" Caireddin asked.

"To curry favor with Cullen, I suppose," Polgar said. "He knew Cullen feared magicians, and would be terrified if one of them got a crown somehow."

"But I still don't understand why you need me," Brangwin said.

"This may not be the only man Annin bound," Polgar said. "Nim was probably living in the castle, but he may have had time to send word to others in the city."

Brangwin looked into the hallway. The guards had returned to the prison, no longer needed. "All right," he said finally. He had to order this motley group, he saw. "Lirden, you should have left Pergodi days ago. It's still dangerous for you to be here—you should go somewhere safe."

"I'd like to help," Lirden said. "Can I do anything?"

"You can, actually," Caireddin said. "You could look after Angarred. She's in the bedroom—she was touched by Drustig's crown."

Lirden nodded and left them. "You too, Caireddin," Brangwin said. "You should leave."

"I'm not going anywhere," Caireddin said.

He wanted to tell her that her swordwork was not good enough; she might have killed one bound man by lucky accident but she would never win out against a crowd of them. But none of the people gathered around Mathewar could fight, or fight well; he had to do what he could with a half-trained girl, a fortune-teller, and a cripple. They reminded him of his hopeless battles in Goss, leading a handful of green boys against an overwhelming foe, though even there it had never gotten as bad as this.

"All right," Brangwin said. "We'll need more swords."

"I'll get weapons," Polgar said, but at that instant they heard men coming toward them.

Because they rode rather than walked, Cullen, Annin, Sorle, and Cullen's bodyguards reached Pergodi Castle before the great mass of Bound Folk. It seemed to Cullen that more should happen after a victory like this one: folks should stream into the streets and call his name, throw him flowers, drink to his health. But no one appeared to know even that a war had ended.

The men rode up to the castle. Once there Annin and Sorle headed to their rooms to clean up and rest after the battle. Cullen's clothes were stained with blood and sweat as well and he thought he might do the same, and he wanted to put the White Crown somewhere safe. But he also thought he needed a celebration, with a large and loud group of men, perhaps, or with a woman. And yet all the time, without his awareness, his footsteps led him toward a part of the castle he had never visited.

Finally he looked around and noticed his unfamiliar surroundings. He tried to turn back, but in the next instant he found himself continuing on. Somehow he couldn't seem to care. The guards following him glanced at each other and murmured, but no one dared say anything.

He heard voices inside a room and peered in through the open door. A man lay there, wearing the Black Crown, his crown. Anger rose within him, so great and deep it seemed to block his throat, leaving him staring and trying to speak.

"You—" he managed to say. "How dare you wear my crown?"

The man—it was Mathewar, he saw now—seemed asleep, or bound. And there were other people in the room, deceitful traitors all of them: his brother Polgar, the fortune-teller, that prince from somewhere in the north, the woman he was going to marry.

"What are you doing here?" he asked. "Did you plan to steal my crown together? You're bound men, dead men, all of you. Guards—arrest them!"

"Polgar!" Caireddin called. "Take Reti's sword." The fortune-teller threw the sword to him. Brangwin, Caireddin, and Polgar moved forward, toward the guards.

Mathewar saw Cullen carry the White Crown into the room, the crown he had drawn toward him from the battlefield. Other things were happening around him but he couldn't focus; he was aware of nothing but the two halves straining toward each other, striving to be whole.

He caught a brief glimpse of his body lying on a blanket, then that too faded and his dream body headed toward Cullen. Even in this strange world in which he moved he felt himself tremble; continuing forward was the hardest thing he had ever done in his life. He had to picture himself taking small steps: one, and then another, and another.

Drustig's laugh flew toward him. He had been unprepared for it, and it hit him like a blow. No, he thought. No, you died, I saw Cullen kill you . . .

But the crowns still bore the imprints of their wearers. He would have to meet Drustig on the battlefield all over again, and at the same time try not to succumb to the impressions Cullen had made while he wore the Black Crown.

The grating laughter washed over him once more, and with it came uncertainty, a loss of confidence. Was he doing the right thing? His plans had made sense on the battlefield, but now, with the two crowns so close, he thought that putting them together might unleash some nightmare power worse than either one alone. Perhaps he was mad; perhaps he had become Drustig in some horrible way. Joining the crowns seemed like something Drustig would think of, an explosion of destruction and chaos.

He heard the derisive laughter again. And again he could not tell which of them had laughed, where Drustig ended and he began. He forced himself not to run; it was like standing still in the middle of a burning house. He felt the flames of madness lash out at him; then he was falling into that place where everything has the same weight of meaning and everything exists at once: battle and birth, jewels and sand, sumptuous meals given for drowned men.

He wandered, lost. He felt for the Black Crown but it was gone. Or perhaps it was still on his head, but it meant nothing in this place, this forest. No, it was a great ocean, with himself in the middle of it, watching strange fish and birds swim by. No, how could he be so stupid? It was the College, with the First Master stepping toward him out of the shadows. . . .

Drustig laughed. How had Drustig become the First Master? And what had happened to him, Mathewar? He had been the First Master, hadn't he? Was he dead?

The laughter sounded again, and with it came the rending of his mind, as if his life were being torn from him. The pain shocked him out of the chaos, made him think again. How had he gotten here? He had come for some purpose, because . . .

Because he had to join the crown. He had to trust to his plans; he could not listen to doubt in this mad place. He laughed at having recovered his thought, then realized that he sounded like Drustig, that he was Drustig. But even in his horror he kept to his task; he searched for his half of the crown again and saw that it was where he had left it, back at his true body.

He took another step forward. The confusion around him grew; he was drowning in it. There was no way out; he could continue only by going on, by ignoring everything else. He took another step, and another.

Finally he faced Cullen. White rays shot from Cullen's crown, growing stronger as it met its double, catching the king in a net of light. Cullen held on to it desperately, overwhelmed by its power but

too frightened to put it on. Through the tracery of light Mathewar
saw his face contort in a scream.

A black radiance shone out from Mathewar's crown. The flames
licked around him, entrapping him. He reached for the two halves
and felt them drawing each other, yearning, craving. He simply had
to let them join.

The idea brought back all his fears of the crown. The combined
strength might overwhelm him, or kill him. He might become
caught in some realm between Drustig's and Cullen's, taking on
Drustig's madness or Cullen's greed and envy.

But he had to do it, had to forge them into one thing. They had
never been meant to be separated; only the unimaginable might of
the Sorcerers' Wars had broken them. Apart, their powers could be
perverted by anyone. And he wondered what secrets were locked
within them, what he might discover next.

He let go. Light flashed out from them both, a light that seemed
made of every color at once. Cullen's crown flew out of his hands
toward Mathewar where he lay on the blanket in the true world.

The two fused together. The crown, whole now, flared with the
color and no color of the light.

Caireddin was no match for the guards; only Brangwin could fight
them as an equal. There were four guards all told, and Brangwin took
them on two and three at a time, leaving Polgar and Caireddin to deal
with one at the most. Even with one, though, she felt pushed to the
limit of her skill.

Cullen stood to the side, holding his crown, gazing at something
only he saw. He would be easy to kill, Caireddin thought, if they
could get to him through the press of the guards.

Polgar proved to be a good swordsman, though hampered by his
bad leg. He watched Brangwin closely, seeming to take orders from
the man's slightest gesture. Brangwin fought deliberately, managing
to turn a guard to face Polgar, and as the guard concentrated on
Brangwin, Polgar lunged forward and stabbed him in the stomach.

The man roared. He dealt Polgar a quick series of blows, one hand
pressed hard against the blood seeping from his wound. Polgar re-

turned them, backing away clumsily, narrowly missing the point of the blade several times.

White lights blazed, and dark lightning flashed in answer. The three strove to concentrate on their opponents. Then Cullen's crown flung itself across the room, and the man Polgar fought turned to look at it quickly. Polgar slipped inside his guard and slashed at him again, and, weakened by his earlier wound, he fell to the ground.

Reti hurried forward and grabbed the man's sword. The death of one of the guards put heart into them all, and they redoubled their efforts, driving toward the enemy.

A guard thrust at Reti. He leapt high in the air, and the sword passed harmlessly beneath him. Brangwin glanced at him, looking astonished but continuing to parry his opponent's strokes all the while.

Cullen moved. No one but Caireddin saw him, and she tried to take a breath to warn the others. Cullen seemed to break free of the spell that held him; he drew his sword and went stealthily toward Reti.

"Reti, to your right!" Caireddin called.

Reti turned. He swung his sword awkwardly at Cullen. Cullen laughed. He parried Reti's sword easily and then danced in and struck at him from every direction, playing with him, netting him in a cage of light.

Two men converged on Brangwin, blocking him in. Cullen pushed Reti back toward Mathewar. Suddenly he seemed to tire of the game. "Did you prophesy your own death, you capering fool?" he said. His sword moved in a blur, and Reti fell.

"No!" Caireddin cried.

She half expected Reti to rise again, laughing at the joke, but he stayed where he was. Cullen turned to Brangwin and began fighting alongside the two guards. "None of you will live to see nightfall," he said, seemingly without effort. "And if I can I'll torture you before I kill you."

Caireddin and Polgar tried to drive through the remaining guard toward Brangwin, but the guard kept them at bay. Caireddin gasped for breath and struggled against him. The floor beneath her was slippery with blood.

Incredibly, Mathewar laughed.

He thought he understood everything, and then whole vistas opened
out and he saw more, and then more. The crown showed him everyone alive and all the connections between them, all their loves and
hates and jealousies and desires. And everything moved and changed
constantly, twisting and shaping into what seemed like chaotic snarls;
but sometimes he saw a pattern weave through it, so beautiful it took
his breath away.

He went on and on, exultant, through wonder after wonder. He
came to the root of all magic, underneath where everything joined
together, and he saw that there was truly no difference between his
magic and Angarred's. All the old divisions melted away, between
women's magic and men's, spells of being and of illusion. He could
become a leopard if he wanted, or a bird, or an old boot. He could
free the Bound Folk. It was easy; it was all so easy.

This must be what Tobrin sees, a part of him thought, the part that
was not exclaiming over each new discovery. And yes, this knowledge and power were dangerous; he realized now why Tobrin had
kept it from him. He saw, amused, that Tobrin had deliberately closed
himself away from this realm while they played kettim, so as not to
have an unfair advantage. And that was why (more understanding,
and yet more . . . ) the old man had let slip that he had never been to
the mountains, something he never would have said otherwise, and
because of this admission Mathewar had wondered if there were
magical talismans in Goss or Ou that had not been captured within
Tobrin's Stone, and that had led to his guesses about the crown, and
to knowledge Tobrin had not wanted him to have . . .

And still he had not tasted all the delights before him. Now he
traced the links and twists and bindings and saw them open out, a
complex ever-shifting web moving through the present and into the
future. No, not a web; it was a forest of trees, all of them constantly
growing and spreading and putting forth new green shoots. Or a vast
impossible candlestand, new lights branching off at every moment,
thousands and thousands of them, each light a human life.

He saw that every branching represented a place where a choice
would be made, all the different futures splitting off from each

choice. But some lines stayed the same throughout the years, and these he followed to the end as if beglamoured, unable to turn away.

So that was who his daughter Eliath would marry; he laughed to see it. But here Berren died tragically young; his heart froze within him at the sight but he could not stop, eager to see everything, know everything, take it all in. And here were the country's rulers, and all the secrets of the court, the petty lies along with the great conspiracies.

He stopped at this line for a while, studying the Harus. So that was why . . . But what would happen after that, would they continue to rule? He hurried on to the present, a jumble of lines all intersecting, an impossibly snarled knot. Something was happening now, something that would irrevocably decide the fate of Karededin and Goss and Ou. The line of his own life split near it, one branch meeting the knot and the other leading away.

He traced some of the strands back: Cullen and Polgar and Brangwin and Caireddin and Reti . . . Reti. He forced himself away, unwilling to see.

He did not want to return to the world of action just yet. The two lines of his life met up farther on. Should he follow it, all the way to the end?

He hesitated only a moment, and then traced it to his death. And here was Angarred's life and death . . . But he wrenched himself away from that one, unable to bear it if she died untimely, like Berren.

The thought of Angarred finally roused him from his enchantment. Something had happened to her, he remembered; she was in danger somehow. He headed back through the line of her life to the present and found her wandering lost, still trapped within Drustig's spell.

He went to her and brought her slowly through the unmapped regions of madness. "Wake now," he said softly. He turned back to see what else lay in the newly discovered realm of marvels.

But before she returned completely to the world she heard raw noises nearby, the sound of sword clashing on sword, and he heard them as well, through her. "What is happening?" she asked. She tried to rise from the bed but fell back, weak. "Don't go. Something's wrong here."

He didn't answer, caught by a hundred dazzling revelations. "Matte," she said insistently. "Stay here. They need you."

He felt annoyed; she didn't, couldn't, understand. He had so much still to see. He made a motion as if to shrug her away. "Matte!" she said. "Listen to me!"

He stopped. He would hear what she had to say and then leave her. "Matte," she said. "You said once that I always come to rescue you. Do you remember what happened in the mountains?"

He did, and remembered the other nightmares as well. She would always bring him back, he had thought, no matter how far he went, how long he traveled. And he saw that she was right: he existed in a kind of fevered madness here, unable to let go.

He needed to act; he had seen that already in the branching lines. He had to force himself away. There was one last thing he had to do, one person to free, and then he could return to the difficult world.

# THIRTY-TWO

It felt as if he were opening his eyes, though he knew they were already open. For a while he could not grasp what was happening before him, still half walking in that other realm, dazed by its splendor. He saw the wonders of that realm in his left eye, and the realm he now found himself in with his right, and he struggled to focus.

Drustig of all people had helped him, he realized. In fighting against Drustig and the crown he had not only regained his magic, he had discovered whole worlds he had never guessed existed. If Drustig had not forced the madness of that other realm upon him, had not prepared him for wonders, he would have drowned in astonishments, like a miser crushed by his gold.

The two worlds merged together, and he saw both at once. Cullen and three of his guards had pinned Brangwin and Caireddin and Polgar to a wall. "Take them to the prisons," Cullen said. "I'll deal with Mathewar."

Mathewar sat up and leaned against the wall. Cullen jerked back at the sight. Mathewar knew so much now; for a moment it was difficult to decide among the many ways he could end this. He raised his hand and Cullen's sword flew to him. Then he held the guards immobile and captured their swords as well, and Polgar and his allies subdued Cullen.

"What—" Cullen said, sputtering. He lunged toward Mathewar, but the other man stopped him effortlessly.

"What happened?" Caireddin asked. The three of them stepped away from Cullen, trusting Mathewar to hold him. "Where were you?"

Mathewar shook his head, unable to explain. The great pattern still wove through his mind, all the thoughts and deeds and words and lives and deaths. "Reverberations and concatenations," he said. "Plots and plans."

He looked down and saw Reti sprawled on the floor. "No," he said. "Oh, Godkings, no."

"Can you—can you heal him?" Caireddin asked.

He shook his head again. He had no power over illness and death. Could he have prevented this? Had Reti died because he had not left that other realm quickly enough?

"Are you still trying to teach me about responsibility, my friend?" he asked. "Is this one of your stories? It's not as good as the others."

Lirden came to the door from the bedroom, supporting Angarred. Angarred looked well, praise the Healer. He took the crown from his head; suddenly there was only the room before him, the world he had once thought of as the real one, and for a moment he felt bereft. He started to rise, to go toward Angarred.

"Give me that!" Cullen said, seeing the crown. "It's mine. I'm still the king here. You're under arrest, all of you!"

Mathewar sat back, putting the crown beside him. No one else moved. "You can't hold me like this," Cullen said. "I did nothing wrong. Polgar's the criminal here. Tell them, Brother. Go ahead—tell them how you killed Jerret."

"I didn't—" Polgar said.

Mathewar raised his hand and Polgar quieted. A servant walked into the room. He had short brown hair, cropped as unevenly as a mowed field. He looked from one person to another, puzzled, though an awareness was beginning to form in his dark eyes.

Polgar moved first. "Jerret!" he said. He went toward the boy as if to hug him. Several people gasped.

"No!" Jerret said. "Stay away! He—he bound me. He came into

my room wearing half a crown—I thought it was a joke, but then he said something and I—I went away somehow. . . ."

"There, I told you," Cullen said. "Look what he did."

"I had to do it, Jerret," Polgar said. "My father wanted to make Cullen king, and he'd ordered some of the Bound Folk to kill you. It was the only way I could think of to keep you safe. No one ever looks at servants."

Jerret noticed Mathewar then. He ran to him and nearly fell against him in his need to hold him. "Careful," Mathewar said.

"Is he telling the truth?" Jerret asked.

"Yes."

"What should I do?"

"You know that already," Mathewar said.

Jerret got to his feet and stood as straight as he could. "How were you going to free me?" he asked Polgar.

"I didn't know," Polgar said. "I'm sorry. I stole the crown from Cullen and gave it to Mathewar—he was the only person I'd ever heard of who'd freed someone, and I hoped he could help you."

"You stole the crown?" Jerret asked. For the first time something like a smile appeared on his face.

"Twice. The first time I took it to bind you. Fortunately Cullen kept it in the same place I had."

"He helped with more than freeing you," Mathewar said. "I was able to stop Cullen because of him. And with the crown I could stand against Drustig."

"Still," Jerret said. "You bound other people, didn't you?"

"Yes, milord," Polgar said.

Jerret turned to Cullen. "Did you become king, as Noldeth wanted?" he asked. For a moment he looked stricken; until his binding he'd thought of Cullen as his friend. Then his expression became grave, the face of a man about to mete out justice.

Cullen didn't answer. Jerret glanced at the signet ring the other man wore and nodded. "I thought you were dead, milord," Cullen said quickly. "I thought Polgar killed you. Someone had to rule, and I was the only one capable of it. What would you have done?"

"I would have sent for Lord Ezlin, for one thing," Jerret said.

"I've done nothing wrong!" Cullen said. "I didn't kill anyone. Polgar was the one who killed—I thought he killed—"

"Did you know he was going to do it?"

"No, of course not. I would have stopped him if I could have. I never wanted you dead, milord. But—"

"You lie," Polgar said. "Our father told us we had to kill Jerret or he would send the Bound Folk to do it. You were there in the room with me when he said it."

"I don't know what you're talking about, Brother," Cullen said. "I never heard him say any such thing."

"He's lying, milord—" Polgar said.

"It's my word against his, milord," Cullen said. "You can't hold me like this—I haven't done anything—"

"You said that already," Jerret said. "Did you bind people too?"

"You never objected to it," Cullen said. His tone turned spiteful. "You didn't mind conquering Goss, or taking their wealth and using it for yourself. How do you think we managed to do that, if not with the Bound Folk?"

"No one ever asked me if I wanted those people bound."

"You never told us to stop."

"Yes, I did," Jerret said calmly. "I told you and your father to stop a number of times. Noldeth said he had."

Cullen glanced from Jerret to Polgar and back again. He looked desperate, as if he could see the trap closing in on him. "Caireddin," he said. "Tell Jerret I'm not the monster he thinks I am. I'm a good man, a good king, caught in difficult circumstances. I did the best I could."

"He's exactly what you think he is, Jerret," Caireddin said, speaking with difficulty. " 'Monster' is a good name for him."

"Caireddin!" he said. Anger flared briefly in his eyes; he forced himself to become calm. "I thought you cared about me."

"I do care about you," Caireddin said.

"There, you see?" Cullen said.

"I care about you because my mother stole Iltarra's pearl. It—"

"What are you saying? You're talking nonsense."

"It was part of the crown once—see, there's an empty setting where it should go. It isn't strong enough to bind anyone, but it has just enough power to draw one person toward another. Iltarra used it to get lovers—I always wondered what men saw in her. And my mother used it to make me fall in love with you."

"That's ridiculous. You don't want to admit you love me now that I'm no longer king. You're the worst sort of slattern—you care only about power, gaining it, keeping it. You'll promise yourself to any man who has it. Watch yourself, Jerret—she'll be coming after you next."

Mathewar had learned so much about the people before him, their hopes and loves and fears, that he was able to predict almost exactly what they would do next. Jerret said nothing, but Mathewar knew he was remembering his love for Iltarra, the memory as painful as grasping a blade. She had not needed any pearl to bind him to her, Jerret was thinking; she had probably not used it with most men. Caireddin could not see how Iltarra had ravished them.

Mathewar raised his hand. "There," he said to Caireddin. "You're free now."

"Oh, thank Marfan and Mathona!" Caireddin said. "He's a horrible man." To the astonishment of everyone except Mathewar she threw herself into Brangwin's arms. He seemed startled for a moment and then held her. "I'm sorry, I'm sorry," she said.

"Sorry about what?" Brangwin asked.

"About all the bad thoughts I had about you, when I thought I loved Cullen."

He looked at her, bemused, and then smiled. Mathewar saw how rare that smile was, and how Caireddin loved it, in part for its rarity.

"Very pretty," Cullen said sourly. "Now release me, Jerret. You have no right to hold me here."

"You wanted to kill me," Jerret said.

"It's my word against Polgar's. I never wanted to harm you."

"You're lying," Jerret said. He glanced at Mathewar, who nodded slightly. "But you're right, I can't prove it. Still, there's the Bound Folk. You admitted to them, at least."

"Yes, but if you imprison me for that you'll have to do the same to Polgar," Cullen said. He smirked, as if he neared the end of a game of kettim and saw that he was winning. "He bound more people than I did."

"There's another matter, though," Jerret said. "Your treason. What happened to Lord Ezlin?"

Cullen went very pale. Jerret looked at Polgar. "Tell me," Jerret said softly.

"Cullen waged war against him, my lord," Polgar said. "When Ezlin came to Karededin to claim his inheritance. He's in the dungeons now."

"Ah," Jerret said. "And some of the witnesses to my ceremony still live, thank the Godkings."

The young king said nothing for a long moment. Mathewar remembered Jerret's question about putting Annin to death, and his own answer: that a king could kill only lawbreakers. Now that it came to it, though, Mathewar was pleased to see that Jerret looked troubled; killing would not be as easy as he thought.

"I sentence you to death," Jerret said finally.

Cullen made another effort to escape but could not break Mathewar's spell. "You can't—you need me—" Cullen said.

Jerret turned to Polgar. "You," he said. "You tried to save me, and you stole the crown as well. I can see that you wanted to make amends. Still, you bound all those people in the mines—you even tried to bind Mathewar. I sentence you to—" Everyone waited; the air grew taut with tension. "Two years in prison."

"You're very generous, milord," Polgar said. "I thank you for your mercy."

"Generous, yes," Cullen said bitterly. "As I said, Polgar bound more people than I did."

"Silence," Jerret said. "The king has spoken. Where are the guards? I want these two men taken away."

"I'll summon them, milord," Mathewar said. He did not move or speak, but a few moments later three guards came into the room. Jerret gave them orders; Mathewar touched them briefly so they would not wonder at seeing the king before them, alive again. They led the prisoners to the cells below.

"My lord," Brangwin said diffidently to Jerret.

Jerret turned to him. "You seem to have saved my life, but I'm afraid I don't know who you are," he said.

He looked at Caireddin fully for the first time, and Mathewar knew that he was struck by her similarity to Rodarren. Expressions came and went on his face: recognition, shock, yearning, and finally an attempt to put on the mask of a polite courtier. "I don't know you either," he said to her.

"I'm Prince Brangwin of Goss, milord. This is Lady Caireddin, the daughter of King Tezue and Lady Efcharren, and the woman at the door is Lady Lirden."

Jerret smiled. "I thought you were a myth, a rumor," he said to Caireddin. "And as for you, Prince Brangwin, I'm pleased to learn that my advisors were wrong. They told me all the Gossek royal family had died, but I see that one of them still lives. I seem to have friends I never knew existed. That is, I hope you three will be my friends."

"I wanted to ask you, milord, what you plan to do about Goss," Brangwin said, growing bolder.

"Apologize, for one thing," Jerret said. "Return the lands to the Gossek, try to mend what the Harus destroyed. Free the Bound Folk, if Mathewar can do that."

Mathewar nodded. Jerret had been clever, he thought, in blaming the Harus for the war with Goss. Probably Jerret would never tell Brangwin the full truth of the matter, that they had invaded with his enthusiastic approval. And Mathewar had to admit the boy was right; Brangwin did not forgive easily, and Jerret had, after all, changed his mind.

"We'll talk about this later, I promise you," Jerret said.

"I'm pleased to hear it," Brangwin said. "And what about me? Will you send me back to the prisons?"

"What?" Jerret said.

"Cullen imprisoned me, milord," Brangwin said.

"No, never," Jerret said. "I'd still be washing floors if not for you. No reward can ever be great enough. But right now I want to see how the castle has changed in my absence, and to show myself to the people. And then I want to sleep for a long time. Mathewar, can you summon more guards for me? And my steward—is it still Dobrennin, or did that poisonous family kill him too?"

Brangwin bowed and left, and Caireddin and Lirden followed. As they waited for the steward Jerret asked more about Cullen and Polgar, and about the clash of swords that had freed him. "Where did that crown come from?" he asked, pointing at the crown at Mathewar's side. "What is it?"

"Drustig had a half crown as well, milord," Mathewar said. "I think Noldeth found his half in Ou and told Drustig about it, and then when the Harus were exiled Drustig went looking for the other half. Apart, the two pieces had a malign power, but together—their power together is far greater than either one alone. I think the College will be studying this crown for years to come."

Jerret scowled. "I shouldn't have exiled them, then," he said. "I should have kept them close to me so I could watch them. I had no idea they'd grow so powerful in Ou."

"You did the right thing to exile them, I think."

Jerret said nothing for a while, though he looked pleased at Mathewar's praise. "Who is this man?" he said finally, indicating Reti.

"A hero. He fell in your service."

"I'll give him a fitting funeral," Jerret said. He caught Mathewar's look and grinned. "Not like Lord Noldeth's, I promise."

"I think he has his own customs," Mathewar said. "But you could ask his people."

"What about these other dead men?"

"This is one of Cullen's guards. And the other man is one of the Bound Folk."

"I'll send people to take care of them. And I'll give you new rooms."

Jerret fell silent; a shadow seemed to pass over him. The decisions he had had to make had kept him from thinking about his binding, but he was remembering it now, Mathewar knew. He had been one of the Half-bound, able to break away from his rote movements for tantalizing moments only to return to work and oblivion. And in the time wrested away from his binding he had learned a great deal.

Jerret tried to laugh. "You told me to work and sacrifice, but I'll wager you never thought I'd work this hard. And sacrifice so much, more than anyone I've ever heard of."

Jerret had changed, but he still had only a vague idea of how dreadful life had been for his subjects, Mathewar thought. He kept silent, though—the boy would learn soon enough, when they freed the Bound Folk.

The steward knocked at the open door. He looked puzzled, wondering, Mathewar knew, how he had come to be in this part of the castle. His expression changed when he saw Jerret; he seemed about to faint with shock.

"My—my lord!" he said. "We thought—"

"I'm not dead, Dobrennin," Jerret said. "As you can see."

"But how—?"

The guards arrived. Jerret gestured to Cullen's men, the ones Mathewar had frozen. "Mathewar, can you do something about these men, or do you want them to stay like that forever? And when they're free I want"—he pointed to several of his own guards—"you three to take them to the prisons. I'll deal with them later."

Mathewar freed the men, and the guards moved forward to surround them and take them away. "Now what, Mathewar?" Jerret asked. "Who should I show myself to first? This will be fun, don't you think? And you can tell me everything that happened while I was gone, and who in the court seemed especially pleased by my death—"

"I'm sorry, milord," Mathewar said. "I'd like to be with my wife now—she was ill for a while. And I'm certain Dobrennin knows more about the court than I do."

"Of course," Jerret said. Mathewar could see him trying not to look disappointed. He bowed to Angarred. "May the Healer watch over you, milady."

"I'll see you tomorrow, milord," Mathewar said. "We'll talk then."

"Good," Jerret said. He bowed again, and he and Dobrennin and the rest of the guards left.

When they had all gone Angarred came forward from the doorway. She was afraid of him and what he had done, Mathewar saw, and trying hard not to show it.

"What are you doing sitting on the floor?" she asked.

He laughed wearily. "I can't get up, actually," he said. "I'm exhausted. I had to fight with Cullen and Drustig, and then join the crown together. . . . I'd hoped no one would notice."

She drew nearer. He raised one arm like a child, and she bent to help him up.

Lirden went to her room, leaving Caireddin and Brangwin alone. They stood a moment, and then Brangwin bent and touched his lips to hers. She moved closer, and he put his arm behind her neck and drew her to him.

He smelled strongly of the sweat of battle, but then, she thought, so did she. Then she stopped thinking awhile; she found herself on a stone seat beneath a window with no memory of how she had gotten there, kissing him urgently. She felt as if they were breaking through all their guises—royal heir, fop, courtier; prince, warrior, madman—growing closer and closer to some ultimate truth.

A long time later they pulled away. "What will you do now?" she asked.

"I'll talk to Jerret, see how much he's willing to help Goss," he said. "And then I think I'm going home." He shook his head, amazed. "I suppose I'm king now. I never allowed myself to think of this—I was always so certain we would lose." He hesitated. "Would you—would you like to come with me? We haven't known each other very long, I know, but royal marriages have been founded upon less. We could, I don't know, cement the alliance between Karededin and Goss."

She began to answer, but he shook his head again. "What an idiotic thing to say," he said. Her heart seemed to die within her, but he went on. "I used to be a poet, but all my words seem to have deserted me. All I can say is that I love you, and I would be honored and extraordinarily happy if you would marry me."

All together it was the longest speech she had ever heard from him. "Yes," she said. "I love you too."

They kissed again. It was far better than the wenching she had done with her companions, she thought; she had never known anything to feel as good. Her lips felt pleasantly bruised.

A while later she said, "Do you know, I have no real idea of what you look like. Can you cut all that hair before we get married?"

"What if you're disappointed? What if you run away screaming?"

"I'll take that chance."

"I'll tell you what, then—find me some soap and water and I'll cut it all."

She grinned and took him by the hand to her apartment. It was only when they neared her rooms that she realized her mother would be there.

"Caireddin!" Efcharren said as they came inside. "What is going on? There are all sorts of rumors—Jerret isn't dead after all, they say—"

Caireddin said nothing. She walked past Efcharren, toward a basin of water and a mirror farther into the apartment.

"Caireddin!" her mother said, following them. "What's wrong? What have you heard? You can still marry a king—it will just be Jerret instead of Cullen."

She couldn't keep silent any longer. "I'm marrying Brangwin," she said. "And you're not invited. Ironic, isn't it—you've always wanted me to marry a king, and you won't be there to see it."

Efcharren looked stricken. "What—what do you mean?"

"I know about the pearl, Mother. I know what you've done. Where did you hide it, as a matter of interest?"

"In my mouth. But Caireddin—I did it for you. I did everything for you. You had to marry Cullen—I just wanted to see you happy with him."

"I didn't have to marry Cullen. As you can see."

"Caireddin, please—"

"That's all I have to say to you," Caireddin said. She turned to Brangwin. "Do you think you still have your room in the servants' quarters? We could go there instead."

"Probably," he said. "I haven't been gone that long."

He placed the mirror over the basin, and the soap on the mirror, and then carried it all out of the apartment. "I wouldn't mind having her at the wedding," he said. He led her up several flights of stairs, each meaner and narrower than the last.

"I would."

He hesitated, and then said, "Someday she won't be there, and then you might wish you had been kinder to her."

"I don't understand," she said. "You vowed revenge on people for years, even innocent people like Mathewar. How can you know about forgiveness?"

"I learned it from you. In the end, after I lost battle after battle, I came to hate everyone, even, as you say, those who were innocent. And then, because you told me to, I let go of my hatred for Mathewar, and I saw how easy it was. It was like letting go of a burden I never knew I had."

"Don't tell me you've forgiven Cullen."

"No. But I wish I could. He's a small-minded man, a man who became trapped in a role too great for him." They went down a poorly lit hallway and stopped at an unpainted door. "I learned one thing about hatred. It twists you—it eats away at you, until there's nothing inside but hatred. Until there's no one you can love, or trust. I don't want to see that happen to you."

"She's not coming to the wedding," Caireddin said.

He opened the door. The room had a pallet stuffed with rags, a chair with a broken back, and a chest.

He set the basin down on the chair and added soap to the water, then took a dagger out of the chest. To Caireddin's alarm he began to run the dagger through the water.

"What are you doing?" she asked. "You'll cut yourself."

He propped up the mirror and scraped at his beard. "This is how I shaved when I was a soldier," he said.

She watched him in silence for a while. When most of his hair was gone he turned from the mirror to face her. "Oh," she said. "Oh, holy gods—"

"What is it?"

She shook her head. She wanted to back away but forced herself to stand. "You look—you look wonderful," she said. She studied the sharp lines of his face, the straight nose, the keen dark eyes that seemed darker against his naked face.

He smiled one of his rare smiles. Uncovered, it looked radiant. "Then what's wrong?"

"Well, why—why do you want to marry me? You could have any-one—"

"I don't want anyone. I want you."

"But I'm nothing. I'm plain, I'm not beautiful—"

"Why do you think that?"

"I know it. I've seen myself." She moved to the mirror. "Look."

"You look like Queen Rodarren," he said. "She had a terrible scar, you know—it ran all the way down one cheek." He traced his finger down the side of her face to show her; her skin felt warm where he touched it. "And she was still the most beautiful woman at court. I saw her just once and I've never forgotten her. Dozens of people must have proposed to her over the years—she didn't stay unmarried because of lack of opportunity."

"Yes, but she was the queen—"

"Look," he said.

He went to the chest again and brought out a small coin, then held it up so she could see it. At first she didn't understand; it showed Queen Rodarren's profile, the side without the scar, just like any number of coins minted during her reign. Well, of course she looked good; every artist in the country had vied to flatter her.

Then she turned back at the mirror and saw how alike they were. And if Rodarren was beautiful, then . . .

She shook her head. She was not ready to change a lifetime of thinking.

She must have given Brangwin this coin as part of his wages, she realized. And then he had given it back to her, and given her an understanding of herself with it. It seemed a trick of magic, that he had changed something of little value into something priceless.

He sheared away the last of the beard. She leaned over and kissed him, smelling soap, and beneath that, his own scent. His smooth skin was a shock, and she raised her hand to stroke it.

Things moved quickly for a while. Jerret talked to his councilors and advisors and soldiers, and listened politely as they claimed undying loyalty to him. He commissioned several makers to write ballads telling the populace what had happened, and then rode through Pergodi, waving to the great cheering throng, proving to anyone who still had doubts that he was very much alive.

Mathewar freed Talethe at once, so that Jerret would have a friend to help him navigate the intrigues of the castle. And he spoke often with Jerret, working out ways to heal the wounded realm. There were perhaps three thousand of the Bound Folk left, Mathewar told him, and he cautioned Jerret against freeing them all at the same time. In their despair at their wasted lives, he said, they might rise up against him.

In the end, Jerret freed around a hundred each day, calling them together in groups of twenty or thirty between the work of governing. Mathewar broke their bonds, and then Jerret spoke to them, and others in the castle tried to ease their return to the world. Mathewar set to work creating a talisman that would allow Jerret to break the connection to the Bound Folks on his own. He had no intention of staying in Pergodi for the four weeks it would take to free them all; he had other work and other people who needed him. For one thing, he had to bring the newly joined crown to the College.

He had seen some of Jerret's probable future, and he knew that the boy-king could be left to finish the task. The effort of speaking for so long would make him nearly lose his voice, and he would become known as King Jerret the Whisperer. But he would also be admired and loved, and the people would never forget their gratitude at being delivered from the Harus.

Jerret and Brangwin spent hours behind closed doors, discussing the future of Goss. No one knew the extent of Jerret's promises, how much of the looted wealth the king promised to return, but when they emerged Brangwin looked satisfied. A court wit said, "He lost every battle but won the war," and this was repeated until the next amusing remark drove it from people's minds.

At the end of a week Brangwin and Caireddin left for Goss, and the fact that Efcharren did not ride with them kept the gossips busy for days.

Lirden began venturing down to the prison cells again, this time to visit Polgar. Their friendship surprised everyone, and folks murmured that Brangwin would never accept one of his family marrying a Haru. But Mathewar, when asked his opinion, said only to give him time. He had seen a future where Brangwin would marry Caireddin, where love for Caireddin and their children, and care for his country, took the place of his finely honed revenge. Mathewar said nothing of this; he was beginning to realize that speaking about the future could change it, that he would spend a good deal of the time in watchful silence.

Jerret arranged a hero's funeral for Reti, as he had promised. The folks from the three caravans came, and other Travelers, more than anyone had ever seen at one time. They sang their haunting songs to Mother Mathona, then Remi got out the bottle of Mathona's Tears and he and Mathewar drank and talked about Reti. Remi told Mathewar that he saw more traces of Mathona wherever he looked, that he thought her time on earth would come soon. Mathewar listened doubtfully, but he said nothing.

Mathewar went back over his actions while he wore the crown and saw that he could have done nothing to prevent Reti's death, that he was still wandering lost when it had happened. He felt great relief; he had learned a little about responsibility, but he did not think he could bear it if he had to carry guilt for Reti as well as Embre.

Iltarra disappeared; no one knew where she had gone. Angarred felt certain she would regain at least some power; she was not the sort to be kept down for long.

And then finally Mathewar and Angarred were ready to leave for the College. They stood on one of the lower roofs, looking over a parapet onto the courtyard below. Jerret had promised to come and bid them farewell but he was late; he had a great deal of work to do.

Brisk wind blew across the heights, gusting through their clothes and hair. They had said nothing for a while, watching as the religious carried out the statue of Jerret that had once stood with the other dead kings. Even from above they could see the displeasure on the faces of the religious; they had rejoiced at the miraculous return of King Jerret, of course, but they also had railed against those who dared to deceive them. Because of Polgar's tricks they had lost a good deal of their authority; no one would ever quite believe them again when they announced that a king had ascended to the Celestial Court.

Suddenly Mathewar laughed. Angarred turned to him questioningly and he said, "Do you see that man there, the one leading the horse to the stables? He thinks his son is dead, but the son was bound and will be freed tomorrow. See how downcast he looks? That's how happy he'll be when he sees him."

Angarred stood without speaking for a while. Finally she said, "Is this what our life is going to be like? You laughing at nothing and then telling me the future?"

"There's no reason to be frightened," Mathewar said. "I—"

"You see, that's just what I mean. How do you know that I'm frightened?"

"Because we know each other. I can tell what you're thinking sometimes, and you do the same for me."

"Is that all it is?" She hesitated again. "What happened to you when you put on the crown?"

She had not asked him that before, and he knew that this was because she had been afraid of the answer. He chose his next words carefully.

"I saw the future," he said. She gasped and put her hand to her mouth. "But it's constantly changing with the choices people make, becoming something else, so what I saw was just the future from that moment in time."

She nodded to show she understood, though she looked doubtful. "The farther I get from that time, the more choices that are made, the vaguer everything is," he said. "So that in a while whatever I saw will be changed utterly."

"And then you won't know the future?"

"A bit of it. Not very much."

"Will—will you ever wear the crown again?"

He thought of the crown, now packed away incongruously with their clothes and books and presents for their children. "I don't want to," he said. "I saw what Tobrin sees, I think, and I understand now how terrifying it is, why he warned me against it. It's too easy to change the future, once you know it, and the changes won't always be for the better."

He hesitated. He knew he would take out the crown as the time got closer for his son Berren to die. He would do anything in his power, would remake the world itself, to prevent that from happening. He said only, "But I might have to, if the realm is in peril. Probably not for years, though."

"Did you see us?" she asked. "Me and you and the children?"

"A little."

"What—what will happen to us?"

"Nothing much. Very little happens to most people, you know."

"You're holding something back, I can tell. You know something you're not saying."

He looked at her gravely. "Angarred," he said. "There are some things that I will not be able to tell you. I'm sorry. I have to be careful that I don't change the future, as I said."

She tried to laugh; it sounded like a sob. "Well, will we be happy?"

"Mostly, yes."

She sighed. "You're different," she said. "Those things you did when Cullen attacked you . . . Sometimes you seem like a stranger."

He turned to her and put his hands on her shoulders. Their eyes were nearly level. "We've always trusted each other, beyond question, beyond foreknowledge," he said. "I'm different, yes, but so are you. And we've returned from worse—you saved me in the mountains, and again when I was lost in the places the crown showed me. No matter where we go, one of us will always come for the other. We'll always find a way back."

They held each other. Their hair, amber and gold, streamed out in the wind and mingled. And that was how Jerret found them, a few moments later. He made a good deal of noise to get their attention, and even Mathewar was surprised to see him.